PRAISE FOR **BOWLAWAY**

"Death and life, frosted with macabre comedy. . . .
[McCracken] lures us in with her witty voice and oddball
characters but then kicks the wind out of us."
—*Washington Post*

"Populated by strange, excellent characters, and unfolds with
all the offbeat coziness and heartache of a great American fable:
molasses floods, workplace fires, surprising heirs, and all."
—*Vanity Fair*

"[McCracken has] considerable gifts as a novelist
[and] instinctive access to the most intricate threads
of human thought and feeling."
—*New York Times*

"*Bowlaway* is that most improbable of literary phenomena:
a buoyant, joyful, rollicking yarn of sadness and loss. . . .
Gloriously vibrant and boisterously surprising."
—*Boston Globe*

"Reading Elizabeth McCracken—the gorgeously-put-together
sentences parading the pages like models on a Paris runway;
the crazy, original insights; the definitive, wholly fictional
pronouncements—is like going on an automotive safari."
—*Newsday*

"McCracken's delightful prose and rich historical details
make this the perfect book to get lost in."
—*Real Simple*

"A comic marvel. . . . Rolls a strike
right through the heart of the American epic."
—*O, The Oprah Magazine*

PRAISE FOR *BOWLAWAY*

"Wildly entertaining. . . . [A] wonderfully unpredictable multi-generational saga which revolves around a Massachusetts bowling alley. . . . *Bowlaway* celebrates the oddest of oddballs and the freakiest of freak accidents with wit and heart. To read McCracken's inimitably clever sentences and follow her quirky narrative twists is to be constantly delighted."

—NPR

"An oddball masterpiece. . . . Elizabeth McCracken holds a funhouse mirror up to the Great American Novel. Whimsy and weirdness spark at *Bowlaway*'s edges. . . . This is McCracken's masterpiece, a story of reinvention. . . . The author has reframed the family saga for the misfit: that truest American character."   —*Entertainment Weekly*

"Whimsical, enchanting. . . . The sort of novel with which you fall in love. . . . Every page seems to provide the kind of writing that makes a reader stop cold, savoring the moment. . . . [*Bowlaway*] takes your hand and hurries you into an inviting, curious world, leaving you happily bereft at its end."   —*Seattle Times*

"*Bowlaway* snatches up every individual that finds joy or tragedy in proximity to the bowling alley and allows them to be observed tenderly and precisely. . . . McCracken's love of language is the *catching* kind. . . . In *Bowlaway*, the journey through McCracken's lush, piercing prose is the destination."   —*Austin Chronicle*

"In an enthralling, magical story that spans generations, award-winning writer McCracken imbues a candlepin alley with the ability to bowl over sexism."   —*Ms.* magazine

"People who don't yet know the work of Elizabeth McCracken, prepare for delight. . . . *Bowlaway* spirits readers into an astonishing world. . . .

McCracken's prose—canny wisdom laid on in swaths of fearless, quirky, galvanizing language—gives consistent joy. Almost every page glitters with quotable treasure. . . . [A] finely wrought, moving saga."

—*San Francisco Chronicle*

"[A] strange and brilliant tale."   —*Philadelphia Inquirer*

"Townsfolk cast small balls at straight pins in hopes of bowling away their troubles, but this being McCracken, a novelist who balances the sweet and the dark, there's ample heartache in their collective future."

—Vulture

"Elizabeth McCracken marries the everyday with the otherworldly. Her electrifying voice brings to life a cast of bizarre characters who lean on, help and flee one another. . . . Heartbreaking and beautiful. . . . *Bowlaway* is an epic of the wins and losses that make up the average life."

—*Paste* magazine

"If you think 100 years is an awful lot of time to spend in a small, family-owned and operated bowling alley, think again. In fact, bowling offers the perfect narrative arc. . . . [McCracken writes,] 'Turn the page!' Believe me, you will."   —Bustle

"A story equal parts sorrow and wonder, magical realism and cold, hard reality. . . . McCracken's gift is to deliver that pain wrapped in astounding sentences and characters who leap off the page. . . . The book is best read pen in hand, ready to underline standout sentences."

—*Texas Observer*

"It's impossible not to fall under McCracken's spell. *Bowlaway* is a rare treasure, a perfect and precious gift."   —*Nashville Scene*

"Elizabeth McCracken's *Bowlaway* is so deliciously weird and wise and alive. It's a page-turner set in a bowling alley, a grief-haunted and hope-raddled book, and a gloriously fresh paean to the 'perversity of love.' I loved it—what a generous pour of humor and sorrow and wonder."

—Karen Russell

"McCracken has one of the more distinctive literary sensibilities readers will likely encounter; playful, inventive, and fearless, she's drawn to oddball characters and the eccentric fringes of American family life. . . . A playful, powerful meditation on the proposition that life itself is strange." —*Library Journal* (starred review)

"To tell a good tale, you need drama—and in this area, *Bowlaway* spares no expense. . . . McCracken's prose is well-tooled, hilarious and tender, thoughtful and jocular. Her characters inhabit their world so completely, so bodily, that they could've truly existed."
—*BookPage* (starred review)

"[McCracken] is a beloved bard of the eccentric. . . . McCracken writes with exuberant precision, ingenious lyricism, satirical humor, and warmhearted mischief and delight. . . . This compassionate and rambunctious saga about love, grief, prejudice, and the courage to be one's self chimes with novels by John Irving, Audrey Niffenegger, and Alice Hoffman." —*Booklist* (starred review)

"Stellar. . . . McCracken writes with a natural lyricism that sports vivid imagery and delightful turns of phrase. Her distinct humor enlivens the many plot twists that propel the narrative, making for a novel readers will sink into and savor." —*Publishers Weekly* (starred review)

"McCracken understands the vast variety of ways to be human. . . . Parents and children, lovers, brothers and sisters, estranged spouses, work friends and teammates all slam themselves together and fling themselves apart across the decades in the glorious clatter of McCracken's unconventional storytelling."
—*Kirkus Reviews* (starred review)

BOWLAWAY

BOWLAWAY

A NOVEL

ELIZABETH McCRACKEN

ecco

An Imprint of HarperCollins*Publishers*

BOWLAWAY. Copyright © 2019 by Elizabeth McCracken. All rights reserved. Printed in the United States of America. No part of this book may be used or reproduced in any manner whatsoever without written permission except in the case of brief quotations embodied in critical articles and reviews. For information, address HarperCollins Publishers, 195 Broadway, New York, NY 10007.

HarperCollins books may be purchased for educational, business, or sales promotional use. For information, please email the Special Markets Department at SPsales@harpercollins.com.

A hardcover edition of this book was first published in 2019 by Ecco, an imprint of HarperCollins Publishers.

FIRST ECCO PAPERBACK EDITION PUBLISHED 2019.

Designed by Suet Chong

The Library of Congress has catalogued a previous edition as follows:

Names: McCracken, Elizabeth, author.
Title: Bowlaway : a novel / Elizabeth McCracken.
Description: First Edition. | New York, NY : Ecco, 2019.
Identifiers: LCCN 2018025083| ISBN 9780062862853 (hardback) | ISBN 9780062862860
Subjects: | BISAC: FICTION / Literary. | FICTION / Family Life. | FICTION / Historical.
Classification: LCC PS3563.C35248 B69 2019 | DDC 813/.54—dc23
LC record available at https://lccn.loc.gov/2018025083

ISBN 978-0-06-286286-0 (pbk.)

19 20 21 22 23 LSC 10 9 8 7 6 5 4 3 2 1

For Gus
&
for Matilda
with love from your old mother

1

THE FOUND WOMAN

They found a body in the Salford Cemetery, but aboveground and alive. An ice storm the day before had beheaded the daffodils, and the cemetery was draped in frost: midspring, Massachusetts, the turn of the century before last. The body lay faceup near the obelisk that marked several generations of Pickersgills.

Soon everyone in town would know her, but for now it was as though she'd dropped from the sky. A woman, stout, one bare fist held to her chin, white as a monument and soft as marble rubbed for luck. Her limbs were willy-nilly. Even her skirt looked broken in two along its central axis, though it was merely divided, for cycling. Her name was Bertha Truitt. The gladstone bag beside her contained one abandoned corset, one small bowling ball, one slender candlepin, and, under a false bottom, fifteen pounds of gold.

The watchman was on the Avenue of Sorrows near where the babies were interred when he spotted her down the hill in the frost. He was a teenager, uneasy among the living and not much better among the dead. He'd been hired to keep an eye out. Things had been stolen. Bodies? No, not bodies: statuary, a stone or two, half a grieving angel's granite wing.

The young man, being alive, was not afraid of body snatchers, but he feared the dead breaking out of their sepulchres. Perhaps here one was. Himself, he wanted to be buried at sea, though to be buried at sea you had to go to sea. He'd been born on a ship in Boston Harbor, someone had once told him, but he had no memory of his birth, nor of any boat, nor of his parents. He was an orphan.

The woman: Was she alive or dead? The slope worried him. He'd had a troubled gait all his life—the boat, or an accident at birth had caused it—and between the slick and the angle he might end up falling upon her. "Hello!" he shouted, then, "Help!" though he believed he was the only living person anywhere near.

But here came another man, entirely bundled, suspiciously bundled, dusky wool and speckled tweed, arboreal. From a distance, dark, and the young man expected him to brighten up the closer he got but he never did.

"What is it?" the stranger asked.

The young man said, "The lady," and pointed. "She dead, you think?"

"Come," said the stranger, "and we will see."

The slope, the frost. The possibility she was dead. The young man said, "I'll call a doctor, shall I."

"I'm a doctor."

"You?" He'd never heard of a colored doctor before. Moreover the stranger had on his back an immense duffel bag more vagabond than medical, and looked as though he'd been sleeping rough for some time. He had a refined accent from no region the watchman could place.

"The same."

"Better get another."

"Now, now," said the man, and he took hold of the young man's sleeve, and the young man resisted. "How strong a fellow are you?"

"Enough," said the watchman.

The foreigner, the doctor—his name was Leviticus Sprague, he'd been educated in Glasgow, but raised in the Maritimes—caught him by the wrist, to tow the boy—he *was* a boy, his name was Joe Wear, he was just nineteen—skitteringly down the hill. Almost immediately Dr. Sprague regretted it. The boy was unsteady on his feet and cried out as he slid. "Careful," Dr. Sprague said. "Here, take my shoulder. Difficult for any man."

How in the world had the woman got there? The frost around her had not a footfall in it. With the green grass beneath, it looked like a foam-rough sea, jade and fatal, and she going under. If she *had* dropped out of the sky, she'd been lucky to miss that obelisk.

"Look in the bag," Dr. Sprague told Joe Wear. "See if that tells us anything."

Dr. Sprague knelt to his patient. He saw the curve of one eye tick beneath its lid. The eyelashes of the dozing are always full of meaning and beauty, telegraph wires for dreams, and hers were no different. Dr. Sprague marveled at their fur-coat loveliness. He took hold of her bare wrist, which was, against logic, warm.

She blinked to reveal a pair of baize-green eyes and the soul of a middle-aged woman. When she sat up from the frost it was as though a stone bishop had stepped from his niche.

"Hello," she said pleasantly to Dr. Sprague.

"Yes," he said to her.

Then she turned to Joe Wear, who had fished from the gladstone bag a small wooden ball and a narrow wooden pin, and was regarding them, then her, wonderingly.

"Ah good!" she said. "Give here."

He did. She held them like a queen in an ancient painting, orb and scepter. She was alive. She was a bowler.

"A new sort of bowling," she declared.

"Madam," said Dr. Sprague, but Joe Wear said, "Candlepin."

"Of a sort," she said, with a papercut tone. She set the pin and ball on the ground beside her. Then, to Joe, "You're a bowling man."

"Have been. Tenpin. Worked at the Les Miserables house."

From the Avenue of Sorrows a voice called, "Ahoy!" A policeman, a middle-aged anvil-headed man, with gray hair that shone just a little, like hammered aluminum.

"Let us get her to her feet," Dr. Sprague said to Joe Wear, and they pulled her upright as the policeman doddered down the frosty hill on his heels. She left her dead shape behind in the grass, a hay-colored silhouette, as though she'd lain there a long time. The dead grass persisted weeks later, seasons. From the right angle in the Salford Cemetery you might see it still.

"What's your name, missus," the policeman said to the woman, once he'd got there.

She got a thinking look.

"You haven't forgotten."

Still thinking. At last she said in an experimental voice, "Bertha Truitt. Yes, I think so."

"Better get her to a doctor," said Joe Wear.

"*I'm* a doctor," said Dr. Sprague, and he took her by the hand, where her pulse was, her blood, her bones.

She smiled. She told him confidingly, "There is not a thing wrong with me."

"You were inconscious," said Joe Wear.

"We'll take her to the Salford Hospital," the policeman decided.

Joe Wear couldn't shake the alarm he'd felt upon seeing her in the morning frost, the pleasure when she'd opened her eyes. She had been brought back from the dead. Her nose was now florid with life, her little teeth loosely strung. He wanted to slap the grass from the back of her dark jacket, as though she were a horse.

"But what were you *doing* here," Dr. Leviticus Sprague asked her. Poor man. She admired how their hands looked folded together. "Darling sir," she said. "I was dreaming of love."

Our subject is love because our subject is bowling. Candlepin bowling. This is New England, and even the violence is cunning and subtle. It still could kill you. A candlepin ball is small, two and a half pounds, four and a half inches in diameter, a grapefruit, an operable tumor. You heft it in your palm. Candlepin bowling is a game of skill: nobody has ever bowled a perfect string, every pin with every ball, all the way through, till you've knocked down 130 pins in a row, multiplied and transformed by math and bowling into a 300 game. Nobody's got more than five-sixths of the way there. Nobody, in other words, may look upon the face of God.

This is bowling in New England (except Connecticut). A game of purity for former puritans. A game of devotion that will always fail. Tenpin balls (what most people think of when they hear the word *bowling*) are the size of hissing cartoon bombs. Tenpins are curvy and shaped like clubs. Candlepin balls are handsize. Candlepins are candleshaped. Bertha Truitt's gravestone would eventually read INVENTOR OF CANDLEPIN BOWLING, THE SPORT OF LADIES AND GENTLE-MEN, and so she was, no matter what the history books say, if history books care at all for the game of candlepin. Most don't but this one does, being a genealogy.

Maybe somebody else had invented the game first. That doesn't matter. We have all of us invented things that others have beat us to: walking upright, a certain sort of sandwich involving avocado and an onion roll, a minty sweet cocktail, ourselves, romantic love, human life.

Our subject is love. Unrequited love, you might think, the heedless headstrong ball that hurtles nearsighted down the alley. It has to get close before it can pick out which pin it loves the most, which pin it longs to set spinning. Then *I love you!* Then *blammo.* The pins are reduced to a pile, each one entirely all right in itself. Intact and bashed about. Again and again, the pins stand for it until they're knocked down. The ball return splits up the beloveds, flings the ball away from the pins. *You stay there.* The ball never does, it's flung back by the bowler, here it comes flying, *blammo.*

You understand. It only seems unrequited.

The policeman brought the so-called Bertha Truitt to the Salford Hospital, where it could not be determined whether she had amnesia or a privacy so pigheaded it might yet prove fatal. Did she want to stay in the hospital? Of course not. How old was she? She wouldn't say. Did she know anyone in town? Possibly: she hadn't gone door-to-door to ask. How long had she been in the cemetery? If they didn't know, she surely did not. Where *had* she come from?

"I'm here now," she said.

Lie down, lie down.

"Will you let me go if I do?"

All right.

The Catholics came to see her, and members from the Hebrew Ladies Sewing Society, and some Presbyterians. She didn't need or seek charity; they just wanted a gander. Newspapermen came to interview the curiosity but found only a pleasant plump woman whom nobody could account for. Those the city was full of. The mayor visited; his deputy had suggested that the recent reports of a strange creature stalking the fens on the north edge of the city—the newspapers called it the Salford Devil—had been this woman, looking for a place to lie down. The Salford Devil had red eyes and brachiated black wings, was the size of a dog, or a swan, or a malnourished child, had a long tail with a tassel (like a zebra or giraffe or a sphinx) or one that opened like a fan (like a bird). Bertha Truitt had none of these things, and on the second day of her hospitalization Moses Mood, the owner of the hardware store, swore he saw the still at-large Salford Devil steal a poodle where it had waited for its owner outside the public library. A real poodle, a pony-size one.

Bertha Truitt confounded people. She was two things at once. Bodily she was a matron, jowly, bosomy, bottomy, odd. At heart she was a gamine. Her smile was like a baby's, full of joyful élan. You believed you had caused it. You felt felled by a stroke of luck.

Nobody who knew her came to visit, though the nurses noticed she was always peering down the ward with a hopeful expression. She had no recognizable accent, no regional manners, no cravings for a certain cabbage salad known on only one side of the Mississippi. When asked about her past, she waved it away. "I'm here," she said. "Wherever that is."

People began to dream of her. Not just her fellow patients, though they were the first, they dreamt of Bertha Truitt sneaking into their beds, lowering the mattress, raising the temperature, dissolving in the daylight. She got into the dreams of the nurses and doctors, then people through the town. One man swore he saw her fly through the air on her back, naked as a piglet, using her impressive breasts as wings.

Really?

Well, maybe more like rudders, he allowed. Otherwise I stand by it.

It was just a dream, his wife told him, as wives did everywhere in Salford, husbands, too, parents who could not imagine where their children had heard of the smiling lady who whispered in their ears at night, *I have a game for you.* And, *it is possible to bowl away trouble.*

The other patients hung around her bed to be smiled at. This included Jeptha Arrison, a lumpheaded young man who'd been hospitalized after swallowing a bottle of aspirin, one pill at a time, like consuming a tree twig by twig. Soon enough he was found sleeping under Bertha Truitt's bed. "Let him stay," she said, and though it was the woman's ward he was left alone. Jeptha Arrison began to sleep abovedecks at the foot of her bed. "I like it here," he said to Bertha Truitt. "The hospital. My ma told me I once nearly died in a hospital but now I think they do me good."

"You have a fine head," said Bertha Truitt. She gave him a look of admiration.

"Ought I become a doctor?" he asked.

"Heavens, no," she said. "No, you're not suited for that at all. I meant the shape of it. I was speaking phrenologically." She touched his temples with the gentling tips of her fingers. He would have done anything she suggested.

It was the early years of American sports. She weighed the ball in the palm of her hand; she got Jeptha Arrison to set up her single pin, thin as a broomstick, all the way at the end of the ward. Again and again she knocked it over. "You have a problem," she would say. "Bowling can take it away like this." Knock it over again. It was impossible, the floor tilted to the south, the agitated footfalls of the sick sent vibrations through the boards, yet she managed it every time. Bertha Truitt told her visitors that the pharaohs bowled, of course they did, the pharaohs did everything first. Martin Luther bowled, before he was devout; Henry VIII had lanes built at Whitehall Palace. Rip Van Winkle was watching his neighbors bowl at ninepins when he fell into his famous sleep.

"As for me," said Bertha Truitt, "I'll build a bowling alley. What is this place."

"This place?" Jeptha asked. He pointed at the bed he sat on. "Salford, or—"

"Salford," Bertha Truitt said. "Massachusetts, then. Yes."

THE BOWLING ALLEY
UNDER GLASS

S alford was a city hard north of Boston, with a sliver of coastline just big enough to ramshackle the houses and web the occasional foot. Like Rome, it had been built among seven hills; unlike Rome, it was a swampy place, a city of fens and bogs. Eventually the founders knocked over most of the hills, shoved them into the bogs, declared them to be squares, and named each for the former hill at its heart. Pinkham Hill became Pinkham Square; Baskertop Hill, Baskertop Square. As for the bogs, they were nameless, then gone.

Former bog dwellers were left to wander the municipality. Prosperous beavers in their beaver coats muscled around Gibbs Square, looking as though they meant to withdraw their funds from the local banks; nesting birds lamented the coarse new immigrants in their neighborhood, like them bipedal but unwilling or unable to fly. Frogs hopped like idle thoughts past the saloon. Sometimes they went in: you had to check your bucket of beer before you poured. Animals, flushed from Salford's pockets, were everywhere. Perhaps the Salford Devil was only some Yankee platypus whose habitat had been replaced by the dime store.

A whole colony of little bogbirds had been ousted from the swamp that became Phillipine Square. In their place was a vaudeville house, a grocery store, and a trolley stop, though the whole demesne still smelled of bog: damp and up-to-no-good.

Here Bertha Truitt declared she would build her alley.

"I am at home in a bog," she said. "A bog is a woman by its nature."

"And hills?" asked Jeptha Arrison worriedly. Jeptha of the Hospital! He had a sack of a head, damp eyes an eely gray, and a face that altogether seemed something caught in aspic. He stood next to Bertha on the new sidewalk of Phillipine Square, though the road wasn't yet paved, and looked down at his shoes, frilled at the edges with mud. "That'll make me sick."

"What will?"

"Filth," he said. He asked again, "What's a hill?"

"Also a woman. There is no part of the earth that isn't. Yes," Bertha Truitt repeated, "I am at home in a bog."

Hire Irish to lay brick, a doctor had told her in the hospital, and now she believed it like a superstition. The Irish called her Truitt, which they made a single syllable, *Troot*, and so she was known by most people: not Bertha Truitt or Miz or Mrs., not The Truitt Woman, not Mrs. Sprague once her husband arrived. The lack of honorific *was* the honorific: Troot. Troot runs a good house.

It took her two months to build the bowling alley. Nobody had seen a building go up with such speed, brick by brick, like knitting a sock. Truitt walked through every day, a distracted but bemused look on her face, as though she were looking not for progress but for a particular person long missing, and was preparing her face for the joke: *What took you so long* or *I knew you'd turn up eventually* or *Hello, you.*

Two stories and a cellar to the Truitt House. Look through the glass windows at the front, like the historic dioramas at the Salford Public Library. The title of *this* diorama is the Bowling Alley at Dawn. Eggshell light outside; inside, murky workingman dark. No windows except at the front: neither the rising of the sun nor its inevitable setting matter here. Balls turn. The earth (being a woman) might or might not.

There are six lanes to bowl upon. The floors are built of rock maple. At the end of the lanes is a ledge—a high wooden bench that runs the length of the wall—for the pinboys to alight upon while the bowlers bowl. Once the bowling alley has opened for the day, the pinboys will sit on the ledge like judges, or vultures, but not yet. Between lanes are three elevated cast-iron tracks—the ball returns—so the pinboys can bowl the balls back to the bowlers. The Bowling Alley at Dawn is a tidy place. The pins have been set. Only one pale matchstick pin has fallen over in the first lane. Impossible to know whether this is the carelessness of the pinboy, or the artist who made this diorama.

Nobody watches or waits. Nobody stands behind the wooden counter at the front—a large oak structure like a pulpit, with a spectacular cash register that looks ready to emit steam-powered music, a calliope of money. Nobody sits at the bar along the other wall, though the jar of pickled eggs glows like a fortune-teller. The tables and chairs in the middle of the room await lollygaggers. The ceilings are warehouse high, so that the eventual smoke coming off all those eventual people (cigarette, cigar, desire, effort) might be stored aloft. Six fluted iron columns for support, three left, three right. In the corner the first of the coin-op entertainments, a standing sculptoscope. Drop in a penny, bend to the brass goggles—you might expect to see a stereoptical Niagara Falls or Taj Mahal, but in the Bowling Alley at Dawn you see instead the Bowling Alley at Dawn in further miniature, complete with diminutive sculptoscope with its minuscule stereoptical view of the Bowling Alley at Dawn.

Below, the cellar is divided into rooms for storage. It smells of bog. The only thing of note is a broad-shouldered cast-iron safe, painted with flowers and the name of its maker (EXCELSIOR SAFE & LOCK CO., SALFORD MASS.) in excruciatingly beautiful cursive.

Upstairs, above the alleys, storage rooms east and west, with an apartment in the middle. When the sun rises—if the sun ever rises in the Bowling Alley at Dawn—the light will fall through the immense sash windows at the back onto the good furniture: an Eastlake sofa, an enamel table with turned legs, an iron bed. Even this room feels like a storehouse, the domestic objects in it arranged like unused furniture, the bathtub near the kitchen sink, the stove near the front door, the toilet in one of the closets. At the front of the building, the staircase down to the alley's foyer, every step white, every riser green.

"For *you*?" the Irish foreman had asked Truitt, when shown the plans for the apartment. She had sketched them on what seemed to be the grease-stained wrapper of a sandwich; her governing aesthetic was symmetry. The foreman was embarrassed by how protective of her he felt, to own this emotion for which Truitt would have nothing but contempt: *I do not need protection, Mr. Dockery, I look after myself.*

"For pity's sake," she said. "No. It wouldn't suit me at all. I plan to install a man."

She'd found her man already, of course: Joe Wear, late of the cemetery. She had known from the moment she'd met him that he was a bowler to his very soul. He had that knack for pointless devotion; his body was built on bowling angles.

He'd visited her once in the hospital, had told her, "I won't pinset. I pinset at Les Miserables. I could manage a house." She turned to him with a gleaming expression, bright and greedy and promising as a collection plate. He said, "I never meant to end up in a graveyard. Bowling"—his voice broke, he repaired it—"is what I got."

She hired him on the spot. All during construction he came to the alley, to give advice, to shake Bertha Truitt's hand. Every handshake was a test, he knew. She was a prophet of bowling but she needed other people to love it, too.

"Jeptha Arrison will be the Captain of the Pinbodies," she told him. That was her own word to describe the boys and men who set the candlepins. "Everyone else is yours to hire or fire. Do a good job," she told him, "and one day the alley will come to you."

There was something wrong with Jeptha Arrison—he was minuscule but had an enormous and lopsided head—and Joe Wear wasn't sure he wanted to be joined to him in an alley wedding. There was something wrong with Joe Wear, too, but he knew how things worked. Everywhere else women bowled behind a curtain, to protect their modesty, to protect men from the spectacle of feminine sport. A steel curtain, so that you couldn't even see the outline of waist or ankle.

"You want women in here, you'll need a curtain," he said.

"Well," said Bertha, "I invented the game, so I suppose I make the rules."

"How's that?" he said.

"I invented this strain of bowling."

She was older than he was, and would pay his salary, and for a moment he thought about agreeing, then found he was already saying, "Looks like ordinary candlepin to me."

"It is not."

"In Worcester—"

Truitt barked. With laughter? Not quite. With anger? No,

she *barked*, a noise that meant *who's there* and *I'm here* and nothing at all.

"I have never been to Worcester," she said.

"Anyhow," said Joe Wear. He could feel the long muscles of his arms spasming, and he crossed them. Not everyone would give him a job, never mind one of authority. He should be grateful and agreeable. But hadn't he saved her from foolishness once? Hadn't he been hired for his knowledge? "You'll need a curtain," he said again.

Bertha Truitt knew it was wrong to protect somebody else's modesty. Your modesty was your own. "No curtain, Joe."

"You'll get gawkers."

"Let 'em gawk."

That was that.

Gawkers, gapers, gogglers, oglers! She couldn't see them, she was ogle-blind. She rode a bicycle around the city in her split skirt and never wobbled even when the sidewalk boys hooted at her. She still found her way into people's dreams, still dissolved in daylight. Perhaps she was a succubus or a vampire, the way she snuck into dreams and returned to Salford in daylight, reading the funny papers on the sidewalk, laughing so loud the pigeons scattered. She even appeared in the Salford *Bugle* itself, beneath the headline NEW BOWLING ESTABLISHMENT INVITES ALL WOMEN. In the photograph accompanying the article, Truitt seems to be in mourning, as all women of a certain bustline do: her very bosom grieves, and is brave, and soldiers on. Upon this bosom a bowling alley was founded.

She must have had ancestors. Everyone does. She seemed to have arrived in Salford sui generis, of her own kind, though of course genealogists don't believe such a thing exists. No generation is ever spontaneous. We are none of us our own kind.

"I have been parented by pamphlets," Bertha Truitt liked to say, not thinking that a bad thing. The pamphlets were outdated, quaint, quite often hateful. She was the oddest combination of the future and the past anyone had ever met.

Every month she opened the alleys for a fete. Beer and beef, oysters, pints of ice cream, brandy, a cake riddled with cherries, pies of all sorts (pork, treacle, kidney), more beer. Each fete lasted the entire day, was serially every kind of gathering: in the morning, a party for children, then a ladies' lunch, then a tea, cocktails, then (as the day began to unravel) a light supper, a frolic, a soiree, a carousal, a blowout, a dance, and as people began to drink themselves sober, a conversation, an optimistic repentance, a vow for greatness, love. Sometimes the party circled around and began again, though on those days you had to be careful Bertha Truitt did not offer beer to your child: she liked children, but she made no concessions to them. These were the stories told later. Married people would say, Well, we got married three years ago, but we first met—we really *met*—at Truitt's at either 10:00 or 2:00 A.M.

Truitt herself told no stories. In the middle of each party, she stood and picked cherries out of her slice of cake and looked hopefully at the door, happy enough at who she saw but never, it seemed, satisfied. Month after month, whoever she waited for stood her up.

The women of Truitt's Alleys bowled right out in the open, a spectacle: LuEtta Mood, Hazel Forest, Mary Gearheart, Nora Riker, Bertha Truitt.

Nora Riker was a round-headed square-bodied woman of twenty-nine, as alfalfa-scented and jostling as a goat. She was married to a similarly sawed-off hard-cornered man named Norman. In public they wrestled. There didn't seem to be anything carnal in it nor any meanness; they tumbled like goats, like Airedales. Even playing whist they shoved each other, guffawed. Even dancing. She was looking for a game she could beat him at.

Hazel Forest was a suffragette like Bertha. At least, Hazel thought Bertha was; they had met on a march, though she later realized that Bertha would join any march at any time, if she happened to be nearby: she liked the chance to walk and holler simultaneously. Hazel had the spectacles of a suffragette, and the bitter sense of humor, made bitterer by her job as a surgical nurse at the Salford Hospital. She'd surveyed the inside of bodies and was always threatening to tell other women what she had seen.

Mary Gearheart was the youngest, seventeen. Her father owned the vaudeville house. She had small eyes and a big mouth, like a carnivorous mouse. She bowled to keep her hands busy. To keep the throwing, smashing part of her brain busy, too.

LuEtta Mood was beautiful. She'd heard it was possible to bowl away sorrow.

Truitt bowled because the earth was an ocean and you had to learn to roll upon it.

"I do not wear the corset," Truitt told LuEtta Mood, Mary Gearheart, Hazel Forest, Nora Riker. They had never met a woman like her. She spread her wings to display herself. "The corset confuses the organs. Besides, the game of candlepin is a boon to the female form. It trims the waist, firms the arm, and lifts the bust. Regard me."

The women did, worriedly. Bertha Truitt was a plump five and a half feet tall, her uncorsetted torso rhomboid, sensual. They all knew the story of her arrival in the cemetery; Mary said she'd heard she'd been found with the body of her dead child, and that candlepin bowling was the peculiar way she'd gone mad with grief.

"Sorry," Mary had said to LuEtta Mood, who had her own dead child, and LuEtta waved the apology and the fact away.

They had no idea how old Truitt was. Older than them, younger than their mothers, mesmerizing.

"Now watch my form," Truitt said. They did, they did. Her shoes were off, her hat was on—already she was famous in Salford for her hats, which she had special made. Today's hat was navy blue and waffled; today, she was a member of a foreign navy. She bowled in rolled shirtsleeves. Her right forearm was carved of oak, her left one of marble. Seven steps, and then delivery. Jeptha Arrison, up on the pinboys' shelf, wrung his hands. They all watched the ball make its way down the lane.

"You got a wrong foot approach there, Troot," called the orphan Joe Wear. What he meant: usually a left-handed bowler makes her last step with her right foot; Bertha Truitt bowled and stepped with her whole left side. It shouldn't have worked. She knocked down six pins. Joe gave a low whistle and Jeptha Arrison echoed it, like bird-call, a nervous avian declaration.

"Thanks, Joe," Truitt said lightly, to the pins—Joe wouldn't have been able to hear her—then turned to look at her team. Like Nora Riker, she wanted to win. She just wanted to win everything of all time.

The invention of a sport: here is a ball, now throw it through that net, if those other guys'll let you. Here is a bat: somebody's going to throw a ball at you and you knock it away and run, if those other guys'll let you. Here is a tiny ball and a stick and out of view beyond that grassy hill is a ball-size hole: you figure it out.

Here is a ball. Heft it in your hand. Nobody's going to stop you. Some man might call out with advice, too much advice, but in the end it's your game to play and your game to win.

Bertha Truitt picked up the second ball of the frame and tested the weight in her hand, a little toss, then brought it up and touched just the plump underside of her chin with just the cool curve at the top of the ball. She looked at how the pins lay, four standing, inter-laced with the dead wood. Then she bowled.

The ball knocked over three more pins, and Joe Wear whistled again, lower, graver. He came over to watch; he stood behind the women, who sat on the rush-seated benches as though at church. LuEtta Mood asked, over her shoulder, "Is that good?" In the dark of the alley her hair shone like polished brass. It irked Joe Wear.

"I'd say so."

In those days to knock down nine pins in candlepin bowling was a feat, no matter your age or sex or waistline. The balls were smaller, the pins narrower, the approaches not oiled or even varnished, just rough fricative wood.

The third ball knocked over the last pin. "Ten box!" said Joe Wear.

Jeptha Arrison dropped down to the wood to reset, fetched the balls and bowled them back along the return, started resetting the pins on their metal deck.

"Good roll, Troot!" he called. "A real good one."

"All right, pinbody," she called back fondly. Nobody had a more interesting head than Jeptha. "Set 'em up."

The women watched Bertha Truitt bowl an entire game till they fell into the rhythm. You set your brain to bowling time and got caught up in the serial nature of it. Three balls a frame, ten frames a string. They hadn't realized that bowling was so full of suspense. A story: our hero (the ball) sets out on his journey (the approach), travels the length of his world until he runs into trouble, acquits himself well or badly, end of chapter.

Turn the page!

The only pause was at the end of every frame, when Jeptha Arrison jumped down to pluck the balls from the pit, then set the pins back up on the plate.

"Seventy-seven!" Joe Wear called out when Bertha had finished her first string.

"No thank you, Joe!" Bertha Truitt called back. "No score, thank you!"

Well, that was like a woman, wasn't it. No score.

What she wanted was a kind of greatness that women were not allowed. If they were allowed a small measure of it, they had to forsake love. She forsook nothing.

CEMETERY MATTERS

Of course she was looking for somebody in particular. She looked for him in the hospital—he was a doctor—and as she built the alley, and as she rode her bicycle along the streets of Salford. She had built a building and put her name on the front as advertising. Naturally she went to the cemetery, where they had first met, and looked for him there. All of the details were not clear in even Bertha's mind, though she remembered the cold of the cemetery and the decision to lie down, to open her coat to let in the chill like a guest. Some days she could conjure up the whole Bertha-shaped stretch of the cemetery where she'd lain and think of it with affection. Her birthplace, in a way. No need to reflect upon what had come before. She'd been found. Marching forward had always been her habit. Only in a bowling alley did back and forth get you anywhere.

She was looking for the other man, the fellow her own age or a little younger, whose name she did not know. He had got into her head, though all he'd done was take her pulse. Still, he did that caressingly, the tip of his finger a bow against the stringed instrument of her wrist.

PHEBE PICKERSGILL, HERMANN SWETTMAN, SUSANA PETERSON, DELILAH FOREST, wife of, daughter of, aged 81 years, aged 18. Bertha Truitt thought they, the dead, were just the same as her, they'd also gone onto the next life. Or else the dead were the people she'd left behind, all life spans ending this date, this year, everyone she'd once known dead except her, a convenience. She could astound herself sometimes with the sudden iron of her heart. Cast iron, ringing like an anvil. Not all the time. At all important times her heart was flesh.

She thought, *When I finish building Truitt's, that's when I'll find him*, and that was true, nearly to the day.

She saw him in the cemetery, walking the avenue of willows that led to the ornamental pond at the center of the park, and then her heart was neither iron nor flesh but pond, ready to receive and conceal anything tossed into it. He was a handsome, tubby, mustachioed black man, in a green suit with an orange windowpane check. The expression on the man's face—he hadn't seen her yet—was thoughtful and pleased, full of a self-kindled light. She felt a plunk in the pond of her heart and went to him.

June. The sun whetted its rays on the gravestones. The fish in the ornamental pond didn't know they, too, were ornamental. They swam up to catch the light.

"Hello," she said.

He said, in a voice quiet as a comb, "I knew you'd turn up eventually." One wing of his black mustache was longer than the other. There was nobody looking after him. "I am glad to see that you are well."

"I am." She couldn't think of the next thing to say, so she offered to give him a reading. A reading? Of your head: phrenology.

"No thank you," said Doctor Sprague.

"Why not?"

He gave her a careful look. Later she knew all the angles of this particular expression, the subtle widening of the eyes, his condescending affection, the way he bore the burden of knowing too much. He was a man of facts. Even his poetry was highly accurate. He said, "Phrenology is not science."

"But it is!" said Bertha Truitt. "There have been many words written on the subject."

"Words are not facts. A man who requires inferiors will find his own head superior, he will write encyclopedias on the subject."

"But you have a splendid head," she said.

"Your Dr. Fowler would not say so, on account of my race."

"Oh!" she said. "Truly? Then he would be mistaken."

She was giving his head a look of admiration and hope, and nervousness, so he took off his derby and aimed his head at her. His splendid head. He liked to think he was immune to compliments, but he wasn't.

This was a long time ago but they were still not young. Bertha, particularly, was not. She would be older till she died.

She read the territory of his scalp not through the close-cropped hair but beneath it. The back of his neck smelled of bay rum, his windowpane coat of tobacco. No, don't smell, she reminded herself. That tells you nothing.

People misunderstood phrenology, thought Bertha. It was exercise. The stevedore, lifting a great deal of weight, changes the shape of his torso; the philosopher who lifts heavy thoughts, the shape of his head. Look at the portraits of Benjamin Franklin in his early years and at the end of his life, see the difference. Look at Dr. Sprague's magnificent forehead, knotted with thought, evidence of all his education, the poetry he wrote, the patients he saved. She went to the knobs at the back of his head, to the prominences, as was her habit.

His area of Amativeness was well developed, as was his area of intelligence. His Alimentiveness was worrying. His Self-esteem was very bad indeed. His Hope—but now she could discern nothing abstract. Was that a scar? What had happened to the man?

"That bad?" Dr. Sprague asked, then, "I told you."

"Hard to say," said Bertha Truitt. She wanted to dally. Her belief in phrenology was draining from her, she could feel it spin down the drain. And yet: as her fingers circumnavigated Dr. Sprague's skull, she *did* know him, there was no way to know him but through his head. She hadn't taken off her kid gloves, a mistake she recognized as her little finger grazed the apex of his ear. So she removed them, tucked one in each armpit. She worked the ambits of his skull. He was kind, and lackadaisical, devoted, careless. He was melancholy. He liked to drink (this she determined from the smell of sweet ferment coming through all parts of him). He would do anything for her, to the best of his abilities. He would love and disappoint her.

"Now you," he said, and doffed his gloves.

She pulled the pins from her hair. Maybe this was really how you read somebody. You applied your head to that person's fingertips, and the person poured themselves into your brain, chin, neck, shoulders—and you knew everything. She stared at his shoes (good brown brogues, one toe scuffed across the perforations) and felt the mechanism of her soul flutter and falter. He was unconvinced, but what if her skull revealed her to be venal or petty or dumb? He was not touching her as though he believed her to be venal, petty, dumb. She closed her eyes. The two living people touched only fingertip to scalp; the dead beneath them lay foot to foot and head to head.

"All right," he said at last.

She opened her eyes, squared her shoulders. His lopsided mustache twitched fondly. "You needn't have taken your hair down," he said, plucking the pins from her hand. She felt the heat of his forearms against her neck, through his jacket, as he tacked her hair back up. She could tell it was a bad, tender job.

She was not beautiful, thought Dr. Leviticus Sprague. Not in the way he had been raised to think of beauty. Her skin was custard. Her hair was the color of bruised fruit. Her face looked like an anthology of other faces: an odd nose with a bump halfway down its slope, a thick upper lip that cast a shadow over its thinner downstairs neighbor. Narrow chin. Broad forehead. Even her eyes were mismatched, the right one bigger, prone to widening to show the white all around the iris, he would never stop noticing. It always made his heart chime.

He had been alone a long while. He had never lived with a woman he was not related to—his grandmother, his mother, his sister—which is to say he had never been regarded the way this woman, this Bertha Truitt, regarded him, with an ardent curiosity. In his way he had loved her not from the moment he saw her in the frost but from the moment she had looked at him and he understood she might love him back. *Love him back* came first: he was a cave, happy to be a cave, and she a swung lantern come to light him up. When he'd heard her tell the policeman her name, he'd thought she was lying: she'd read it off some headstone. But he'd walked the cemetery a dozen times since then, and never found a single Truitt. The unsteady boy with whom he'd found her had gone. He could not go to the Salford Hospital to ask what had happened to her, not because he would be turned away as a visitor but as a doctor. He would not ask.

But here she was. She was so *odd*. Mismatched in her soul, and pleased with the effect.

"It's a humbug," he said. "A lie, start to finish."

"But tell me your findings."

She would always be stubborn in the face of his reason. He would always surrender.

He said, "I could not find a single flaw."

"Do you bowl?" she asked him.

He laughed then, with his whole head. She wouldn't have known he was a laughing man. "Well," he said. "I *have* bowled."

"I mean candlepins."

He nodded. Candlepins existed also in Oromocto, New Brunswick, Canada, where he was from. An elegant sport, he'd thought when he'd watched it, and like most elegant things that white people favored also essentially feebleminded.

"*I* bowl," said Bertha Truitt. Then she touched him behind his ear, beneath the brim of his hat.

MRS. MOOD

Everyone talked about what a merry person Truitt was, but LuEtta Mood could see that the merriment was trained on a trellis of sorrow. It was a companionable sorrow, the sort you might never have to discuss. It drew LuEtta Mood in. Sorrow had interested her since childhood, long before she had any sorrows of her own. Then she met her own unhappiness and wondered where the earlier interest had come from, ignorant as it was.

Her husband, Moses Mood, was known almost reverently as the homeliest man in town. As a child he'd been shot in the ear by his brother, and the resulting scar made him look not blown apart by violence, but as though something deep in his head had tunneled its way out and, famished, lapped and then gnawed at the basin of his ear. When he'd woken up after the injury, age eight, his father said into his good ear, "Well, Mo, this will be the making of you," and Moses Mood decided it wouldn't. He would not be kinder than he might have been, but neither would he be ruined. The scar would mean nothing to him. So it didn't, except for this: he was like a snake-bit man who concluded he must learn to dominate snakes, so it might never happen again. He loved guns. The snake charmer always dies of snakes eventually.

The scar was not the source of Moses Mood's homeliness: he would have been a bullet-eyed dogtoothed man no matter what, with dark eyebrows worn away at the edges. He grew from injured child into a slow-moving self-satisfied fellow whose lower teeth bulldoggishly revealed themselves when he laughed. He laughed indiscriminately. He seemed to ladle his laughter out like a phi-lanthropist feeding the poor. All would benefit from his laughter; all should receive it. Beautiful LuEtta Mood (the former LuEtta Pickersgill) was used to getting more of everything. She was so young and so lovely she had never questioned why that was. Not till she married did she notice that the bolt of affection she re-ceived from her husband was not wider, nor longer, nor made from better stuff than what he gave to everyone. So she resolved to love him for *that*.

Then her own sorrow arrived.

The sorrow's name was Edith; the sorrow had been born sick and lived sixteen months. It wasn't the sickliness that killed her: she had been scalded by a cup of coffee while visiting her grandmother Mood, had wandered into the kitchen to find it on the table. LuEtta hadn't known you could die of scalding. "Our Edith was not made for this world," said Moses Mood. He meant to comfort his wife, forgive his mother, comfort and forgive by diminishing, and LuEtta Mood rejected the comfort and diminishment both. Forgiveness was his own affair. She had a locket with a lock of the baby's hair inside, so fine and short it was like dust, it could not be kept together in any way. Red, from a certain angle. It had gone with Edith's blue eyes.

What was LuEtta's duty, according to everyone else? To go mad with grief. To soldier on. To exist the rest of her life as a paradox, a human woman who suffered what everyone said was the worst thing and yet continued to live. Sometimes Hazel Forest, who after all had learned about death at the Salford Hospital, tried to talk about Edith, and that was the worst, to listen to a woman talk as though she understood when clearly she did not. Though of course all those years when LuEtta herself had been interested in the sorrows of other people that was just what she'd done. She'd offered up her sympathy as a way to keep herself safe.

Also her duty: to have more children.

It had been two years and she hadn't had another child and she could see the pity and impatience people felt for her across their mouths like a handkerchief held up to filter out disease—what was she doing, walking around outside, when she should be quarantined in her marital bed? If another baby had followed, people would have forgotten about Edith; or she might've been talked about from time to time with a weak happiness. LuEtta didn't want people to forget about Edith; she didn't want them to remember, either. She wanted Edith to exist the way any child did.

That was why LuEtta Mood bowled, to give people something else to know about her. Joe Wear was right, she brought in gawkers, mostly mannerly, men who came because where else could you see such a good-looking girl dewy with sweat and happiness, and not pay a cent, and not have to go to confession? LuEtta Mood swung around and smiled at the spectators. Then she rolled.

Soon enough she was better than Bertha, and Bertha bought a new machine to stand by the sculptoscope, a combination grip tester and spirometer. See how strong Truitt's hands were, after years of bowling! See how mighty her lungs when she blew into the tube! No woman or man could beat her at the machine, including LuEtta. Let LuEtta bowl. That was fine. Truitt was still a record holder.

Mary, Hazel, and Nora (the poodly one) bowled as though they were delivering the mail, politely, dutifully, inaccurately, but Lu-Etta Mood rolled so hard and true, you wanted to write a folk song about her.

She did not love bowling—no, she did, she loved it, only this love was inseparable from her love for Bertha Truitt. The fascinating greenness of Bertha Truitt's eyes. That particular smile—not the smirk, which was bonny, but the big beaming smile that seemed both private and magnanimous. Her very peculiar clothing—she always wore the divided skirt, but sometimes she had a divided petticoat beneath shushing and surging as she bowled. The way she called LuEtta by her full name, LuEtta Mood, *now LuEtta Mood pay attention to your follow-through*, and LuEtta wished she could hear her old name, her real name, in Bertha Truitt's whiskey voice, *LuEtta Pickersgill*, though even Lu herself knew it wasn't near so lovely.

"But where did you come from?" LuEtta Mood asked her.

"I'm here now," said Truitt, her customary answer.

Dear LuEtta wanted only to assemble Truitt accurately. A born-in-Texas Truitt was different from a born-in-San-Francisco Truitt, a widowed Truitt different from a never-married. Even three years of living one way or the other would sharpen or dull other facts.

One morning when LuEtta turned she saw a stranger, a black man wearing a tweed suit. The tooth of the tweed was dulled by dust, though overall his appearance was neat. His feet were propped up on a canvas bag that looked military but smaller. He read a book too small for his hand, a Bible or instruction manual; he had another book in his breast pocket. A long, curved pipe smoked in his hand. He frowned—no, only his mustache frowned. His actual face was at ease. He gave no indication that he knew he was in a bowling alley. He scratched the corner of his mouth with the stem of his pipe.

"Who's *that*," LuEtta said warily to Bertha Truitt.

Without looking, Truitt picked up a ball and said, "That gentleman is my husband."

"I mean the colored man," LuEtta clarified.

"Just so," said Bertha. "My husband, Doctor Leviticus Sprague. Dr. Sprague is from the Maritimes."

How could this be? LuEtta had heard the rumors of a husband, but Bertha Truitt was Bertha Truitt, alone on her bicycle, bending the paper to laugh at the Katzenjammer Kids, a singularity. Even when LuEtta dreamt of her, she never imagined interrupting that singularity, never saw the two of them in a kitchen somewhere, sitting on a sofa, sitting on the edge of a bed—nowhere but the bowling alley.

Maybe the man wasn't colored. Maybe the Maritimes were a place where white men were dark, like the Azores, or Sicily.

"Congratuations," LuEtta said. "No, really. When ever did you get married?"

"Sit, Lu," said Truitt irritatedly. Truitt held the ball as though it were an intimate thing she couldn't reckon with as long as someone stood near. LuEtta felt a flare of shame, jaw to cheekbones, at having got her so wrong.

She went right to the man, Truitt's so-called husband.

"I'm LuEtta," she said.

The man looked up. He nodded, and smiled, and conveyed to LuEtta—who had a sympathetic heart, it was her downfall, she saw the best in everyone but could never figure out how to get it out of a person, she could just see it glittering away inside doing nobody any good, this was the lesson of her marriage—a radiating, painful shyness. He had a face plumper than the rest of his body. LuEtta fought the urge to touch him.

"Nice to meet you," she said. "I hear you're—you're married to Bertha."

"She tell you that?" He shook his head, but smiled again. "Well, I've never known her to be wrong."

"It's a pleasure to meet you," she said.

"Yes," he said. Then he corrected himself. "Yes, a pleasure. For me. As well as you. Excuse me." She thought he was about to stand up, but instead he put his pipe in his mouth and returned to the book.

He was definitely not a white man.

When Bertha was done, he stood to join her. They did not speak, they did not touch. They walked out not together but adjacent. How they always moved through the outside world together: close enough to not lose track of one another though neither glanced the other's way, far enough to be blameless strangers if they passed the wrong sort of people. On the street at the same time as though by coincidence, but the sort of coincidence arranged by the gods, and between them a space of such evident magnetism that no reasonable person would have breached it.

B owling was new to the territory: superstitions grew like ivy on the walls of Truitt's Alleys.

It's bad luck to spit in a bowling alley.

It's bad luck to drink beer in the middle of bowling one frame; wait till the pinbody resets the pins before you touch your glass.

If the bowler on either side of you has a bad leave, wait till she finishes the frame to bowl, or you too will be cursed with a bad leave.

It is terrible luck to be born in a bowling alley.

Bad luck to eat fish in a bowling alley: eat only beef, venison, fowl.

A nonbowler who spends time in a bowling alley must never pick up a ball: he is as a priest in a maternity ward, on entirely different business, and must remain pure.

Do not speak of a nonbowler in a bowling alley. Worst sort of luck.

(For who? The bowlers, the pinbodies, the nonbowler himself?)

That's enough now.

Where had he been? Mary Gearheart heard he'd been out walking. (Her father ran the vaudeville house: she could sniff out the freak acts.) He had walked from Boston to New Brunswick, Canada, where he was from, and then back, a distance of 1,100 miles. He was a pedestrianist: he'd won walking races, though this had not been a race. It had taken him a hundred days altogether, but that included ambling. Ambling and rambling, swims in rivers, visits to relatives. It was a religion. It was a disorder. It was a habit, like drinking or bowling. He was a physician, educated in Glasgow. Did he walk to Glasgow? In a way: he walked for miles on the ship that took him there. Did he speak Scottish? Scottish is not a language, Mary. I think it is, I heard a Scotsman speak it.

The women pictured him sloshing across the surface of the ocean in seven-league boat-bottomed boots. They pictured him striding to Canada, a fishing pole shouldered like a rifle.

He might have been deaf, the way he never flinched at the sounds of the alley. He had a double chin so replete that strangers wanted to test its bounce with a finger, or wished he'd grow a beard for modesty's sake. "Dr. Sprague is from the Maritimes," Truitt said whenever she introduced him. She said this as though *The Maritimes* were a chronological location, not geographical. In a way she believed that this was the case, though she couldn't have explained it.

"That's my husband," Bertha Truitt said, to the police who wondered whether she needed help, the greengrocer, the ladies of Truitt's Alleys, anyone who asked. He did speak, at the same rumbling pitch of the rolling balls, maybe why she loved him.

Jeptha Arrison said, "There's the smartest man I ever met." But Jeptha was so amiably stupid everybody was the smartest man he ever met. It was a worldwide tie.

"Nobody can think that much," said Joe Wear.

"He writes poetry," said LuEtta Mood. At first she'd resented Dr. Sprague: she felt she'd dug out a little space next to Bertha Truitt and here was this man stepping into it. She had thought terrible things about him, even wondered whether their marriage was legal (in Massachusetts, it was) or actual (a different question entirely).

But Lu was as muscular in mind as in body: she made a decision. She would protect him. She said to Joe Wear, "He's published two books. He writes the poems in his head as he walks."

Joe Wear frowned with such vehemence it made the women laugh. "No doubt he does. Myself, I have a job. I have no use for poetry. I don't see what's so funny, ladies."

He was a feral child, Joe Wear, brought up in bowling alleys by bowling alley operators. He had gone to work for Bertha Truitt because he understood she would not try to mother him: he had no use for mothers, having never had one, only a photograph and a maiden aunt and a general ungainliness caused by the doctor's forceps (according to the matron at the Dolbeer Home for Destitute Children) or the umbilical cord around his neck (according to the maiden aunt). Not a limp but a liquid lumbering walk. He seemed to need tightening at his joints, or else he'd been overtightened. It did not stop him. It would not.

No mother, no imagination. He could not see how things could be improved or changed, and so he'd follow his employer's directions to the letter. She had found him at the lowest point of his life, ruined by love. Or not yet ruined, but the ruin hung over him like a guillotine blade. The blade hung there still. She had stayed the execution but did not have the power to pardon him.

Do a good job, Truitt had said to him the day of his hiring, *and one day the business will come to you.*

His employer, singular: Bertha Truitt. Old Levi wasn't anything to him, married or not. Still, his presence worried Joe Wear. Truitt was a fraud—she went around claiming she'd invented The Game, when everyone knew that wasn't so—and now she'd married a colored man, which showed she was a woman of bad judgment, too. Joe

Wear worried somebody might burn Truitt's Alleys to the ground. Nobody did. Rich people were allowed to do things, he guessed. One day he'd be rich himself and live how he wanted.

No curtain at Truitt's, too many women, but he had lodging above the alleys and Truitt trusted him. He had never been trusted in his life. It was a perturbing sensation.

They were alike, Joe Wear and Bertha Truitt, foundlings for whom the rolling ball was the feel of a hand on a forehead, a light touch of love on the back. Bowling gave you something to think about besides your regrets.

THE ODDITY

D r. Sprague had no theories about architecture, and so he let his wife draw up the plans for the house on Somefire Hill, near City Hall, half a mile away from Truitt's Alleys, along O. S. Fowler's architectural theories: octagonal, with large rooms, a stepped-back third floor, an octagonal cupola at the top. It wasn't a good-looking house but a spectacle. Not a folly (people could live in it) but a folly (who would want to). The walls were filled with lime and gravel and ground rice, and stuccoed with a combination of plaster and coal dust. *A Home for All* (the pertinent pamphlet, fished from Bertha's gladstone bag) promised it would make its occupants happy. Bertha oversaw the construction, the frames built and filled with mortar. She got the Irish in again. "That lime'll eat up my boots, Troot," the foreman said, and Bertha said, "Never mind your boots, I'll buy you more." There were more rooms and closets in the house than anyone in Salford had ever seen. The neighbors called it the Wedding Cake.

Bertha named the house Superba, which she insisted was Latin for *superb*. Unlike Dr. Sprague, she had no classical education. "It means arrogant," he said. "The feminine form." Oh no, she said, people made that mistake all the time, but her interpretation was the correct one.

It was hard to arrange the furniture in the pie-shaped rooms, and Bertha shifted the chairs and tables clockwise around the floors as though measuring time. The one interior staircase, spiral, was in the middle of the house, just as Fowler recommended—fewer steps, less wasted time—which meant they met there several times a day. They loved each other, it was fine almost always, but a staircase amplifies ill will, and a spiral staircase tangles those feelings round. When they fought, Dr. Sprague took the exterior stairs, which were built into the plaster outside, all the way up to what Bertha called the cupola and he called the belvedere and the reader might think of as a widow's walk. You couldn't see the exterior stairs till somebody was on them. Dr. Sprague seemed supernatural, sprinting up the outside of the Wedding Cake. The neighbors worried that someday he might climb their houses in just such a way, as though it were a talent he and possibly, terrifyingly, all of his race had.

(He crawled into their dreams, too, like his wife. Not into dream beds but into dream kitchens, where the dreamer would find him at the table, drinking from a glass of water, waiting—the dream–Dr. Sprague listened to his neighbors as they confessed to him first their medical problems, then marital; the failures of their bowels and their affections. The dream–Dr. Sprague was interested, and did not interrupt, and so they kept talking as he nodded, and just before they woke up they felt awful that they planned to boil the glass or even throw it out, so unnerved were they by the colored doctor's lips upon it.)

Sometimes Leviticus would send Bertha a note in the dumbwaiter, and she would answer through the speaking tube that fed into the closets and ran along the dumbwaiter shaft. The speaking tube opened with a squeal of air that signaled an incoming call. He would be in the belvedere, composing a poem in his head. He composed everything in his head, music and poetry and watercolor paintings, and then it took a maddening few minutes to set his notions down on paper—except those compositions he forgot on the stairs down, dozens of them he reckoned, because he forgot everything when Bertha called his name.

Their bedroom was large, bedrooms needed to be, else your own breath could kill you in the night or make you—that most dangerous thing, according to health specialists—*sluggish*. A slugabed. A mucousy terrestrial mollusk. No, thought Bertha, they would not be slugs. She had a sort of canine back that responded to scratching: Leviticus knew all the spots. He liked to be bit. Once, during a thunderstorm that had woken them in the night already lovingly biting and lovingly scratching, she looked up and caught sight of the mirror's reflection above the dresser, both of Leviticus's dark hands around one of her white breasts, and said aloud, *this is what other people see when they look at us*, and it was as though their iron bed had been struck by lightning. But their bedroom was safely on the second story, and she merely lovestruck. Bad for the health to sleep directly under the roof because of chilling breezes, bad directly over the cellar because of the noxious gases off decaying vegetables.

They never lied to each other but the past was behind them, the past was a patient beyond saving.

"When I get a home, I want a cat," Leviticus had said when they met. They took in a swollen vicious little tortoiseshell who'd been mewling around the pear tree and soon the foot of the bed was filled with kittens, whom Bertha named after famous Italians—Donizetti, Botticelli, Raphael—though she didn't like opera and knew nothing of painting. The mother cat was the Mother Cat, as crabby and duck-voiced a creature as ever lived. Her undercarriage had been loosened by kittens and swung when she ran up the stairs. For Bertha she had no time at all; the Mother Cat's love was for Leviticus alone. She looked like a carpet bag his own mother had carried. In his lap, she gave herself entirely to love; she purred, bade him pat and scratch, rubbed her cheek against his jaw.

"She reminds me of someone," Leviticus told Bertha.

"Leviticus," she said. "For pity's sake I am not a cat."

"Then what animal are you?"

She went silent a long time.

Finally he answered for her: "A sphinx."

D r. Sprague opened a practice in the next town over, Foxton, in a black neighborhood called West Hills; he had admitting privileges at the Plymouth Hospital in Boston, which his friend Dr. Garland had founded when no other hospital around would allow in black doctors. None of the white people in Salford could imagine it, the way he could hear wrongness in a body. Leviticus's siblings were musicians but he had perfect pitch for the anatomical: gurgle, hush, echo. He knew all the body's misdirections, the stomachache that meant an ear malady, the limp that meant your shoulder needed tending. His expression was scientific as he worked, his hands gentle, impersonal. You were not your body, but if you were to persist, your body must be attended to. His patients loved him. They asked after his wife. "She is very well," he told Faucenia Brooks, Chickie Barksdale, O. V. Orlebar.

"Come to church," said O. V. Orlebar. He meant Shiloh Baptist, where O. V. was a deacon, and Leviticus did go a few times. He'd been raised in the faith. His father had been a deacon, too. But church was his childhood, his family, whom he knew he'd turned his back on. His parents were dead. His younger siblings were still on the family farm in Oromocto waiting for him to come home. (That was where his own money had come from; his people had been farming in Oromocto since 1776.) No doubt his siblings—Almira, Benjamin, and Joseph—would think church was the first step north. Most of the parishioners at Shiloh Baptist were from America's South, people of surpassing kindness and foreignness to Dr. Sprague, above all because they believed in God and everlasting life.

Leviticus Sprague despised Truitt's Alleys, though he would never say so. To be surrounded by people! Not just the fellow in the next lane over, but the pinbodies, the lollygaggers. The racket. The repetition of it. The troglodyte conditions. The smoke and spit of white men gathered together. The dirty looks. The ill feeling, which itself seemed made of smoke and spit.

The thing that had worried him about married life was the idea of somebody *looking* at him all the time. Out in the world people looked at him, more now than ever because he was married to Bertha. One of the things he liked about being a doctor: when people had their eyes on him they were thinking of themselves, what he might say about their health, what conclusions he had about a boil or a tremor—they did not care about his body, only theirs. But Bertha watched. She believed him to be her territory. When they ate dinner, the second that Leviticus got gravy caught in his mustache, or ketchup on his chin, Bertha would say, "My darling," and gesture to her own face. The very *second*. He could not explain why this bothered him, other than a mustache was private property. "How is it?" Bertha would ask at the first bite, when the grub was still unfolding on his tongue. And meals were innocent. *She was always watching.* She did not tell him to give up his bad habits but she noticed them. Another pipe, Leviticus? Another glass of whiskey?

He brought all his bad habits to the belvedere. There Dr. Sprague opened the eight windows of the octagonal cabin, smoked his pipe and his du Maurier cigarettes, drank his Gibson's Finest, read books on the history of the Maritimes, and with the wind whistling through, and the smoke puffing out the top, it was as though Superba were a great kettle, or a steamship headed upriver, a conveyance of industry. Up there he could not be seen and he was himself.

In the mornings he would walk. He was a man of nature, he could go miles along the river, all the way to Waltham, or through the Salford Fens north to Foxton. At the start of a walk, alone and moving, the sun at his back or cold rain down his collar, he was more himself than under any other circumstance, until he had walked so far he was *not* himself, not a *self*, but joined to the world. Invisibly joined. Had a religion been founded on this, purely this, he would have converted. (Unlike Bertha, he did not have the need to found or invent anything himself.) Proof of God? Proof was in the world, and the way you visited the world was on foot. In winter you came to the ice floes like shattered monuments in the river; in spring you walked into a blooming dewy magnolia bush. Your walking was a devotion. Most days he rose early and left Bertha behind, asleep, and walked for three hours and was back to fix her breakfast. What happened in those hours? O only the shift from the sky dark and aerated with stars to the layered morning light to the sun gilding the river and regilding the already gilt dome of the courthouse, only the invention of morning, only Bertha in her dreams bowling, bowling, he could tell by her trembling arm and wrong-foot approach.

One early morning as Dr. Sprague walked along the edge of the fens he heard an animal rustling amid the marsh grass. What might it be? Something wild, he hoped. He'd been too long in a city looking only into the hostile eyes of men.

At first he thought the creature in the fens was a big cat. A hillocky beaver. A faun. Through the sandy grass he saw a pair of eyes, at first too wide-set for any earthly creature. Then the face looked distressingly human, though he could hear the steady *thack-thack* of a muscled tail, a noise neither warning nor comfort, and the unfurling sound of wings or a parasol.

"Hello?" he said. Dark green eyes. A narrow-bridged nose. Leviticus stumbled on the solid ground before the fens; his gloved hand plunged into the muck as though into a human body during surgery, he could feel a beating heart beneath, and he was on the creature's level. He knew her, the face was hers, in a seizure he believed it. Despite the muck, the dark, the seizure, the beating earth, what he felt was love, and he said her name.

The thing hissed and fled: oily waddle, blurping noise of a stout body sliding into swamp. Not his wife after all. But the love didn't ebb. *Bertha*, he thought. *No, an animal, or a spirit.* He ran home. There, Bertha was turning over in bed, sleepy, dream-damp. "What is it?" she asked. He wanted to tell her. Then he said, "I thought I saw you by the fens."

She gave a burbling half-awake laugh. "You saw the Salford Devil, maybe."

He said, severely, he never was severe, "There is no such thing," and climbed muddy beneath the counterpane. He felt above the covers, then below. "Where's the Mother Cat?"

"Maybe the Salford Devil's got her," Bertha said matter-of-factly.

"Not the Devil," said Leviticus. "We do not believe in the Devil."

"I didn't realize our beliefs were yoked together," she said. "Anyhow if she's gone she'll be back, full of kittens. The cat, Leviticus," she said. "Not the Devil."

"That cat's too old for kittens," he said, and he made the clicking noise with his tongue against his teeth that always conjured up her and all cats from the corners. She didn't come, only her children, Donizetti, Raphael, Botticelli.

The Mother Cat didn't come home that afternoon, or that night. The next morning Dr. Sprague went through the neighborhood on all fours, clucking his tongue, with a herring on a string to toss beneath bushes. Had it been the Mother Cat, twitching in the fen? Where could she be? He went into people's backyards, peered under their porches. "Mother," he called, "little Mother." "You'll get yourself shot," said Bertha, "and over a cat, when we have three more!" Eventually he did find her, but dead, beneath the roses in the backyard, intact, untouched: she had crawled there to die. He wept, he couldn't stop. The Mother Cat had a way in bed of sleeping in the crook of his knees, so he could not move; she spent the evenings purring beneath his book, nudging the book with her head. He missed her bodily—

"We'll get another mother cat," said Bertha.

But he would not be comforted. "Another does not exist!"

"Grief is not for cats."

"Do not, Bertie," said Leviticus. "Do *not*." He couldn't finish the sentence: whatever she was doing was too awful to be named.

She wouldn't stop. "Grief is surprise. Grief is, I wasn't prepared. Grief is, It's not fair."

"It isn't," he said, but uncertainly.

"That cat was old as Moses and died in a rose bower. You are not griefstruck. You feel sorry for yourself. I feel sorry for you, too," she added. They looked at each other and understood: this was how they might mourn each other, she clear-eyed, striding forward; he weeping and inarticulate. It was what each would have wanted of the other.

But *was* Bertha Truitt the Salford Devil? Did the Salford Devil make itself up piecemeal, gull's wings, duck's webbed feet, twitching cow tail? Did Bertha all alone transform so she could study him?

Ever after Leviticus took his flask with him. He walked off the liquor as he walked off everything. Soon the memory of seeing the creature was as though a dream, or a childish imagining, something he'd made up once to give himself a thrill. Something he kept in his pocket even now.

A WOMANHOUSE

The first indication of Bertha Truitt's condition was the spirometer's reading. She held the record for both grip and gust—when you set a record, your coin was returned; if you failed you were given an electric shock instead—and though her grip was strong as ever, one day when she blew into the tube—*Hygienic!* the spirometer said, inaccurately—the machine rebuked her with electricity. "No," she told it. She tried again. Another shock. She did everything she could: she imagined her lungs as bellows, and then as bagpipes; she quieted her mind and tried to still her other organs (hush, liver; settle down, pancreas); she tried to empty every inch of her body down to the soles of her feet to make room for more air that she could then expel into the spirometer. Shock, shock, shock.

Though she didn't really believe that her husband knew more about her body than she did—all those years of experience she'd had with her carcass, and he only a handful—she walked home to him from the alley. Even now, three years after the last lick of paint had been put on it, the very sight of Superba lifted her—mood?—no, it felt more bodily than that. The angles of it pleased her, straightened out her spirit level, brought her plumb. So did Dr. Sprague's roses. Whatever had lifted inside her was not her lung capacity: she was so out of breath by the time she got inside she couldn't force a word into the speaking tube. She just opened it so it squealed upstairs, and he came down in his green dressing gown, the one that made him look like a handsome billiard table, with the quilted lapels.

"I am dying, maybe," she said.

"I believe just the opposite," he told her. "Sit, Bertie." She sat, but on the arm of the davenport. He knelt on the floor beside her.

He'd seen the spread of Bertha's nose, the puff of her ankles, took notice of tenderness of both the physical and spiritual kind.

"The opposite of dying is living," she said.

"Is making life," said Leviticus. "Bertie"—she stared down at him—"you are with child."

"With?" she said. "*With?*"

She made allusions to her age, which she then remembered she'd vowed not to reveal, and began to say, you see my mother never, and remembered she'd vowed not to discuss her parentage, either. A change-of-life baby! After all, the octagonal home had been designed by O. S. Fowler to encourage procreation, even in a woman such as Bertha Truitt, at such an age.

Leviticus, kneeling, touched her right ankle with such gallantry you would have thought that the site of the miracle.

"Impossible," said Bertha. "No, I refuse to believe it."

"It isn't a matter of belief."

"I do not believe in the unseeable," said Bertha. She heard the lie and decided to clarify. "I do not see a child and until I see a child I will not believe one exists."

At first the pregnancy was like an idea she had, present, indefinite, entirely hers. A wait-and-see thing. Doomed, maybe. A bad idea. Then it was like a train ticket somebody had folded into her hand without telling her the destination, and she'd been put on a train and had to keep her fist shut till the conductor came through. Then as though somebody else's bag on the train—*here, hold this*—had been settled into her lap so she couldn't move around the way she liked, the bag's owner striding off into the next car. Soon enough it was as though that stranger had picked up the bag and had sat extraordinarily close to her, but in a clever way, so that she could not complain, call the conductor to have that person removed.

Her bowlers looked at her sideways in the bowling alley. Her togs were designed for the ordinary fluctuations in her weight—all her life she was a pony, put on weight in winter to keep herself warm, lost it, lost *most* of it, in the summertime. Now her divided skirt was overburdened. She'd broadened all over. Mary Gearheart said it was a growth, her own mother had died of such a thing—

"I don't think so," said LuEtta Mood. "That it's a growth. I think Truitt's going to have a baby."

"Banana oil," said Mary. "Bullshit."

Mary Gearheart might say anything at any time. Nobody ever asked her questions: she spewed. She spoke of her own cramps and bleeding and bowel movements, of her husband—she wasn't *Gearheart* any longer, but Phillips—she was so frank about the various ways her body ticked and dripped and gushed and gurgled and stretched and smelled that she appalled even Hazel Forest, who believed in medicine but had her limits.

Mary Gearheart Phillips was pregnant, too. "See," she said, and she lifted the white duck middy blouse she bowled in, and knocked her knuckles against her stomach. "Hard. My mother died of a growth big as an ottoman," said Mary. "And it was soft. You could sink a fist in. I have hair on my toes, and my lip, and"—her voice dropped to a sizzling whisper—"nipples!" She talked about her own body as though gossiping about a girl at school she wished to humiliate.

"It's natural," said Hazel Forest.

"It's *disgusting*," said Mary Gearheart happily.

"It's not a growth," said LuEtta Mood.

LuEtta had recently decided she would be a wonder instead of a beauty. She had seen beauties go mad in middle age, as their beauty turned less live and more monumental, beauty still but mostly to mark the space where greater beauty once had been. But wondrous was wondrous, even when you outgrew it.

Lu bowled. She bowled against women and men. One spring she bowled against Minnie Barden, famous in her own Massachusetts town, in a ten-string trolley tournament: five strings at Truitt's, get on the streetcar to go to Ripton Lanes and finish it out. LuEtta won by seventy-eight pins. She brought the trophy back to Truitt's.

"One day you'll bowl a perfect game," said Truitt, stout, ungainly, who'd never been ungainly.

"It's not possible," Lu said.

"Of course it is," said Bertha. "On tenpin lanes they do it regularly. This is why The Game"—when bullheaded she called it *The Game*, there was no other; when tenderhearted, *Our Game*, a private pleasure—"why Our Game is better. It is harder. It is arranged to disappoint. But LuEtta Mood, you must not be disappointed. The world is prodigious. There are more things than are visible to the eye."

"Truitt!" said Lu. "You mean God and spirits and such?"

"I mean quite the opposite," said Bertha. "I mean the natural and exhausting teeming world."

Well then. She would broach it. "When will Dr. Sprague be back," she asked, for he was off on one of his walks. "How are you getting along?"

"Lonely," said Bertha, and as she said it LuEtta herself felt lonely as a rung bell, longing for the clapper's strike again. "What's that look on your face, Lu? I like to be lonely. I have been lonely for most of my life."

"I didn't mean," said LuEtta. "I'm sorry. *I* don't like to be lonely. You do?"

"Oh, people like all sorts of pain," said Truitt. "I could tell you. They pay for it. They like to be footworn and exhausted. I know a woman who loved the feel of starvation."

"Truitt," said LuEtta.

"Bowl," said Truitt.

"You're going to have a baby."

Truitt shrugged. "Perhaps," she said.

"Perhaps," said LuEtta.

"We will see."

"We will see."

LuEtta wondered whether Bertha Truitt would be overtaken by ordinary life. She wondered what she herself would do, if Bertha Truitt disappeared into motherhood. People were careful around her when they spoke of babies, but other people's babies never made her miss Edith more. Edith was an organ that existed inside Lu-Etta, far away from all womanly organs, tucked up in her rib cage. For a while after Edith died LuEtta had wanted another child very keenly—Edith the Organ worried for her mother, had suffused Lu-Etta with that desire. Quick! Before this is the story of your whole life! Another child! But then Edith the Organ simmered down, and was herself.

LuEtta wasn't sure whether Truitt knew about Edith. She'd assumed so these years, assumed that Truitt's extra affection for her—everyone saw it—was sympathy for the loss of Edith. It was pragmatic Bertha who allowed LuEtta to think—just some early mornings, just some lunchtimes—that one day she might leave Moses Mood. Walk away, on to the next life. The presents Bertha gave: a wooden toy brought back from somebody's trip to Germany with two bears who took turns chopping at a log when you pulled a string; blouses made up specially, with coppery trim that matched LuEtta's eyes. Truitt's love for LuEtta lit up Moses Mood's lack of it. His regard was for tools: hammer, wrench, awl, plane, rasp, angle, gun. A wife was a tool for the production of children, and LuEtta Mood was faulty. She would not leave him but she could believe she would.

Truitt liked to name things without naming them. The game. The place. The bog. The place in the bog. The bog and the boglands. The gentleman. The ladies. The baby. The bowler. The ball. The wood: you must learn to read the wood. The world: the world stops for the game. The place. The city; the Commonwealth. The old pinbody. The dead. The afterlife. The time. The death of me. The almighty, the very death, the bitter end.

They had been two childless women together. *I had a baby who died*, thought LuEtta, but she knew that the moment to tell Truitt had passed, if Truitt didn't know.

There was no name for Edith but Edith.

When Bertha's time had nearly come, Leviticus performed the Leopold Maneuvers, his hands on Bertha's stomach. "Who's Leopold?" asked Bertha. "Ssh," said Leviticus. They were in their bedroom. She wasn't aware of how much more of the bed she took up but she was clear about how much more of the world, and it was terrible. He was ascertaining how the—not *child*, she insisted, not *baby*, she didn't want a word that suggested the future in any way. Well, not *visitor*, said Leviticus, not *guest*, nothing that suggested transience. They settled on *stranger*, which seemed equally wrongheaded to both of them. The Leopold Maneuvers were a way to ascertain certain things about the stranger: direction, presentation.

Bertha lay back on the bed. She would have liked to discuss the peculiarities of a woman's body with LuEtta. Impatience with husbands. Pregnancy, its terrors and pleasures. Bladders, blood. Women told these truths to each other. Bertha knew they did, but she had never told anyone and nobody had ever told her and she didn't know how to start. Leviticus's hands, cool and dry, were on her skin at the top of her abdomen. An intimate distance. He nodded, worked his way down. His left hand cupped the right side of her immensity, then he reached up and took her hand and laid it in the same spot. She could feel a heaviness, a curve that was not her but beyond her. "The stranger's spine," Leviticus said in a fond voice.

No, she thought, *let us not*. She didn't hate certainty, she didn't hate mystery, but she couldn't bear the mongrel state between the two, knowing only some things—the stranger's head was pointed downward!—but not everything—who? *Who?* Even to call the event *the stranger*—as soon as she got used to it, she hated it. Leviticus's hands worked their way down. He was not really touching her but it still hurt. He pinched. She jumped. He'd covered her feet with the old quilt and she felt staked as a circus animal. The living being inside of her *was* an idea she'd had, her own dear idea, grown round and meddling. He tilted his face to the ceiling. In other examinations he had struck and sounded her, but now he just palpated, looking for shape instead of echo. His hands never left her body.

"Like head reading," she said.

"Nothing like," said Leviticus.

"Who are you examining?"

"*You*," he whispered to her immensity. In English it could be plural or singular. English was a fine language for prevarication.

Later that afternoon, Bertha Truitt thought, *I am heaving with child. Child*, she thought again experimentally, the entity that ordinarily tried to kick and shoulder Bertha out of the way, though Bertha was all around. Now she could feel no movement, only a lightning pain that was her body and not what her body contained.

The pain sent her to the spiral staircase to the belvedere, where Dr. Sprague had gone to smoke a pipe. A disaster is coming. Get yourself high up. The baby, too. The baby? Yes, she was starting to believe it. She wanted to see her husband's reassuring face. The iron stairs were narrow and she had never liked them. Her frame did not bend. It marched, it bowled, but it did not bend. Even at the best of times if she dropped something she would not stoop to pick it up. Her bosom sometimes had to be moved around a tight corner like a chifforobe through a doorway.

She assessed the staircase with fury and then thought, *Dominate it, Bertha, give it no quarter.*

She went right up, paused only a moment, *victory*, to rest her breasts upon the floor of the belvedere, and took one more step, and stopped.

"Leviticus," she said, "I'm caught."

He was there reading a book. He put it on the little green table by his fringed armchair and regarded her.

All her life her widest part had been her bustline, which she used, as a cat uses its whiskers, to gauge where she might fit. No longer.

Oh, Bertha: wedged in the aperture of a belvedere.

She hollered, a wild noise, and Dr. Sprague understood why she'd chanced the staircase. By her expression he could tell that she was now a different person, as all women are in the act of childbirth. That is the great change, Dr. Sprague knew, not the baby, who is the same object on either side of the experience. One *hopes* the same object: alive and mothered. Here in childbirth Bertha was somebody who would say—she was saying now, *I will stay here forever if I must, get away from me, get away from me, leave me alone.*

He never was intended to deliver this child. That job belonged to Hazel Forest, who was bored by childbirth, and the hired girl, Margaret Vanetten, who was now in the kitchen. Dr. Sprague was too softhearted.

"Turn, I think, to the right," he said to her. "Perhaps—"

"Hazel!" she said, and also, "get the hired girl!"

He couldn't shout down the stairs at a white woman who wasn't his wife, hired girl or no. He would have to retrieve her in person. He went out the window, down the ribbed raked octagonal roof. Had he dropped his pipe inside? Had he remembered to douse the match? He almost went back in: he was terrified of fire. No time. Late winter, ice and snow. His insides leapt but he kept his feet careful down the exterior stairs of the octagon. The wet seeped through his leather slippers. Then he burst through the back door into the kitchen, where Margaret Vanetten was weeping with onion-cutting for supper.

"Margaret," he said. "My wife. If you wouldn't mind. The time has come."

She looked petrified; she was a girl, only, big nosed and pale and fresh from the convent. She believed in God; she believed God was an old-fashioned man Who surely would turn His head away from childbirth. What would she need? She wiped the knife on her skirt and put it in her apron pocket in case. "Yes," she said, "yes, but where did you come from?"

He pointed toward heaven, but he took her through the house. The sky outside was darkening. The blue hour; *l'heure bleu;* but all hours are blue. "Follow me," he said to the hired girl. "This may be tricky, but we will have gravity to aid us."

Bertha's legs were still there, though she was naked from the waist down.

"Mother of God!" said Margaret Vanetten. "Shall I get the lard?"

Bertha was part of the house, the house was part of her, they were a mythical domestic creature. The structure had fastened around her like an exoskeleton. That was what happened when you had a baby, she told herself. (She was almost certainly going to have a baby.) You became part of the house.

She felt her body a floor beneath her but near the ceiling. She could hear the voices below, too, humiliating, then not humiliating. She understood she might never feel mortified again. Then everything shifted, and it was as though the house were wringing out her torso: a tremendous unfastening fart, and her legs and feet were soaking, and she scuttled scrapingly up into the belvedere.

"Oh," said Margaret Vanetten, "oh, oh, don't worry, Doctor, we will get this settled."

The two of them went up the stairs and found her there, on the floor, stroking her own hair off her forehead, a comfort, a tic. She'd got up but there was no way to get her out except in two pieces. The pipe smoked, cupped safe in the ashtray.

"All right, Bertha," Leviticus said. He had found his doctor self, the one that was bored by childbirth, too. "Nothing to worry about."

"If all goes right," she said. She wore a white smock hitched up around her hips.

"Everybody on this earth was born," he said. "It's the one thing we all have in common."

"Not only," said Bertha darkly.

If all goes right, she said again and again. Every third time the words were flattened with fear. A bog was a woman; a woman was a bog.

Margaret Vanetten the hired girl thought she herself might die of fright. She had never seen so much in her life, so much fluid and woman and marriage. It smelled of spilled whiskey up here. Something sterilized, surely. Then she thought: I will know this baby her whole life, I will love her more than anything or anybody. (She was certain it was a girl.) If we live through this—by *we* she meant only the baby and herself—I will love the child perfectly. "*Don't* be scared," she said.

Bertha said, "But I am," and Margaret Vanetten hugged her, and was flung away with such fury she skidded across the floor to the baseboards. "Don't touch me!" Bertha Truitt commanded.

"Onions," whispered Margaret unhappily, smelling her own fingers. "Yes, ma'am."

In the belvedere Bertha Truitt hollered. It sounded to her like somebody hollering in the other room. *Quiet that woman. I am trying to die.* Her old self rolled around the boards of her brain; she couldn't get at it; she had a sense it was about to drop off the edge.

She was dying. Her soul was leaving her body. *A* soul was leaving her body. A body was leaving her body and it didn't want to. A person.

Who was it, this person?

She thought, *If the worst occurs I will leave. I will walk out of the house and into the city.* Another thing she didn't have in common with her husband. He would have disappeared into the countryside.

She loved Leviticus but she'd left things she loved behind before. Things could go wrong. She knew that well. The sky around the belvedere had turned nacreous: pink, weak gold, blue in the hollow of clouds. "Go get a lamp," said Dr. Sprague to the hired girl. The house had electricity but the belvedere didn't. The air smelled of salt and disaster. Bertha found herself thinking of Joe Wear. Why on earth? He was capable and unsentimental, unlike Leviticus, unlike the hired girl. He would solve this problem. Also he had survived his own birth, evidence you could escape utter calamity. He'd told Bertha his survival had been a question: "I was blue, they said. Cord round my neck. So that's why."

The Salford Devil was only a woman, birthing or grieving, alone or plagued by company.

She was a creature with two heads, half woman, half infant. "That's good!" said Leviticus, as though she had said something. Then woman and baby were just two naked people in one room, same as the other two gaping, bloody, entirely clothed people. No, thought Bertha Truitt, you weren't anybody's mother till you looked that person in the face, and she waited, she waited, and then she thought, ah yes, the child was dead, the death was like hearing someone reading a bad-news telegram in the other room, and wailing, though the wailing was hers: she should have known not to count on any kind of luck in matters of love, so she said, "Leviticus," and "Ah!" he said, "Bertha," and handed her an object, it was a baby, a live one, beating like her heart, thatched top, broad shouldered as a bread box, "Our Minna."

They had agreed to name a girl baby Minna. She could no longer remember why.

1907, February 22, Washington's birthday. The date cannot be argued with: her birth was recorded at City Hall.

THE DARLING

The babies Margaret Vanetten had previously known had been such little dear dumb animals, but from her earliest hours Minna was peculiarly human. She had a look to her that communicated everything, and Margaret understood. There's her hunger cry. There's the wet. Hold her head, Miz Truitt, she doesn't have the muscles to do it herself, she's just a little loaf of ham.

Margaret had originally been unsure about working in the strange house for the strange couple—was it natural, their marriage? was it right?—but Minna was the answer, a blessing, an amendment, an agreement, and also, as it happened, Margaret Vanetten's purpose in life.

"Those curls'll fall out," Margaret had told Bertha, because she'd heard that was what happened. You admired a newborn baby for her hair and then it dropped out and both of you were disappointed. But Minna's hair stuck.

Rosy and squinched Minna, milky sweet, with her smell that

sent Margaret swooning—though the scent turned out to be a particular brand of detergent that Dr. Sprague had shipped to him from Canada in the same box as his whiskey. "Nothing in America like it," said Dr. Sprague, who wrote love poems to his girl:

> Daughter, you are little, waking
> In the slant light of late morning.
> I am here to meet my sweetheart:
> Glint-eyed, round-faced, dimpled darling.
>
> Who knows, baby, if you hear our
> Prayers for you, our dreamy dreams?
> Every hour we tell the hour
> By the sun's unlikely beams
>
> Through our windows: you're our sundial.
> You're the measure of our days.
> Your ears are flowers, I whisper in them,
> Your eyes as green as chrysoprase.
>
> Minna, mine, remember this if
> Babes remember things they hear.
> My heart, eight-sided, every angle:
> Is my Minna's. She's my dear.

(The poem was in Minna's desk when she died, written in the sort of cirrocumulus penmanship that sets you to dreaming no matter the words.)

Bertha Truitt was a mother, a loving one, but perplexed. Minna in her mother's arms looked up. Anybody has seen it, a baby reading a face, careful as a phrenologist: that round chin means you're my mother, that wide forehead means you're my mother, that ear close to your head, those green eyes! What a scientist Minna was. What inventions and conclusions. She had the advantage. She had known Bertha's literal depths, had elbowed her organs and heard the racket of her various systems. She had measured time by her mother's diet and respiration, her exercise, and then Minna was born into the wide world and Bertha was so behind in knowledge she would never catch up.

So every morning she went to her place of business, to remember who she was. Of course she brought the baby.

"I'll come along," said Margaret.

"The laundry wants you," Bertha Truitt told Margaret, as though the laundry were a man at last asking for her hand in marriage, "and the alley wants us."

People inexperienced with babies couldn't understand how that baby slept so peaceful amid all the noise. Mary Gearheart wondered if she were deaf. Nora Riker wanted to toss her like a football. Hazel Forest dispensed advice about her mechanics. LuEtta Mood saw her beauty, knit little round caps for her dark hair to spring out the bottom of. She wanted to pick the baby up to feel the dense loveliness of her. But people, women especially, are leery of mothers of dead children, or too gentle around them. The bereaved mother is a combustible gas, the baby is a match; which one is dangerous makes no difference but best keep them apart. LuEtta couldn't think of a way to ask that didn't make her seem more dangerous. She saw she might never be allowed to hold anyone's baby again. She peered over people's shoulders into the pram, and admired Minna: plump thoughtful mouth, hands in dowsy fists. Oh, a fast asleep baby was faster asleep than any other animal. The women of Truitt's Alleys had children, too. Mary Gearheart her slack-jawed darling Patrick; Nora Riker a bald-headed drooling detestable boy named Philip;

Hazel Forest the mismatched twins Hollis and Ivy. Only LuEtta Mood remained childless, childless in the present tense.

Bowling was Minna Sprague's lullaby, like Rip Van Winkle before her, the low thunder of the ball down the wood, the clatter of the pins. No matter how far Minna Sprague got from Truitt's Alleys—and she put oceans between her and it, and graduate degrees, and husbands—her heart was set, like her mother's, to alley time, though it would make her furious to hear it.

Scatterbrained Jeptha Arrison was always picking up the baby and threatening to bring her to the pinbodys' shelf. One day Joe Wear found her snoozing on the cast-iron ball return. Joe scooped her up and went to talk to Truitt. "This ain't a place for a baby."

"And why not? You look fine with a baby, Joe Wear."

"Babies need peace and attention."

"What do you know of it?"

"I don't know what babies need, OK," said Joe Wear. "I run this alley. Miz Truitt, do I run this alley?"

Of course he did. She didn't know the least bit of the way the place worked. She relied on him and he'd never put his foot down till now.

"What I know is babies need a place to think," he said. He held the baby tucked in the crook of his arm. "And to not be carried off every which way. A baby who grows up in too much clatter is miserable. Hm," he said to the baby, who'd started to fuss. He reached down and touched his finger to her cheek. Minna looked taken aback, then dubious, then—as though she finally got the joke, your finger, my cheek—she smiled and revealed dimples, left and right. You got shocked with love, when a baby smiled at you. It was a religious experience. Joe Wear renounced it.

"Here," he said, and he handed her not to her mother, but to LuEtta Mood. Every woman in the place—it was morning, they were all women—quieted.

—

The two of them had never discussed their understanding, Joe a lifelong orphan, LuEtta the mother of a dead child, but they shared a ruthless sentimentality. "Would you, Lu?" he asked, and she did. The baby was solid with sleepiness. She yawned. LuEtta handed her to Truitt. "Here she is," said LuEtta, as matter-of-fact as she could make it, the way you always do, when someone has trusted you and you want to be trusted again.

"All right, Truitt?" Joe Wear said. He hadn't smiled once during the entire transaction, but a week later he presented Bertha with a jointed cow carved from a candlepin. Even the tail was articulated. Even the udders.

Everyone knew Minna Sprague was no ordinary child. She sat up at three months old and she said her first word—*lightning*—at seven months. She could read, it was said, at a year and a half, not taught, just off the marquee of the Gearheart Olympia Theater. Leviticus Sprague had been a prodigy himself, though his mother had accomplished this with drills and blows, until his sister, Almira, was born and their mother decided she'd rather a prodigy of the musical sort. Minna would not be put to work, but what was the harm in saying interesting things to her? Interesting things in French, perhaps? Then Bertha caught him at it.

"Italian, if you must," she said.

Well, his own Italian was not so good, though his accent was flawless. They learned together.

They would educate Minna at home. "With governesses," said Leviticus, worried that Bertha might teach her. "Margaret Vanetten will serve," said Bertha.

No, of course not. Dr. Sprague would teach his Minna. Who else? They met in Dr. Sprague's office on the third floor—he'd all but abandoned it for the belvedere—and read, or went over tables and maps. Bertha loved pamphlets; Dr. Sprague was devoted to reference books, atlases and dictionaries, anatomy books with transparencies and paper cutouts of the human body as red and pink and promising as dime-store valentines: you could lift the paper liver right out of the paper torso. Scientific treatises with gatefold appendices; giant dictionaries printed on cricklingly thin pages. They read next to each other, asked each other questions. Her mother was given to stroking Minna, which she loved, scratching her back, braiding her hair. Her father merely filled his office with his physical presence, which draped all around her, along with his pipe smoke. She leaned back on his shins, or absentmindedly untied his shoes. She was drawn to music and art, and needed to go to museums, which Dr. Sprague loathed: he did not object to the exhibitions but to the humanity that had come to regard it.

Margaret Vanetten took her to the Harvard Museums to examine the stuffed bison, whale, the dissected flowers blown from glass, the honeycomb like their own house, multisided, made of cells. They went to the art gallery, where Minna was drawn to the Mother and Childs. She particularly liked one flat-faced Byzantine rendition, where Mary looked like a tarnished ladle and Christ a bronze coin balanced on her knee. Their bodies were turned to the observer, and they looked at each other out of the corners of their eyes, as though the minute the museumgoers moved on they would gossip—but if Minna tarried, thought Minna, she might be included.

Certain paintings made Minna feel loved. Needed. This painting, for instance, required her above all other people to look at it. Sculptures were haughty; landscapes were tureens of soup, nice enough, sustaining for a while, but too democratic in their purpose. But the right painting—the *Mother and Child* by the Master of Nervi, for instance—was like music, a kind of flattering invited intimacy. She knew she couldn't explain this to Margaret Vanetten, who always seemed to be examining her for highfalutin notions that, left unremarked upon, might develop into delusion, or suffrage. Margaret did not want to strive to understand the world. She wanted the world to simplify, so that she might understand it.

"Margaret," Minna said one afternoon, looking at her *Mother and Child*. She was six years old then. "Where were you born?"

"In Salford, I expect, or nearby. I was left with the nuns. So I don't know."

"Don't you remember?"

"Being born?" asked Margaret, laughing.

"Yes," said Minna.

"Nobody remembers being born," said Margaret, and added, "and a good thing, too."

"*I* remember." She turned her body to the painting one last time. "All right. Let's go. You were there, Margaret. When I was born."

"I was indeed."

"I *remember*," said Minna as they walked down the marble stairs, softened in the middle from generations of footfalls. "It was dusk. It was in the belvedere."

"Your father tells you too much," said Margaret uneasily.

"He doesn't. And he didn't. I remember. It was before he put the smoking stand up there. My mother was hollering, and then she quieted down." Minna got thoughtful. "It was dark inside Mama— ordinarily I could see shadows, like on a lampshade—but then I saw some light—"

"Minna—"

In the vast atrium of the gallery, Minna turned to Margaret. The museum was closing. Gravity was working on the gallery-goers, shaking them down from the upper floors. "You smelled of onions," said Minna.

At that Margaret put her fingers to her nose, as though they still might be soup-fragrant. "Yes," she said, despite herself.

"*Now* you believe me," said Minna. "I'd gotten very crowded inside of Mama." She demonstrated with her elbows. "That's why I was born early. I remember all of it."

Was this terrible news, Margaret wondered, or splendid? All those things she had whispered, when she'd thought the infant Minna didn't understand English, when she seemed a well to drop wishes into. *Minna, I love you. Minna, nobody loves you but me. I love you best, I always will. Little grubby girl. Little darkling. Beautiful Minna, you are mine. Shall we run away together? Shall we go where nobody will find us?*

What she wanted to ask Minna now: Do you remember loving me, back then? She knew that six-year-old Minna loved her, in a dutiful, condescending way, as children love things they know they will outgrow. But did she remember that particular baby love she had for Margaret? You're a wonder, Dr. Sprague had said to Margaret, when little Minna quieted in her arms. You are surely good with babies. You have her figured out. But it was only that Minna loved Margaret, and Margaret loved Minna, and they made each other happy.

"It was shocking cold, being born," said Minna. She threaded her arm through Margaret's, and they walked out of the gallery and into a chill evening, like that of Minna's birth. Their own breath manifested in clouds in front of them; the clouds tore apart. Minna was still child enough to huff, to conjure up more fog, and Margaret joined her, two teakettles set to boil. Minna would know how breath did that, make itself known in cold weather; Margaret wanted to ask.

"It was *shocking* cold, being born," said Minna again.

"It always is," said Margaret.

By then Minna had forsaken the bowling alley entirely. As a child she'd visited every now and then, to watch her mother on her lane, but she couldn't bear it. It wasn't that she couldn't concentrate over the tumble of the pins but that people insisted on interrupting her. *That's a big book for a little girl!* Or *Look at you and your pigtails.* Or *You're Truitt's daughter. Truitt's and that man's.* As a baby she had loved being peered at, admired, but at heart she was not like her mother: she minded being a curiosity. At least if she were one—and she *was* a curiosity, also at heart—she wanted to orchestrate it herself. She would not go to Truitt's. I can't read there, she told her parents.

"Novels have ruined many a young woman," said Bertha. "That's a quote."

"From what on earth?" said Leviticus, whose idea of domestic life was the family reading together, in silence, until such a time as he found something interesting he wanted to read aloud.

"You're not too good for your mother's bowling alley," said Margaret to Minna, knowing that she was.

Leviticus knew it, too. Bertha didn't know it, and wasn't. You're never too good for the things you love, no matter how low. But Minna was better than Truitt's. He was, too. They *had* to be better, and this was the thing that Bertha never understood. She could be low, and not care, she could oddball around town all she liked. They had to be better. They had to keep their eccentricities to themselves.

Music Minna pulled out of the air. She sang, all the time and for hours.

> Who know what a cat loves?
> I know what a cat loves.
> Not mice even though they're delicious.
> Not lizards or roosters or fishes.
> Cats love fire because
> What cats do fire does.
> Purrs and skulks and stays up late
> Pounces twice to celebrate.

One of Minna's songs could last half a day, and her father nodded, pleased, and paid attention every third verse, and her mother would maddeningly try to sing along—"I know this song!" "You do not! I'm making it up!" "No, I'm sure: I heard it in the long ago"—and Margaret would be driven to distraction—"Such a clever girl," she would say, "but you'll wear yourself out"—but for Minna, inside Minna, the feeling was athletic and exhilarating, like climbing a tree, but the tree was the song, and grew up from the center of herself: it kept coming and coming, though she never knew the next line, neither words nor tune, till she'd sung it. That was the joy. She had to concentrate—not to *make up* the next line, but to *perceive it.*

Her house was like that, too. She sounded it the way her father sounded a body: thrummed the heels of her hands against the metal staircase that led to the belvedere (she was not allowed to go up without permission), *rat-a-tatted* her fingernails against the window-panes, whispered secrets into the obtuse angles of the milk room to see whether her voice would travel all around and back to her, the way her father said sound traveled under the dome of St. Paul's in London. She sang down the bulkhead doors. She sang in every closet in the house. The house was a drum. It was meant to be struck. Margaret Vanetten was always saying, "Oh, you want a sister, you poor thing," but Minna didn't, she didn't want to share the house or her parents or any part of her childhood.

"I think the house is a drum," she said at dinner. Margaret Vanetten had tried to civilize them, to insist they sit in the dining room and make conversation with each other, but as a family they were hopeless, and preferred the kitchen, and ate like castaways. Dr. Sprague's table manners were passable—he ate with knife and fork and never ladled food from the serving bowl directly into his mouth, the way his wife did—but he read books right in front of everyone and seemed surprised when asked a question.

"Daddy," said Minna. "Do you think the house is a drum?"

"Do I think what, my Minna?"

"The house is not a drum," said her mother, idly picking up a clot of mashed potatoes with her fingers. "It is an octagon."

"A drum might be octagonal," said Dr. Sprague.

"*Might*," said Bertha Truitt.

"*I* think," said Minna, "that at night, when we are asleep, the house turns on its side and rolls around the world, and all the furniture spins out to the edges."

"What happens to us?" said her mother, amused but also concerned.

"We spin out, too."

"That's called centrifugal force," said Dr. Sprague.

"That's called quite an imagination," said Margaret Vanetten.

"You're right," said Dr. Sprague. "It's a *beautiful* imagination."

"I meant—"

Minna sang, "The house is a wheel, the wheel turns around, the cats yowl about, we all sleep so sound—"

"The child needs a sister," sang Margaret Vanetten in her iceberg voice. She saw the looks on the faces at the table and understood that she had spoiled the moment, but she wasn't sure how. "I wish you'd get out of my kitchen," she said, bitterly, to nobody, "so I could do my job the right way."

Bertha felt Minna's head nearly every day but didn't read it, though it was a head finer (as Fowler said of all children's) than any adult's. Wouldn't you want the best for a head like that? People would judge her on it anyhow. They already did, they looked at Minna and thought different things about her, depending on who she was with, mother, father, nurse.

Did a child need secrets? Yes, Bertha believed; everybody needed dark thoughts, they were the lime in the mortar of your head. They held up the good thoughts. She knew now that phrenology was not real. It wasn't true that your connubial love resonated from one side of your brain and your jealousy from another—but even now she could *feel* those thoughts, the good and the bad. Hear them, too, her brain a gyring xylophone that rang when struck.

She loved her child entirely, perfectly. Her husband, too. She had never intended to marry the way some people never intend to go to sea. It struck her thataway, something you couldn't change your mind about for months if you didn't like it. Marriage to Dr. Sprague *was* an ocean—one of those peculiar foreign oceans so full of salt it buoyed the leaden. She was in the middle of it. She could not sink if she wanted to.

They were happy, that is, until the flood.

OVERTAKEN

1919. All around them candlepin houses had closed because of the war. Bowlers had been drafted; pinbodies, too. Truitt's Alleys had survived, welcomed back the wounded Salfordians, Freddy Pearlman who'd gone deaf in an ear, Pinky DeMuth who'd lost half his jaw and hid it with a kerchief, Martin Younkins who'd lost his left leg, Jack Silver who'd lost a hand and part of a forearm and bowled with the ball tucked in the crook of what was left. They formed a team, the Salford Half Nickels.

The same year, Bertha Truitt bought a Stanley Steamer. The Stanley factory was six miles away from the alleys, run by the Stanley twins. Machines! You shouldn't love them, but Bertha did. The controls with which you lit the boiler, let the steam go; the hissing noise of it. Mechanical Bertha, who had loved her bicycle, loved her motorcar better. She was steam powered, too, all human beings were, some set to simmer and others to boil. Listen to Bertha Truitt percolate! The things she would do, with her steam-powered notions. Doubt her? Feel: there's her boiler. Why she never corsetted: she'd been built by her inventor particularly, she wasn't going to choke her source.

Leviticus wouldn't get into the thing. He mocked her for her superstitions, but he had his own: he thought cars of any sort about to explode, with malicious intent, at any time. "Internal combustion!" he said. "A terrifying thought." Bertha insisted that a steam car was the safest sort, being water powered, but he wouldn't believe it.

Dr. Sprague favored nature, Bertha liked the works of man. She had a love of factories and shipyards, of railroad lines and cemeteries. Cemeteries particularly: she had been delivered to Salford in a cemetery, had married because of one. She was, really, a Victorian, though it was 1919, Victoria long dead, and Bertha never her subject anyhow. She still dressed in her old-time togs, divided skirts and waistcoats, and was a curiosity on the street. It was a form of armor, a way to get men to do business with you.

This morning she wore a green vest and one of her many-sided hats, a dark blue one that made her look like a minuteman or like a medieval sorcerer, depending. Some couples grew to look like each other, but Truitt, getting ready for her drive on a January day in 1919, looked like her house: octagonal, indomitable. She was going to Stearn's Warehouse to investigate some rock maple for new and bigger pins. The new pins would have a groove in the middle, Joe Wear's idea so pinbodies could grip them better.

"Come with me," she said to Leviticus that January morning. She had just started the car. It was a complicated procedure: you lit the boiler with a little torch, then got in the car to pump the steam from the boiler in the back of the car to the engine in the front. Later Leviticus would not know whether to be glad or destroyed that he had not gone with her. At any rate he had never ridden in the steamer and never would.

"In your motorcar? Bertie."

"I'm an excellent driver." Pump.

"So you say. No, thank you. An explosion will be the death of me, but not today."

He believed this and also he had a bottle of whiskey in the belvedere. Prohibition was coming: only one more state needed to vote the Eighteenth Amendment in, and it would come any day, and the law would go into effect a year later. The way he drank would be his undoing. He knew that. He told patients who drank less that they had to stop; his organs were half-unraveled with drink. Meanwhile he had bottles sent down from friends in Gaspé, the finest Canadian whiskey.

Finally the car was ready to go. She drove off. Once she was gone, he ascended to the belvedere and looked for her car on the street. She had already turned toward the river. He lit a cigarette and doused the match with water. He was terrified of fire, poor man. That's what everyone said later. Poor man, to go that way: he must have been terrified.

n Boston, Bertha parked the car on Commercial Street and went for a walk in the Copp's Hill Burial Ground. Cemeteries reminded her of bowling alleys, especially Copp's Hill and the Old Granary, with their tilted stones, the various projectiles sailing between them (tourist children, birds, genealogists). Dead wood: one of the differences between candlepins and tenpins. In tenpin bowling the dead wood, the knocked-over pins, is cleared between balls, spirited away by the pinsetter. In candlepin the dead wood lays where it has fallen for the whole frame, laced between the upright pins or flat out in the gutter. Dead wood can help you, if you know where to strike it, to knock it into standing pins. If you hit it wrong, though, it can absorb all the momentum of the ball, send it spinning in place out of reach of all other pins.

She's not dead wood yet, Bertha Truitt. She's moving through

Copp's Hill, looking at the names on the stones. Shem, Goody, Increase. Plenty of Williams and Sarahs, too. In cemeteries she feels like herself, whatever *that* is, without hearing the voices of other people like an electrical charge that makes her act otherwise. People who report seeing the Salford Devil describe, variously, a flying badger, a mammoth skunk, a mass of bats shaped like a bat. She believes wholly in the Salford Devil, and the shifting is evidence. It is a reactive animal.

Her, too. She is the Salford Devil—*like* the Salford Devil—a different person depending on who finds her, matronly or alluring, a chatterbox, a silent thoughtful woman, funny, humorless, shy, bold. Not on purpose: that is the charge pulsing through her. She feels no long story in her soul. She has a serial self. First one person, then another. Boxcar Berthas, one after the other. Once she had been an heiress to a factory that made boots for the Confederate Army; not anymore. Once she had loved an Italian. No longer. Once a man who believed in God. So long, so long, say goodbye, see you later, tomorrow, soon, around.

Bertha walked in Copp's Hill. She thought of Minna's thewy golden brown hair, a shade lighter than her skin; the careless length of Minna's legs overlapping her own on the davenport; the hot breath with which she filled Bertha's ear when whispering into it. Minna was twelve and it took all of Bertha's will not to treat her like a baby, carry her down the stairs and tuck her into bed and feed her from a spoon, sing nonsense to her, nibble at her neck. She still believed that she owned every inch of Minna. She was her author, her *inventor*. Out in the world, everyone said, *Oh, isn't she her father's daughter.*

Well, she missed them. She needed to go home. Tomorrow she would send Joe Wear to talk to the foreman at the lumberyard, sort everything out. The things she did, just to prove that a woman could! Honestly: the intricacies of maple bored her. Joe could talk about maple, how it was different in the floorboards than in the pins.

He could touch lumber and know its character and history, water damage, tendency to splinter or warp. Bertha could only look at the man selling the wood and judge him. She was good at this but not infallible. Joe, with wood, was infallible. Send Joe.

She went to her roadster and lit the boiler and climbed in. She waited for it to start up. It purled in the way that unnerved Leviticus. She wished he were in the seat next to her. She missed him more than she was sympathetic to his fear.

Just now he would be in the cupola, pulling on a bottle of whiskey. She knew he drank. She liked to think he didn't hide his drinking: they simply didn't speak of it. She wouldn't have expected him to give up alcohol for her nor would she ask him to give up his pantomime teetotal. Only sometimes did it bother her—when he fell twice a year into alcoholic melancholy, or when she reflected that he would die before his time. Then again, being so much younger than she, his scheduled time was long after hers, and drinking might even it up, a pair of scissors snicked across two lengths of ribbon at once. She supposed a better love would have wished him a long, long life without her, but her love was deep and true and bottomless and in the end (she didn't know that it was the end) not all that good. She had loved him immediately for the following reasons: his quietude, his broad forehead, the deep lines in his lower lip, the way his pinker upper lip was half-masked by his mustache, his mustache itself, the certainty of his medical knowledge, which she did not always believe. She had loved him next for the erotic scrubbing curve of his tummy, the way he hated the word *tummy*, his carelessness in all things (coins spilling from his pockets, food down his shirtfront), his love of cats—no man she'd ever met loved cats so much, whispered more endearments in their ears; she'd forgiven his foolishness over the Mother Cat, what a lot of fuss over an animal whose time it was. His love of Minna, of course, which was just as it should be and no more (despite her eccentricities Bertha believed the love of a mother and child, and husband and wife, were more important than father and child: in this she was a woman of her time). Most, first, ever: his admiration of her. That was evident the moment they met, and despite her pleasure in his admiration she had thought then it showed her own weak character, to find admiration so lovable. Now she knew: in marriage, what else mattered but admiration? And of course she admired him, too—loved him, knew his follies, lusted for him even now, felt it quicken her step—but most of all she admired him. It was the one marital affection you were allowed to take out in its true state and display to the dinner guests.

As for the affections you weren't supposed to show in company— *even now*. Bertha Truitt, in her dotage—though she never would have used the word—miles away from the man, felt flush with him. In their early days he had been decorous, polite, the way he'd been while reading her head, but by nature he was a nuzzling, nestling, insidious man, and eventually every county of his body had rubbed against every county of hers—unlike Savior Ercolini, who had always been extraordinarily specific in his physical affections.

Now why had she thought of *that* man? He was another life.

Gunshots. She'd parked on Commercial Street near the elevated train tracks. She thought they were gunshots anyhow, six sharp metal reports. Then she heard the roar of an enormous animal. You couldn't tell whether the animal was rampaging or dying, at first.

An elderly woman pushing a pram nearby turned to Bertha. "What was that?" she said.

Bertha said, "It sounded like—"

But then the woman screamed.

Not gunfire but a spitfire of rivets popping sockets on the tank atop the Purity Distillery Building. The tank was full, had been full, was now unburdening itself of two and a half million gallons of molasses in all directions. It had already killed two children and a horse, had done that straight off.

Bertha knew how to swim in water. She knew how to find the pocket of air in an upturned boat. She knew to stay indoors in a lightning storm, to go to the basement in case of tornado, she knew that salt or a wool blanket would smother a fire. She knew how to protect her heart—that is, her brain—from the various inflammations of dissatisfaction. She knew to look a mad dog straight in the eye and show her teeth; she knew never to try the same thing on a bear.

She had planned for disaster, just not this one. She could not make sense of it.

Nobody could. People tried to outrun the flood, but which way was safety? No guessing. The molasses scooped the baby from its pram; it turned a big man into a missile and sent him through a trolley windshield.

Drive, Bertha. Put the steamer in gear, turn the wheel.

The molasses smashed the door of Bertha Truitt's motorcar, wrenched it off the frame, and dragged her out. She couldn't hear anything over the sough. The smell was overwhelming, a kind of sweet lumber. It painted the back of her throat. *Slow as molasses.* The molasses wasn't slow. The molasses had grip and intention. You couldn't swim against it. You couldn't punch your way out. It plucked her hat from her head, which hurt worse than anything, the yanked hair, the *indignity*. It had the finicking audacity to unlace her boots, the animal strength to turn the car over. Then the molasses pushed her down beneath its surface and blacked her eyes and shut her up. Above her it swept an entire house, whole, out to harbor. The baby stolen from his pram; scrap iron; stray dogs: all passed over Bertha Truitt like the shadows of birds. She had already thought of Minna, of Leviticus, of the winding cats including her favorite, the black-and-white Donizetti, who was bony and old now, she *would* miss him, she *would* grieve, and now the cats were multiplying in her octagonal memory, they clogged the spiral staircase and filled the dumbwaiter and she was just on the brink, the brink, of thinking of her parents, and of her sister, and of lost Nahum—now, how would they find him to break the news of her death? she had worked so hard to banish him from her memory—and then another clobbering wave of molasses lay itself over the first, and her brain lit up like a lightning storm, then went over green, then was struck entirely dark.

n the old days, the disaster happened. When a stranger called or wrote or traveled by train, you learned of both the disaster and your ownership of it.

In Salford, in what was not yet known as a widow's walk, the widowed innocent Dr. Leviticus Sprague looked down Mims Avenue and wondered when Bertha would be back. His ticking punctual Bertha always knew the hour. Her heart kept excellent time. His did not. He hadn't brought up his watch. The fact is he did not drink so very much in those days—more than most men, but less than many. He kept his senses, his wits, nineteen times out of twenty. Now the January sunlight cut through the eight windows of the cupola—no, let's be honest, only four, that's as much as is mathematically possible—and he felt warmed from the inside and the out.

Superba did not have a phone. At six o'clock someone knocked on the door. Margaret Vanetten answered. A policeman stood there, holding an object like a sodden corsage. The molasses had taken Bertha's hat to the shipyard and pasted it to the side of a tugboat in drydock. Her name was stitched inside. They had not found anything else, not car, not body, not laced shoe.

Margaret Vanetten climbed to the darkened cupola, a place she'd been forbidden. She hadn't gone there since Minna's birth.

"Dr. Sprague," she said. "She was a wonderful woman—"

Margaret Vanetten had got ahead of herself. She always did, that one.

WE REGRET

Leviticus Sprague would not come down from the cupola. The women of Truitt's Alleys stood on the third floor of the Octagon and shouted up the little wrought iron staircase, which they didn't want to climb for fear of embarrassing him or themselves. They didn't know about the speaking tube. Not one of them had been in the house before.

"She might be alive!" LuEtta Mood called.

"You should go look for her!" bellowed Hazel Forest.

Getting Dr. Sprague out required a man. They would have asked Joe Wear, but nobody could find him—Truitt's was dark and locked, and if he was in his apartment overhead, he didn't answer the door. Jeptha Arrison was not a man to send on any mission. Finally Nora Riker's husband, Norman, was dispatched. They thought Norman would know how to talk gently but firmly: jostling Nora had died the year before of flu.

"Drunk," Norman Riker said when he came back down. He didn't say anything else.

So the morning after the flood LuEtta and Mary and Hazel went downtown to look for Truitt. They'd been young women when they first met her, and she middle-aged; now they were middle-aged, and she—they had no notion. They loved her but were unaccustomed to this particular strain of love, worry on her behalf. They felt helpless with their lack of experience.

"I hope we don't find her," said LuEtta.

"Well," said Mary Gearheart. The vicious little girl had grown into a deadly calm, censorious woman. "Well, LuEtta, I hope we do, and I hope she is healing."

"I only meant," said LuEtta, but she couldn't finish the sentence. She knew what it meant to find a person alive but beyond saving.

"Ssh," said Hazel. She was a nurse. You could not pronounce death without a body. "Girls, let's look."

Truitt wasn't at the Haymarket relief station, where living victims had been brought, browned by molasses, their skin mottled like oilskin. Everything was dulcified, awful. The pillows and floors were smeared with molasses, the doctors and nurses with molasses and blood. People sobbed but quietly. Gummed wheels stalled the gurneys; the sticky floor sucked at the soles of shoes. Truitt might be walloped, unrecognizable. Two unidentified women had been brought to the relief station, neither of them Truitt. One of them, an old lady, regarded the bowlers with one dark eye—was the other plugged up with molasses, or plucked out?—and said, "I can't get out, I'm trying to get out, Rachel."

Outside, the streets were brown, glutinous. They heard gunshots. Real ones.

"What is that?" asked Hazel.

"Horses," said Mary. "Trapped. They're putting them down, poor things. Mortuary next, I suppose."

The dead bodies were easier to look at than the live ones, since there was no longer anything to struggle against. The molasses turned people to pillaged antiquities, or bugs caught in insufficient amber. Louder than the relief station: filled with wailing, with no injured to disturb. After the women had toured the place and stepped outside, they gasped for breath.

"What I meant," said LuEtta to Mary and Hazel, on the trackless trolley back to Salford, "is I wonder whether she ran away."

"From *home*?" said Mary, in a voice of wonder.

"*To* somewhere."

They began to discuss it, at first with concern, then titillation. She had done it before, landed in Salford, Bertha ex machina, rumors of a fled marriage and a child left behind. She had begun again so entirely, with such enthusiasm, they hadn't held it against her. Perhaps this was her rhythm: take on a life, live it, shed it. If they could imagine her escape, then the gold shining behind her car was sunshine, not molasses, and she had nothing in common with the people they had seen that day, the man who had a spear of iron pushed through his chest, the old woman in the care station, alive, a ruined rowboat, crushed and washed far from harbor and longing for her Rachel.

They could picture Truitt in her Steamer. She's driving west, to Chicago maybe. To Texas.

"No," said Hazel. She had married, had her twins, divorced, had gone from spinsterhood to respectability to scandal herself. She would have run away if she could have. "New York."

"Her passenger seat's full of candlepins," said Mary Gearheart.

"No," said Hazel, certain of it, "bowling's done for her. She's gone to be an artist's model."

Mary Gearheart laughed.

"And why not?" asked Hazel.

"*Truitt?*" said Mary Gearheart. "Naked save a bowl of fruit?"

"Surely Truitt's the *artist*," said LuEtta.

"Oh!" said Mary Gearheart, and Hazel, grateful and sorry not to have thought this herself, said, "Of course she is." It was Hazel who believed that nudity and freedom occupied the same territory, not Truitt.

They felt ecstatic for her escape, and judgmental. They'd spent too long arranging their lives around their husbands and children, trying to mine happiness from the happiness of other people: always the first to wake up and the last to go to bed, always the least favored piece of chicken from the dinner platter. But *they* wouldn't leave, LuEtta, Mary, Hazel. Maybe one day they'd go to New York and look for her, in the bowling alleys, in the public parks, a theater, a museum. When they didn't find her, they'd stay another day, look in restaurants and opera houses. Of course they'd go back home to their families, once they had satisfied their curiosities.

The syrupy soles of their shoes skicked against the floor of the trolley.

"Maybe they'll never find her," said Mary, hopefully, because Mary of all of them knew she was dead, knew that for a while *missing* was better than *dead*, until it became worse. She touched Hazel's elbow, and then Hazel knew it, too.

LuEtta shook her head. "We'll look again tomorrow."

"Oh no," said Mary. "I could not make myself do that again."

Hazel said, "Ah me," and began to cry.

Nobody had ever seen her do such a thing, she who had watched so many people cut apart, the salvageable, the beyond repair, the good-as-new and the never-the-same. LuEtta and Mary took her hands. Somehow even their fingers were gummy, not the full muck stick of their feet but a remembrance of the stuff, enough to scent a love letter. "I'm sorry," said Hazel, who now could not even dry her own tears or hide her face, "I'm sorry."

"We'll look again tomorrow," LuEtta said. Hazel and Mary shook their heads.

So only LuEtta went to the relief station at Haymarket the next day, then the makeshift mortuary, then to the North Mortuary on Grove Street, where people killed by more ordinary things came as well, measles, old age, dropsy. On the third day she found Bertha at Grove Street, dusky sweet, her arm crooked over her head: the molasses had pulled her hat off, her boots from her feet, had knocked two teeth off-center from her now gaping mouth. The mortician had not yet begun to wash her with the bicarbonate of soda that would make her look like the twentieth-century person she was. Her silhouette was unmistakable, heavy bosomed, split-skirted, indomitable, brought low.

Vesuvius, Pompeii. What else could knock Bertha Truitt from this world? From the first, LuEtta had found herself praying: keep Bertha alive even if not here. Keep her in the world. She had never bowled a perfect game. She had never voted for anything. Hazel and Mary felt ordinary grief, for Truitt, for the children who'd been killed in the flood, for themselves for witnessing it all, for Truitt's daughter, who'd lost her mother. *That daft woman*, Moses Mood called Truitt. No, please, keep her here. Bertha would teach LuEtta how to drive, the way she'd promised. She would bring LuEtta into Superba, into the cupola: they would sleep on the roof of the house, as Truitt said she did in the summer weather. They would bicycle. They would march for suffrage. They would hold in the palms of their hands the calamities of the past—Edith; whatever had happened to Truitt—and would talk about them, but only if they wanted to: the conversation would not be momentous. None of that had seemed possible when Truitt was around. Now it was impossible unless Truitt was returned. That was why LuEtta went to the infirmary before the mortuary, even three days after the flood, when nobody could possibly be rescued alive from the wreckage and muck.

Not Mount Vesuvius, but the tank of the United States Industrial Alcohol Company. Not caught in ash but molasses. Twenty-one people had been killed, but they wouldn't know that for another four months, when the last body was pulled from the harbor.

Truitt looked ancient, a prehistoric woman lugged from a bog, a primitive who had not known what death was, exactly. You knew it was a disaster, yes, but not the universal one. She was LuEtta's second dead body, though she had not been allowed to see dear Edith's face, so badly burnt. Edith had not needed to be claimed. She was only a dead child, no mystery at all.

"Bertha Truitt," LuEtta said aloud. She meant it as an address. The mortuary employee took it as identification. She would not be covered with a sheet till the molasses was washed from her skin, the clothing cut from her body. Sorry, thank you, say goodbye.

The night of the molasses flood, still drunk, Leviticus wrote to his sister in Oromocto. Send the child now before there is news, he decided, get her far away before he knew something to tell. Anything might be put in a letter, later. Nearly nothing could be said aloud.

Minna was in bed. When did she sleep? They had not instilled good habits in her. You might find Minna sacked out in the parlor at eight in the evening, or awake in the kitchen at midnight. Her sleeping was deep and total, once she gave in, mouth agape and eyes open an unsettling crack. Leviticus stood outside her bedroom door and heard nothing. Then he found Margaret in the kitchen. She was making sandwiches. He knew her well enough to understand that this was an emotional response in her: anticipation and grief, worry, rage, all sent Margaret Vanetten to the bread bin, the icebox, the kitchen table. He examined the sandwiches to see if he could discern what drove her at the moment. Brown bread, butter, cheddar cheese. Her expression, too, was inscrutable, a cheddar-cheese and butter face. She turned it to him.

"Margaret Vanetten," he said.

No tears, but nerves.

"Meg."

"Yes," she said.

What should she call him? She reminded herself that it depended on what he asked of her. Bertha issued commands, but Dr. Sprague (he was still Dr. Sprague to her) asked questions. Bertha was kind, but didn't believe, exactly, that Margaret Vanetten had an interior life. Dr. Sprague was kinder, and he did believe in Margaret's interior, her soul, her sorrows and ambitions, which frightened him: he could look her in the eye for only seconds.

If Bertha Truitt was dead, Margaret must be bold. She might finally be allowed to mother her girl the way she wanted, with the full force of her love—she might be a *mother*. For years Margaret had flattered herself by thinking she was as *good as a* mother, she was a second mother, motherly, motherlike, mothering, but that, she understood now, wasn't enough. She would have to make the claim. It was tempting to believe that if you made yourself small and light, beneath notice, you might be allowed to persist nearly anywhere. But meek women were tossed out and forgotten: that was something she'd learned from Bertha Truitt herself. What women needed to do was take up space. Become unbudgeable. She would never be the woman of a fine house like this—but why not? Of course she wouldn't marry the Widower Sprague—but why not? She didn't have a family to be scandalized.

She knew the next question would be important. He had put on a clean shirt and tie to ask it. *Would you be willing to stay, in another capacity? To give Minna all of your attention? Of course I would employ a new hired girl to take on your domestic duties.* Or: *What will I do without her, Margaret?* Or: *Margaret, tell me: am I an unredeemable sinner?* Or: *What will become of us?* Or: *Will you, Margaret?* Will I what. *Will you?*

He said, "I am sending Minna to my family in Oromocto for a while. I have bought train tickets for you and her. Would you be willing, please, to pack and take Minna to the station by eight, and explain to her—"

She was smiling. Even from the inside she could tell it was a daft smile. "No," she said.

He nodded.

"I mean," she said, "I won't explain. You'll do that when you say goodbye."

"Ah, no," said Dr. Sprague. "No, Margaret. What good would come of her seeing me like this?" He put out his arms to display himself. He believed that the ruin was already total, and patent, but not even a day had gone by. He was drunk, yes, but he was often drunk. In the days to come he would fall apart in all the ways a man can when nobody is looking, but for now he wore a staid green wool suit, with the dark tie he'd put on to go down to talk to the policeman.

"It's a terrible thing, to say goodbye," he said.

"It's worse not to," said Margaret.

She wasn't sure that was true the next morning. She had packed their trunks. She had put on what she imagined were traveling clothes, though she had never traveled. Perhaps she would turn in the train tickets at the station, and they would go anywhere they wanted: to Cape Cod, to look at the whales. To Coney Island to ride a Ferris wheel. Meanwhile she would make sure her charge said goodbye to her father.

He hollered down the belvedere steps, "Bon voyage!"

"Come and say goodbye," said Margaret in a stern voice.

Silence from above.

"Then we'll come up!" she shouted, and that got him going.

Minna was alone at the foot of the stairs when he climbed down. She'd grown as tall as him. For her twelfth birthday he had bought her a snare drum, much to the dismay of Margaret Vanetten, but better to strike the drum than those steel stairs he now stood at the bottom of. "Women aren't drummers," Margaret Vanetten had said. "She's a girl," he said. "Look again," said Margaret, and now Leviticus saw she was right. On her way, anyhow. But she would be a drummer.

"You're going on an adventure," he told her.

She nodded. Her bronze hair was still in the tight plaits Bertha had put in the morning before. They pointed like daggers down her back, ceremonial ones that would bring her luck. When Minna was serious, she didn't look herself: she was then only a reasonably pretty child with no surprising theories. Only when she laughed or sang or drummed was she beautiful, beautiful because odd, with a gap between her front teeth and a wide mouth. Her nose and its seventeen freckles: she was golden, gold, golden, and he put his hand on her shoulder to keep from crying.

"Are you coming with me?" she asked.

"I'll stay here."

"What about Mama?"

"She'll come along eventually. You'll go with Margaret. You'll meet your aunt and uncles. That'll be something!"

"Yes," she said, meaning *no*.

"Minna Sprague," he said. At any moment he could say, *me too, I'll come, too*, and be tucked into bed by Almira. "Love you, Minna dear," he said, and she laughed at him, they were not a family who said such things, they scorned people who declared their love for one another instead of showing it through deeds. Margaret, for instance. Minna could only imagine he was joking. "I will write you," said Dr. Sprague. "Will you write me?"

"Of course," she said. You could sign a letter *love*. That was easy, or easy enough.

Later that day, Minna and Margaret already gone, he imagined he might start walking toward her straightaway. Let the train go, let it race ahead. He might outpace his own terror, and by the time he got to Oromocto he would be Minna's father, a widower, a brother. (But what if Bertha were alive!) A colossal walk. A memorial parade. He would blaze a trail and every mark a remembrance.

Or else he could stay home and drink.

Thereafter his fatherhood manifested in packages sent north— perhaps this was why Minna remembered him so fondly, he was a genius of generosity, she had so many keepsakes from him, and none from her mother, from whom she was never parted till death. He remembered what she liked and never duplicated anything. A leather-bound set of Shakespeare, a long necklace of jet, silk dresses. He wrote love letters and love poems. Bertha's money he left alone in the bank, having plenty of his own. It was one of her vanities, that she was rich and so he could practice medicine among the poor of Salford. He had never told her he still owned a farm in Oromocto, run by his brother—he had so many people he'd given up for his marriage!—enough that Minna would never have to worry.

His sister, Almira, wrote back, *Now you will find out how sorrow shapes a life.*

But sorrow doesn't shape your life. It knocks the shape out. It severs, it unstuffs, it dissolves. It *explodes*. That was what he couldn't get over. It had exploded the logic of his brain as well. An explosion! The car—oh, he knew—no, not a car, a tank. So the explosion killed her? No, not exactly, the deluge. A tidal wave? Of sorts. Of *sorts*? Of molasses. She drowned? Yes, or she suffocated, or was bludgeoned. She was a wonderful woman, your wife. He hadn't had so many people refer to his Bertha as *wife* when she was alive. What was she now? Past tense. She wasn't anything: no wife, no mother. Intolerable.

She'd been frightened of certain things, particularly once Minna was born. House fires, for instance, and tidal waves. Bees. Hurricanes, reasonably. Highwaymen. Drowning in all its previously imaginable forms: bathtub, ocean, pneumonia. Being buried alive.

Falling down stairs. *Should have built a bungalow*, she always said, watching Minna spiraling on the spiral staircase.

She didn't fear her Stanley Steamer. He blamed it.

Margaret Vanetten had written him a card, left it behind when she and Minna had gone to Oromocto, a full three days before Bertha—but was it Bertha? he wasn't sure whether he wondered this metaphysically or actually—before a body fitting the description of Bertha was pulled from the muck. Margaret had copied from an almanac the following words: *We cover a bird's cage to hear it sing, night brings out the stars, and sorrow reveals to us many truths.* He had disagreed with it instantly. Other people's sorrows might bring out the stars. One's own sorrow made everything in life counterfeit and pointless.

He went to the belvedere to write. Poetry, he thought at first, and he did write some:

> Bertha, darling, are you going
> Down the alley, out the door?
> Round the corner, 'long the sidewalk
> To our lifetime's distant shore.

> Bertha, honey, I beseech you,
> Leave your Levi nevermore.
> He adores you wholly always.
> Never lost but gone before.

But even he had to admit: Bertha cared nothing for poetry. "Too few words," she'd tell him, "and half of 'em only chosen for the rhythm or rhyme." What Bertha loved was myth. He would say, of her notion that the human brain was many different organs and not merely one, "I have seen the human brain, Bertha, and that is not true."

She would answer, certain, "I believe it to be true," as though the belief was what made it manifest.

He should have gone to look for her when her bowling women begged him to, when that stiff white widower he had never even met had come up the stairs to say, "Come now, Levi, pull yourself together and look, before you regret it." He hadn't looked. He could exist in Salford because he was a blindered man. Like a horse he could keep on because of what he would not turn his head to see, the hatred and the gossip, the terrible indifference, the bald curiosity. Even now: he would turn around to look into the past. He would write the Myth of Bertha, as she might have written it herself, and every page would be happy.

He wrote:

The Life of Bertha Truitt

—and then he stopped, in tears: it was *the life* because she was dead.

No, Leviticus. This is your work now.

Believe your nonsense: make it true. That was behind it all, all those awful pamphlets she collected, *A Home for All* and *Fowler on Matrimony*. You wrote to persuade yourself, because the ideas in their way were beautiful. To sleep beneath an octagonal roof would make your marriage harmonious; to choose your beloved based on the shape of his head meant some scientific destiny guided your life. The brain was such a terrible closet, packed full, uncatalogued. Who wouldn't want it organized?

He wrote her life. He lied a lot, in the ways she herself lied: omission, aggrandizement. The first day of work was dreadful, Bertha distant, as though she had not told him a single secret in their married life and would not now. Who was that woman, whom he'd met in the Salford Cemetery sixteen years before? He did not know anything about her. The next day he felt the heat of her, standing behind his chair, breathing on his neck the way she did, and the next day—as though it were a phrenological faculty, the seat of Berthaness—he knew everything and wrote everything. Her feet as she bowled felt little and sweet; her bust interfered with her swing; when Minna was a suckling baby she bowled with cabbage leaves in her brassiere. What a strange thing, to be a woman in this world! He'd never really thought about it.

He did not go downstairs unless he had to, just sat up in the belvedere and wrote and drank. His daughter's birthplace, where Bertha had been stuck with the entire house below her like a hooped skirt. He didn't need the entire house, not ever again.

In the belvedere he fell asleep deathlike: no dreams, no rest, those minutes excised from his life. He was awake and then suddenly he was struggling awake again. You could not dream sitting up. It was architecturally impossible. Bertha worried about being buried alive—and she was! she was!—but he wouldn't have minded: it would have been no big change for him. He would close his eyes and would remember these things, in this order: *I am alive, I am a human being, I am not in bed, Bertha is dead, I am sitting up, I am in a chair, I am in a glass box, the Almighty might see me from any angle, birds, too, it is Monday, I am alive.*

The cats would curl on his lap, but he ignored them. They purred less. They looked for love elsewhere.

The book took him three weeks, and when it was over he wept, because his time with Bertha was over. He looked around the cupola and saw how wild he'd gone, the empty bottles, the stink of his body. Of course that was why he'd sent the child out of the house. He had a memory of pissing down the speaking tube. Let the house fall to ruin: it had anyhow.

He sent the manuscript off to his publisher, changed the name of the house to Supersum—that which is left behind, superfluous—and went to the shuttered bowling alley, to sleep on Bertha's lane.

2

AN ALLEY MARRIAGE

Joe Wear knew two people who died in the Molasses Flood: Bertha Truitt and a Scotsman named Virgil Fraser who (according to the Salford *Bugle*) had been working in the navy shipyard as a builder. It was Virgil who'd taught Joe Wear wood; it was Virgil's death that devastated him. When Joe Wear saw the name listed among the dead in the afternoon paper he took to his bed, sick with longing. Not for Virgil as he was—they had not seen each other in twenty years, the math was astonishing—but the young Virgil, the younger Virgil, with whom Joe Wear had shared a bed for some days when they were on the razzle (as Virgil had called it), drunk as newts (as Virgil said). Joe was sixteen. Virgil might have been twenty-three, or thirty-two, or forty-five. (His age was in the paper: he died at fifty-two. So thirty-six, when he and Joe had known each other.) They'd met when Virgil'd come to the Les Miserables house to repair the maple approaches for the alleys, and Joe was a teenage pinboy. The first night they'd drunk and slept and woken up in the same bed, that was all. Virgil's room was at the top of the building, made smaller by a mansard roof and larger by a dormer window that overlooked Scollay Square. The second night Joe woke up in the dark to that question of young love, but in Virgil's burled voice: *Are you awake?* Beneath the slant of the eaves Joe was not sure what the right answer was—neither which answer was true (was he awake?) nor which might lead to what he wanted to happen, which was for Virgil to take: what. Liberties, or Joe himself. He wanted Virgil to *take*. Virgil put his mouth to the back of Joe Wear's head. Joe thought it was a kiss though it was slipshod. Then Virgil bit him on the shoulder: *wake up*. Well. Joe turned over. "There you are," said Virgil, reaching down, taking hold of Joe matter-of-factly, "and there you are."

Virgil kept his thinning hair cropped so close you could only see what he had left—a magnificent head, a pair of rococo ears—not what he had lost. Days, Joe went to work and set pins. Nights, he took drunken inventory. The staves of Virgil's ribs were prominent in his barrel chest. He was missing two fingers, half a thumb, and three toes. It seemed rude to ask where they'd gone, and Joe—leaning back off the single bed, peering at the elevated train tracks, Virgil's incomplete hands clamped on his shoulders—was holding on to what manners he had. He'd always laughed at his Irish aunt's clinging to the scraps of linen that had come over with her (handkerchiefs, soiled napkins), but now he understood that you clung to what survived. If it had survived, it was durable enough. It might be the making of you.

Virgil never asked Joe, either, the cause of his rolling, irregular walk. People always wanted to know, as though they could not make sense of Joe himself, could not hear a word he said, without that piece of information. As though he were a different person depending on the timing of the event: before birth, at birth, childhood, last year. Depending on the cause: in utero shock, a violent father, a runaway horse, an act of bravery or cowardice, fate, luck, fault.

"Don't worry, lad," said Virgil in the morning, seeing Joe's stunned face. "You'll outgrow it, you'll be fine."

Then came the afternoon of his monthly appointment with his maiden aunt Rose, who'd visited Joe in the Dolbeer Home for Destitute Children but had never taken him home. They were the last of the family, she liked to remind him, she too old and he too odd to marry and have children. An old maid and a cripple: the family would wither. In the meantime she lived in a round room at the prow of a pie-cut building near Copley Square. "My turret," she called it, though it was on the second floor, and instead of a moat she looked down into the triangular interior of a Rexall sign.

Monthly they met at Shaw's cafeteria, where Rose liked the chop suey and Joe got the chipped beef. She was not so very old, not even forty, though she had the high color and querulous voice of a woman of eighty. He thought she had been married once—her name was Rose Friant; he'd been told his mother's maiden name had been Daisy Crump—but like Virgil's digits the missing Mr. Friant seemed a subject too personal to broach.

"An appetite!" said Aunt Rose, watching Joe eat. "You're usually such a persnickety fellow." Her eyes were bright and teasing. "Are you in love?"

It was true that he ordinarily extracted his chipped beef shard by shard from the cream sauce; it was true that today he ate with so little attention to anything that his shirt cuff trailed in his plate and painted the table. Now that she'd called attention to it he saw that he'd eaten the lot. She was still ferrying bits of celery, ribbed like her stockings, to her careful mouth.

Love: what a thing. To kiss a man and grab a man and to give yourself over to a man—that was something (as Virgil said) that was perfectly normal. Plenty of it at the Dolbeer Home in his childhood. A game you'd outgrow, and, like all games, sometimes childish fun and sometimes overwhelming fun and sometimes unasked for, awful, shameful. But love: that was the perversion, he understood. That is what would keep you out of Aunt Rose's heaven. Joe shook his head and gnawed at the side of his thumb.

They sat near the plate glass windows by the street. The world was bright. Joe despised it.

"One day, Joe," said Aunt Rose. "Here—what goes on? Your thumb."

He took his thumb from his mouth and examined it. "A splinter," he said, surprised to see it. He showed her.

"Well, don't use your *mouth*," said Rose, "your mouth is filthy." With one hand she took hold of his thumb, and with the other she rummaged through her purse. Maiden aunts have supplies in case of shipwreck, sewing kits, horehound drops, dry socks, so that they might earn their place on the lifeboat. She produced a needle and, without asking, began to coax the splinter from the side of Joe Wear's thumb.

"Be brave," she told the thumb.

"I will," said Joe himself.

"You always are." She did not look at him. "There." She wiped the splinter away on the ivory napkin on her lap, then turned his hand over and gasped. "Riddled with them. Joe! Didn't this hurt?"

He wasn't sure.

She moved her chair closer to his. What did other people see? A woman old enough to be the boy's mother holding his hand, a boy too old to have his hand held. A gypsy reading a palm. A man and woman joined in some sort of serious enterprise. A good woman praying for a sinner's soul. A sinning woman asking for absolution. Joe Wear felt flush with guilt, not for what he had done with Virgil Fraser in a rented room near Scollay Square but for bringing it here, into the lap of Rose Friant, now fishing splinter after splinter from his hand with such care you might think each a relic of the true cross. One by one she dug them out—"now the other," she said, "the other hand, Joe"—and set them on the napkin and clucked. His hands were so calloused it mostly didn't hurt, though every now and then she dug past the armored skin to the layer where he lived. Where did the splinters come from? The pins, the balls, the approaches; the bedrails, the dormer window frame, the bentwood chair, the tiny desk, the boardinghouse floor; swapped over direct from Virgil Fraser's own splintered body. All of those places. You could not tell which splinter came from where. You could not keep them apart and you could not tell them apart. He wanted to wrench his hand away from his aunt and run from Shaw's and back to Scollay Square: he later thought it the greatest act of bravery that he stayed put.

"You could build a boat," she said at the end, but she didn't let go of his hand. What would she have done, had she known where those hands had been? Had he even washed them? She patted the inside of his wrist and looked at him with those very blue eyes, bluer because bloodshot, and said, "It's all right, Joe. You might meet a girl who doesn't care. Shake my hand!"

"What?"

"Shake it. You can tell a man's character by his handshake." She closed her eyes assessingly. Then she opened them and looked at the splinters on the napkin. "Don't forget me, Joe. You owe me a kindness. Androcles and the lion."

What had she divined about his character? He said, though he did not remember, "My mother used to tell me that story."

She smiled piteously at him. The pity was because he still believed that his mother and her stories belonged only to him. She said, at last, "I know she did."

That afternoon at Les Miserables he got into a fever of pinsetting, set them so fast all the other pinboys sat back and watched him swing from pit to pit, standing the pins on the plates, tossing the ones that had split and grabbing new, sanding the bottoms on the fly so they'd keep their balance. It was true that the pins reminded him of Virgil Fraser, it seemed certain that he would never be able to take hold of a bowling pin in all innocence again. How had he ever? What they'd done had seemed necessary, incendiary in the room; it still seemed incendiary, and he was worried that he might burst into flames, and the cause of death would be *sodomy*. That was the word that came into his head. It was biblical. He had never read the Bible. Maiden aunt Rose would find out and send the news via prayer to her dead sister. Even so he wanted to go back to Virgil Fraser and the hard smell of him, his knockabout affection. The bentwood chair, the dormer, the bed. It was this that shamed him, not that he'd done such things but that he'd do them again, and he the only hope of his family.

He was burning. Was it with shame or love? Either might kill him. Physical pain, too: he knew in the morning he would be laid low with spasming muscles, unable to climb back on the shelf before the balls came at him. (There was a meanness at Les Miserables. The bowlers sometimes aimed balls at the pinboys for laughs.) He hoped every snatch of a pin replaced one of the splinters that had been stolen from him: he could touch nobody with his tender tended hands, including Virgil Fraser, a man who now seemed made of wood: barrel staves, bowling pins, sanded or ebonized or unvarnished. His sawdust breath.

After Joe came off his shift, he quit Les Miserables. He would walk away from this life and begin again. He would find a job where he was beneath notice or desire, where nobody would aim a weapon or a look at him. At the end of the week he found a job in Salford, a city five miles away, in a cemetery, surrounded by the dead, who (it turned out) did not withhold judgment. *As I am now, so you shall be. Weep not for me. She was without sin.* The dead were arranged by families, husbands next to first and second wives, unmarried people buried at the feet of their parents, all these stones paid for by somebody, after all. A crowd of dead people was as much a crowd as a bowling alley, he thought, until the morning he found a live woman amid the stones. He went to visit her at the hospital, and there she offered him a job, and lodging, and her odd smile, offered her hand for shaking. He took it.

You can tell a man's character from his handshake, Aunt Rose had said. He didn't know about a woman's. Her hand felt like rock maple; his own, as though Rose with her needle had drawn out not splinters but his very bones. This woman was offering him escape from Virgil Fraser, his corrupting, compelling influence, the particular smell of him, his dangerous jokes, his ruinous affection—*was* it affection or was it just pastime for Virgil? He had known the minute Virgil Fraser had turned him over in bed that he was at a fork in the road, *yes*, *no*, and that his life would be made of such forks: he just didn't know he'd come to another so quick.

"Will you join me," said Bertha Truitt, as though it were not a question but persuasion, and then that's what it was. "Do a good job," she said, "and one day the business will come to you."

Joe Wear left behind his rented room and moved to the apartment above Truitt's Alleys, where he thought of Virgil Fraser hourly. Then daily. Then, after some years, weekly. Then only when he was startled by a tall bowlegged man coming through the front door: Virgil's here for me at last, he'd think, nearly leaping over the counter and into the arms of the stranger.

n January of 1919, Joe Wear lay in bed in his room over the alley and grieved alone. Nobody knocked on his door. Nobody told him what was expected of him. For the death of Bertha Truitt, Old Levi would be given flowers, and bunting, and notes of sympathy. Actual sympathy. What would Joe Wear get? He had not said the name Virgil Fraser aloud in nearly twenty years, or ever. He had gone to see Aunt Rose at Shaw's every week, until *she* had fallen in love with a widower with three small children, *she* had become a mother, *she* had moved to New Hampshire to begin her life. If he had given up Virgil for her (though Virgil had not been his to give up), if he had given up not just another life, but life itself, how could she have left him for the bald and birdish Mr. Birch, who owned a choker of summer cabins ringed round a lake?

She had, though. Come stay in a cabin, she told him. What would Joe Wear do in a cabin? All she owned, the coral necklace, the fine Irish linen, the sense of propriety: it would be left to her stepchildren.

Do a good job and one day the business will come to you.

"Don't fall in love with that woman!" Aunt Rose had warned him twenty years ago, when he'd told her about Bertha Truitt. She did not believe that women should own businesses. But if he had fallen in love, or at least into marriage, the alleys would now belong to him.

He'd asked her only once how she'd come to be in the cemetery. After a pause she'd said, "You're an orphan, Joe, aren't you?" "Yes." "Well, I was orphaned from myself." "I don't know what that means," he said, but he did. A terrible thing to be orphaned from yourself. Why he and Truitt had an understanding: they both had been.

"Orphaned from myself," said Truitt, "and so I left myself on the front doorstep of God. But you found me first." "And your husband." "First, Joe Wear. I always remember you found me first."

One day the business will come to you.

She had said that. He was certain. It had seemed a preposterous promise when she made it, but Truitt had turned out to be a preposterous and trustworthy human being. If you looked hungry she would have a turkey dinner delivered. If you admired her hat she would have it duplicated for you, even if you were not in the habit of wearing ladies' hats. She lived in a world not of sips of whiskey but cases, not of sandwiches but roast pigs.

He stood up in his bed and leaned on the iron headboard. He could feel the springs beneath his feet. All those days in bed had turned his muscles to starched sheets. They hurt to move. He wondered whether they'd hold him.

In his absence, he was certain, Truitt's Alleys had stayed idle. The pins would have been cleared into the pits at the end of the night, the balls rolled back along the returns, the ashtrays emptied and stacked and left so for days. Old Levi wouldn't have opened it, nor Jeptha Arrison. Only Joe. There might be a scrim of handprints, noseprints, on the plate glass window, bowlers wondering when Truitt's Alleys might rouse itself, if ever, now that its mistress was gone.

Maybe he owned it. Maybe the business had come to him.

He went crotcheting down to open the alley under his own orders.

Somebody had hung a wreath of roses and carnations on the door, and a black ribbon on the door handle. Joe hesitated, then removed the ribbon and got his keys out.

The place would need a full scrub: he would have to enlist Jeptha Arrison. No, he thought, he would do it himself, this first time. It might be a kind of ceremony. It might be just the exercise his body needed. He went to the corner to punch on the lights and then saw, in the corner, like a ghost, Old Levi sitting in the dark. He turned to look at Joe and gave a small forbidding nod. Joe turned the lights on anyhow.

"Open for business, you think?" Joe asked.

The same unfathomable nod.

Joe Wear had never liked Old Levi, the way he kowtowed to Bertha and at the same time was so full of himself, walked right in like he owned the place. Acted like he didn't care what Joe Wear thought about him. It would be bad for business, a brooding drunk colored man in the corner. He'd aged in the way of furniture, Joe saw: threadbare in places so you could see the angles of his frame, creaking at the joints, and all his padding shifted.

"You happy there?" Joe Wear asked.

Old Levi held the sides of the round table, waiting. "I'm not happy anywhere," he said at last.

If Bertha had left a will—surely she would have, she would never miss a chance to explain exactly what she gave away and to whom and in what quantity—she would not have left the alley to Old Levi, who would find it an albatross. He wouldn't want it; she wouldn't give it to him. Nor to their little daughter. There would be a will and it would be read. Until then—

"—I'm not fired," Joe said.

"Not fired, no." Old Levi's voice was mild as milk, as though to cool the fire in Joe Wear's. "You go ahead and open."

"Listen, Sprague—"

"*Doctor* Sprague," he said. So he did care, at least a little. "If you are seeking employment elsewhere—"

"No, Levi, I ain't. I'm not fired?"

"Not fired," said Dr. Sprague, irked at the fellow's tone. But the point was to keep Bertha's alley as it was, and that required this fool.

They both looked toward the front door, saw the three women goggling their eyes with their hands, peering in. They'd been drawn by the lights of the alley, on for the first time in two weeks. Now they straightened up and turned their backs, as though they'd only stopped on the sidewalk for conversation.

"Don't worry, Mr. Wear," said Dr. Sprague, so polite it sounded insulting. "I'll die soon enough."

"I'm not waiting for that."

"Then what?" asked Dr. Sprague.

"Not waiting for anything," said Joe Wear. "Waiting for the work-day to be done." Once the bowling started, surely, the man would be driven away, would go home to his own people up in Canada. "Heartfelt sympathy," Joe said, then added, "to you. For your wife."

He waited a while for an answer, then went to open the door for the women.

"Ladies," he said, in a bitter voice, and he was overwhelmed with the smell of molasses. The women brought it in, slowed by it, by the sticky click of the gummy soles of their shoes against the alley floor.

The women—Mary Gearheart, Hazel Forest, LuEtta Mood—had read the paper every day for a funeral notice. Would it be at Cedrone's Funeral Parlor? At the alleys? Not at a church, surely: Truitt had no use for church. She said so herself. They had to do *something*, even if it was just to bowl upon Bertha Truitt's own lane. They had hung the wreath and the ribbon and had gone home to bowl in their sleep. Now they were here.

LuEtta Mood saw Dr. Sprague in the corner of the alley, and she thought about running. She had identified Bertha's dead body; she should have gone directly to the Octagon to break the news. Instead she'd let the police do it. She had never written him so much as a note on the loss of his wife, when she should have been better, when she knew what a note or a word might mean to a person terrified and terrifying in grief. She had never understood Dr. Sprague but she had never tried.

Now she went to the table. "Dr. Sprague," she said. He lifted his head.

He'd lost weight. His double chin, once curvaceous, nearly embarrassing, was gone; his mustache had taken on different, doleful angles. What happened in a marriage? Her own had fallen like a cake, if ever it had risen, and since Bertha's death she'd been dreaming of escape, and only now realized it needn't be a dream: leaving is something one might do. "LuEtta Mood," she said of herself. Then, "I was a friend of your wife's."

Had she spoken to him in the past year? At the other end of the building, Mary and Hazel had begun to bowl quietly, which is to say badly, a pin at a time. Jeptha sat ready to set—now, when did he get here?—and neither he nor the women looked over. LuEtta knew she had to bring them back something.

"We were wondering," she said, "if there will be a funeral."

"Memorial service," said Dr. Sprague. "Eventually. Not now."

There was a carelessness to Dr. Sprague that alarmed Lu-Etta: he would attend to things when he got round to them and no sooner. He might not have done a single thing: the body itself, ant-sweet, caved in, glowing like a saint's, might be stored in the house. Still, she thought, her loss of Edith gave her the right to talk to him about the loss of his wife. "And the burial?"

"Done," said Dr. Sprague. "The Salford Cemetery."

"Of course."

He looked at her as though she had expressed an opinion on a dream he'd had.

"I'll look for the stone, if it's there," said LuEtta.

"In a year, in the way of her people."

"Her people."

He nodded, said nothing more.

Then she sat down at the table. Why she hadn't gone to see him after finding Bertha at the mortuary: because to do so she would have had to relinquish her own grief, fold it like a flag into a neat triangle and hand it over. She had not been ready then and she was not ready now. She tilted her head to see what he was writing; he turned it so she could read.

BERTHA in colored pencil, built not out of ordinary letters but something like architecture, ivy winding up the exterior wall of the *B*, and the *R* covered with pink roses and eyebrow windows, the *A* blushing peachily, alight with a sunset. She wanted to take it; he had it pinned to the table with his thumbs. He said, "Not lost but gone before," and she said, "Yes. My condolences."

He frowned. In his doctor's voice, he said, "*Not* lost." Then he looked at her, and more gently said, "Bertha said you lost a child."

She nodded.

"I'm sorry." He examined her face a moment, as though troubled by it. "You could still have another, should you wish. Should your husband wish."

"Thank you," she said, though—she told herself later, away from the alley, fixing Moses Mood's dinner, chicken livers and buttered noodles—it wasn't as though permission was what she lacked.

Leviticus watched the women bowl. He loved Bertha, his thoughts never wandered to the loveliness of the other women, but it did wander. Inattention: his sin, as ever. Whatever was in front of him, he'd rather think of something else. He woolgathered, dreamt— sometimes he was stringing spondees and iambs on a line of poetry, but often not. He was vacant. He was walking along a street in Fredericton he'd last walked decades before. Remembering poems he'd memorized years ago, his own and other people's, like reading old letters found in a trunk: nothing new, and everything new.

If he'd belonged to a confessing religion, he would have gone to confession. *Bless me father for I have—what were we talking about?*

Instead, like many sinners, he devoted himself to his sin. He sat in the corner of Truitt's Alleys. Flask in pocket. Eyes to ceiling. A memory of Bertha trailing in from time to time and then her crushing death.

You could only hope she'd tasted sweetness in some way.

Can we forgive him everything? Everything? Even the cats? He left them behind. *They're wild animals*, he told himself, but if so they were wild animals locked in an octagonal house. Or: *Margaret Vanetten's let them go*—it was she who fed them—but Margaret had been sent on the train with Minna, and her employment expired the moment their feet hit the train platform in Fredericton. Every time he remembered the cats—when Minna wrote to ask how they were doing—he thought, *who am I to feel sorrow for a cat, when Bertha is dead.*

He thought of the Mother Cat, whom he searched for, whom he found, whom he wept over, to Bertha's disgust.

There is no animal like a cat for grief. They have the stamina for it, the disregard for convention. A dog would try to talk you out of it. The cats would have been a comfort to him. He could not bear to be comforted.

Bring me Donizetti when you come to visit, Minna wrote, and he wrote back, *I could not live without him.*

He planned to leave Salford only in his coffin, or in a sack of ash.

BERTHA TRUITT'S
AFTERLIFE

She was seen walking down Mims Avenue walloped and alive. She was seen walking along Atlantic Street but ectoplasmically, looking for her hat. She peered through the plate glass windows of Truitt's, her jacket pockets paying out silver dollars like a one-armed bandit. Her body in the coffin was cast of molasses; she herself had swum through to safety. Her body lay in her old bed in the Octagon preserved in syrup. Her body had been torn into six pieces—head, arm, arm, torso, leg, leg—and was packed and buried in a round rubber ball. She had told her lady bowlers just the day before, If I disappear I will return to you in the Salford Cemetery: come look for me, no later than noon on March 1, by the Pickersgill Obelisk. Eventually so many people came looking for her there they had to keep the gates locked.

She ruffled the fenny weeds on the north side of town. She changed her name to Abigail Patrick and lectured on temperance on the streets of Nantucket.

She was the unnerving heat on your February pillow slip, the unnerving ecstasy that woke you at 2:00 A.M. pawing at the bedclothes, trying to find your way through the curtain and back into that humiliating, beauteous dream.

She flew through the sky naked on her back, using her enormous breasts—

—yes, Earl, you said that before; we didn't believe you then.

No, thought Leviticus, it wouldn't take any time at all to accomplish, dying. Joe Wear was a rough man, without people or love. Naturally he wouldn't understand what it meant, to be dying of grief. To *want* to die of it. To wait patiently. His publisher had turned down his book about Bertha with an irritated note: *yes, yes, but to what end?*

Most days he sat in the corner of Truitt's Alleys. Other days you could only hear him rummaging in the basement among the old pins, the chipped vulcanite balls. He did not seem to ever go home. The Phantom of the Alleys, the bowlers called him.

They lived together in this way, Wear and Sprague. Upstairs, Joe moved his bed to the other side of his rooms, so that he could not hear the snoring—Joe suspected that Old Levi slept right on Bertha's old lane, without blanket or sheet, only the memory of his wife to pillow him, the feel of her ball rolling down his spine. Other times Joe would wake in the night with the old certainty that he was the only person in the building: he felt strung in bed. *I'll die soon enough*, Old Levi had said. Joe Wear worked hard not to wish for it. Nothing good could come of wishing for another man's death. Why had he said it? Why had he put it into Joe's head?

In the morning, he looked at Old Levi. "You make people uncomfortable," Joe said.

"I know it."

Joe Wear nodded. Then he said, knowing it fully for the first time, "I make people uncomfortable, too."

Nothing would move Leviticus Sprague, who all his life had felt an odd sense of calm about his place in the world—his mother had instilled it in all of her children, and it had a religious underpinning that he most days ignored—which is to say, he cared very little about the opinions of other people. He was not sure he believed in them. People, yes, but not their opinions. He was patient. He could wait for anything, forever. He did not think this was a virtue. Why stay in godforsaken Salford? He still might move to West Hills, join the Baptist Church. Or get on a train to Oromocto himself, go home to Minna, to Almira, Benjamin, Joseph. He was the only one of the siblings who'd married. Now it was too late. (But why is it too late, Leviticus? Because it is. Because Almira would say, *That's all right, what counts is you're home*. As though they'd been waiting for him to be rid of Bertha.)

Dr. Sprague sat at a table in the corner of Truitt's and he drank. He'd closed his practice, informed the Plymouth Hospital. His friend Cornelius, who'd founded the hospital, tried to talk him out of it, but halfheartedly. Dr. Sprague had lost interest in the world and Dr. Garland knew that you could not practice medicine that way.

Soon enough his organs felt replaced with the implements of bowling, his blood balled up and rolling through his veins, his lungs full of wood. He sat at his table and watched the bowlers. The women still came, in their athletic outfits, which made them self-conscious, now that Bertha was not here to outdo them in sartorial strangeness. The bloomers, the middy blouses that had made them eccentric near her now made them feel dressed as children. The self-consciousness was a sign of decay: the memory of Bertha was falling apart.

—

Finally Dr. Sprague went to Joe Wear with his proposition. "I have a job for you, Mr. Wear. Might you be interested?"

"Already have a job. I work for you. You tell me what to do and I do it. So go on."

Dr. Sprague thought this over. "No," he said. "This is different altogether. I will pay you."

"You already pay me."

"*More*," said Dr. Sprague, not kindly. "It's a job I want done with care and I think you're suited for it. I need a body."

Joe Wear shook his arms out then hugged himself. "*Un*suited—"

"Limbs is what I mean. Legs. Wooden ones. I have in mind a monument for Mrs. Sprague."

"Your mother?"

Dr. Sprague was standing at the oak front counter, a position he never took up. He looked at Joe Wear with such consternation it was almost a compliment: he'd expected better. "No," he said, "no—my late Bertha's."

"Oh, Truitt," said Joe Wear.

"Just so."

"I'm unfamiliar."

"You just—"

"—unfamiliar with her *limbs*," said Joe Wear, which made Leviticus Sprague laugh, a phenomenon with which Joe Wear was likewise unfamiliar. He would have thought that Dr. Sprague was anatomically incapable of laughter, like a friend of Joe's from the Dolbeer Home who'd insisted he couldn't cry because he'd had his crying glands removed after a childhood fever: previously Joe had thought all bodily waters—tears, sweat, spit, piss—were pulled from the same bodily well.

The laugh was silent and mouth borne, like a sneeze. His shoulders kept still but his stomach jumped. When he'd composed himself he said, "Yes, I imagine you are unfamiliar, Mr. Wear. I am building, as I say, a kind of monument. The head I will manage. The legs, her arms—well, I cannot get past the disappointment of anatomy. But I thought of your work with wood. You once made a cow for Minna, I remember. A little one, with a swinging tail. She has it still."

"Does she?" said Joe. He had not thought of Minna since she'd left. She'd seemed like none of his business. "Well then. Sure."

"Don't make her out of bowling pins."

"Bowling pins or nothing," said Joe Wear, and Leviticus Sprague was about to argue except for the planning look on the man's face, which suggested that he knew exactly how to solve this problem.

"But wood don't last," said Joe Wear. "In a monument, I mean."

Leviticus was silent a long time. Then—mockingly? in order to be understood?—he said, "It don't last forever, but it don't do badly. Legs first. When you're done we'll look them over and then discuss arms, hands, feet, and the like."

"Life-size?"

That startled Leviticus. For a moment he imagined a figure Bertha's size and felt the wrongness. No such thing as life-size: you'd always be fractionally off, and the difference would be heartbreaking. He drew a shape in the air. "Yea high," he said. "Yea wide."

"So smaller."

"Smaller," said Leviticus. "Has to be."

Across Joe Wear's table, old battered bowling pins, made of rock maple. He decided to go in calf first. He'd turned down Old Levi's new wood but accepted a selection of artist's tools, hammers and chisels, little planes, little rasps, sandpaper in various levels of irritation. The rock maple pins were hard to carve but strong as Truitt herself. Beneath the white paint, pale wood. It did not take him long to realize that the attitude of the leg would make a difference. Old Levi wanted the legs jointed at knee and ankle. He himself would work on the torso. That made sense. How would Joe Wear know how to make the womanly parts of a woman? Who would ask another man to make his wife's body?

Begin with the lower leg. That seemed safe. He used his own muscles as models. A calf shaped itself one way standing, another sitting, another with its foot slung up on the table. What was this monument of Dr. Sprague's he was building the pedestal to? He carved the curve of a calf, with just a suggestion of the shinbone. Gave it one comely ankle, lump of bone, notches in the skin up the Achilles tendon. He planed and sanded. Sprague had offered him an anatomy book but he did not like to look. God built bodies from the inside out. Only He could do it. Joe Wear worked his way in. He found he couldn't stop. Wood and work had always mesmerized him. In the dark of the night he finished the ankle and wondered about a foot. How would it fit in? His own legs were knock-kneed, left more than right; his feet pigeon-toed, right more than left. His wooden legs he vowed to make perfect.

Joe Wear hefted the calf. Was it like Truitt's? He wasn't sure. Truitt's calf. In actual life they had scarcely touched. She was The Great Handshaker, and no person at Truitt's could entirely avoid her pivoting bustline, which came brushing by no matter what. She was bold with her body, always had been—never a hugger but a backslapper, an elbow patter. She might even tug your hair, if she were particularly fond. But she paid attention. Joe Wear was a tightrope walker. He balked at the hands of others. She left him alone.

Here was her calf, or somebody's. He tucked it under his pillow when he went to bed. The next day when he saw Dr. Sprague, he lied without knowing why: "I'll start tomorrow."

All day long he thought about the calf: when he gazed at the bowlers, when he was meant to keep score for the leagues. What next? Calf, then calf, then thigh by thigh? Or all one leg at once? How would he devise a knee that both worked and looked kneelike?

That night he made a left calf so the right calf would not be lonely. Later he would think, *A right thigh might keep a right calf company, too, Lord, Joe Wear, you needn't always go for the obvious companion.* The second calf was harder, because it had to mimic not just life but its maple partner.

For a week he could think of nothing else. Would he carve a kneecap out of wood, to hide the hinge of calf and thigh? At what angle did upper leg meet lower? He wanted the legs able to support whatever weight they had to, though Dr. Sprague had given him nearly no specifications—legs for a monument; if those passed muster, arms for a monument; if those passed, feet and hands. He decided he would make the legs with feet straightaway. The Salford Half Nickels still bowled at Truitt's. Joe thought if he got these legs right he might offer to carve a wooden leg for Martin Younkins, who got around with crutches and a pinned-up pant leg. Maybe then he could do an arm for Jack Silver.

He watched the Half Nickels as they bowled, to see how their legs worked, whole or abbreviated. He examined the women in their skirts and bloomers, their angles and inlets. LuEtta Mood was a terrible stand-in for Truitt except for the fact that neither of them cared what they looked like as they bowled. He felt he'd never been so aware of what other people looked like in his life. He took the information back to his room over the alley and worked.

Heel, toes, arch, instep. Bare, every tendon visible, though in his heart he knew that stout Truitt's tendons would have been hard to see in her fubsy feet. He thought of making a portrait of Virgil, in negative: three wooden toes, two wooden fingers.

The thighs he did last, being the most personal territory. He had to get to know the rest of the leg before he dared.

You've done both legs."

"I couldn't understand one leg without the other, so. No paint or varnish yet. Wasn't sure what you wanted."

He set the legs on the table in front of Dr. Sprague. He wasn't sure of anything other than the cleverness of the joints, of which he was proud; he felt a rush of regret that he hadn't articulated the toes, or thought about how the top of the legs might fit into a torso.

"Extraordinary," said Dr. Sprague. He took them into his lap. They looked smaller there, but all right, plausibly half the length of Truitt.

"What you wanted?"

Dr. Sprague shook his head. He palpated the knees one at a time. He bent the left leg so he could hold its foot. "Mr. Wear. Bowling pins?"

"Yessir."

"Then there is glory in bowling pins."

"They like her?"

"Not at all," said Dr. Sprague. "Arms next."

"How's the head?"

"It'll have to be better now."

"What're you making that out of?"

"I'm still in the experimental stage," said Dr. Sprague. "I am not the artist you are."

Joe Wear found the elbows dull at first. Who is sentimental about an elbow? Who would recognize a beloved's elbow among a dozen unknown elbows? One can't even really know one's own elbow, not by direct sight, not investigate it with both hands. He spent so much time contemplating the meaning of elbows he came right round to them. He was an elbow himself: useful, unseen, in service to others. Still he might rub up against something meaningful.

Now he felt bolder around Dr. Sprague. The man had asked a favor and Joe had complied. *Glory*: that was the word he'd used. Joe might ask him things, too. He began to bring little brown sugared and cinnamoned doughnuts in the morning, set the paper bag on a table. Mostly Joe ate them, but every now and then Dr. Sprague would accept one.

"How is it?"

"Quite remarkable, actually," Dr. Sprague would say, his mustache flocked with sugar. Sometimes Joe thought all the man ate was what Joe brought him.

"What'll you do with this place?"

"Just this."

"Why not sell it?"

"It was my wife's," Dr. Sprague said. "Not mine to sell."

"It *was* Truitt's. It's yours now."

Silence.

"Yours now," said Joe. "Unless: she leave a will?"

Dr. Sprague shook his head.

"So then what."

"Let it go to hell," said Dr. Sprague.

"You could sell it," said Joe. He didn't have enough money to buy it, but maybe someday. "Why don't you go home?"

"Too far away, in time and miles and all the ways. They'll sell it after my death. I hope you'll stay on till then, Mr. Wear. Or—"

"—or what—"

He hesitated. Then he said, "As long as they don't find family."

"What family?"

"Bertha's family. Descendants."

"Minna?"

"No, not Minna. No, never Minna. This place—no."

Dr. Sprague had heard of wills that prevented children from marrying certain people, or required it, going into certain lines of work, or devoting themselves to charitable works. He could write it into his will. He could leave the bowling alley to whom he liked. This place was quicksand, it would swallow up any good person who stepped onto it. He saw that now, it was what had killed Bertha, not the steamer but the errand, off to attend to the alley's needs. He was being swallowed up himself. Minna must never own it, not even to sell. Still, he imagined that Bertha would want it to be Truitt's down the ages. She had loved Minna more than the bowling alley, but she had looked to the bowling alley for her immortality.

He said, "Not Spragues. Never Spragues. Truitts."

"Are there other Truitts?"

"The lawyers will look."

"What if they don't find anyone?"

"Then it will be for sale."

"Highest bidder?"

"Mr. Wear," said Leviticus Sprague, "you are meant for better things than this."

"Owning a bowling alley is a better thing."

"Owning a bowling alley is something I wish on no man," said Dr. Sprague. "I base this on my personal experience."

The head itself did look like Bertha, when Joe Wear saw it, though Dr. Sprague would not show it direct. A pale head, jowly like its inspiration, pink lipped, and full of sorrow. Later Joe would wonder what it had been made of, plaster, clay, papier-mâché, tin, silk, tallow, white chocolate, glass, wood, porcelain, felt, cotton, wool; he found his memory could not tell him whether it reflected light or transmitted it. He watched Dr. Sprague set it on one of the little tables by the lane, then cover it with a cloth.

"It was a terrible thing to make her head," said Dr. Sprague. He put his hand upon the cloth. His hand was enormous; Joe Wear had never noticed that before. A candlepin ball would disappear inside it, a tumor would. "She believed in phrenology."

"In what now?"

"She never spoke of it? The study of heads. Nobody believes in it any longer. She did. There has never been the least bit of evidence. Always a danger when you look for a scientific explanation for your beliefs, rather than form your beliefs based on scientific evidence, though I suppose it is the same sensation. But I discovered that when you try to mold somebody's head it does feel as though you are mapping her soul. This is my ninth attempt, as bad as the others. It's an unspeakable thing to believe you can judge a person's character by the shape of her head."

"Why?" said Joe Wear. "People judge your character by the shape of your body all the time." He stretched out one stiff leg. "*I* know. Lame, fat, spindly. You, too," he said.

"Judged or judging?"

"Both."

"You may be right, Mr. Wear." Dr. Sprague toyed with the cloth over the head, but he did not lift it. Then he picked up one of the arms and held it like a baby in his own arms. He looked like he was wondering what to do with it: swallow it like a sword, put the wooden hand to his cheek.

They'd become alike, Wear and Sprague, two men drowning in privacy. They weren't uncivilized—even gone-to-seed, there was an irritating civility to Dr. Sprague; Joe Wear followed certain rules, so as not to go wild altogether—but they were untended. Either could disappear and nobody would notice; each believed this was true only of himself.

"Where will you put her?" asked Joe.

"Oh, nowhere."

"Thought you meant her for a monument."

Dr. Sprague turned and looked at Joe Wear. The sorrow was of course and always his. "Maybe eventually," he said. "I'll leave that to the lawyers."

That was the last Joe saw of the effigy for a long time. What was that dummy's purpose? He thought it might be supernatural. Calling down the spirits, the old gods, to take those wooden elbows and make them bend. Old Levi must have stored her away somewhere clever, because no matter how Joe Wear hunted he couldn't find her.

As for Dr. Sprague: once they'd finished the work he could as usual only see how he failed. "I'm sorry, Bertie," he said to the wood, which was not Bertie, he knew she was not Bertie, but perhaps she could pass along the message, perhaps that was what he believed: every portrait is a kind of telephone to its subject.

CONFLAGRATE

At first the neighborhood gossips believed Joe Wear had set the fire. Then the police did. It had sparked in the corner of the alley, where Leviticus Sprague had sat for all these months—where he was sitting, in fact, when the fire broke out, though it was after hours and Truitt's Alleys was closed. Nobody knew how Sprague lived, exactly: whether he bathed himself in the shallow men's room basin, slept upright in a chair at that round table. Had Joe Wear wanted to kill Leviticus Sprague he could have done it any number of ways, thought the neighborhood gossips: poison, suffocation. Even patience would have done the job.

You didn't have to burn a man to death.

No, of course: the man had set himself on fire. Smoking, maybe. His shirtfront had been wet with whiskey or tears or tears suffused with whiskey, and that was that. So much for his so-called intelligence. His wife had been dead nearly two years. Maybe he'd done it on purpose.

That morning, Joe Wear had opened the door to the alleys and was knocked back by an appalling smell. The smell had been in his nose already, he realized: distant sugar through the floorboards but obscene close up. Sweet with Hell and flesh beneath. All horrifying odors are nearly pleasant in tiny doses. Now he thought he might faint from it.

In the corner, the darkened mystery.

Incinerated chair. Melted table, the metal stem drooping like a dying thing.

No sign of a man except the object on the ground.

The fire had burnt so fast, so hot, it put itself out. The chair was gone, the tabletop was gone, the wood paneling was gone, all of Leviticus Sprague was gone save the leg, which was there whole, untouched, on the ground. It was a shock to see it. A shock to see anything so human, so dead, and so forsaken.

A leg still half-dressed in tweed. Old Levi's leg. Had it been a fake and Joe unaware? A bit of brown ankle showed. Skin made to match the original person. Was it the wooden Bertha's, swollen up with smoke? Must be. But how on earth? He reached down automatically to feel it.

ord God. Lord God.

hereafter everybody said: Joe Wear won't say word one but you should hear the guy shriek.

The strangest of all strange things: there was a cat in the alley, a little black and white girlcat, no evidence of how it got in. Was it the soul of Dr. Leviticus Sprague, the way some people said a dove was a soul? A piteous, inexplicable thing: Donizetti looking for his master. But Donizetti was old and male. This cat was half-size, with his same Holstein markings and chittering voice.

The insurance company sent an inspector, and the inspector found no cause for the fire. No accelerants, no source of heat. Just ash and leg.

They arrested Joe Wear anyhow and put him in one of the cells in the basement of City Hall. The cot was familiar, made in whatever great factory had produced the beds for the Dolbeer Home for Destitute Children, an industrial concern that employed prisoners and orphans to make mattresses for prisoners and orphans, stuffed with the thin horsehair dreams of prisoners and orphans. Of course he slept. The fire had exhausted him, burnt up his ability to do anything but lie still and be washed over the cataract of sleep.

He could even hear the sound of the policemen saying, "Lookit. How can he sleep like that?"

"Sleep of the innocent."

"The innocent don't sleep in jail."

"You think he did it?"

"Did what? He did something."

Three days passed before they let him out. No evidence tied him to the fire, which had killed only a foreign colored man already half-dead. Besides, Joe Wear had an alibi, said the officer as he unlocked the door.

Did he? Joe Wear wondered. In dreams he set the fire. The dream-fire burnt so hot he believed he'd been dreaming of fires for months before the spark. But he also knew he wouldn't have been able to make a fire so canny and brutal, to incinerate only the human matter and not take down the alley. Take down himself.

"I explained I was with you," said Jeptha Arrison to Joe Wear at the Salford Police Station. "Let us take you home."

They rode the trolley back in silence, went to Truitt's Alleys, walked up the narrow stairs to Joe's apartment. Jeptha tried to fit through the door at the same time as Joe and nearly got them jammed in the frame. One big room with a bed, a little icebox he never used, a sink, a stove, the bathtub right there in the open so the place didn't need two sets of hot water pipes. The toilet was in a closet by itself. The place was tidier than Joe had remembered leaving it, his bowl and spoon washed and dried by the sink, the chair pushed in. Meaner, too. It was a mean place.

For a moment he thought someone had flung one of Bertha Truitt's black-and-white hats in the middle of the bed. No: a cat curled round itself.

"What's that doing there?"

"Dunno," said Jeptha. "Been around, is all. Bertha's."

Joe sat down on the bed and pulled the animal close, one of those accordion cats that got longer when you picked it up by the middle. It circled itself back up in his lap.

"Thanks, Jep," said Joe. "Go on home."

But Jeptha was going through the kitchen, locating food Joe had not put there. Some fruit, a paper sack of peanuts, which he shook. "Are you hungry."

Joe gave a confessing nod.

"'Course you are. Hungry myself. I will fix us some tuck." Jeptha hunted around the sink looking for dishes. He peered in the cupboard, the bathtub.

"Only the one spoon," said Joe.

"Bowls?"

"The one bowl." Shame, to have Jeptha here to see that, though it had never been shameful before. Joe sat at the table.

"We'll share so," said Jeptha.

"You shouldnta lied."

"Nor did I."

"Well, you did, Jep. You said I was with you."

"And so you were."

"I don't—"

"I do sometimes," said Jeptha. "Good thing too."

An electric chill swept over Joe's shoulders and down his torso. The cat felt it and jumped to the floor.

"Here I was," said Jeptha. He conjured up a paper carton from the always empty icebox. "In your place, right here. I am catfooted. You know that, Joe Wear. I do come in sometimes."

"Here," said Joe. "*Here.*"

At that Jeptha looked nervous. He handed Joe the bowl. "Not all the time. Try that. Peach Melba. Well, I call it Peach Melba. It's good. My turn next."

Joe set the cold bowl in his lap where the warm cat had been. Peach, vanilla ice cream, raspberries, salted peanuts. He'd never tasted anything like it, so delicious he felt tears in his eyes. Jeptha watched him hungrily.

Rumor was Jeptha had been a jockey who got kicked in the head. That made sense, the smallness of him and the tangle of his brain. His head seemed to change shape depending on the season. In the fall he might pass for handsome till you noticed how oblong he was above the neck; in spring his noggin was a sack of flour; in summer, a boiled pudding slumped in the heat.

(It felt that way on the inside of Jeptha, too, changeable. He thought different things depending on the slant of light. He believed things that were not true—that he could understand the awful thoughts of horses—and did not believe things that were fact—that he would one day die. He had a headache all the time. Sometimes all he thought about were the pins, the way they played in the gutters of his sight. The very sound of them knottering together rearranged the headache and made it, if not better, then more interesting.)

"I'm a sneak," said Jeptha now. "You sleep like a sweet baby, with your little arms thrown over your head." He put his hands in the air to demonstrate but didn't take his eyes off the bowl.

"Don't do that," said Joe.

"Well I know you are an innocent man."

This set something ticking in the back of Joe Wear's head. "Was it you?"

"Pardon?"

"Set the fire."

"Oh no. Joe! No! No: spontaneous combustion." Jeptha was still looking at the bowl. "Leg is how you can tell."

"Tell what?"

"Cases like this. Careful you don't—"

It was a staggering amount of ice cream. Joe kept eating.

"You'll headache yourself," warned Jeptha. "Cases like so. A fire burns that hot, that fast, now, why weren't any of the other chairs touched? And nothing but combustibles all around, lanes, pins, balls? And how come it happen when he was all alone? And the *leg*," said Jeptha. He touched his own. He seemed to consider how it might look, burnt free of his body.

Joe looked up from the bowl. The cat rubbed against his shins consolingly. "You're a ghoul."

"No sir I am not. He just went up. Only other explanation is the Pukwudgees. But I don't reckon they'd do it."

"The who?"

"The little people. Most mischief is Pukwudgees."

"But how did you get *in* here?"

"Keys. Boss gave them to me."

"Boss?"

"Truitt. She loved me, Joe."

"She did." Joe looked at the dark beams of his ceiling. Jeptha had been the alley's first employee, there forever and always. Before even Joe. He might have been born in the pits. Bertha had doted on Jeptha Arrison, had treated him like a child: she bought Jeptha sacks of candy rock and nut zippers, sweaters when it was cold. She let him walk the baby. *Poor Jep,* Bertha had called him, with great delight, as though he were a stroke of luck.

"Do you know," Joe said, "I always dreamt she left it to me. In her will. You, more likely."

"The alley?" Jeptha scratched his Adam's apple with one finger. "Not to me neither. Nahum Truitt more likely."

Joe put his spoon down. "Who's that?"

"Her son. Think he's Maineward. The lawyers are looking. When Bertha died the alley went to the doctor, and the doctor's will leaves it to Nahum. If he exists. Not everyone says so. They think he might be a figment. But he's not. Bertha confided in me. Joe Wear: I know secrets."

"Do you," said Joe uneasily. A son. The possibility of Truitts he'd known about, but never a son. If he'd known, he'd never have felt hopeful, or angry. He would have walked out years ago. It was getting dark out, but neither man reached up to pull on the light.

Jeptha laughed. "Some people think I'm a figment, too, but I'm here. I did not mean to watch you sleep, Joe. Good thing I did, hey?"

Those years ago in the Salford Hospital, when the patients on the ward dreamt of Bertha Truitt crawling under their covers: that was Jeptha. He'd stolen her perfume, Fleur Qui Meurt, dabbed it behind his ears as he'd seen Bertha do. In the night he sat on beds or sinuated underneath. He was all sorts of unexplained phenomena, Jeptha Arrison.

"You've eaten the lot," he said now.

Joe looked into the bowl. "I'm sorry."

"You were hungry," said Jeptha, as though this was the worst accusation he could make.

And who's to say that Jeptha Arrison had it wrong? If Doctor Sprague had had one wish in the world, what would it have been? To die, not quietly, but in a way that let everyone know: I loved a woman so and grieved a woman so that I burst into flames. All anyone ever wants is evidence. She had not written him a single love letter and she had not saved his. By god the woman hated words.

There he is at his table. The bowlers think he has given up. They think he isn't doing a damned thing except drinking and scrawling notes on jagged scraps of paper. (The man can afford more than scraps. Why must he be so perverse?) The women bowlers think he might at any moment turn the boat of his grief back to shore. Right now he's drifting; soon he'll find some purpose; he'll remember his daughter, or the memory of his wife will be one he wishes to honor with good deeds and happiness and responsible fatherhood. But the men think otherwise: a certain dead-eyed look in a drunkard means he's done for good, and no legislation or temperance Mary will save him. Both men and women think: *there's a clock wound down*. They only disagree over whether his gears are jammed for good.

But *we* know: grief looks like nothing from the outside, it looks like surrender, but in fact it is the most terrible struggle. It is friction. It is a spiritual grinding, and who's to say it cannot produce a spark and heat that, given fuel, could burn a good man to the ground?

ALMOST DONE

Ads were taken out in newspapers all over New England—Orono, Maine; Portsmouth, New Hampshire; Mystic, Connecticut; Boston, Worcester, Providence. Nahum Truitt was not flushed from any of these places. Joe Wear ran the alleys. He oversaw the rebuilding of the first lane, though it did not take much: new bench, new floor beneath, new table. Time and smoke and the greasy clothing of bowlers would take a while to shellac the new wood: there was a halo there. Joe Wear thought about what he might do, if the alley were his: rip out the bar, which had buckled and which since Prohibition they did not really use, add two more lanes. Meanwhile he hired pinboys, paid their salaries, paid his own, took the profits to the bank, and awaited the appearance of Bertha Truitt's son. No will existed for Bertha Truitt, but Leviticus Sprague had been more thorough. All he owned to Minna, except the alley, which he left to any close relatives of Bertha Truitt who weren't Minna

Sprague. From the bowling alley she was disowned. It was Jeptha Arrison who offered up the name Nahum.

What had happened to the leg? Buried by itself in a coffin, cremated to match the rest, filed as evidence at the police station.

"You reckon he's haunting us?" said Jeptha, as though he were a girl wanting to be asked to dance. "I always wanted to meet a ghost. I mean, of a fellow I knew already."

"No such thing," said Joe. "No such person." Though he wondered. Objects in the alley had found their voices: the toilets sang in the middle of the night, the radiators shook their chains and hissed. Since the fire he felt widowed, or married. The only way two men *could* marry, thought Joe Wear, is if one were a ghost.

Jeptha closed his eyes. He said, "I been waiting for a ghost all my life. I'll be one, if I'm allowed."

"What do you mean?"

"I was born here, and I'll die here," said Jeptha Arrison. "That's what I mean."

But he had his own parents, a pair of doting old Yankees who liked to watch their Jeptha set pins. Mother Arrison, stout and sharp nosed, stood by the front door, holding her pocketbook up near her face to ward off the smoke.

"Mrs. Arrison!" said Joe Wear. "It's a pleasure. Tell me—" He tried to come up with a question. He landed on, "Where was Jeptha born?"

"We live in Attleboro," said Mrs. Arrison coldly. "We have always lived in Attleboro."

Joe tried to decide if that was an answer.

"Oh, look at him," said Mrs. Arrison. Her voice had been ice but now it was edged with melt. She would have been in her sixties then, and Jep a man of forty. There he was at the end of lane eight, as though on a stage, setting the pins. The smoke and distance made him black and white; the noise of the alley made him silent. He stood on one leg, Buster Keaton among the pins, humming his own accompaniment. Pure grace doing a dumb job. Pure love, too. He set the pins down as though they were sleeping children. He looked at them as though they were works of art.

"We almost died, Mr. Wear," said Mrs. Arrison. "Both of us. When he was born. Now there he is. He loves it here. We thought *she* might leave him something in her will. Not the whole alley, but mention it, mention he should be here always, no matter." Mrs. Arrison's eyes were damp as oysters, as salty gray. Then, as though she trusted Joe: "Whatever happens, you must keep him here. I believe he'd die if he had to go."

"All right."

"I mean it," said Mrs. Arrison.

"Mothers always mean it," said Joe Wear, who had little experience of mothers.

Across the city of Salford, like the drifting ash he might have turned to, the particulate Dr. Sprague entered dreams. He ran up walls. He alphabetized canned goods. He cured two headaches. Twenty different people heard him warble "Somewhere a Voice Is Calling," though in real life nobody had ever heard him sing a note. He kept Jeptha Arrison company and he came to Joe Wear and said, *Thank you for staying, Mr. Wear, I know you'll regret it.* You mean I won't regret it. *Did you not hear me the first time.*

Hazel Forest dreamt that he appeared and parted his shirt and then his stomach to show a weeping wound, and parted the wound to show a dripping cauldron. He said, *You're a nurse, you should have known.* But you're a doctor! she told him. *Yes,* he said.

Mary Gearhart came down to breakfast to find him there,

explaining that he was actually a wax figure from the museum: why he went up in flames like that.

LuEtta Mood dreamt that Dr. Sprague met her at the public library, in front of the dioramas (*Salford in the Time of the Pilgrims; Shakespeare's Globe; Salford, Like Rome, Is Built on Seven Hills; Salford in the Time of the Revolution*). He said to her, *You're pregnant.* She could hear her mother's voice calling down a dream hallway, *Where's Edith, where is she?* though in real life she never said Edith's name aloud. *I'm not*, LuEtta said to the dream doctor, and then, when she woke up, she did the addition in her head—weeks, symptoms—and it seemed a bewitchment. She was old to have another child, in her late thirties, though younger than Truitt had been.

Not sorcery. Not a miracle. As with most unbelievable things, it was mere and shocking biology.

Why not be Nahum Truitt? The ads had been placed. The lawyers were waiting. He was the right age.

"I am Nahum Truitt," said Joe Wear. He was alone in the rooms above the alley. But if he owned them! Not such a grim place. The windows were big and showed the blue of the sky over the grocery store roof. The rough brick walls reminded Joe of beloved lost roughness. "Mother was ashamed," he said, and that he couldn't believe. "Ma Truitt."

So what if Bertha Truitt had never shown him any motherkindness while she fussed over Jeptha? That was her, he practiced saying, that was mother: not one to spoil.

He had never really owned anything. He knew he still did not. He looked at the hissing stove upon which he heated canned soup, the tiny icebox he never stocked with ice. The furniture had been bought by Bertha, and there you could see some affection very much like Bertha herself: horsehair heart and velvet skin. Well-made furniture. Through the closet behind the toilet was a ladder that led to the roof, where Joe Wear liked to smoke. He went there now.

He sat down on the tar of the roof. "I am Nahum Truitt," he said again. He tried through the seat of his pants to feel in possession of all that was beneath him. "I once was Nahum Truitt. Nahum Truitt is my name by birth."

He had never thought himself the hero of any story. He was the janitor, the handyman, a mechanical. Perhaps it was a matter of assuming the center of the story. You cannot smash your life around the way you like it but you might step into somebody else's carefully made life. Step into it, like a pair of pants.

Unlike Jeptha he had no inconvenient parents to disprove him. Joe Wear's folks has crossed the ocean with their baby, caught TB, and died in Boston Harbor, or so he'd been told. He had once seen photos. His so-called parents were a pair of playing cards in his memory, visible only from one angle, and even then outlandish. A man who looked twelve years old, bad freckled, with burnt eyes; a woman apparently fifty, ruined by life, with a crude hairdo that seemed carved of wood. They had died long ago, they had been born in a country Joe didn't remember. Perhaps *they* had been the frauds. Perhaps he himself had never drawn breath in Ireland.

What he knew: he had been raised in the Dolbeer Home for Destitute Children. He'd been lonely all his remembered life. He had an aunt Rose—but maybe she was no relative, which was why she so easily renounced him once she had a family of her own. (He thought in a searing moment: What if he was on the right track but the wrong pony? Who was that lady who said he was his aunt? She could be—

—No, Joe. Claim one woman at a time. But he knew, and the pain it caused him made him believe he deserved anything he claimed.)

He'd keep Jeptha if it suited him, Mother Arrison.

After seven months a man who said he was Nahum Truitt arrived in Salford, holding on to an old newspaper as though it were proof of identity. The *Providence Journal*, not the Orono *Messenger*. "Live on Vinalhaven, you hear of it?" the man said. "Island off Rockland. How this thing got over there I do not know. Ferry? In the belly of a whale? I minister at the Church of the Woods. You hear of it? Not all my life. I were a fisher of fish before I were a fisher of men. How I ended up on the island. The real fish drew me there. But then I had an experience. You see? Came to know. Came to *understand*. I can see as I look at you," he said, "you've had some hard times your ownself."

"Listen," said Joe Wear. "How—do you mind—how old a man are you?"

"Not so young as you think. The salt air's preserved me!"

Preserved, thought Joe Wear, *in the way of beef jerky*. He was a tall gray-bearded fellow in a minister's collar, weathered as old clapboard. A feral man, as though he'd been found in the woods and cleaned up, beard pruned, burrs combed from his sideburns, forced into a suit and pushed into society. He blinked like a circus bear; his hands were brown as paws. The only youthful thing about him was the pure density of his gray hair.

The godliness was beyond belief, but not so beyond as everything else: his height, his tiny yellow brown eyes, the pink beneath the leather of his cheeks, and the fact—so far as Joe Wear could tell—that he was a good ten years older than Bertha Truitt. One thing for sure: Dr. Sprague was not his father. He was a big unruly white man.

"You got kids?" the man who said he was Nahum Truitt asked Joe Wear.

"Bachelor. You?"

"Grown and gone, much to the unhappiness of their ma."

"Who raised you?"

"*My* ma."

"And—well, who was that?"

Nahum quirked his head. "Your lady employer. Bertha Truitt. Till I were grown. Well, I thought so. We had an argument. Had I been less stubborn we would have spent our lives together. Had she been less stubborn. She would have known the love of her grandchildren, and the love of a daughter in the form of my wife. But I were fifteen and thought I could look after myself. And you know what?"

"Tell me," said Joe Wear.

"I could! More's the sorrow. I regret it, I do. I regret the reason." He leaned across the wood of the counter. "The Negro," he said. "She intended to marry him. She said, 'He will be your father.' Well, sir, my mother herself raised me without a bit of God. She raised me hard-hearted and hardheaded and hateful, may she rest in her peace. I found the family Bible propping open a window and I took it out of spite. So I were a sinner when I walked away and I am now as you find me." He touched his collar. "Now I would forgive her. I do forgive her. God has forgiven her, too."

"He was a fine man," said Joe Wear, who felt grieved to realize this was true. "None better." That might not have been. Joe himself: he was not a good man, he was looking in a mirror and it was awful.

"Drank," said Nahum.

"Well."

"I partook myself before I found my way. I forgive him for that. I realize now indeed the brotherhood of all men, and that it is a sin to despise a person for the color of his skin. God made us all. Nossir, I realize now, I disliked that fellow for other reasons entire."

"What about your father?"

The man was silent. Finally he said, "I'll leave Our Lord God to judge him. Bertha Truitt raised me, named me Nahum. About a year in there she thought she were a Mormon."

"*Truitt* did?"

"Our Bertha. Had me baptized through a hole in the ice in

Joeson City, Michigan. Plunged in herself right after. Didn't take except I do believe the cold got in my veins. Therefore Maine. You've been to the state of Maine?"

"You have a sister," said Joe Wear.

"Been told so," said Nahum, narrowing his narrow eyes. "But I don't know about that. I am here to know our Bertha. I am here to know who she knew, to shake the hands she shook. I come down to give the place a lookover before we decide to up and move. See if this place needs Nahum Truitt, you understand."

Joe Wear was doing the math and it didn't seem possible, not any of it. He picked up a pencil; he didn't write the numbers down but it helped to doodle as he added in his head. Minna was fifteen now, or thereabouts. No, not possible that she and this fellow had the same mother. There had to be forty years between them.

No God, Mormon God: he couldn't even keep his story straight. Some con man come down from Maine in a fake dog collar to seem respectable. Saw the ad. Figured there was money in it. Amazing, really, there was only one fraud.

There had almost been two, Joe reminded himself.

"She were terrible young, she had me," said Nahum. "If you're doing the math. She were fifteen and a sinner. God has forgiven her. And as I am now fifty years of age, she were sixty-four at her untimely demise three years ago."

"She never was," said Joe Wear.

"But she *were*," said Nahum.

He pulled from some drawer or cabinet in his greatcoat a book clad in dark green leather, gilt at the edges. "Look here." HOLY BIBLE said the cover. Joe Wear had always thought the actual title must be something longer, and HOLY BIBLE just a nickname, but there it was. Nahum opened the cover. There, in Truitt's inimitable handwriting, was her own name. Flourishes and serifs, a rehearsed signature, ready for contracts and admirers. *Bertha Truitt, born 1855 at—*

But the place of her birth had been scratched out. Indeed, the entire family tree had been bowdlerized. That she had parents was inarguable, but they were listed only as *Mother* and *Daddy*. *Daddy* had died in 1861. Neither had birth dates. Beneath the blue of Bertha's pen you could see the faded loops of somebody else's. Joe took the book and flipped through, to see whether Bertha had likewise corrected the Bible, or had inserted herself into some of the more thrilling stories, but she hadn't.

"Where's your name?" Joe asked, looking again at the back, *Bertha Truitt*, a few other names at the edges of the family tree, *Sissy* and *Bachman* and *Anthony*. A forgery? No, nobody else could draw such a *B*, with such vigorous ringlets.

"Lost interest," said Nahum Truitt. "Far as I know she never did read the good book. Propping up a window, as I said. Luckiest break I ever got. So," he said. "I am most ignorant of bowling. You'll enlighten me?"

At night Joe sat at the kitchen table and let the black-and-white cat pace the top, butting up against him. What was at the corner of a cat's mouth, that they needed so much affection focused there? Never mind. He did not think the cat was the ghost of Leviticus Sprague, as some of the bowlers suggested, but he did believe the spirits were acquainted.

The man who said he was Nahum Truitt had no interest in The Game, not the business side nor the playing of it. He would say, when Joe Wear explained something to him, "I understand only the souls of men." Sometimes he'd watch the bowlers and examine their movements with such intensity he ruined the game. You almost thought he was studying how to be a human man. He took a room at the YMCA down the street, though Joe Wear offered the apartment. "You pay rent?" asked Nahum. After a moment, Joe said, "Part of my wages." "Well then, no need," said Nahum, "moreover: the place has a case of cats."

"This is till we get settled elsewhere," he said sometimes, or "Till we decide for sure concerning the Commonwealth of Massachusetts." He referred, always, to *the Commonwealth of Massachusetts* and *the State of Maine*. Either he felt there was a strong distinction, or he just liked the lard of extra words. *We* was royal, or referred to him and his wife back in Maine, or the partnership of Nahum Truitt and God: there was no telling. His beard thickened. The stand of his hair seemed to be cut daily, but from a distance. He gave up his minister's collar and took to wearing dark pants and a vest striped like mattress ticking. He drew no salary from Truitt's Alleys.

"That's all right, boss," he'd say to Joe Wear. "You just put it in the bank."

He'd vanish for weeks then show back up, sometimes wilder and sometimes barbered. "A great success!" he'd tell Joe Wear. "Our revival. We saved dozens of souls up in the State of Maine. Oh, at first they resisted, at first they clung to their bottles and their gambling, to their sin, to their darkness—isn't that a terrible thing, Joe Wear, how the darkness fools you into thinking it's a boon, fools you into thinking it's *interesting*—but they come to us eventual! Hundreds!"

"I thought you said dozens."

"I reckon hundreds," said Nahum Truitt.

At any moment, Nahum Truitt might drift away, end up on a boat or in the belly of a whale, go back to the Church of the Woods and his Wife of the Woods and whatever else (children, grandchildren, a lobster farm) was in the Goddamn Woods. Nobody believed that this so-called Nahum Truitt was a child of Bertha's. The height of him, the denunciations, the way he *talked*. You could die of boredom. You *longed* to. They imagined Nahum Truitt would close the bowling alley and convert it to a storefront church, or a mission.

Instead, he merely wanted to ban women. He'd come to the conclusion on one of his forays to the Woods in Maine.

"Men need a place to come together in fellowship," said Nahum.

By now Joe Wear knew a few places where that happened. Once liquor got pushed into the basement he discovered that's where Massachusetts kept a lot of interesting things, but he didn't think that was what Nahum had in mind. "They need a place of recreation and exercise where they may speak their minds to one another without interference. Are we bowlers? Yes, we are bowlers, but we are also Christian men, and when Christian men gather in a place of understanding and decency, they may come to know God."

"What would your mother think?"

Nahum frowned. "You tell me."

"She wouldn't like it."

At that Nahum looked nearly moved. "Yes," he said sadly. "She would hate it. That was like her. What would she say?"

"She would say," said Joe, trying to conjure her voice up. He could not even quite disinter her face from his memory, though he would recognize her particular lolloping walk from a distance. "She would say, The game is for all, Joe Wear."

"Not to *you*," said Nahum. "What would she say to me?"

But Joe Wear couldn't imagine. At last he tried, "Nahum Truitt, let women bowl."

"We shall install a pool table," said Nahum.

"We shall?"

"Get a pool table, Joe Wear," said Nahum. "Get two, so that more men may commune. But first, clear out the gals."

THE ANGEL
OF THE ALLEYS

Mostly the women had gone anyhow, home to their children and families, to speakeasies, to other hobbies. LuEtta Mood came every Saturday with her new baby strapped to her back so that you could only see his comically fat head. The first time, pregnant with Edith, she'd been unnerved that she had a living thing inside of her; the second time, a mortal one. She'd denied her imagination at every turn and so had been surprised by a boy who looked nothing like Edith, with the black hair and pug nose of a foreign prince. She did not feel as though she knew him yet, though he was six months old.

"Sorry, Lu," said Joe Wear, the first Saturday of Nahum's reign. "New rules. No women."

"*Rules?* On whose authority?"

"New owner. Mr. Truitt. Who else's?"

LuEtta Mood was taller than Joe Wear. She leaned over so she could rest her bust on the glass counter in a territorial way. "This is Bertha Truitt's house," she said. Her chin was substantial. It possessed a certain force when she pointed it at him.

Then Jeptha Arrison was pattering down the gutter like a tightrope walker.

"Lu!" he called. "Lu!"

"Hello, Jep. Now, Mr. Wear," said LuEtta, who'd never called him so, "you tell your new boss you informed me but I said no." She pulled out her shoes from her satchel. "I came to bowl. I bowled here opening day and I will bowl closing day. Call the police if you like."

"I'm not going to call the police," said Joe, irritated.

LuEtta made herself tall as she could. She fluffed her bloomers to their full blossom. "I won't go."

"*Won't* she?" said Jeptha Arrison, in a voice of terror. "*Won't* she? Joe, me neither, I won't go neither, I'll stay with Lu and the babby."

"Were you asked to go?" said Joe. "Are you a woman?"

"Not so's I noticed," said Jeptha.

"You'll pinset for me," said LuEtta, and Jeptha put his hand to his chest and said, "'Pon my honor and always."

W ho's that gal?" Nahum asked Joe that afternoon. "I recall saying no women. Our mission is a bowling mission, I remember distinct I told you this, and we preach to men. Men fail to speak their minds when women are around, for fear of contradiction. That woman there looks especial contradictory. She especial contradictory? She looks terrible contradictory and contrary."

"She's all right," said Joe. He disliked it when Nahum stood behind the counter with him: the man was an elbower and shoulder shover, a whisperer of confidences that added up to nothing, an animated overcoat who only wanted you to don it, no matter the weather. "Won plenty of trophies in her time. I wouldn't bother with Lu. Worry about the cats."

"Cats and *women*," said Nahum. "Which is worse? Both species cold as ice and fishy to boot. Gal! Gal! Gal!"

Lu didn't turn her head.

"I'll get her out," said Nahum, darkly. "What's that fool doing setting her pins? Hey! Hey! Pinboy! Don't set her pins." He elbowed Joe Wear in the elbow; it hurt. "Is he deaf?"

"Might be, all these years. He's all right."

Nahum looked at Jep. "If that's all right I hate to think."

But Jeptha Arrison was not all right, he was struck, he was vibrating, he was pinsetting for LuEtta Mood, connected to her as though by piano wire. The ball, he swore, was still warm from her palm, faintly whiffish of her perfume.

He loved her.

Jeptha Arrison had not been kicked in the head, leastways not by a horse, not actually. His father had tried to make him a jockey but Jeptha didn't care for horses, their oil derrick heads and black eyes, their mouths all the way at the bottom of their snouts. "I like cows," he told his father at the Rockingham Track, where he'd been brought for employment. Jeptha's father had looked around, shook his head. A skewbald mare sneezed and whips of sticky spit lashed from her mouth. "Well," his father said, "I don't know any of those ladies, you'll have to find cows yourself. Marry a farm girl. I don't know any of those, either."

"I won't marry a farm girl," Jeptha said.

"Dear Jep," said his father, "you won't marry anyone."

But *oh yes he will* said his mother, and by the time Jeptha Arrison was twenty he was a married man and by the time he was twenty and a half he was a widower. His wife, Bessie, had been a schoolteacher, had loved him with an antiseptic, what-will-I-do-with-you love. She liked especially to tuck him into bed with fierce hands like hoes that jammed bedclothes around him. "You cozy, Mr. Arrison," she'd say. They'd been married for six weeks when, while in

Baskertop Square, they stopped to look at the men constructing the monument on top of Bledsoe Hill, one of the two hills that had survived the leveling of Salford. The monument was a tower to commemorate a Revolutionary War battle that Salford had supplied the guns for; it looked like a saltshaker. "Almost done!" said Bessie, and at that moment the masons on top of Bledsoe Hill lost their grip of a cart holding a block of granite. It roared down the hill and, in almost a deliberative way, took Bessie out of the square and married her to the tobacconist's wooden Indian and sent them both—Bessie, the chief—through the tobacconist's glass window in a calamitous shatter.

Left-behind Jeptha gasped on the sidewalk. He'd been holding her pocketbook. He still held it.

"Glory!" said a woman who'd seen it happen. She tried to take the pocketbook from him, as though he'd stolen it. For a moment he even thought she was Bessie, come back to claim what was hers: the purse, her Jeptha. About the same womanish shape, and Jeptha was awful at faces. Then he saw she was older, and redheaded, and herself: she tugged and he tightened his hold and they wrestled till the woman said angrily, "You're bleeding!"

His knuckles were scraped, one toe was broken, that's how close he came to dying. He couldn't even get dying right, he told himself later. He'd let her die alone.

All his life Jeptha had confused the word *widow* and *window* and now here they were: he was a windower. He wanted the murdering block of granite as a headstone but the city wouldn't let him. He would have carved it with the words BESSIE ARRISON. ALMOST DONE. Instead they trucked the stone back up and put it in place, and they trucked Bessie to the morgue and the cemetery. He didn't know what happened to the Indian. Her people put up a little marble cenotaph that said:

BESSIE
BELOVED DAUGHTER
& WIFE

"Beloved wife, too," he told his mother-in-law, and she said, "Yes, that's what it says." She pointed at the BELOVED, then at the WIFE, as though grammar could explain. "*Most* beloved," said Jeptha.

Oh, he knew he upset people. Bad enough when he was Only Jeptha; troubling when he was Jeptha Married and sharing a bed with a woman; once he was Jeptha Bereaved he was untouchable. He worked at the track—his father had a friend—but in the canteen. He was a man apart and knew it. Even the horses started to look at him cow-eyed. To watch your wife die before you! People were suspicious of him so that they would not have to pity him. Even the horses. Especially the horses. In his grief he swallowed aspirin and was sent to the hospital, where he found Bertha Truitt. She took him in, built the bowling alley around them both.

There, he was just big-headed Jeptha Arrison: who imagined he had a past? Always Jeptha, ever Jeptha. Only his parents saw, in his fastidiousness with the pins, his exactitude and grace, a man recreating the world, ten pins at a time and ten frames a string, all day long till the lights went out. A man born for love.

LuEtta Mood, at home, nursing the baby, tried to conjure Bertha Truitt up: what she might have said to the man who insisted he was her son. There was no Bertha to him. He was leather and gristle, mean-eyed, lazy. Anyhow it was Dr. Sprague who'd left the alley to him. Bertha might object. She might have chosen somebody else. A woman. A collective of women. LuEtta herself, even. Why would Bertha Truitt allow her beloved bowling alley to be owned by a *man*? She only ever seemed passingly interested in the male sex: she loved her husband, and Jeptha Arrison. Ordinary male Salfordian bowlers she ignored so far as she could, though she had a soft spot for the men returned from the war, who'd lost part of an arm, all of their hearing. They were nearly noble enough to be women. When it came to most men, she took their money and turned down their advice. The former they were stingy with; the latter, profligate.

"He says men need a place they can come together without women," Joe Wear had said. But wasn't that the whole wide world? Where did women have? Truitt's had been hers for all her grown-up years, even if her teammates had fallen away. Indeed, perhaps women did not need a place to come together but to be alone. That's what Truitt's was to her: a thunderous place where she could think in peace. A place her husband hated.

She was, still, an excellent bowler, the baby on her back where she couldn't see him but could feel him breathe and so knew he was alive. She had forgotten how many minutes of motherhood were devoted to this question, even before Edith's accident. Alive now? And now? The deeper Edith's sleep the shallower her life, it seemed. The extraordinary stillness of a sleeping baby! Look for breath at the stomach, flush at the cheeks. Then LuEtta would leave the room, come back. She lost hours to the question. Alive now, now, now?

These days she didn't have hours. She strapped the rude baby to her back. Away from the bowling alley she dispensed love to him through every part of her body, her neck and face and breasts and stomach. At Truitt's she let her disinterested back pick up some of the mothering. He was an animal, asleep. She bowled well. You should never have to give up something you're good at.

She met her old teammate Hazel Forest at Coop's Tearoom. "It's unbearable!" said Hazel. "I haven't been in a year or more, but what would Our Bertha say?" Hazel was old, but with children still little: she had an exhausted air of experience, someone who thought a lot of things but actually knew very few. If you asked her how to make a cheese soufflé she would tell you about the rivers of blood running down the gutters of Paris during the French Revolution, as though you should be able to divine a recipe from that.

"We'll chain ourselves to the ball returns," said Hazel.

"You can't bowl in chains," said LuEtta.

"We'll take up *space*. We'll interfere. They want a quiet place to gather as men? We won't let 'em. We'll get cymbals. Horns! *Hatchets*."

"Hatchets?" LuEtta said in a panic. "We don't want to destroy it."

"Why not? It's not ours anymore. Why preserve it?"

Why not? It was Bertha's place. She'd left it to them. Bertha was four years dead, and LuEtta's love for her was spilled molasses. Before the spill she'd known she'd owned it, up on a shelf, contained and unopened. Now it was everywhere, it got everywhere, the stick and smell, the uselessness because spilled. *You talk of that woman too much*, Moses Mood told LuEtta as she read about the lawsuits against the Purity Distillery Company, owners of the burst molasses tank. She wanted them to pay for killing Bertha, though she didn't want the exact dollar value of Bertha's life calculated by lawyers. *She's dead*, said Moses. That was true. *And I am alive*. LuEtta wasn't sure. Some days she thought she'd married a man killed years ago by a bullet, dead but still talking.

"What good does ruin do?" LuEtta said to Hazel at Coop's Tea-room. "If we want to be allowed—"

"I've seen that man. That is a man who hates women for their very womanhood. He is the Devil."

"We might change his mind."

"He would rip himself in two before changing his mind," said Hazel. "*Bertha* marched."

"Not in her own house. In her own house she bowled. So we'll bowl."

In fact Hazel did not want to bowl: her shoulder was bursitic. She was older than LuEtta Mood, and she'd been divorced eight years now. Golda Bastian, like Hazel a nurse at the hospital, had moved in to help, but it was clear that Golda hated children with the pure passion of a bigot. "I'll bowl with you," said Hazel.

She lasted a single afternoon.

Men came from all over by car, by trolley, to see the Angel of the Alleys. Time had blunted the point of her chin, and bowling, as Bertha Truitt foretold, had proved a boon to her form. She wouldn't give up, LuEtta. She bowled alone. She got there in the morning and bowled till night, in white culottes and a blue-trimmed middy blouse. Bertha Truitt had bowled alone plenty and the men had never wanted to intrude on her solitude. LuEtta was different. Soon enough men started to challenge her. That is, they tried to flirt and she said, "We'll play for it."

"Play for what?"

"Conversation," said LuEtta. "You lose, you leave me alone."

"All right," the challenging man might say.

She was a spectacle, just the sort of thing Joe Wear used to despise, but he found he didn't mind so much. He even found a wedge of admiration for her.

Thereafter, nearly any time of day, you could find LuEtta Mood taking a stack of cash off some frowning man, the frowning baby strapped to her back. That imperious baby! He seemed to disapprove of everything, though silently: he would issue his orders for your execution later, through his trusted ministers. Good thing he would never remember this, it was terrible to be so bound by duty and age, and soon enough the baby—did he have a name? nobody ever heard her mention it—kept his eyes averted, as though the sight of her pained him, as though she were dying in a hospital bed.

Duty. You would sit close, you had to, but to watch your mother do something so grim and personal meant you'd remember her no other way.

One afternoon Moses Mood met them on the sidewalk outside of Truitt's. He had not been on the streets of Salford for a year or more. His assistants ran the hardware store; he stayed at home and worried. He'd had black hair once, so black that people wondered where it had come from. Now it was white. *Turned white overnight*, people said, *from the shock*, but it was only that they hadn't looked at him in so long, not really. He'd lost weight, and the scar on his cheek had been laid bare. Lu wanted to touch it, as she had in the old days. He put his hand up to hide it.

Moses Mood had thought the baby would make things better. Would eat up some of her affection for the dead Edith's, so that his husband's portion would outweigh either child's. No: that gobbling baby ate up every bit of spare love and attention, and then she took him to the bowling alley and stayed away all day. He was a year old now, as baby a baby as ever, as gobblingly greedy.

"Lu-Etta," Moses Mood said in his slow furious voice. "Lu-Etta." He shook his head and chuckled. There was never such a man for chuckling. "Come on home, it's dinnertime."

What was he wearing? Shirt and tie, he wanted to look good, but with a little shawl around his shoulders because he was cold. It was March. He had a pistol in his pocket, a little one.

"I'm hungry," he said, with a small awful smile, small as the hidden gun.

"You know how to cook," she answered.

"You walked right out of the house, no food in the icebox. I looked for you. I yelled for you. Then Snodders calls me on the phone and says, She's down at the alleys again."

Of course she had taken to the alleys, married to a man like that! For years she'd been trying to please him and he would not allow it. She had sewn or knitted or crocheted all of the baby's clothing (she had made the very shawl that Moses Mood wore) to the wonder of her friends: nobody's stitches were tinier, and Moses Mood could only say, *Look at the little fellow in his ball gown.* She had cooked him meals for years, and never a compliment. Had sung to the baby: *Was that you caterwauling, Lu?* No matter what she'd done over the years she could hear his response: *Let me do that* and *you'll ball it up* and *this house is a mess, no I'll clean it, I'll clean it, I always do.* When he yelled, she could only make herself smaller on the couch. She'd had a father who hit her. Moses never did but she believed she was the one who stopped him, by her small stillness.

He said again, "No food in the house. I looked."

"You said you were too sick to eat! You said you wanted to lie in bed alone!" For a moment she was a stranger listening to herself berate an old man on the sidewalk and she almost softened to him. The baby on her back turned.

Moses Mood said, smiling, smiling, "I am dying, honey. Come tend me."

"I will," said LuEtta, "soon."

"Then I will take the boy," said Moses Mood. He went back of her and tried to extricate the baby from its wrappings.

"What are you doing?"

"It's no good for him," he said. He got her by the hand. Her bowling hand, which fidgeted in his own. "You bitch," he said under his voice, but now he was not just smiling but laughing. Laughing so he could laugh it off.

LuEtta thought, *We're in trouble.*

Danger was a cloudburst. Ordinarily she read the signs, thunder nobody else could hear, a greening of the sky, a whiff of ozone. Not today. In the past she had merely stayed away. She would put the baby on her back so nobody could get to him, so she would be able to place her body between him and disaster. Were they in more danger because Moses Mood was in public or less? He cared what people thought of him. That was why he laughed. He thought his laughter was charming.

She knew he had a gun because he always did. She wasn't particularly frightened of the gun itself. Not more today than any other day. The baby on her back made it easier to flee, that was another thing. She'd already packed the important object. A year ago she might have thrown herself on Hazel's mercy and asked to move in, but that was before the child-hating Golda Bastian had taken over the house. "Let go, Moses," she told him, though then she realized that as long as his hands were occupied he was not fishing for the gun. She wondered how long she might keep up this dancing. The baby was alive. She could heard the ticking in his chest that came before he cried.

"*You're* not scared," said Moses Mood to his son, or to his wife.

What was the right response to that?

Then the door to Truitt's opened up, and Jeptha Arrison stepped out. He said in a mild, formal voice, "Your lane awaits you, Mrs. Mood."

"No," said Moses Mood. Now he laughed at Jeptha, the idiot who thought he could take a woman from her husband.

"Nevertheless," said Jeptha, in a voice of such chivalry it made Moses Mood step back. "I'll take the babby." The child reached his arms to Jeptha. Moments before he'd seemed tied to his mother permanently. Now he nearly flew through the air to Jeptha. "Please," Jeptha said to LuEtta, and he held the door for her, and the three of them—bowler, baby, pinbody—went into the alley.

"I said *No!*" yelled Moses Mood, though he was alone on the sidewalk. "No! No!" He was going off like a gun, though he kept the gun quiet in his pocket; he felt its weight. No! No! What direction would he fire in?

When the news came some weeks later that Moses Mood had shot himself in the other ear, LuEtta was staying with Jeptha and his parents in Attleboro. Mood had left two notes, one that said *I belong to the ages* and the other *Lu, I do not blame you, you see I could not live with myself either.*

"You saved me, Jeptha," said LuEtta, and he said, "You saved yourself."

But that was after Nahum Truitt had made LuEtta Mood bowl for her soul.

RATTLED

uEtta felt something poke her calf as she got ready to start her approach. She figured it was one of the cats; there were three now, all black-and-white, prowling Truitt's. The cats were the only thing that made the baby laugh, which convinced LuEtta that he, like his father, might have a mean sense of humor. Cats don't laugh back. But the baby was silent, and it wasn't a cat, just Nahum Truitt on his knees and one hand, jabbing at her with a pool cue. His beard was a thicket. He'd left behind a blue chalk print on her white sock. She pulled her leg closer to her body and cleared her throat, but Nahum looked fixedly at the end of the cue and crawled closer, poking, his pink knit necktie lapping at the floor like a tongue.

"Mr. *Truitt*," she said. He didn't answer. He poked. "Mr. Truitt!"

He used the cue as a cane to pull himself to his feet and turned to the men bowling on the next lane, the Salford Half Nickels, the men returned from the war. They were practicing for a tourney in Boston at the Sheaf House.

"Care to join me in a prayer?" Nahum asked them, plucking a ball from the return. "You're churchgoing men, I know, but once a week is not enough, you see your wives every single day and you see your pals twice a week, you better find more time for God! Who's with me?"

The men looked uneasily at each other. "The YMCA has a team," said Jack Silver, not a churchgoing man. "Perhaps—"

"The YMCA does not need saving!" said Nahum Truitt. He looked at Jack Silver, who had a ball tucked in the crook of what was left of his right arm. "You bowl thataway? You've got a good arm just the other side of you."

"Right-handed," said Jack Silver.

"But you're *not*," said Nahum. "The only hand in your possession is of the left variety."

"I am a right-handed bowler," said Jack Silver.

Nahum frowned. "It unnerves."

Jack Silver gave the ball a toss in his abbreviated arm and said, "Your nerves are no concern of mine."

Nahum shook his head. "All *right*," he said. "Whatever serves." He looked at LuEtta. "I will bowl with the men," he said over his shoulder to the Half Nickels, as though declining an invitation, and went to stand directly at the foul line. He bobbled the ball from hand to hand as he stared at the pins. Nobody had ever seen him show the least interest in the game. The men worried he would pitch the ball overhand instead of bowling it.

"Sure you want to do it like that?" called LuEtta Mood.

"I'll do it thisaway," he said, and flung the ball hard to the side, directly into the gutter.

"You see," said the captain of the Half Nickels, Pinky DeMuth, unsure whose side he was on, "you have a three-step, or a five-step, or a seven-step approach. Stand back here—"

"I'll do it thisaway," said Nahum again. "Gal," he said in a grand voice. He rested the ball on one hip. "You gamble, I hear."

"I play money games," said LuEtta. She and the baby were lodging with the Arrisons now. She needed the money.

"You'll play me."

How did a grown man know so little about women! To command her like that, and she the best bowler in the alley. Martin Younkins leaned on his crutches in a thoughtful way and said, "Well Truitt, you might—"

"Gambling's not a sin?" LuEtta asked.

"Not *nearly*," said Nahum. "No, it is not, for what is God besides a gambler? He is locked in a game—"

"I'll play you," said LuEtta. The baby as usual was on her back. A child now, really. Still silent and unamused. How did she stand upright with that weight tugging at her? "Dollar a string, progressive."

"One game," corrected Nahum. "For your tenancy in the alley."

The men of Truitt's Alleys were divided about LuEtta Mood, each one of them divided, not down the middle but cut into pieces like a pie. She had been there longer than any of them: she was practically a piece of equipment. An outdated piece, the lone woman left in the alley. Had to watch your tongue around her (though she never did flinch no matter what was said: she'd heard worse). What did Mr. Mood think of his wife? Didn't she belong at home? (They didn't know she had left them.) She was quite a sight. She was a beauty. She was not as beautiful as rumor had it. It was hard to concentrate on your own bowling when she was there, and these days she was always there.

Nahum Truitt they plain disliked.

So when the two agreed to the bet, the Half Nickels weren't sure which was the Devil and which bowling against the Devil. They just knew souls were at stake.

"One game," said Nahum Truitt again. "Everything on one game, and whoever wins lets the other alone."

LuEtta looked at him. "Meaning I own the alley if I win."

Joe Wear said, "No—"

"All right," said Nahum. "Why ever not. You beat me, gal, and I happily sign everything over to you."

Martin Younkins shook his head. All the men did. They wanted a piece of that action! "That ain't fair," Younkins said. "She wins, she gets a whole bowling alley, but he wins—"

Nahum took a heroic stance, so noble and statuary you thought a pigeon might alight on his head. "That is how much it means to me, that my alley be free of the feminine influence," he said.

"Jiminy," said LuEtta, but she could feel her juddering heart in her chest. She might win the alley. She reached behind and felt the baby's ankle for luck.

"You want to take that child off?"

"No," said LuEtta. The baby was sleeping. "This is how I'm used to it."

"One game," said Nahum again.

LuEtta Mood had a 103 average, higher than any of the Half Nickels, the Diamonds, the Greystockings, the Kings. She had no trouble at all bowling against Nahum Truitt for her soul: she bowled for her soul every day. She was one of those dead-eyed gamblers, in other words, who bet against themselves every time. Dead-eyed in aim; dead-eyed in the light gone from her as she bowled. Bowling was what she had and she needed it to have a happy ending and that had looked unlikely for a while now. Owning the alley might do it.

Nahum gave her a condescending rolling-wristed gesture. Ladies first.

Every time LuEtta had picked up a ball in the past twenty years she went through these steps. First she felt lucky: she knew that this ball would be a good one. Then she felt cursed, and could see the ball journey down the lane only to drop into the gutter at the last minute. Then she felt scientific: luck had nothing to do with it! Then as superstitious as an ancient, there were forces all about her that wanted her to win but only if she appeased them in the right way, *I honor you spirits of the bowling alley, I love you, deliver my ball.* Only then would she actually bowl.

She had a three-step approach, absolutely ordinary, and a languid elegant follow-through with her bowling hand. She downed six pins with the first ball. With the second ball she picked up the spare, not neatly, but in pieces, the wood against the nine pin, the nine into the two, the wood spinning into the seven and one. At the end of the alley Jeptha jumped down to the deck to set the pins. The first thing he did was kiss the second ball, still warm from LuEtta's fingertips, still warm from its triumph.

The men didn't know he was in love with LuEtta: they believed Jeptha was a child, Jeptha liked games, Jeptha wouldn't know what to do with a full-grown human woman, Jeptha loved only the pins. It was true: Jeptha's pinsetting was brilliant, perfect. He was never the least bit off. When Jeptha Arrison set your pins, you knew how they'd fly, every time.

This time LuEtta took three balls to knock down seven pins. Nahum's turn.

The Salford Half Nickels winced to watch Nahum Truitt bowl. He had taken off his jacket and rolled up his shirtsleeves, tucked the awful organ-pink necktie into his vest. An ossified man, all knuckle and claw: he held the ball with the tips of his fingers. Generally it was against Joe Wear's ethics to let a man bowl in such an amateurish way. (Joe had locked the front door and joined the crowd to watch.) The man didn't have a chance against the Angel of the Alleys anyhow. Few men who visited Truitt's could hope to touch her, never mind an awkward inexperienced man of God. God himself (surely a tenpin man; surely God loved clarity, the promise of perfection) might have a hard time against LuEtta Mood.

What would she do when she won the alley? Cast out all the men as Nahum had wanted to cast out the women? Drive them out with a stick like snakes? Leave it to the cats and girls?

Bertha Truitt had never done that. Bertha Truitt had not seemed to care for men but did not find them a nuisance, had spoken to them as though she were their equal, and that was maddening, but LuEtta Mood had the infuriating air of superiority. She thought she was better than. Leastways, she was trying to convince herself of it.

There was the ball clutched in Nahum's fingers, daylight all around it. He took his place at the foul line and bowled. No approach, no follow-through, and yet he knocked 'em down. Three pins, then five pins, then two for the ten box. Martin Younkins marked it in chalk on the board.

The pinboy, a malnourished flop-haired ten-year-old named Leslie Bish, had been eating rock candy off a string, and now he set the candy on the shelf and jumped down to roll the balls back to the boss. His hands were never clean, and he set pins loose and sloppy. He took no pleasure in it: they might as well have been milk bottles at the carnival, saplings planted along a path. Sometimes he kicked one or two over as he worked. Even if he'd done it well, there was nobody to praise him beyond Jeptha, and the older boys had told him to steer clear of Jep, not because he'd interfere with you but because once he got a notion you were a listener he would never stop talking. Leslie Bish's mother needed the money he made. That was true of all the pinboys except Jeptha himself, who tsked on his shelf and regarded the pins with sorrow.

He looked after the pins because he was not allowed to look after the pinboys. They wouldn't let him. "Go away, Jeptha," they said, though he was the only man among 'em and he felt he'd earned the right to boss 'em around a little. How did it happen, that he had been bossed around by men when he was a boy and by boys when he was a man? Never mind. He would tend his lane.

Jeptha Arrison spoke to the pins. Loved them. Bowling he didn't care for, he had never bowled in his life, it was a foolish waste of time though he would not say so to the bowlers he adored. But the pins he understood. Here comes the interloping ball, once, twice, third time, then he jumps down—Mother Jeptha! for he is as a mother to them—to tend to his darlings, his pinlings, his knocklings, his flocklings. "Here dear," he says to the ten pin, the five pin, the three. He remembers where they stood even now that they've tumbled. "Here four, here five—oh dear, no, you have split yourself. Poor thing, you're broken beyond saving." See him toss the pin away.

Not mother then, but God. Mother is more powerful, mother can heal with love because she plays favorites. When you've split in half God will not pretend you haven't. God Jeptha sits above the pins and waits. When the world is destroyed, he resets it. Makes it stand again.

Leslie Bish's sticky fingers would spread sugar everywhere: down the return to the bowler, then onto the lane, then back to the pinsetter's hand. It would degrade every part of play. Jeptha nearly called out to Nahum to say this. A money game was a serious thing, it required honesty and evenness. But LuEtta's place in the alleys was at stake, and so he kept quiet, the first sin Jeptha Arrison ever committed in the name of bowling but not the last.

Nahum bowled again. First ball two. Second ball five. He'd knocked over one more for sure with the third, but the six pin was still thinking about going down, the six pin was fighting off sleep— and Leslie Bish jumped down early and kicked it over himself.

"Hey now!" Nahum Truitt yelled. "Pinboy! Get out of there."

Leslie Bish raised his head. He was thin and oily as a mackerel. He was only ten but he'd been fired before, for sleepiness and inaccuracy. He reached to scoop up his rock candy, but it was already stuck to the side of his pants and with gravity's help was trying to undo his pocket.

"All right, Wear," Nahum Truitt called. "You'll set for me."

"Ah no," said Joe Wear. "Jeptha'll set for you both."

"Not that moron. He'll fiddle it. You'll set for me."

Why did Joe Wear agree? He should have gone out the door with Leslie Bish to drown his sorrow in rock candy or needle beer. Instead he walked down the lane. He felt everyone judge his lubberly gait.

"'Lo, Joe," said Jeptha, but Joe shook his head.

Once Joe Wear had been the pride of Les Miserables, but that was years ago and moreover this was not a wager he wanted a hand in. Already he could feel the splinters he'd picked up setting. What if LuEtta *did* win? Would she fire him? Sell the alley at a good price? She was better than anybody in that alley except Joe Wear himself, who bowled every night, and even on his days off went to the Sheaf House in Boston for the money games there. *He* should be bowling for ownership of the alley.

"I'll do for both lanes, you like," said Jeptha, but Joe had already finished. He had spent plenty of time in the pits over the years, checking the metal plates the pins stood on, cleaning up shattered pins, surveying the wood of the lanes from all angles, but he hadn't sat up on the pinboys' shelf since he was a teenager. He was stunned to measure just how much bigger he'd grown. Up close Jep was almost heartbreakingly graceful, going from toe to toe, a hummingbird amid the trampled blossoms.

"I *could* set for both, Joe Wear," he said in a hurt voice.

"'Course you could."

"I'm honest as the day is long."

"I know it."

"My love is for the game."

"I don't doubt that."

"I'm honest," said Jeptha again. "I can't go back to the horses. No man can, once he's left them. It's the alley for me, Joe. I was born here and I'll die here."

"You weren't born here," said Joe Wear.

"In a *way*."

"No," said Joe. "No man is born in a bowling alley. Anyhow LuEtta will win and I will be fired and you may be the manager."

Jeptha shook his heavy head. "He's spooked her. She's done for."

Then it was Joe's turn to jump to the plate to set. Nahum had left just the king pin. Joe was altogether too big a man for this job, a pigeon impersonating a hummingbird, his big boots with the iron in the heel clanking against the plate. Still, his body remembered the odd pleasure of the task, tucking a pin in his armpit while he set another, letting the tucked pin roll down the inside of his arm into his hand. Candlepins had no up or down: unlike ten pins, you could set them on either end. Of course, he, Joe, could fiddle it. He could set the pins in such a way that Nahum could never knock them all down. He could rig it so LuEtta would win for sure. He looked at her. She did not seem spooked. She was bowling as true as she ever had, ahead by eleven pins.

"You done, gal?" Nahum Truitt bellowed.

She stuttered on the approach, her steps too long, and the sleeping baby gave a shuddery sigh, and LuEtta was at the foul line and over it. He yet could win.

The men of the alley watched Nahum Truitt's expression, neither negative nor positive but zero, the face of a man who knows that any emotion might get him killed. His posture was rigid. His grip had changed, and he put some English on to spin the ball, a tenpin trick rarely seen in candlepin alleys. Some people thought it couldn't be done, but here was Nahum doing it. He stopped talking to the Salford Half Nickels. While he waited to bowl his next two frames, he put his hands in his pockets and watched LuEtta unmovingly.

Then he bowled. Spare, nine, and it was clear Lu wouldn't catch him. He seemed almost bored by his ability.

It was not God, Joe Wear knew, though of course Nahum would say it was. He was just that good and had hid it, a hustler who'd been waiting to make his move. Every time he disappeared from Truitt's it was to bowl and hustle in somebody else's house.

Joe had cleared out plenty of cheats in his years at Truitt's, men who snuck in weighted balls or wrongly sized, but Nahum owned the place, and as far as Joe could tell he wasn't cheating, he'd only hustled himself into a bet he was pretty sure he could win. It was too late, even, for Joe to fiddle at setting the pins to give Lu a chance. You could see her heart was no longer in it.

The men of the alleys had abandoned their lanes, their racing forms. A dozen forgotten cigarettes burnt in the tin ashtrays stamped at the bottom TRUITT's. LuEtta bowled, a tall gal in white leather shoes, her ankles in their thin socks indecent. Her blond hair was brassy. Her form was exemplary. She looked like a deer burst through a window at a train station. She didn't belong there, she had to go, they would never stop talking about her, they needed to show her the door, for her sake, too. If you were the last of your kind why *would* you stay.

You stay because of your stubbornness, learned from your mentor. You stay because you think you'll stop being the last of your kind if you just get by: another of your kind will come find you. One woman surrounded by two dozen men, not one of whom would fight to keep her there, no matter she was Salfordian born and bred, no matter her long association with the eponymous Truitt of Truitt's Alleys, the one true Truitt. O Bertha, a stranger who came into Truitt's Alleys now would think Nahum was the significant Truitt. They would think the lone woman was the toothache. When there were plenty of women they caused no trouble at all—why, they were barely noticeable. One woman was an insult, a poison, a gal, a girl, disposable—she would be carried out and dumped in the gutter. The actual gutter, the one of the street. Jeptha Arrison on his shelf looked like he was praying over a four-horsemen leave, a line of pins LuEtta could convert to a spare if they jumped right, but what good would it do?

LuEtta Mood shook her head and shivered. She tried to tell herself that her luck today, two spares, two ten boxes, was a kind of enchantment. To believe it was skill and physics meant she was, as Nahum said, done. What would it have meant to own Truitt's Alleys, if the man actually gave it up? Leaving her marriage for good. Never leaving Salford. Honoring Bertha—she longed to feel Bertha here but she couldn't.

In the end the man beat the woman 117 to 101. The loser offered her hand. The winner wouldn't take it.

"Well then," said LuEtta Mood, and every man in the place saw how ruined and relieved she looked. "I'll go."

"Aw come on," said Martin Younkins. "He didn't mean it."

"I meant it, every pin," said Nahum. "I meant she must go, she must go, this marks the Common Era in Truitt's Alleys, we may begin our mission."

"It's a *bowling* alley for Chrissakes," said Jack Silver.

"Yes, for His sake," said Nahum. "I do not blame you, gal, for your blindness. I myself were raised to believe there were no difference between man and woman or if yes then it were a small difference, that man and woman were as business partners and everything agreed upon but that an't true. Indeed, the female sex is smarter and foxier as has been so since the Garden, and therefore the male of the species must be stronger. Only then is it even, in life as in marriage. Goodbye," he said to LuEtta Mood. "It is time for you to go."

"Give me—"

"*Now*," roared Nahum. He looked sideways at Jeptha Arrison. The man had a daft canine look on his face, openmouthed, trying to make up a mind. Best smack him across the snout. The man even shook hands like a dog, offered it up at a soft-wristed angle, and Nahum took it. Jeptha's hand seemed to grow in Nahum's, till one hand engulfed the other. He stretched to whisper in Nahum's ear. *Poor soul*, thought Nahum, *ignorant of the ways of the world, and me, a stranger, the only one he can speak to.*

"I believe," whispered Jeptha Arrison to Nahum Truitt, "I *believe*—"

"What is it, child?"

"I believe you're going to hell," Jeptha whispered, his voice calm as tar, and when he leaned away the assembled men assumed from the look on Truitt's face that Jeptha Arrison must have finally bit somebody. LuEtta was already on the sidewalk. Jeptha leaned in again and said, "Me, too. I fiddled the pins for you, boss."

Then LuEtta and Jeptha were out on the sidewalk in front of Truitt's Alleys.

"Well, Lu," said Jeptha. "I suppose there's nothing for it but get married again."

"To who?" LuEtta asked wonderingly.

Jeptha took her hand and LuEtta, like Nahum, felt its strange transforming properties, years of pinsetting tenderness and perfect timing. Who had ever understood her so well? The baby woke up then. She could feel his limbs reassemble after a long sleep.

"To us," he said. "I mean, each other. Will you, Lu?"

She meant to say, *I'm already married.* Her husband was still then alive. She meant to say, *Don't be silly, I have a child, you cannot be a father.* Instead she felt her torso open like a birdcage, and some part of her, either terrible or necessary, went flapping toward heaven, or at least past the belfry of the Methodist Church.

"*Will* you, Lu," he said again.

Yes, in a way, she would.

nside, Nahum knocked the Zeno's Gum machine off the front counter with one furious elbow. "Gum is for idiots and imbeciles," he said to the stunned men. "They mistake a piece of gum in their mouths for a thought in their heads."

JOE WEAR EVAPORATES

In the middle of that night, Joe Wear woke to the shift and shuffle of somebody sitting on the edge of his bed. He'd grown up in an orphanage, he'd been woken in the night by strangers a dozen times. In sleep he was always the same abandoned child found by the wrong person: his first instinct was to pretend he was unconscious till such a time as he could not reasonably do so. Then the grown-up part of him drained of dreams. "Jep," he said, but it wasn't Jep.

"These are no bad lodgings," said Nahum Truitt.

"Suppose not," said Joe. "Do something for you?"

"Oh, nothing," said Nahum. "Not bad lodgings at all. Not a bad bed you have here." He gave a clattering phlegmy sigh. "I have been turned around in the dark, Wear. Give me this."

By *this* he meant Joe's left hand, set on the old flowered counterpane, and by *give* he meant he would take it in both of his. The kitchen light tossed a bit of pewter from its tin shade onto the bed. Nahum's hands were as tendinous as most men's feet; Joe's hand was the leather mitt of a laborer, muscle and threat. He thought about punching Nahum, what it would mean, how it would feel.

"You're an oblique one, an't you, Wear?"

"Beg pardon," said Joe, not a question.

"An invert. Not of this world. Listen, I recognize."

His touch on another human being was as ungainly as on an inanimate object. The bones at the back of his hand stood out in shadow like the ribs on a lady's fan. "I can cure you," he said, in a voice that might have been threat and might have been seduction. "I've done it before, Wear."

"Cure?" said Joe. "Of what? Of myself?"

"We are all afflicted with the disease of us," Nahum agreed. "We are dying of it."

He took one of his hands away and Joe was grieved to realize he missed it. *Turned around in the dark.* What direction were you headed, when you went into the dark in the first place and then got turned around? Nahum put his free hand behind him, on Joe's ankle, then lay back across Joe's thighs, and in this way they made a cross in the bed. "My mother wouldn't forgive me, for all that I have done," said Nahum.

"Bertha?"

Nahum said nothing. Then, to the ceiling, "I am going to the State of Maine. Will you come with me? You need forgiveness, too."

Joe said the same nothing.

"You will not," said Nahum, as though putting his foot down. "For what? For murder."

"I didn't ask you for what," said Joe, though his blood turned to mercury at the accusation.

"No man deserves to burn to death," said Nahum. "Not even that one. You thought you got away with it."

"No," said Joe Wear, to all of it. The accusation was as awful years later as it had been at the time. The way falseness made you doubt yourself, it deformed your very shadow, the grammar of your soul. He'd been led to believe that innocence was a pure feeling, cleansing, it would spirit away guilt and cowardice. That wasn't true. Innocence stung. It'd be easier to be accused of things he'd done.

Nahum's weight across his legs hurt. Still the man was talking. Had he ever stopped? Did he, ever?

"I shall retrieve Mrs. Truitt, of whom I so often fondly speak. When I am back we shall change things."

"When?" asked Joe.

"I am going today."

"Today?"

"This morning. It's morning."

Joe looked at the windows and saw it was true. From the alley below came the sound of balls being bowled along the returns.

"What's that?" said Nahum. He startled from the bed and staggered to the kitchen table.

"Jep, I imagine. He comes in nowabouts most mornings."

Nahum looked like he was about to leap to the tabletop like a treed cat. "That moron's come *back*?"

"'Pears so. You'll need him."

"Pinboys are everywhere."

"He'll die here if he's allowed."

"By God." Nahum slapped at the kitchen light and sent it swinging. Joe closed his eyes against the hammering flash. "This *place*," said Nahum. "I was not meant for this place."

"Salford?"

"The entire wicked world," said Nahum. "You know what that fool said to me before he took the gal away?" He turned to look at Joe with his squintish sulfur eyes. "You know what he had the nerve to say?"

Joe shook his head.

"Never you mind what he said, Wear," said Nahum. "I expect he regrets it still."

When Nahum Truitt returned from Maine with a set of luggage and a woman in a lavender traveling suit, it was Jeptha Arrison behind the glass counter who said hello. Spring—a verdant backed-up burble that ran down the streets—was lapping over the threshold of Truitt's and inside. The woman's hat was felt and bell shaped and trimmed with artificial violets.

"This is Mrs. Truitt," Nahum said to Jeptha Arrison. "She will be your mistress."

"She'll be my *what*?" said Jeptha Arrison.

"Your boss," said Nahum. "This is Mrs. *Truitt*."

"This is Maragret Vanetten," corrected Jeptha. "Hello, Meg! How ever have you been?"

"The *former* Margaret Vanetten," said Nahum, perturbed. "Yes. Currently Mrs. Truitt. We were married at the Church in the Woods. We have honeymooned at Boothbay Harbor and now we have returned to leap into marital bliss."

"We've leapt!" said Margaret.

"Apparently we've leapt."

They were holding hands. Nahum's beard had been topiaried into a kind of basin into which the former Margaret Vanetten could nestle her head. She did just that.

"Hello, Jep," she said. "I didn't know you were still here."

"Hello, Meg," he said again. Then to Nahum, "Where's your wife, boss?"

"Here before you, as I say," said Nahum. "A Mrs. Truitt of one week, but nevertheless and for the rest of her life."

"*Meg* is?" said Jeptha.

"Call me Mrs. Truitt," she said, as though granting him an intimacy.

"But where's your *wife*?" Jeptha asked.

Nahum Truitt removed Margaret Truitt from his beard, so that Jeptha might better look. "I am a widower, Jeptha Arrison. I've told you that. Dead these ten years. Dead without issue. I were alone in the world, until I met my Margaret. Jeptha Arrison," said Nahum. "You said something to me. As you left."

Sometimes Jeptha's pale eyes were glitteringly blank. Then there was a drawing together of his features, a suppressed smile, a near rakish intelligence visible there. "Well, boss, I helped you out. You don't think you could beat her straight forward, do you."

Nahum nodded uncertainly, though that wasn't what he'd meant.

"Not Lu. The angels are on Lu's side. But I was on yours."

"Well," said Nahum, glancing at the current Mrs. Truitt. "Perhaps this will cure her of feminine athletics."

"She'll bowl yet but elsewhere. No, they'd kill her. From the pit I could tell all. For instance, what might *you* do?" Jeptha looked at Nahum with what seemed to be fondness. "Even you don't know, my guess."

"Jeptha!" said Margaret Vanetten Truitt.

"Never mind," said Nahum grandly. He slapped the counter. "Today our new life begins. Where's Joe Wear?"

"Don't know," said Jeptha.

"Well, ask someone."

"Someone knows nothing same as me," said Jeptha. "Gone."

For years the Half Nickels would say, "Joe Wear would know the answer to that," but Joe Wear was nowhere around. He had left not one forwarding detail. He wasn't the last of his kind but he'd been acting like it, for decades now. Buried alive. Where would he go? Elsewhere. He took his head full of bowling straight out of Massachusetts, and did not return for many years.

The future is coming. It always is. We have generations to get through first, marriages and divorces and widowhoods and remarriages, the yoking of families, the unyoking. The disappeared and misattributed. The pathetic life spans of dead children, the greedy awful life spans of the very old. *She came to a tragic end.* That's as true for the plummeted teenager (a Barcelona balcony, a broken romance) as it is for your great-aunt, dead at 103 after years of silent confinement, who has turned, it seems, into soap and slough. You will be born soon. You're promised. What damage you'll do to the family tree is in your hands. That's for later. Patience.

3

BETROTHED
AND BEHOLDEN

Once upon a time, happily ever after, was never seen again. Such things are only true in the storybook world, not ours. Once upon a time there was a little girl—no, there have been millions of little girls, at all times. They lived happily ever after—but after the disaster, your happiness is always shadowed by the closeness of your escape. Never seen again—you can't stop seeing the dead wolf opened like luggage on the bed, his turned-out stomach embossed with the pattern of your grandmother's lace bonnet, his intestines perforated by her kicking heels. The dead are seen over and over, and most of the living.

Once upon a time there was a girl. Then she was again.

She was a parcel of a person, Margaret Vanetten, left and stored and sent away, sent away again. Left by her mother on the steps of the Little Sisters of the Poor. Raised by nuns who thought they might make a nun of her—nuns are more discerning than wolves, they don't think any old naked left-behind baby is automatically one of them. Sent by those nuns to be in service to rich peculiarities living in a ridiculous house. "Are they adopting me?" she'd asked Sister Catherine.

"Adopting?" said Sister. "Margaret Mary, you are fifteen years old."

Margaret waited for the rest of the answer a long time. Seventy years later she would die waiting.

On the train north with Minna she had watched New England fly by and thought: *we could get off anywhere.* Hadn't she raised that girl from a baby? Shouldn't she be allowed to have the child instead of those Canadian strangers? She and Minna could make a life together. People might not believe the colored child was hers; then again, the baby's own mother was lily white, just like Margaret (though Margaret suspected there was something dusky and foreign in Bertha's past: Jewess, or Persian). Minna might pass, for Jewish, or Persian. She was born pale—Margaret knew because she'd been there—though she'd darkened up, with olive skin and green eyes. But where would they go? There was no house in the world that would take Margaret in, apart from the octagonal one from which she'd been cast out. From which she and Minna had been cast out. How could Dr. Sprague have done it?

On that northbound train she dared herself to think about getting married, having children. She was twenty-seven already, spinsterish at her toes and fingertips, singularity creeping up her limbs. She might marry somebody small, modest. Somebody like limping Joe Wear, who was likewise employed by Truitt: she might be allowed as little as him. A pinboy's worth of happiness. They would have little candlepin babies. They would take in Minna: a girl needed a mother and father, even queer ones such as themselves would make. Minna would have brothers and sisters at last.

Dr. Sprague had paid for a compartment with a fold-down bed that folded up into seats. *Your mother is dead,* Margaret thought at Minna, though nobody knew that for sure. The girl had her diary in her lap. She didn't understand it was a history book. Her mother had put her golden brown hair into two plaits the day before, the last record of her motherlove, now unraveling at the top.

"Do you think they'll recognize me? My aunt and uncles."

"I imagine so," said Margaret. "Family knows family." My darling. My dearest. You don't need to go with those strangers, Minna, Margaret wanted to say.

They had been in Canada a long time already and had more Canada to go: Margaret, from Massachusetts, found this upsetting. The bigger the place, the more claustrophobic. They might never get out of Canada. She felt it close over her head like a coal mine.

At the train station in Fredericton, Benjamin Sprague stood next to his creamy green REO, one foot propped on the running board, looking like his brother except taller and thinner and unmustachioed and in a pair of new two-tone shoes of the sort Dr. Sprague never would have worn, shoes to go to the city in, and also he was lighter skinned, and with a nose that had once been broken—really, they looked only as alike as cousins, but he had the Sprague gravity. Margaret wished he would make decisions for her. "What news?" she asked him. The damp guarded look conveyed to Margaret that Bertha was dead, but they would wait to tell Minna. She started to sob. She reached to gather Minna in her arms, to whisper the scalding secret in her ear, but Minna had already climbed into the back of the Sprague motorcar, a fine sedan, and regarded her old nurse with dry eyes and a little horror.

"Minna!" said Margaret. "Will you write to me?"

The girl nodded.

"You're homesick," Benjamin said to Margaret in his deep voice, both sympathetic and imperative. He offered her a red paisley handkerchief, which she accepted and stuck in her pocket, though she knew that's not what he'd meant. "You should go on home."

She looked in her purse as though for her life. "I don't have a ticket," she said in a waterlogged voice. She wanted to be taken in with Minna, raised up by the Sprague siblings. Stranger things had already happened. But she understood that she and Minna had not been cast out together. Margaret had been cast out. The girl had been saved.

Benjamin Sprague pulled a roll of bills from his pockets. "For your service," he said, handing her the bills, fake, clearly fake, no, Canadian. "Your folks'll miss you. Thank you, I should say. Thank you for bringing our Minna to us."

"Give me your address," she said, "so I may write to my charge."

"Charge no longer," he told her, but he wrote it down on the back of a train schedule, in curvilinear script. Ah, there was the family resemblance: the strong Sprague *S*, the weak Sprague *e*. She folded the timetable and stuck it into her coat pocket.

She had no folks. She had no people. She waited for Benjamin Sprague's REO to pull away and she walked into town, found a room in a hotel for women, found a job in a restaurant, stayed there for an entire year in case Minna needed her. She sent a note to Benjamin Sprague:

> *Dear Mr Sprague or are you also Dr, I shouldn't be surprised with*
> *an educated family like you, if Minna wishes to find me I am working*
> *at Bach's Cafeteria, I am there most days but will come anywhere.*

Later she would remember this year as the loneliest and most peaceful of her life. She waited: for Minna, on customers. The Spragues would surely come to her. She wrote to Minna every week, till an envelope came back that said RETURN TO SENDER. No more explanation than that.

Benjamin Sprague was exactly right: Margaret Vanetten was homesick. She was homesick the same way she was anything else, from birth and forever. Born missing the womb, left off at the convent—she'd never had a bed to herself before going to work for Sprague and Truitt, and at first she couldn't sleep for all the rooms and doors in that house.

She had loved Dr. Sprague like a father; she would never forgive him for sending her away. For all she knew, Minna had gone home once the worst of her father's grief had passed. Two weeks, or two months—of course she would go back, taller but still a child, to comfort her father and sleep in her own bed. Now this envelope. She was the sender. Her love had been returned to her. Only Margaret had been forgotten. Only Margaret displaced forever. But Salford was her home, too. Those people could not keep her from it.

Not till she got back did she discover that Dr. Sprague was dead and the house boarded up. She couldn't bear to stop by the bowling alley itself, to be among people who had known for so long what she, an idiot, had not: her life as she'd known it was over and she hadn't even noticed, hadn't felt the difference.

She was a hired girl again, working for a family who lived on Pinkham Square, who told her what a fine house theirs was, belonging to a fine family. In the foyer they kept a family tree, embroidered on linen, framed, enormous, stretching back to 1620. Her own family tree would have read, in its entirety,

Margaret (b. 1892?–d.)

She didn't even know where her last name had come from. "It suits you," Sister Catherine had said, as though it were a left-behind hat. Nobody behind her or ahead, just how Bertha had landed in Salford. Once Bertha had said to Margaret, "I didn't mean to get caught up again in this whole business of families," though Bertha had been cuddling two-year-old Minna at the time, and two-year-old Minna was particularly irresistible, a child who spoke in full sentences but still could see every supernatural corner of babyhood. "I never meant to be a line in the family Bible."

That was all Margaret wanted. To be an ancestral entry. She'd been left at the Little Sisters of the Poor clutching a braided lock of unidentified light brown hair, as meaningless and meaningful an object as ever an orphan has inherited.

Her Pinkham lodging was a closet behind the kitchen. In the Octagon she'd had a second-floor bedroom, same floor as the family, odd shaped but good sized, and she walked to Somefire Hill every day to remind herself of the people she'd lost—Bertha, Dr. Sprague, Minna—as well as the house that had lost them all. Uninhabited, the whole place, every room. Could she break in? She still had a dress hanging in the cupboard, a hairbrush on the dresser. They had broken her heart in turn, the family, they had taken it apart like an orange, first peel (that was Bertha, dying), then the breakapart into pieces (Dr. Sprague, sending her away), then the eating up (Minna, who did not even cry as they separated forever). That hairbrush was hers by rights. The room was.

Then one day a tall bearded man likewise was walking on the lawn around the house. "Curious construction," he said to her, "put up by curious people. Lost on me how people could live in such a space. Warps 'em, I would think. Odd angles here." He tapped his head. "And also." He thumped his heart.

"I could tell you," said Margaret Vanetten.

"You tell me then," said the man. "You tell me everything. I'm Nahum. Truitt. Bertha's child. Whoa, stand up, gal, whatever is the matter with you?"

Margaret had sat down on the lawn in shock. "You're alive!"

"So far I am," he admitted. "You might keep me live longer."

"I'd figured you for a stillborn," she said and then covered her mouth with her hand. What a thing to say aloud! Then again, she'd never heard about *Nahum Truitt* from Bertha, only from Jeptha Arrison.

At this the man sat down next to her on the lawn. He didn't have to worry about grass stains on his dark pants, though she could feel the stains on her own. She remembered, all of a sudden, being a child and learning that grass could do that, paint your clothing green so you'd never forget it: what a wonder that was. The man's face was long, sad, sincere. "No," he said, "that wasn't me. No. I survived. Lived. *Out*lived."

A squirrel came up to regard them. There were always squirrels on Somefire Hill, brown brawny ones, but this was their squirrel, and it sat back on its haunches, and under the circumstances it was impossible to ignore how much such a squirrel looks like a preacher come to marry a couple, consulting his tiny Bible.

Oh, she was a rotten judge of character, she knew it, she never foresaw who would stand up for her and who would betray her and she alternately believed that she would be looked after by good people, and that she was doomed to be taken advantage of by callous ones. Regarding this man she felt both things at once.

"Well I'm glad," said Margaret. Because that sounded forward, she added, "No mother should outlive her child, it's unnatural."

He put one hand to the back of his neck. "What happens in nature is natural. Commonest thing in the world. The Lord God has his reasons."

"Are you Catholic?" she asked.

He said, "Small *c*."

She took that to mean yes, but not devout. By the time she found out otherwise it was too late, a week later, at their wedding in Rockland, Maine. Overwhelming in a way: the thumping oak of his voice, his height, his furred body—somebody should have told her that men could be so bodily whiskered. That skeletal Maine minister who married them, perhaps. The conductor who took their tickets for the train. Not that it would have changed her mind but just to sit quietly ahead of time and contemplate.

She was a married woman and everyone knew. Nearly all of the time it delighted her, his size, his rumbling overgrowth. Not a boyish iota to Nahum Truitt, and that conferred upon her (she believed) a seriousness, that she had married such a man.

Nahum was not interested in tales of his sister, lost somewhere in Canada; her name was not to be mentioned. Neither was Bertha's, nor Dr. Spague's. Why had he married her at all? She had imagined she was a way into his family. She'd known them, still possessed a store of love for them all kept in fine shape in the cupboard of her heart, that she might divide and share. No: he was not interested. He and she were the Truitts now.

Astonishing how quickly one's origins fly to dust. Salford had forgotten that Bertha Truitt had been found unconscious in a cemetery without the expected underclothes; Salford forgot, mostly, at least for a time, that Nahum Truitt's maternity had ever been in question, that Margaret Vanetten had been the hired girl. The new Truitts ran the bowling alley and lived in the little quarters overhead. They moved to the apartment above the alley, where Joe Wear had lived, which he had vacated so thoroughly it was as though he had never existed—all but the toilet by itself in the closet, a cubicle of such filth that Margaret preferred to use the ladies' room downstairs in the alley.

A mile away, on Somefire Hill, the Octagon stood empty, a board over the front door and cataracts of dirt across the windows, though the grounds were kept tidy enough, the lawn mowed. "It were built to pagan specifications," Nahum said, when asked. "We'll have nothing to do with it." Storehouse for ghosts, or more likely the Truitt fortune, because the one thing nobody forgot was money. There must have been treasure in every obtuse corner of that house, and the new Truitts misers who wore all black (him) and all purple (her) because neither color showed dirt. Saved on washing. The Octagon surely held their hoard.

W ell," said Margaret Vanetten Truitt, once installed in the bowling alley, "let us get to work. Mr. Arrison. Tell me what you know."

"The pins," he said. "The pins and the pins. You take the stool, Meggie. Joe Wear knew the business of it but I only know the pins. *Except—*" he said, in a voice full of meaning.

"Yes," said Margaret.

"I am acquainted also with the bowling balls. Acquainted, but my love is for the pins. Let me help you up."

He did, onto the high stool behind the front oak desk. The back of the desk was a warren, and Margaret now its warrener.

"There's money for you." Jeptha indicated a stack of bills rubber-banded together in a cubby. "There's the bank book. Joe Wear would know all but he is gone."

She took the afternoon to go through each cubby. She found more cash that hadn't made its way to the bank. In those days they still kept score on chalkboards hung on the wall, but there were scraps of paper upon which Joe Wear had mapped interesting matches, or imaginary ones. You could tell they'd been written with the stubs of pencils.

In the bottom row, she drew out what she thought at first might be a forgotten sandwich. One of Dr. Sprague's, no doubt; Margaret had always found him peculiarly forgetful about sandwiches. A wax paper packet, still a little greasy. She unwrapped it and found a stack of letters. From Minna, to her father. The return address was not the farm in Oromocto, but Paris. Another foreign country.

Oh. She held the envelopes as though they were Minna's hands.

Yours. Not hers. Thick cream paper. Sealed with blue wax, dramatic, like Minna herself, severed by Dr. Sprague. Men were bowling on their lanes. She pulled out one note, just enough to see the date, *September 10, 1919*, mere months after Minna had ridden off in the green REO. So all that time she'd waited in Fredericton, all those letters that Margaret had written: Minna was already gone.

She would not read them. Of course she *would* read them, just not yet. Sitting at the oak desk at Truitt's Alleys, she wrote to Minna Sprague, 44 Rue du Temple, Paris. She wrote on the long paper that spun off a spool, used for receipts. She folded it into an envelope. Would Minna recognize the address in the corner? Margaret herself wouldn't have: she thought of the alley as being in Phillipine Square, but the actual address was 74 Mims Avenue. She added *Apartment 1.* She omitted *Truitt.* Why? Oh, she would explain things soon enough but for now she meant to be only Minna's Margaret, and not Minna's, what was she—she burst out laughing. She was Minna's sister-in-law.

Well, Margaret understood relics. She jettisoned the wax paper and tied the bundle with blue ribbon. She hid the bundle at the back of a bottom cubby, where Nahum would never find it.

She got a letter back, from Minna, Parisian Minna. *Dear Margaret*, she wrote. *How extraordinary to hear from you!*

It was a short letter, well spelled, unsentimental. No blue wax seal. It explained that she had moved from Oromocto with her aunt a few weeks after her arrival; her aunt could teach her the cello—of course Minna should play the cello—but Minna's voice required training and of that Almira Sprague was ignorant. Her father was dead, had Margaret heard, of course she must have heard, being back in Salford. She signed herself *as ever.*

Margaret read the letter five times. Then she was out of words and she allowed herself to read Minna's letters to her father.

She could tell the difference. Minna's letters to her father were strange casseroles, made of language, yes, but only sometimes in English: words of such foreignness they felt like cold spots in the warm lines of Minna's sentences. (Latin, French, Italian, probably, even little prickly lines of what Margaret assumed was Greek.) Also sudden bars of music, pencil drawings, watercolors. Was it that Minna and her father didn't understand each other, so she wrote in as many languages as possible, hoping to find the one in which they were both fluent? Or was it that they understood each other so utterly that this was how they communicated? She wrote in rebuses and code. One letter began, *My own Papa! This is a lipogram. It's lacking. Do you know what it lacks, my darling Papa? Hint: a small thing, but without it you & I cannot sign our patronym, nor you your first.*

Minna's letter to Margaret was in ordinary English. *Dear Margaret*, she wrote. *How extraordinary to hear from you! You say you would recognize me anywhere. I wonder. I am quite made over. In answer to your question: no, I don't think I will ever come back to Salford. Not ever. You must understand that it is a place of terrible memories for me, worse than you know. Not ever,* she wrote again, and here she underlined it, and underneath the word *ever*—silly to think so, and yet it was true—Margaret could see a hint of the child she'd known. The paper was torn. So *not ever* and yet in a way here she was. Not ever and as ever.

For every five letters she sent to Minna she got one back. They were matter-of-fact, as though to a distant friend, enough, the way you might send pennies to the electric company when you owed hundreds of dollars: not square, but you wouldn't be cut off. Margaret tied her letters, her paltry archive, with blue ribbon, too.

N ahum made over Joe Wear's old apartment, moved the toilet to the other side of the apartment, added a sink. Bought a fine new electric icebox with a monitor top.

"What else would you like, Meggie?" he asked. "Say the word."

She would like not to live above a bowling alley, with the smoke that came up through the floorboards. She would like to say, "Now that we are married, we can bring Minna home!" But Minna was a far-off dream, and Nahum was real, and she loved him. You gave things up for love. The nuns had taught her that. What she wanted was the house and she imagined Minna owned it and she imagined Minna should give it to her, after all she'd done for her.

He left alone the kitchen-side tub, that he might sit at the table late at night and watch Margaret in her bath, so little all he could see was her head on the lip at the higher end, one languid dripping hand on the edge, until the moment—it was staggering suspense, you never knew when it would happen—she would chide herself for sloth and stand streaming, as though hoisted in the air, not a freckle on her pale body, not a mole, not a scar, immaculate Meg!, even when she fell pregnant, once (that was Roy, professorial even as a baby), twice (Arch, a flirt, also from birth). No little girls. That was for the best, little girls didn't belong in bowling alleys. Leave the bathtub, watch the boys like otters in their evening wash, always (Nahum thought) on the verge of drowning each other: you knew, when you were that young, that the point of life was to win no matter how you managed it.

It seemed a bewitchment to Margaret. A storeroom became a bedroom. A hired girl a wife. A woman could become a mother, even without meaning to. Some days she closed her eyes and tried to remember that other path, the one she'd been on, which she'd thought she hated. A single woman who had to work to keep herself alive. That whole year in Fredericton, waiting for the Spragues to come for her, washing dishes, putting aside her whole paycheck so she could build a home for Minna and herself and whoever else came along. When she remembered that girl she'd been, she saw the light all around her and thought, *You were so miserable! And for what?*

Orphaned, taken in. Alone, married. She did not know who she was. Her soul was a goldfish, a little thing inside the bowl of her body. She always had to concentrate to find it before she said her prayers.

DREAMS CARVED
OF WOOD

H is older brother, Roy, was a self-contained child, sedentary and bookish, but Arch Truitt opened things. Doors, cupboards, purses, pockets of trousers left on the floor, pockets of occupied trousers, packages of powdered soap. He was an investigator, a rifler. It confounded his parents, who both had assumed that children knew the line between the childish and adult world, and would ask permission to cross it. Roy had been that sort of child, at least when it came to the physical, but here was Arch, butter-blond and blithe and laughing. Even so when they found him, at four, in bed asleep with the doll, they assumed Roy, then five, was to blame. That doll was as big as Arch. Bigger. How could he have carried it there without the sound of her wooden heels against the wooden floor?

Margaret, standing over the bed, was the one who'd discovered the child and the doll. The doll's head was on the pillow next to Arch's, though faceup. His lips were at her neck. Her head, crudely sewn of white duck, was a lopsided bulb, not much of a chin, not much of a nose, though the face itself had been hand-painted and was poignant.

"Holy!" Margaret whispered before astonishment shut her up.

She'd thought at first it was the Salford Devil, come back from the stories and curled into her child's bed. It was a put-together thing, same as the Devil, with one beautiful carved wooden arm outside of the covers, plus that worn bolster of a head: it reminded her of a woman she'd once seen with hyacinth blue eyes and a jaw swollen by a purpling growth, a woman deformed and beautiful simultane-ously, not one state despite the other. The doll's eyes were green and large, the mouth, near where the head tapered into something like a neck, sherbety, lips parted to show little painted teeth. The doll was having a good time. Margaret uncovered the body—a white duck torso, happily unpainted but buxom, unnippled, unnaveled, unnel-lied; wooden limbs that looked real. Arch was still asleep, one hand on the doll's large lopsided right breast.

By then Roy was awake, and Nahum stood in the door of the bedroom. "What's going on?" yawned Roy. The summer heat had pasted his nightshirt to his stomach. "What's *that*?"

"It's Bertha," said Margaret.

"Bertha?" said Nahum, stepping awkwardly into the room, which he generally considered a place for women and children; bedtime and awakening were a mother's job. But intruders fell to fathers, and here was an intruder. He tossed aside the blanket.

The doll was calm and barefoot. Unlike china dolls who showed their teeth, she seemed unworried, like she was about to pick up a check. "Bertha," Margaret said. "Without a doubt."

"Well," said Nahum uncomfortably. "She got fat. Archie," he said. "Archer. Wake up."

He wouldn't, he only snuggled in, gripped the one breast harder. Margaret turned away.

"*Arch*," said Nahum, and walked through the back door of the boy's dreams, and made everyone there scatter, the dogs, the man with the mechanical swan, the miniature women, and Arch was up and blinking. "Who's her?" he asked of the doll. He touched her painted hair, her painted ear rememberingly, and answered his own question. "I found her."

What do you do with an effigy like that? Where could it go? Margaret wanted to install it in the alley. Nahum wanted to burn it; he knew he couldn't burn it. Drown it, but dolls don't drown. Give it away, though what child, other than Arch, would cuddle a thing like that? Put her in a rowboat and send it down the Salford estuary. Put it in the fens and let the animals decide. Bury it in the Salford Cemetery. Seal it in a wall. Put it in a chair and offer it sweets. Build it a little house where it might be happy forever. Give it to the prop mistress at the Salford Theater, so that it might tread the boards. Donate it to a ventriloquist who might make it a better head—no, no, best not give it the power of speech, uncanny enough silent. Buy it a train ticket to Hollywood. Try to find her people. Write letters to her breathing double—no, her double was dead, of course, though surely only Bertha would know what to do about the wooden Bertha.

Nahum hated the thing and kept locking her in the basement. Arch loved the thing and pulled her up the stairs to cuddle her, took her back to his bedroom. Roy alone was indifferent, though it amused him to use her to model items from the lost and found—scarves, hats, spectacles. Margaret sewed the doll a suit: a divided skirt, a double-breasted vest, rolled sleeves, an annular hat, and sat her up on the oak counter at the front of the house.

The worst was Jeptha Arrison, who sometimes when he finished his pinsetting shift took the seat next to her at a table, and held her hand, and said nothing. Once he set the doll out along the glass counter at the front and rubbed linseed oil into its joints. "Oh dear, oh dear: her brains is coming out." He poked some horsehair stuffing into the seam of the doll's head. "She does not like that."

"Doesn't she?" said Margaret, spooked by the feminine pronoun. "That smells flammable."

"She's fine," said Jeptha. "Our girl's not the type to burn."

Margaret was uneasy, looking at Jeptha massaging the doll's knees, feeling his own knees for reference, returning to the doll. "Where did she come from?"

"Heaven," said Jeptha.

She shook her head.

Nahum looked broodingly at the doll. "It is a cursed thing. I cannot see an end to it that does not call down terrible luck."

Her face was pale, her limbs were tan. You could see every knuckle, hear the blood beating beneath the varnish. Sometimes bowlers took her into their laps. They weren't respectful. It would have been better if her expression hadn't been so jolly.

Her face got grimy. Someone bit her breast. Somebody drew on pubic hair, which Margaret with averted eyes bleached out with a brush. There were rumors the doll was found in a different place in the alley every morning.

"Boris!" sobbed Arch. That was what he had named her. "Boris!"

Finally she disappeared. Nobody took responsibility.

But who *is* Bertha," Roy wanted to know.

"Nobody," said Margaret. "Founder of the alleys. Original Truitt."

"Original Truitt," said Roy. "So—a relative? We're related to the founder? Bertha Truitt."

"Well," said Margaret. "Yes."

"How?"

"For heaven's sake," said Margaret.

"Papa's mother? We could do a family tree."

"No use," said Margaret. "We've been pruned."

"But—"

"Who are you looking for, for heaven's sake!" said his mother. "Aren't I enough for you? And your father. Greedy," she said to Roy, "that's your problem."

(How she talked too often: she thought something mean, thought, *you can't say that*, and then she was saying it, knowing it awful, so she didn't even get the pleasure of meanness.)

Margaret looked at her son. He was pale and freckled and red-headed and looked like nobody she'd ever seen before in her life. She thought, accusingly, as she often did, *I made you*. Any trace of Bertha Truitt had been stored in the cellar before Margaret had come back to it; there was no trace in Roy himself, except perhaps the plumpness. "Roy," she said. "I can't tell you. Don't ask Papa. I don't know what else to say."

"Why not can't I ask?"

"You know why," said Margaret. Roy didn't know *why*, but he did know *that*. His father had a way of stopping questions before you asked them.

But they couldn't keep Bertha out that easily. Not just by never saying her name aloud. If Roy went looking—*when* Roy went looking— he would find the scrapbooks, the framed newspaper clippings, the monogrammed wallets, the photographs. Bertha herself was still everywhere, and Nahum, on dark mornings, could believe that the doll had assembled itself out of leftover emanations.

The bad luck snuck in bit by bit, misfortune to trial to catastrophe— or else it had always been there, like a basement infestation driven at last up through the floorboards. Or else it was only the luck they deserved, having not looked after their wooden matriarch. One afternoon, the strength tester that Bertha had so loved to dominate threw up a fountain of sparks when Jeptha Arrison squeezed it. It was the last place you could put your hand and pretend, for a moment, that you were shaking hands with Truitt, put your mouth to the tube where her mouth had been. The bowling balls, yes, it was possible, but balls were rotated through the lanes, they rolled back at odd angles, were eventually retired: you'd never know for sure. That was why Jeptha loved the strength tester, and the shock it gave you when you failed to squeeze hard enough (Jeptha never squeezed hard enough), a tickling pain in all the public and private parts of him, the curve of his cheeks and his giblets and oysters. Then the machine sent him to the hospital.

The three black-and-white cats who lived at Truitt's—a mother and her children—died one after the other after eating rats who'd eaten poison laid out at Coop's Cafeteria next door.

Arch caught measles and they were all quarantined. "Quarantine comes from the Latin for 'forty,'" Roy said, he who knew too much of the ancient world and scorned the modern one. Nahum and Margaret got the measles, too, but Roy was fine. He heated up soup and nursed everyone. *This means he will take care of me*, thought Margaret in her fever. *This means I will escape*, Roy thought, *because I can take care of myself.*

The furnace caught whooping cough, whooped, whooped, whooped, never recovered. The pipes in their grief for the furnace froze and burst and wept over lane ten, which warped and rotted.

Martin Younkins of the Salford Half Nickels, the team of war veterans, stepped in front of the Salford *Bugle* truck one cherry-spring evening, league night, the air full of possibility and pollen. "He flew across the road!" said a witness, but he didn't, he was killed on impact, he never flew again. The rest of the Half Nickels heartbrokenly rolled away from Truitt's forever.

—

Nahum blamed the doll. They were not yet ruined—that would come later—but they could not do without luck, which meant he needed to find her. He could never find things, even the wrench in his hand, the name of a regular bowler. The way he misplaced things had always made Joe Wear shake his head. Joe Wear found things. It was one of his talents.

"Wherever do you suppose that fellow went?" Nahum asked Margaret one night in their bed. Astonishing how she'd made their bedroom over, with a knit throw over a quilt and flowered curtains, though the iron bed incarcerated them, and the radiator made a tin-cup-on-prison-bars sound.

"Who?"

"Joe Wear, when he went so sudden."

"He might be anywhere," said Margaret in a cheerful voice.

"Where were his people from?"

"Ireland. All dead now. He might be dead himself. He was a sickly thing."

At that Nahum sniffed the air, as though for evidence, wound the tassels of the coverlet in his fingers. What he wanted was a coarse wool blanket, one that would rub a rash across his neck and onto his cheek; he wanted to yank his wife's knit monstrosity by its useless tentacles right off the bed. He wanted to holler, but he knew it would do no good. His first wife had responded to shouts—she took herself away, for an hour, a day, finally for good—but Margaret was immune to noise. She didn't pay him the least attention when he shouted; she answered in her usual voice. She might even sing her answer. Her conscience was astonishingly clear, always.

"What of the Truitt fortune?" said Nahum now. "The gold, I mean, she come here with." But he didn't really know how money worked, whether it was staggering the money had been squandered or a miracle it had lasted so long.

"Gone. Into the house and into this place. It's been years."

"Disappeared."

"Spent."

"I suppose. But the doll. Where is *she*?"

"Someone stole her as a joke. Perhaps she'll come back. You see, Nim," she teased. "There was another woman here all along."

"She left with our luck."

"No," said Margaret.

"She was the plank what held it up."

"You miss her," said Margaret. "You miss your mother."

"I miss the doll. I require the doll. Some idiot has hid her."

He'd been in Salford eight years by then, and he had never meant to stay, only to secure his fortune and leave. Find the gold, if there was gold yet, or empty the bank account. He had a right. But then he had fallen into the long con of marriage, and lately he realized the gold must be gone. Spent, or swept into the harbor. He'd looked floor to ceiling in the Octagon, though by law he was not allowed to be there, and he had hated every moment of the search. The safe in the cellar of the alley was empty; he slammed the door shut and set the wheel spinning. Then he opened the safe again, as though the wheel might have pulled it up from some deep hiding place. Why had he stayed all those years? Why had he married that funny little woman? For the most appalling reason. He loved her. He could not live without her.

In the morning he would look for the wooden figure. He had hated living with that spurious Bertha but apparently he could not live without her. Much like the actual Bertha. He would look for the gold, too, cellar to roof, but he knew he would never find it. No, he told himself, you must believe that you will, that is luck, too, you conduct it with your brain. No man who felt unlucky was ever luckstruck.

Who was he? Who had he ever been?

Nahum Truitt, just as he said. Never Bertha's son. Only her first husband, from whom she'd gotten her name and from whom she'd gotten bowling. She'd stolen her first candlepin from him, her first bowling ball, then she'd broken his heart and left him for Leviticus Sprague. They had met in Sacco, Maine. They'd parted in Boothbay. She was a tyrant. She was a thief. He loved her yet.

Years later he would die with these truths upon his lips. He loved everyone he had ever loved.

MARGARET OVERCOME

n 1932 Nahum Truitt went to Picardi's Barbershop in Phillipine Square to have the beard shorn from his face. He looked at the long mirror, his reflection surrounded by all the blades of the business, which meant he was, too. He trusted Picardi to put the sharpest blade to his very neck; he trusted himself not to wrest the razor away to do something terrible, to himself or someone else. Time was he wouldn't have trusted himself. Therefore the beard.

Would he look older or younger without it? He'd grown it not to change his age but to hide his face, the nervous smile that had always brought him trouble. A liar needs a beard, but today he would tell his wife the truth.

These things were true:

He loved her.

The Commonwealth of Massachusetts was killing him.

He did not love bowling.

He was not Bertha Truitt's son.

They were flat broke. No, they were at the bottom of a crater.

They would move to the State of Maine, all of them, and there—assured of his luck, once and for all!—he would stop gambling.

They would be happy the rest of their days.

This was it. The last day he could stand Salford. If she did not say yes he would leave her, and the boys, and Massachusetts forever.

He couldn't quite order these facts in his mind. Start with the good news? Interweave? As for preamble:

> *Meg, I have news. I have good news. I have unfortunate—I have come to an unfortunate conclusion. I can explain. I can't. Let's away.*
> *I am not myself, Meg, and have not been since you have known me, and long before. I love you.*

(What about the boys? He loved them but could not say so. Even the thought of it made him furious.)

Nahum had amassed debts. Deep ones, the sort you could drown in. You, and your whole family. If you believed in them. Nahum did not always believe in his own debts. They were a lack of money, they were imaginary, and he had always thought that if he threw just enough money at his debts or outran them altogether he really owed nothing.

Nahum Truitt had lost bets, though he was not alone: the whole country had lost bets, and jobs, and fortunes, so it was harder to work to take money off another fellow to replace what you'd lost. These days he skimmed cash from the day's earnings for dumb wagers. He pitched pennies in the park; he went to watch the dogs run; he went to watch the horses run though when he did he had to wash the smell of horse away, else canine Jeptha would sniff it out, and balk, and tell. He bet on other bowlers all the time, though he no longer bowled himself, worried he would fall again into the hustle—you couldn't both hustle and stay in one place without being well and truly beaten. He had been well and truly beaten in his life, with fists but also bowling balls, thrown by a big Gypsy in Bangor, like bombs going off. He was a pious gambler but now he felt his belief worn away by reality.

When the last bit of lather and bristle had been scraped away by the blade, he examined himself and saw his mistake. His face had lived in the wilderness so long it was unprepared for the eyes of humanity upon it, white, abraded by the razor, his very chin retreating. Behind him Picardi winced. It was that sort of lack of chin. You blamed the fellow for it.

"Voilà," said Picardi in a voice of tragedy. He was a bald barber. He had transferred his tonsorial vanity to his customers.

"Thank you," said Nahum.

"Don't," said the barber. "It's my job."

Nahum, revealed, went to meet the little wife for lunch and further revelation. (Jeptha was running the alley counter; he was still allowed to then.) Nahum would have liked to go to Coop's for his last meal in Salford—he'd never eaten in a restaurant till he was in his forties, and if he were a millionaire he might never eat anywhere else—but his frugal wife insisted on packing sandwiches to consume in the park. Her body seemed to produce sandwiches without her knowledge. "It's not that I don't like restaurants," she always said, "it's just that I prefer my own cooking." This was another inexplicable, terrifying quality of hers that he nevertheless admired. Her stinginess was how they'd managed to limp along as far as they had.

She wanted him to stop gambling, but he couldn't. It was how he thought about the world. Gambling was a series of questions: Am I lucky? Am I favored? Am I unlike other men? Will I die alone? Am I loved? Am I respected? The answers to these questions came at once, and with great certainty. Then the certainty evanesced. That was the good news. You got to ask again. Only the wilderness could cure him, where there was no other man to wager against.

In Salford's Plocker Park—they'd arranged to meet by the frog pond; it was spring and the water boiled with spawn—Margaret walked right past him, despite the black suit she knew very well. What percentage of him had that beard been? For a moment he felt that peculiar combustion of uncertainty and nerve that is the engine of a fraud. He could keep on walking. Either he'd leave for Maine immediate, or he'd stick around Salford, incognito, peering through windows at his family from time to time. But no. There was her dear back. She was looking for him. He would not leave alone. It was possible after all to tell her things.

"Meg," he called.

April in Salford is a tossed deck of cards, every day like the others and unlike them, too. Yesterday it had been sixty-five degrees; today it was brighter but twenty degrees colder. Nahum Truitt's face felt interrogated by both the chill and the sun and now by his wife, who stared at him then seemed slapped.

"Your beard!" she said. "Your beautiful beard! Nim!" Then, ominously: "You lost a bet."

He could never tell whether *Nim* was a nickname or a persistent misunderstanding. "I did not, missus, for heaven's sake, how would I gamble my beard away?"

She had set her basket down and doffed a glove to investigate his face, as though it still might be an optical illusion. "I don't know. But you could do it. Did you keep it?"

He caught up her hand. "It's gone to the barber's furnace," he said, though he did not know if there was such a thing. What happened to shorn beards? Were they ghosts or corpses? "He were welcome to it."

"You lost a bet to the *barber*," she said.

"The barber is rich in beards, the barber can have any beard he likes. No," he said. "This morning I awoke and I remembered what I once said to Joe Wear and I thought I wanted a good clean chin for a good clean start."

"Are you married to Joe Wear?" she asked.

It were a marriage of sorts, thought Nahum. "Listen," he said to her, but kindly. He had been surprised by many things in his life—the bodily cold of his baptism, seasickness when he'd planned to be a sailor, a poison-eyed demon ransacking his camp that turned out instead to be a particularly bumptious raccoon, a naked lady upon a beach who oscillated between beauty and rapaciousness—"Sir," she'd said to him, "have you seen my Larry," and he could not tell whether *Larry* was a child or a husband or some sort of terrible slang for something she was offering up, something he did not want but might should have accepted. He'd been surprised by hunger often, and by fatherhood, and by the invention of the motorcar and by seeing the name NAHUM TRUITT in the Orono *Messenger*—but nothing surprised him more than his particular love for his odd little second wife. He loved her more than she loved him. *Opalescent*: that gets to the heart. Her thoughts were beautiful, but really only ever for show. Maybe that would help, eventually.

"What I said, Meg, to Joe Wear, all these years ago: let us see if the Commonwealth of Massachusetts needs me. I do believe the Commonwealth of Massachusetts has rendered its verdict in the negative. It does not. I were born in the Commonwealth of Massachusetts and it sput me out once and I believe it is getting ready to duplicate the effort. Let's away to the State of Maine, Meg. Can we? To the ocean. Build a house of rock. Our own house. As many sides as would please my darling. A duodecagon. Boys'll hunt and fish. We'll be ourselves. State of *Maine*," he said, and he clasped her chilly hands.

"No," she said.

"But why?"

"Our business is bowling." She handed him a sandwich wrapped in wax paper.

"It is *not*," he said, filing the sandwich in his jacket pocket. "That were an accident we both ran into and now it is bankrupting us. Let's walk away from the wreckage of it. Give it to Jeptha. Leave it to the cats. I were never meant for the world of men. I say, Meg, you must choose."

"Choose what?"

"Choose *me*," he said. "Over the alleys. Let me tell you who I am, Margaret, let me deliver you the truth—I have good news! I have—"

She shook her head in disbelief. "I've written to Minna," she said. "She'll help us."

"Who?" he asked, but he knew who.

"Your sister. I'll write again. I'll ask for help. Give us the Octagon, at least. Let us live there."

"But how did you? Wherever did you locate her?"

She hesitated. "I wrote to her through her uncle Mr. Sprague, who is a friend of mine."

Nahum was glad to see her cheeks flush at the lie of *friend*. Margaret had no friends. "No," he said. "I am done with all Spragues."

"Nim—"

"*No*," he said. "From Spragues I seek nothing, from Spragues I *expect* nothing. Bertha Truitt renounced her own people for them."

"She was an orphan before she met Dr. Sprague," said Margaret.

"Ah," said Nahum. "But not alone in the world, is my meaning.

My meaning is *me*. She gave up *me*. I made her the offer, I said, Mother if you marry him, that's the last you'll see of me, I will walk away, here I go, here I am off walking, Mother, say the word, and she did not, and it were. The last, I mean. Till she died. She hasn't writ back, the girl?"

"Not yet," said Margaret. Then, "Your beard."

"My beard is not the topic," said Nahum.

"Your beard," she repeated. "I can't think of anything else till it's come back."

By then, she'd been through so many abandonments and deaths. Everything in her life had fallen through. She was an orphan, too, of course—you'd think orphanhood was both hereditary and contagious! Well, it is, most people pass it along to their children.

"She's your sister," said Margaret to Nahum. "She loves you no matter what. Shall we sit?"

There was no term for the issue of your first wife's second marriage. He took the sandwich out of his pocket, regarded it, replaced it. He had not had so much as a bite and he was choking on it. To Maine, then, alone, or else he would deliver himself to his debtors, he would sink into them and expire. But if he went, he owed nothing. "My appetite has gone to Maine," he said. "I will see you anon."

He kissed her. Without the beard it felt to both of them at once distant and overwhelming, like jumping off a cliff. Margaret had expected his bare face would be cold but it was as warm as any other part of him, and she almost suggested that since Jeptha wasn't expecting them and the boys were at school, they should go home to bed. But that wasn't her way, and instead she said, "Anon. Is that soon?"

"Soon enough," he said.

I was never made for a world of men. By *men* Nahum had meant *human beings*, as people always did in those days. A world of women would have killed him outright. He had a ham salad sandwich warming in his pocket for supper. It hadn't occurred to him that Meg would say no to Maine. She had only ever denied him things if they cost too much money. He would not get on the train at the Salford Station, where somebody might see him, though who would recognize him without his beard? His face hurt. Heart, too. To Boston, then, to disappear into a crowd. Would he see his sons again? Did they suspect he was a fraud? Roy would, soon enough, and Roy would tell Arch, Roy liked to ruin things. If Nahum had had daughters instead of sons he wouldn't have fooled them so long but he might have been forgiven. Sons didn't forgive. He knew that much. Well, he'd die anyhow. Might as well give them more room at home: they wouldn't have to recoil from him, shrink themselves so as to make space for their unwieldy father. He didn't understand that his absence would be as large as his presence, the exact same dimensions, cast from his body like a bronze sculpture. Durable as bronze, too.

THE NOISE OF
ORDINARY THUNDER

I t's time to train the boys," Margaret Truitt told Jeptha Arrison.

"The boys," said Jeptha.

"My boys. Train Roy and Arch to pinset. We must make some changes here."

The changes Margaret brought to Truitt's Alleys meant it survived the Depression, the way all cheap entertainment did: by its very cheapness. For ten cents you could bowl; for nothing at all you could sit and watch. Mornings men went out to look for work but by the afternoon the lanes were full. Margaret put in leagues, held exhibitions, money games that went on all day, or all week, or all month, best of three or ten or a hundred games. Cocked hat bowling, where only three pins were set at each corner of the pin triangle. Food, too. Margaret never did get far from the ham dinners she cooked for Bertha Truitt and Dr. Sprague, but within the ham arena she was a minor genius—of thrift if nothing else. She roasted the ham in her little kitchen over the alleys, then filled her icebox with ham sandwiches wrapped in wax paper. If she really liked you, she'd offer to run up and fix you a plate of ham and eggs. Three times out of ten the eggs were perfect, frilled and brown on the edges, and the ham nearly hot through; mostly, she pummeled the eggs as she fried, spilled the yolks and tore the whites. Leftover ham was deviled, or turned into hash, used to flavor potato salad, served over spaghetti in a ketchup gravy, chopped into pots of beans. Some people thought she stirred minced ham into her wacky cake, though that was almost certainly not true: she merely used cups of flour in everything she cooked, so that any recipe had a hint of cake to it. Finally the coda to the ham, a pot of split pea soup flavored with the bone, served with dry brown bread. When pea soup showed up for lunch at Truitt's, the men knew that actual ham was coming soon. Margaret was vain about her cooking, she required compliments and gratitude, which she then batted away. "Ah, no," she said, "no, no," but you could tell how pleased she was. She never charged a cent. Everything that involved men was a war, to Margaret Vanetten Truitt: you had to feed your troops.

If asked about her husband she would shake her head and say, "Gone." Let people interpret that as they might. It was as much as she knew herself. She knew they thought she was embarrassed.

She wasn't. Not embarrassed but alight. Chronic, debilitating, volatile: how love always manifested in her.

She might be anywhere at all when it happened, the intimations of his body crawling over her, his breadth and warmth, his fiddle and grasp. The shaggy fog that had always let her know they were in the same building, even if she were upstairs at the sink and he just back from the bank, walking through the alley doors. Now he was gone but they *were* in the same building, if she could just find the right door, which would open into the right corridor, which would lead her to his bed, no matter where in the world. But if there were another woman in it! No memory of a living man could have that power. He had to be a ghost, come to worry or comfort her.

She could not get over him. Any day now, he might return! Then she would kill him. At night, in the same way she'd been staggered to discover, once married, the force of her desire, now she was staggered by her bloodthirst. At night she knew he was alive. She would murder him. Obliterate him. With her hands, with a candlestick, with a bowling pin hidden in the pleats of her nightgown: she'd bludgeon him, stump him, take him apart. Then she'd go back down the hallway to Massachusetts and burn her nightgown in the furnace.

Once she'd read about a woman whose husband had been killed in battle. His heart was taken from his body, delivered from the battlefield to her, and she placed it in a glass box and stared at it seven hours a day. With love? Yes, but of the furious kind. How else could you stare at a heart?

She wanted his. He'd left no relics except his sons, and those she knew she couldn't keep.

t's noble work, setting," said Jeptha Arrison. He'd grown portly; in the striped alley coveralls, he had a prow like a ship's. Roy and Arch wore coveralls, too. Impossible, thought Arch, not to feel great in uniform. Impossible, thought Roy, to feel like anything but an idiot dressed in the same outfit as other people. His own weight was spread around his body, and he disliked how the coveralls made him aware of his undershorts. "Noble," said Jeptha again, as though contradicted. "What's that you have with you, Archie?"

Arch was eleven. For his first day of work he had packed a comic book—*Favorite Funnies*—and a ham sandwich on a folded-over piece of bread.

"You're not going camping," said Roy. "It's not an overnight trip."

Arch saluted him with the deckle-edge of his sandwich.

"I see no harm in it," said Jeptha.

Roy hated the bowling alley and the bowlers, grown men who

called him names. They called him Spot for his freckles, and Tubby and Doughnut and Speedy. They called him Tiny and Babe. In bed he could suck his stomach into concavity and tell himself it wasn't so bad. He could strum the wings of his rib cage, feel the muscles in his thighs. At the bowling alley, though, he was just a fat kid, a sullen boy with odd ears, one gibbous, one flush. His freckles were the splotchy sort. Nobody else in the family was fat, nobody bookish or sour. Where had he come from?

But his brother, Arch: even years later, when he was dead of misadventure, what people said of Arch was that he was *fun*. He loved *fun*. He had his father's bristling hair, his father's hooded eyes though bigger, and limpid, and blue.

For a while Roy and Arch sat on the pinboys' shelf and watched Jeptha as he set the pins with an educated air. Some life in him yet! Training the Truitt boys to pinset gave shape to his weird head, made him light on his feet again.

"One pin," he said, pointing to the front of the steel deck, where the first pin was to be stood up. "Two pin. Three, four, five, six, seven, eight, nine, ten."

"All right," said Roy. "I know how to count."

Jeptha turned and frowned; his white hair had comb marks in it. "The pinbody's the boss. Nobody thinks of that. No bowler's so good she can overcome a bad pinbody. You set the pins perfect, every pin where it ought be, just in the middle, then it's science for the bowler: she'll know how the pins'll fly. But a sloppy pinbody means there's no telling. Even just a little off changes the whole game. Some bowlers know it. Some bowlers'll offer you money to set one way for them and another for the other bowler. Cheats, I mean. Don't take money."

"Pinbody?" said Roy.

"What Bertha called us and so me, too, I say *pinbody*. Now, she was a bowler, Bertha Truitt. *This*," he said, and he indicated the alleys, the men at the approaches, their mother the only thing female in the place. "Truitt's was for women. Even your mother bowled in her day."

"*Mom?*" said Arch.

Jeptha nodded. "So then. You set the pins fast as you can but part of the job is you must feel and feel the pins and balls, looking for wrongness. The cracked or wobble footed. The chipped or unbalanced. Honor in bowling is the pinbody's job. Yes, your mother," he said to the boys. Nobody thought Jeptha kept much of anything in that lopsided sack of his head. Sawdust. Folk songs. It was best that way. Nahum Truitt wouldn't have tolerated him there otherwise. But he remembered everything. "She was not the finest of the ladies—bowlingwise, I mean—but she was good, and game. Now, boys, to your stations."

Above the pit, eleven-year-old Arch Truitt closed his eyes. It would be hard to fall asleep. Not impossible. He knew he shouldn't but the sensation of surrender was sneezily delicious. Perhaps if he closed his eyes and held still, he could balance, he could sleep for ten seconds, his body was already asleep, the sleep was reaching his head—

A pinboy is not a parrot on a perch or a horse in a field. Halfway through the first string of his pinsetting career, Arch Truitt dozed off and fell onto the lane. He woke up as he hit the pins, cheek first, was conscious long enough to get thwacked between the shoulder blade by the third ball of the box, rolled by Mack Constable, and was sent back to dreamland by the four pin knocking him on the head. The noise, the beer, the smoke—it took a moment for anyone other than Mack Constable and his teammates to notice the boy on the lane. Mack was a bowler, he'd been trained not to cross the foul line, but he hollered and pointed and then everyone noticed, and everyone was stuck. It was as though Arch had appeared from nowhere, in the family tradition. His right shoe and sock had been knocked clear off.

"Don't move him," Margaret shrieked, "his spine, Roy!"

But Roy was stunned, too, till Jeptha Arrison hurdled the lanes and scooped Arch up, taking care not to skid in the ham of the splayed-open sandwich. He carried him down the gutter and brought him to the benches. Margaret closed her eyes, clung to the counter. If Arch were dead or broken, she wanted somebody else to make the diagnosis. Roy was there. Roy would tell her. Roy loved bad news.

"Is he paralyzed?" asked Roy, worriedly.

"It's nobody's fault," said Jeptha.

"Oh God," said Mack Constable.

Outside: Arch's eyes fluttered as he returned to them. Inside, the world fluttered, returned to Arch. "ARE YOU PARALYZED?" Jeptha Arrison yelled into those opening eyes, and Arch didn't know the answer, he'd never been paralyzed before, he didn't know what it felt like. A long list of things he didn't know: why his head hurt, how he'd got to the bowlers' benches, why one of his feet was so cold, how long he'd been gone from the conscious world, who put that bite of ham sandwich at the back of his mouth right where it could choke him.

The men looked down, Jeptha, Mack, Bill Semb, his brother Roy, Dutch Goldblatt. He could feel the heat of the whole Saturday afternoon league radiating around him. His neck hurt, and his face. He lifted his hand to his cheek and the crowd cheered.

"Not paralyzed!" called Bill Semb, just as Jeptha Arrison twisted Arch's exposed big toe nearly off.

"Ow!"

"The boy is entire!" called Jeptha.

Roy lowered his mouth to his brother's ear. He whispered, "You're drunk."

"I fell *asleep*," said Arch, but his brother was right. It was Satur-

day, June 26, at 2:30 P.M., the Year of Our Lord 1935, the eleventh
year of Arch Truitt, and Arch was drunk, not for the first time.

f not for beer, Arch Truitt might have become a pickpocket, a sneak
thief, a Peeping Tom, a second-story man, a spy: what interested
him were the secret compartments of adulthood, the things grown
people cupped their hands around. Wallets, sex acts, lit cigarettes,
whispers into ears. What things went on! So he went looking, and
the first place he looked was a left-behind beer glass, and what was
there satisfied his curiosity, piqued it, satisfied, piqued, satisfied.

Arch drank beer ends. The warm of it, the way it went down
the middle of your tongue then rolled to the edges bubblier in some
places than in others; the way it spread out first at your shoulders
and then at your hips. It tasted of bread infused with gold, a flavor
inseparable from the way it unlaced his muscles, his way of thinking. It was as though his body ordinarily was a darkened room. Beer
turned on the lights, warmed the furniture. Made him happy to be
there. Filled him with joie de vivre (which is fatal in nearly all cases).
He could drink beer for the rest of his life, he thought.

Margaret refused to let Arch pinset after his accident. "He's
too sleepy," she said, "it's dangerous for him." As though sleepiness
were hemophilia. One side of his body was bruised like an autumn
shadow. "He never fought sleep, not even as a baby," said Margaret.
She said it in a voice of admiration: he was a pacifist in the Army
of the Wakeful. Let others fight sleep, let Arch act as distraction,
sacrifice himself to his pillow and satin-bound blanket.

"He's lazy, you mean," said Roy.

"He's *sleepy*," said Margaret. "He can't help it. Look at him. He's
meant for something else. Great things."

"Aren't *I*?" cried Roy.

His mother looked at him. The truth was, she knew nothing

about fate, or destiny, or even tomorrow, but she knew she needed someone to take care of her and only one of her sons was capable. "Oh Roy," she said. "Not all of us are."

Margaret didn't mean to be cruel. She was only stupid; she'd had ideas put in her head. It felt to her later as though these thoughts had physically been *put* there by Nahum, solid thoughts she never could have manufactured on her own. Arch reminded her of Bertha, friendly and ruthless; Roy of her, a left-behind person who would always strive for love. What was keeping her in Salford, when everybody else had left? Duty. Some people were built for it and others weren't.

A PAINTED KANGAROO
WITH A PAIR OF FALSE WINGS

The wreck of Supersum still stood in those days, boarded up by the city. A colony of birds nested in the belvedere. Nocturnal, pelagic, monogamous, mysterious, ordinary dun-colored birds, but nobody knew what they ate, or where they went.

The Audubon Society wrote to City Hall. Something must be done about the house, they said.

We'll tear it down, said City Hall, who'd been meaning to look into it for some time. They just had to write to the owner first.

You can't! said the Audubon Society. Not now!

Why not?

We'd thought these birds were extinct! To see one—

—are you *sure* you saw it.

—yes, said the Audubon Society coldly. Quite sure. As sure as we can be. Now, these birds only come inland to breed—

Like sailors! said the old woman at City Hall.

Some people, said the Audubon Society, say that they're the ghosts of drowned sailors. They hover over the ocean to feed. They *patter.* They flutter. It's amazing to see, if you could see it, but mostly you can't.

And they're extinct?

We thought the Cross-rumped—what we have here—was. The Ringed might be. The New Zealand: almost certainly. We know so little of these birds.

Then how do you know they're them?

They are no good at walking, said the Audubon Society, ignoring the question. They never really do, their legs are so weak. But their wings! They can fly forever, or so we think. Amazing birds. Little married couples. They trade off incubation of the egg, father then mother then father then mother.

Just one egg?

One egg is enough, said the Audubon Society in a prim voice.

The old gentleman at City Hall believed in the birds. He'd seen something flying home to the belfry in the early morning. What the old man thought: there were birds in the Octagon, and if the Audubon Society believed they were these extinct seabirds, then they *were.* The belief made it so. It was like love.

But the old woman at City Hall had once been a young woman at City Hall. She had been there in 1903, when the Salford Devil had been sighted skulking along the squares at night, killing cats, terrifying women, shrieking at motorcars. City Hall had offered a bounty. What people brought in! An eight-foot gutshot snake. A small boy with his bellowing mother who wanted to teach him a lesson: "I have the Salford Devil here! I've come to ask the mayor to throw him in jail." A curious foreign man presented a kangaroo (where did he get it?) painted the same lime green as the gas station, with a pair of wings fashioned out of a bifurcated umbrella. Most people who brought their devils forgot about the wings, but the wings were the essential part. The foreign man was deported; the kangaroo's fate is unrecorded. One teenage girl carried, in a shoebox painted white, a dead bat dressed in a doll's satin wedding dress, veiled, bouqueted, sides split to make room for its own born wings.

"The Salford Devil!" said the then-young woman of City Hall, before she looked closer and saw the beauty of the folded ears, the furred cheeks.

The girl was hurt. She cuddled the thing. "No, lady. She's an angel. I found an angel."

"We didn't ask for angels," said the woman. "No rewards for angels, and I mean none."

A bat was a bat. A bird was a bird. You couldn't make up a species by calling it by name, not *petrel* for Saint Peter, nor any of the other names the seabirds were known by: *waterwitch, satanite, satanique, oieseau du diable*. Bird of the Devil. Little rock.

Anyhow, said the old woman of City Hall to the old man of City Hall, it was time to write to the owner of the house to straighten out its future.

n this way, some months later, the owner of the abandoned house stood on Somefire Hill. (Supersum's abandonment was finally as notable as its shape.) The neighbors took her for a stranger. They wondered whether to call the police. Bronze marceled hair, skin a shade darker, and a gap between her front teeth that made her look both voracious and elegant. Her tweed coat wasn't the exact green of her eyes, but an altogether more alchemical color, and expensive, nipped in at the waist, the fur trim dyed to green plumage, the pockets angular and shocking. There was nothing about the coat that wasn't magnificent. Its occupant looked like somebody who ate her dinner at midnight.

Over the years Minna Sprague had thought of her old house, dreamt of it. She thought she remembered every room, the pantries and bedrooms, her father's study, the belvedere, the peculiar number of closets, more rooms than any three people could need (she didn't think to count as a resident Margaret Vanetten, whose bedroom had been next to hers). But she couldn't do the geometry, she couldn't make it fit: the second floor in her head was twice as big as the first, as though the house were not an octagon but a nautilus shell, a spiral around the spiral stairs.

The letters from Margaret demanded love, which Minna had sent in homeopathic amounts, and very little else: postcards with her newest address (Toronto, Paris, New York, London, Paris again), reports on the weather, like any tourist. Who cared what the weather was like two weeks ago in Europe? It was something to say, something that cost Minna nothing. But the letters that Margaret sent got worse and worse.

> Minna darling I remember when you were a baby and I held you in my arms. I wish you were a baby again. Your mother come back from the bowling alley or from a trip for a tournament and you just crying for me. I looked after you so, Minna! Such a good baby. You didn't miss your mother at all. Then you got sent away and I thought that was a terrible thing. I was against that. I will say no bad thing against the dead but that was a terrible thing for your father to do when this was the home you knew. Some people will say he was broken but life breaks many people and they do not give up their children no matter their circumstance or family background. Come home, Minna. The house is big enough for all of us. When you marry I can nurse your babies for you, I am still a fine baby nurse. No matter how it looks to other people I don't care. I was as a mother to you and I will be as a grandmother for your babies—Minna, come and I will explain all to you. I know you have love in your heart for me still because you were always such a fine and smart girl. I await your answer and I remain your loving Margaret Vanetten.

The letter that Minna received from the city through her uncle Benjamin was something else again: she was responsible for the house, for the birds inside, unless she wanted to deed it over. Now she opened the kitchen door—when she was little they never used the front entrance, which was boarded over anyhow—and it felt as though the whole weight of the house had been resting on that lintel. She never should have come. She went in farther. She thought about taking off one of her stockings to breathe through, but it was cold and already she was nervous about the neighbors. She didn't remember them kindly. She'd worn her most ostentatious clothes because she knew that the best camouflage was a kind of flagrancy: you didn't have to worry how people took you so much if the first thing they noticed was that you were rich.

The floors were not just dusty but covered in debris—chunks of plaster from the ceiling, bottles left behind by somebody who'd taken refuge there some years before. She understood that the neglect was her own, that she could have hired someone to fix the place up, rent it out. Then again, she'd been a child. What had her aunt and uncles been thinking? Well, they'd been mourning her father, too. The oldest brother. The smartest and quietest one. They did not know what they would do without him, never mind that he'd gone away, had married away, had written faithfully but rarely visited.

She felt she might come across his body, or her mother's, though her mother's remains were buried in the Salford Cemetery and her father's sealed in an urn up in Oromocto. The neighbors had called the house the Wedding Cake because of the tiers, and that was what the plaster was like, ruined cake. She touched a wall and it crumbled away in her hands. The house was beyond saving.

She'd had an idea, when the letter had found her in Paris: she would donate the house and land to the city under the condition that it could be turned into a museum—not a museum devoted to her father (though Salford could do worse) but a history museum, with her father's office preserved. In her father's office, she was certain, was evidence. Of what? Of him, his strangeness, genius, goodness. Her mother she remembered as bosomy and flatulent, hot, grasping, an old woman already, when Minna was a young woman already.

She could go up, look out the window and see what the birds saw, what her father had seen the last day he was happy. Wondering when his darlings would be back—Bertha from Boston, Minna and her nurse from the public library. They'd come down Mims Avenue. "You wave at me," he'd instructed Minna. "You won't see me, but I'll see you."

The stairs were the best-built part of the house, and she climbed them to the second floor. The doors to all the bedrooms were shut. No, she wouldn't open them.

The roof had fallen in. Of course it had: it hadn't been pitched right, and years and years of uncleared winter snow and melt had collapsed it. On the dark desk was a glass of wine that time had boiled the moisture from, leaving one ruby clot at the bottom. The desk was otherwise blank. The shelves were empty. He was beyond saving, too.

In Oromocto, in his family, he was both prodigal and favored, gone away from them but never lost. His picture was in the parlor, the books he'd written around the house, and when she'd been sent there it was as if in recompense, as though she were coming back to lead his life, this light-skinned girlchild instead of their beloved Leviticus. She slept in his bed and inherited his old books and the depth of his siblings' love: she was a loved child in Oromocto. "This was his real life," her aunt Almira always told her. "He was so happy here. That woman made him miserable and left him to die in a bowling alley."

In a way she believed that still, she could feel a sort of misery, like the afterheat of fire coming up through the floorboards. It felt distinct, familial. This was what he'd chosen. The heat of her mother. She missed her mother now, she realized, the bustling bossiness of her. She remembered being—how old? Too big for it, but lying across her mother's lap and sneaking a hand up her mother's shirt just to feel the lovely *fatness* of her, that roll across the tummy, the boiling heat.

You could get *at* her mother, she remembered now. Her father was always out of reach, overhead.

She had known for a long time that her childhood was over, but now it was also lost. No museum. The house torn down. She told herself it had been good as torn down all those years she was away. The city could raze it and take the land—no, that's right, they were worried about the birds. All right. Let the birds take it over, fill every floor with nest.

Then she heard the pounding on the door.

"The neighbors called," said the woman behind the door. "Oh, my Minna."

Minna Sprague recognized Margaret: her brown hair in its childish bowl cut, her little hooked nose, the way her hands clutched at each other, the printer's ink purple of her clothing. "My baby," she said to Minna, very seriously, and then she folded her arms around her. It was an odd feeling, a powdered milk embrace, something like actual love but reconstituted from a packet.

"Minna-bean," said Margaret, a phrase so inane it unraveled the embrace. "How is it? The house."

Minna shook her head.

"Let me see."

Inside, Minna found that porous Margaret Vanetten absorbed some of her terror. It helped to have company as she said goodbye to the house. "This is the front parlor," said Margaret. "Just over the milk room. The kitchen. Oh! The sewing room!"

"Who sewed? Not my mother."

"I did. You did, too."

"Not anymore," said Minna. "I pay people to sew for me."

"Good for you, sweetheart," said Margaret. "I was so happy here."

Margaret Vanetten Truitt opened the door to her room and there it was: the little single iron bed, still made up, the quilt she'd sewn herself grayed with dust. The hairbrush on the dresser top. "And through here—" She opened the door: Minna's room. Another single bed, though grander, with an Eastlake headboard. A good bed. The blue coverlet had been kicked down, the pillow. Margaret remembered making both beds up the morning they left for Canada. Who'd slept here since? "You were happy, too," she said, feeling Minna's doubt. This house went on and on. She still dreamt of it, too. She straightened the covers on Minna's bed. "Do you have children, sweetheart? I should have asked that. I should have asked that first thing. You married?" She'd worshipped that child all along and now she saw how right she was to do it.

"Divorced," said Minna. Margaret clucked her tongue. "No children."

"You're young yet," said Margaret. "Let's go upstairs."

"Oh, it's too sad."

"I'm already sad," said Margaret, in an improbably cheerful voice. They went through: the softness of the plaster, the holes in the roof.

"Shame," said Minna. "They didn't build it right."

But Bertha Truitt had followed every direction. Fowler's advice was just so damnably bad. The wooden houses he scoffed at still stand everywhere in New England, but the gravel and lime octagons have fallen to rubble.

"Where are the birds?" asked Minna.

"Sleeping," said Margaret.

"Margaret," said Minna. "Come with me into my father's study. I want to look in the desk. See if there's anything in there."

They walked onto the wooden floor as though it were ice on a pond. Little steps. They clung to each other as though that would do any good. The desk was leather topped, gold edged, though you could not see the gold for dust. Minna remembered the pleasure of writing on it, the way the leather gave under the pressure of a pencil tip.

The desk drawers were empty save one: in the bottom drawer, a bird's nest, three perfect celadon-green eggs snuggled in.

"Are these the eggs?" asked Minna. "The seabirds. They nest in *drawers?*"

"Oh, no," said Margaret. "These are ages old. Your father collected them. He had dozens. He shut them away from the cats."

How do you disturb a thing like that? Minna wanted to own it and to leave it alone. Her father's hands, a doctor's, had moved it from its first location. You could do that with human houses, too, she knew. It was the eggs that shook her. Inhabited, haunted. Little mausoleums. She took the nest away.

It was among her effects, when she died in New York, fifty years later. Or maybe that was a different nest. All nests look as though they were built in the nineteenth century. She had become, like her father, a collector.

"Somebody stole the stairs," said Margaret. "The iron ones, to the cupola."

"That's where I was born," said Minna. "On the stairs."

"Not quite. Overhead. That's where your father worked, mostly."

They gazed up at the hole in the ceiling. Maybe it was the seabirds themselves who sold it for scrap.

Minna looked down at the nest balanced on her upturned palms. She'd always thought of nests as round, but this one looked polygonal, like the house itself. She'd come to Salford to get the last scrapings of her father's life. Here it was, overhead, in her hands. Unhatched eggs, but beautiful. A former hired girl as a guide. You could hear the wind through the cupola overhead, whistling at a strange pitch. Her father—his private thoughts, his bad habits, his actual self—was above her, no way to get at him. Maybe better that way, to not know our parents, to love them as we move away from them—they're on the shore and we're on a ship, moving away; later we will switch places as they sail away from us, and we say to them, *a little longer.* There were poems above her head, and the corpses of cats, empty bottles, peanut shells, the smell of heartache, a small stack of hate letters sent to the house, which Dr. Sprague had intercepted (not realizing that most such correspondence was sent to Truitt's Alleys: all on the subject of their marriage, written by strangers, which Truitt threw in the furnace). One carpet slipper. A photo of a beloved baby.

Minna looked at the nest in her hands and decided a nest was sufficient. Let everything else rot. Here were her father's intentions.

"Let's go," she said to Margaret.

She remembered Margaret as a cabinet of a woman, functional, extra, but nervous, cedar scented, lavender tinted. A graspingness. *You will always, always, always be my baby*, she said to little Minna. Or was that her mother? The sad truth: she could not fully untangle Margaret and Bertha. One baked inedible cakes. One sang a song called "After the Ball." One carried her around the house long after she was too old and when Minna had said no, that's enough, had burst into tears.

It was hard to walk down stairs while carrying a bird's nest. The fresh air stirred up Margaret's fire. "See?" she said. "Still standing after all this time."

"It's not safe."

"We'll make it safe."

"I've already given it to the city."

"You give away too much!" said Margaret Vanetten.

"I have enough."

"*You* do." Margaret sat down on the lawn as though she might need to be removed with dynamite. She was the one who mowed the grass, as a kind of a promise and a prayer. The house looked like a prison. You could not judge houses or people from the outside.

"Well, I can't keep it," said Minna. When they'd left all those years ago, she hadn't known she would never live in Salford again, never see her parents, never hide in the wedge-shaped closet in her room to listen to the house from inside the house. The closet had smelled of herself, mown hay and milk, a hint of hairdressing. That smell was gone, and Minna—though she stood here in the city limits with her old baby nurse—was gone, too. The Octagon, the Wedding Cake, Superba, Supersum. Within a month the city would raze the place. There was no way to save it, not even for ornithological reasons. It was as though she were seeing the house from a great distance as it moved away, *goodbye, goodbye*. She said to Margaret, "What would I do with a house like this? I have a career I need to get back to. I leave for New York this afternoon."

"Oh," said Margaret, then, "Take," then, in a childish voice, "Why did you even come here?"

Minna saw it then, the look on Margaret's face, Margaret who'd been begging for her to come back for years. What could Minna say?

She knew, of course, that Margaret lived in the bowling alley, that she had married the man who claimed to be Minna's half brother, that she was, in fact, Margaret Truitt. What a thing to have done! All of this she had learned from the lawyers, because her father's will had been very clear on the matter.

She said, "How's your husband."

"Gone," said Margaret. "Come to the alley."

"Oh, no. That is one place I'd never go. Do you have children, Margaret?"

Margaret nodded.

"Well then," said Minna, "that's lovely. Look after them."

"You're the one I love," said Margaret.

"What?" Minna said, scandalized, and she knew that it was true. It was an old love, paid for, but paid in full.

CAREFUL WHAT YOU ORDER THROUGH THE MAIL

Once the war started in Europe, the ghosts came to Salford like any refugees. Displaced persons except no longer persons: there were so many new dead in Europe the old dead were forced out. The locals objected to these immigrants, their old-timey ways, their unfamiliar smells, their unintelligible utterances. Then the locals got accustomed. Then the locals blamed the newcomers when trouble flared up. The ghost at the Gearheart Olympia was thought to be Dahune Doner, a German contortionist who in his act arrived onstage packed neatly in a box, and had been packed into this box by a jealous rival and left for weeks backstage of a Freiburg theater to suffocate and starve; it was said the mortician could not straighten the corpse to fit it into a coffin. The ghosts of contortionists can fold themselves to handkerchiefs. Sometimes this ghost left the Gearheart to haunt a particular compartment at the Automat, and soured whatever sandwich or soup or slice of pie had been put there. America! Soon everyone knew which door to avoid, though the superstitious Automat owner kept the compartment filled with a chunk of poppy seed cake, replaced weekly.

Elsewhere people discerned the ghosts of the slaughtered tangled up with their slaughterers, dark-eyed mothers with their starved children, and, on the fens, a pack of dogs who'd been shot one by one near Tbilisi—even the animals looked different from American animals, their heads too big and bony; even the ghosts of those animals. The souls of animals are usually too small to be detected with ordinary technology (the ordinary technology being the souls of human beings), but in the case of unexpected mass animal death (zoo fires, poisonings) they clump together and form a ghost about the size of a very old person's. The ghosts of children are enormous. The ghosts of the very old are worn thin from use.

Arch Truitt had grown up in an apartment over a bowling alley, and late at night he could hear the ghosts, which he believed were in fact science—radio waves, or radiation, or fine magnetic objects rushing to the North Pole. What but the unseen could explain the bursting sense of joy Arch sometimes felt, despite everything? The notion that he was loved by an intangible someone? His body slept in his bed above Truitt's Alleys but his being was tickled elsewhere and otherwise. Truitt's Alleys had its own ghost. At least people believed lane five did: every now and then the pins fell over, not all at once but in turn, one into another, till all that was left behind was a 7-10 split, two standing pins like fangs amid the dead wood. Anything might have done it. Roy said nonsense, only physics knocked over the pins on lane five. The city was built on swampland. It was a wonder anything stayed upright for more than half an hour.

Arch tried to explain it to Roy. Life itself was strange. Think of things people didn't used to believe! Think of the true things that were even now unbelievable! The Earth was, in fact, round. Duckbill platypuses existed and waddled on the other side of the world, where it was also—this was just a fact—winter, though in Salford it was July.

"It's July in Australia, too," said Roy suspiciously. They were lying in their beds, putting off getting up to go to work. Summers Arch worked the counter while Roy pinset. Roy wasn't fat anymore, though he carried his body around as though he were, ponderously. Pinsetting and puberty had thinned him out.

"Yes, it's *July*," said Arch. "But winter. Tell that to an ancient man and he'd never believe you!"

"Try it on Jeptha," said Roy. "He's the only ancient man I know."

"A *primitive* man. If you traveled back in time."

"I don't deal in hypotheticals," said Roy. "I believe in science."

"I thought science was all about hypotheses," said Arch.

He could feel Roy's fury emanate from the bed, could see it, a cloud rising up, could smell it, the acrid scent of Roy not believing he'd been beat in an argument. Maybe all of the emanations in the alleys were just bad moods of Roy's, kicking over things, mooning and moaning about. Roy's mood even now had legs, and round cartoon boots, and distantly, distantly, Arch knew he was about to fall back asleep even though the morning was under way, he was on the downward slope, his own feet just dipped in dreams: where he learned most of the things he knew about the unseen world.

"Who would want to haunt *this* place," said Roy, but Arch didn't think it was a who, exactly, and anyway, being a ghost was like being drafted: you didn't get to choose where you were sent.

Later that day he saw the ad in the back of his mother's *True Stories* magazine:

GHOSTS?
Extranormal researcher
Seeks haunted properties

> To photograph & investigate.
>
> Please write care of
>
> Box 231, Eureka, California.

So Arch wrote.

The Ghoster arrived three months later, no advance notice, wearing the kind of cabled Irish sweater designed to camouflage sorrow and poverty. His bald head was trimmed with dark hair, and his shoulders were skewed by a camera bag. He had a handsome, hangdog face. He leaned on the counter and said, "What's the best time?"

"We have lanes free now," said Margaret Vanetten Truitt.

"I'm sorry," he said. From somewhere under the sweater his snaking hand located a card. He handed it to her. *Ghosts? Write Box 231, Eureka, California.* "I'm here to photograph the spirit."

"We have no spirits," she said.

His hand went under his sweater again, and from a lower quadrant of his bulk found a letter handwritten on lined paper. "Arch Truitt says otherwise."

"Arch Truitt is fifteen," she said. "He's at school."

The man explained to Margaret that he was well known among those Americans who wished to see a ghost. "I spend my life avoiding them," said Margaret, and he said, "You're a rare bird." He had taken a picture of a woman in a San Francisco hotel who'd died of a plunged elevator. The mystery of it: she was not in the elevator itself, but underneath the car, at the bottom of the shaft, murdered, but by who? He'd photographed her forty years after her death, in the hotel lobby. He took a magazine clipping out of his camera bag.

"There she is," he said. "See? She's tilting her head."

Margaret could find nothing in the photo except flash and blur, but she could feel his longing. "Oh yes," she said, putting her finger to the page. "Yes, there she is. It's a shame! Fresh out of ghosts, we are."

"Maybe the fellow who died in the fire," the man suggested.

"No!" said Margaret. Then, "Nobody died in a fire."

"Murdered, maybe," said the man.

"Arch said that?"

"No, no. Found that out myself. This is Bertha Truitt's place. She had an interesting death, too. I see you're startled. But you see I do my research. What I heard is it was a crippled man."

"A colored man, you mean," said Margaret.

"Not the man who died. The man who set the first man on fire. A crippled handyman who was arrested but let go. Joe the Cripple."

"Joe Wear," asked Margaret. It was a shock to hear the word *crippled*, to realize that's what Joe was to other people.

The man took out a tiny book, and opened it to reveal notes written in a barbed-wire cursive. "He was in love with some hired girl who got fired by the family, and the crippled man decided to avenge her."

"*Me?*" said Margaret.

"Not *you*," said the man, "a long time ago. No, you're far too young." He peered again into the notebook. "'The pins fall over for no reason.'"

Margaret had known that the police had suspected Joe Wear of setting the fire. The two men had been at loggerheads—whatever loggerheads were; Margaret saw Joe and Dr. Sprague like lumberjacks standing on fallen trees gliding down the river, each wanting to go first—no, not loggerheads, they plain hated each other. But Joe Wear had never been in love with her. She knew that much. Didn't she?

She said, "Subsidence."

The man looked out over the lanes. "Possibly. Is that man *dead*?"

Margaret turned to look—a spirit? A ghost? But it was only Jeptha Arrison, sleeping on the pinboys' shelf. Margaret was about to explain, but then she saw him, on his stomach with his head turned toward them, gray in the face. They stared at him for a long while. He gave a rattling sigh, and rolled over. Since the war had started it was nearly impossible to hire pinboys, but then again there weren't many men around to bowl. You couldn't hire little boys any longer. That was illegal.

"Only Jeptha," she said. "I'm Margaret Truitt." She stuck her hand out for a shake.

Just like that the man's eyes were filled with tears. He caught her hand between his. "My late wife's name was Margaret," he said. "I won't need a thing from you. I'll take some photos. Then, depending on what we find, perhaps some moving pictures. I understand, you say, *We don't have spirits* or *we don't want spirits* or *how do we get rid of spirits if we got 'em.* Customers don't like ghosts, you might think, but they do. Look at Salem! Look at the Continental Hotel!" He nodded at the photo of the hotel elevator; he was still holding her hand. "You may find business better than it's ever been."

She didn't want the man to find a ghost but she also didn't want him to go. He was a big man, and Margaret loved big men the way some women loved big dogs. Their very presence comforted her; she thought she particularly knew how to talk to them. "Well," she said. "We could use the business. You start looking. Find me a ghost. Make it a good one."

Arch spent the week following the Ghoster, whose name—he *thought*—was Cadey. He'd imagined a ghost seeker's instruments would be astonishing, made of whiz-bang plastics and fireproof glass and plutonium, with knobs and screens, automatic pens and a clock with luminous hands that had the ability to go spinning back through history. Maybe all that material had gone to the war effort; after all, they had torn down the cast-iron ball returns for scrap and replaced them with wood. What the man carried: an ordinary Brownie camera and a scrapbook filled with snapshots and clippings, a small tape recorder. Similarly, the words *ghost hunter* had conjured up in Arch's head a man of energy, excitability. But Cadey was slow, dolorous, piscine. He seemed to swim through the alley.

"Hetty Dubois," he said, pointing to a page from a magazine. "Died of a plunged elevator. Not *in* it, under. Murdered, but by who?" Arch looked. A figure knit of light: he could see it, her head, her beaded dress, her flat kid shoes, feathered hat. "Here's the Peddler of Ogunquit, Solomon Kamp. Here's little Bobby Kent, hanged in a barn. The Dark Lady of Union Station—we don't know her name, alas. Still a mystery. Perhaps that's why she hasn't moved on. But here she is. See? In front of the newsstand. Her head. Her arm."

"They're *people*," said Arch.

"Of course they're people," said Cadey. "Were. What else?" He looked across the alley. "The thing is, you don't know that you've got the ghost till you develop the film."

"But what do you *think*?" asked Arch. "What do the readings say?"

Cadey shrugged. "Honestly, I don't know. You got a historical case of spontaneous combustion, that's for sure. But whether there's a haunting—" He saw the look on Arch's face. "I'll take more pictures this week. Then we'll know." Cadey tilted his head and pointed his nose at the ceiling.

Arch tried to feel a ghost. His father, or a fraction of him, something glowering and clumsy. He looked at his mother to see if anything had come over her: peace, or unease. He didn't know which his father's presence would induce in her. Cadey touched his own nose as though to adjust it.

"You smell something?" Arch asked.

"Beer," said Cadey, giving Arch a sideways look. "No, I'm divining. The tip of the nose is a sensitive instrument. Why it succumbs to frostbite."

"You feel something, then." Arch examined the air in front of Cadey's face, but all he could really see was the man's nose twitching in a circular way like a dog's. Arch'd only drunk one beer that day, left behind by an old man on lane one, and suddenly he understood that to the old man, *Arch* was a ghost: a beer-thieving phantom.

Cadey sneezed, but angrily. He gazed along the back wall. Jeptha knelt oddly on the pinshelf, glowering at them like a gargoyle.

Grief was what made him handsome. A doleful beauty. Still Margaret thought he was overdoing it. In his camera bag he carried his wife's childhood teddy bear. "Sweet!" said Margaret, and the man pulled out the bear and displayed it. Out in the open the bear wasn't sweet; it was a haunted object, one eye replaced with a horn button, the other glass and accusing, a slip of pink tongue reattached in some battlefield surgery, belly fur worn away to warp and woof. As though only he had evidence of loss in this world.

"Poor love," said Margaret.

"Me or the bear?" asked Cadey. He danced the bear up Margaret's arm.

"You need to stop," she said to him. "The photography, I mean."

"Can't. I'm writing a book."

"Write a book about something else."

"What else is there?"

"I don't know. Marry again, big handsome man like you."

"Ah no," he said. He gave her a dazzling, woebegone smile. She knew it was pity; it felt like love. "I'm done with that."

He was done with lots of things, he told her. Restaurants, candy, newspapers, parties, cars, airplanes, living in houses. He slept in hotels and traveled by train.

What he needed was to fall in love with another woman, but she saw he was too vain. Ordinary happiness would be a dent in his armor. Happiness was everywhere, like dropped coins. You might feel lucky to pick it up and put it in your pocket, but what could it really buy you?

To be haunted! That set you apart.

C lose 'em," Cadey said to Arch. He gestured. "The blackout curtains."

The blackout curtains were floor-to-ceiling black velvet weighted down with metal at the hem, intended to shut out not the outside light from the bowling alley, but the bowling alley light from the outside, in case of enemy attack. Salford held air raid drills all the time, according to the whims of Norman Riker, the air raid warden, who liked—he wouldn't deny it—to make the whole town seem to fall dead at one time, the citizens in their houses or caught in their cars. Did they feel dead themselves, or did they only seem dead to him?

Close them, Cadey called, so Arch went to close them. They were so heavy it felt like the end, the very *end*, every time you drew them.

"Now shut the lights."

Arch looked toward his mother behind the counter. She nodded. That was what the home front was, you could plunge a place into darkness and people would accept it. The dark was patriotic. He threw the switch. He didn't think you could see a ghost in the pitch black, any more than you could see a spiderweb. Such things need light.

Still, in the darkness you could believe in nearly anything. Every person there sensed the six iron columns, cold and dead and clobbering, like ancestors holding the ceiling up. They could hear a ball roll along alley three, let go when the lights were still on, too late to stop it. It wobbled into the gutter. Then silence, then the miniature guillotine sound of the shutter of Cadey's camera. Margaret felt the hand of her mother on her shoulder, could hear at the back of her skull a suggestive whistle; Arch had an intimation of his father, about to bellow; Jeptha Arrison was overcome with thoughts of his dead Bessie, whose grave he still visited weekly. Roy, upon the pinboys' shelf, thought only of himself.

E very boy becomes, at some point in life, a genealogist, hoping to find a king, if only to settle a bet with other boys. At school they'd had to draw a family tree, and Roy's was no more than a shrub, while the other boys had cousins and aunts and uncles, even nieces and nephews. He had a brother, and two parents. His mother was an orphan; instead of aunts, he and Arch had nuns. His father, too, was an orphan, though he knew nothing more than that. He had one pale and ludicrous brother. If he wanted more family, he would have to wait.

He had read the letters his mother kept in the lowest cubby, tied with dirty frayed blue ribbon. He'd worried that they were love letters. From a stranger? Terrible. From his father? Worse. But instead they were from a woman named Minna Sprague who lived sometimes in New York City. From the letters he discovered she was Bertha Truitt's daughter; from the *New York Times* index at the public library he discovered that she was a well-known percussionist and singer. She was also black, which stunned him. Here was a picture of her with Duke Ellington; here, eyeing a seedy-looking Bing Crosby. The royalty that he'd longed to find, when he'd made his family tree, but closer. He would not ask his mother about her, because he wanted to keep the facts of Minna Sprague to himself.

Roy Truitt did not believe in ghosts, but he did in supernatural forces: duty, for instance, and guilt. In the dark he thought he could see things. Not the past, in the form of the dead, but the future, a life in which he did not live above a bowling alley. *Go to college*, said a voice in the dark. *Enlist*. My mother won't let me, he thought, but he knew it was also fear—not of war, or death, but living in close quarters among men who would see all the ways in which he was deficient, the way men always had: his father, the bowlers, the boys at school. His bookishness. His dislike of men. He thought again, *I could just go*. Go to New York. Find Minna Sprague. Just show up at some club, finding the listing in the paper. After it was over, introduce himself. *A kind of cousin*, he imagined saying, though officially he was her nephew. When he listened to her records he could never tell whether he wished she were singing to him, *I love you so dear it's murder*, or whether he wished to be her, singing to someone else. He understood it did not make sense, but he had this idea that he would one day meet Minna Sprague, and Minna Sprague would save his life. She would recognize that he, like she, did not belong in Salford, Massachusetts.

In the dark he turned to look at what he thought was the curtain, as though a ghost might be projected upon it. Nothing. Then he started to lower himself off the shelf. Where were the pins? Where was the cellar door? His mother, from somewhere in the center of the dark, said, "Do you see something?"

Nobody answered.

She said in a rough whisper, "I do."

A noise, an icy one, winding. That fraud, thought Roy, he's trying to terrify us all, though he felt a muffler of cold air wind around him. Roy was halfway off the shelf. Should he go? Then he heard the pins on lane five fall over, not one at a time but all at once, and this startled him so he dropped down and scattered the pins on his own lane.

"Lights!" called Cadey. "Lights!"

Their eyes had been so open in the dark, it was painful to be thrown into light.

The squealing noise was Jeptha. He was crying, and Cadey sat on the pinboys' shelf next to him, was taking the man into his lap. "Ssh," said Cadey to Jeptha. "Ssh. It's terrible, I know." He looked at Roy. "I don't think it's funny," he said.

"I don't—"

"Playing tricks on your family that way."

"*Roy*," said his mother.

"It wasn't Roy," said Arch. He could feel his father, he was sure of it. Even in the light the air was changed, was sharp with dissatisfaction.

"It was *you*?" his mother said to Roy.

Arch said, "I believe in ghosts."

"Lucky for you," said Cadey, "so do I."

At the end of the week, Saturday morning, Cadey arrived with a stack of photographs in a paper envelope and began to lay them out on the front counter, all four sides, dealing them out like some sort of game. He came behind the counter, where Margaret stood—you'd expect a man that big to give off heat but he was cold as an icebox, why he wore that sweater, his fingers as bloodless as stalactites. The Truitts were there. Margaret, who wanted Cadey to stay. Arch, who believed in ghosts. Roy, who did not believe in ghosts but whose innocence could be proven only by evidence of their existence.

"Where'd you develop these?" asked Arch.

"Drugstore," Cadey said sadly. Slap, slap, slap: the photos went down. It was true, you could see what wasn't there, namely women. In black and white the alley looked like a boys' reformatory.

A test. Was there an order to how the man arranged the snapshots? They became children again, who wanted to be first and right and rewarded. At first they could see no light in the pictures and then that was all they could see, glint and glance and gleam.

"I think I see it," said Arch, leaning over a picture of lane five. The ten pin, back right corner, seemed lifted off the ground, no ball or pinboy anywhere near, a pale curl of something at the top. He looked in every corner of the picture, trying to find a face, or a hand, trying to feel a presence. He pointed. "There."

"Nope," said Cadey.

"This one?" said Roy of a photo taken from outside the alley, looking in, planks of light coming off the window. He was a cynic, he reminded himself, but he could still feel the clammy cold that had wrapped around his neck in the dark.

"Left the flash on. *You* should be able to tell that."

"Here," said Margaret, picking up the oddest, quietest picture, a lost tin solider on his side—from this angle the oval plinth he stood on looked like liquid flooding from his feet.

"No," said Cadey, taking it from her hand, "I just liked the composition."

Jeptha wouldn't look. He was shaking his head. "It's a bad business," he said, "sniffing out ghosts. Don't believe in it."

"You're the one who told me!" said Arch, incensed. For the first time in his life he felt fatherless. He felt he might float into the air. "You said always!"

"No, no," said Jeptha. "Oh, you nice Archie. I don't believe in doctors, nor in the FBI, nor in prospecting for gold. I don't believe in looking."

Cadey nodded at that. "He's right. There's nothing. Sometimes no matter how you wish for it, eh, Mr. A?" He raked the photos together and tamped them into a pack.

"But the light!" said Margaret. In the black-and-white movies Margaret loved, when a person died the soul pulled away from the body perfect and monochromatic, as though death were a printing press, the body a plate, the ghost an impression. Of course you could photograph it.

"Smoke and flashbulbs and the angle of the overheads. Sorry," said Cadey. "Believe me, nobody's sorrier than me."

Then they all turned to the pins and hoped. Even Roy did, he closed his eyes and tried to see them fall over, pin by pin.

Arch said, "*I've* seen them." But had he? Had he ever actually been looking at the lane when the pins fell over? He could feel his organs disperse in his torso, a kind of sickness—a thorough bamboozlement. "Roy," he said. Roy shook his head.

Arch couldn't explain it. That ghost had belonged to *him;* it had felt personal and exact. All right, it might not have been his father—but he'd felt *something* flattening itself against the wall so it could sleep with Arch in his bed. (Maybe it was in his bed even now!) Maybe not even human, just a leak in the pipe of the afterlife that happened to drip drip drip on Arch's head.

Not bamboozlement. Or that particular sort: heartbreak. Someday somebody will love you but it'll just be a living girl. A whole string of them. Tough luck.

The Ghoster packed up his equipment that afternoon, the mirrors, the microphones. "It's too bad," said Margaret, as though she were at fault but didn't want to admit it. She gave him an Eskimo Pie from the machine. "Here."

"What is it?"

"Ice cream."

"I don't eat ice cream anymore," he said. He tried to hand it back. "Time to go."

"Eat this one," she said. "Here, I'll have one, too." She got a second for herself.

He unwrapped his and examined the chocolate coating. "They gave us Eskimo Pies in the service," he said. "Taste of home."

"You fought in the war?"

"A little. It's good. It's melty."

"That's why don't unwrap the whole thing. Here, take mine.

I'll take yours. There you are. Where will you go next? Nothing like an Eskimo Pie."

"Heard about a nineteenth-century defenestration in Paterson, New Jersey," he said. He had chocolate on his chin, and she knew the ice cream was as cold in his mouth as it was in hers, and that was something. "Over a card game. Seventy years ago. That death's got some age on it: that's what you need. I figure you get some time on yours, let the spirit come into his own."

"So you don't think it was Roy."

"Don't get me wrong," said Cadey. "I think he's a jackass. But jackassery and spirit activity may be found in the same place. Might even be the spirit that's inclining the boy to mischief. He's young yet. Fresh. The spirit, I mean. He'll show. I'll come back."

She didn't know whether she should defend Roy. He wasn't a jackass; he had other flaws that were worse. She said, "Arch would like that."

"Oh, *Arch*," said Cadey. "You tell Arch to keep a lookout for phenomena."

"Like what?"

He shoved the end of the Eskimo Pie in his mouth so the coating shattered, and wrote out a list.

> Cold spots
>
> Mist
>
> Flickering lights
>
> Inconsolable children
>
> Upset in dogs
>
> Moaning
>
> Misplaced items
>
> Ineradicable mold

Puddles of no known origin

Mushrooms

Somewhere a band playing

He signed it in a florid hand, *Love K. D.*, but he forgot to put down any forwarding information. Who was that love meant for, her or Arch or the ghosts?

"K. D.," she said.

"Yes, Margaret?"

She tried to come up with a question as serious as she sounded, though she'd only been reading his initials out for the first time, wondering what they stood for.

Ghosters, like birders, tiptoeing. Did you see a chickadee, a thrush, a suicide, an accidental decapitation? Don't scare 'em off with your big feet now. They are precious. We need them.

She tried, "What happened to your wife?"

He shook his head as though seeing it. "Terrible."

"She was murdered," said Margaret.

"No, ma'am. But she was sick a long time. One morning I was rubbing her feet, they were always cold, I rubbed and rubbed and the feet stayed cold and I understood that they wouldn't warm. Got up, called her mother, walked right out of the house and never went back." Then he said, "Everyone who dies is murdered."

After a moment, Margaret said, "I don't believe that's true. So you left her there, alone in bed?"

"I had done the hard part," said the man. "Walked away. So you see." He hefted the camera bag. "What about you," he said in a knowing voice. "You are alone, too."

"Do you think," she began. "Can you tell? If he's." She wasn't sure what she was about to say. "If my husband has entered the spirit realm." For the first time she wished it were true: she was tired of hoping.

He stared at her a long time, then said, "Yes, Margaret, he's dead."

"What does he say?" she asked in a little voice.

He caught her hand in his. He was always doing that, as though her hands were butterflies, to be cupped in his own. Then she knew everything about him, the way he held her hand. That man did not believe in ghosts. What a relief, to understand that he knew nothing about the dead.

He was a fraud, but Margaret had a weakness for fraudulence. Fake cakes in the bakery windows lovelier than any real slice, her husband, her Saturday afternoon movie matinees, the packets of saccharine she sprinkled on her cereal.

He said, "Bertha would want women here. You need them, anyhow. Get in some girls to set the pins."

"Girls?" said Margaret.

"I can't talk to the dead," said Cadey. "No man can."

"All right," she said wryly.

His whole face went angular with hurt feelings. His eyes were isosceles triangles. "Really, Margaret," he said. "You don't know. You believe in God and I don't mock you."

"Believing in God is not believing in ghosts," she said, but how did he know she believed in God?

She believed in God for the same reason anybody does: it is unbearable to think that our private thoughts are truly private.

I HAD TO TAKE HER
APART TO MAKE HER FIT

Apart from his accidental electrocution at the hands of the strength tester, Jeptha Arrison had never been injured on the job. Remarkable for a pinbody, right there where the whole calamity of bowling occurred. He'd never taken a ball to the head or a pin to the ankle; had never strained his shoulder sending the balls back on the return; had contracted no infections of the skin or lungs or blood. If you overlooked the tremors that he hid in his pockets, he was in astoundingly fine shape for a man who'd done manual labor all his life. But setting was precise or it was nothing. When he closed his eyes Jeptha could see the pins and their order but his body could not make it so.

He was born in a bowling alley, and he planned to die in one.

That's what he said to his friend William Burling Jeter Jr., who claimed he was the oldest man in Salford, and who was Margaret Truitt's most hated customer.

"You could do it," said William Burling Jeter Jr.

"I *will*," said Jeptha. "That has been my plan all along."

Meanwhile he would listen to the lectures of William Burling Jeter Jr., which was itself a kind of death. Jeet was certainly the oldest man in Truitt's Alleys, a loiterer, a bore, who never bowled but hung around. He had igneous features, hardened, fluid. His dark eyes glinted amid his freckles.

"I did my service for the Union," Jeet said. "Nearly too old for that, too!"

"Are you even *American*?" Margaret asked. Oh, she hated him. She thought he had a kind of Japanese-y look, but that might have been only old age. His accent, too, seemed more geriatric than geographic. "Where did you come from? I don't remember you."

"Been here since the beginning," he said. "I knew 'em all. I was here when Bertha Truitt made her entrance and her exit, and all the acts between. Honey," he said to Margaret. "Come on, honey, smile for me."

"No thank you," she said.

"Some hot nuts, then? Give me a scoop of hot nuts."

"Do you have a nickel?"

He waved away the question. "I'm the oldest man in Salford."

"I doubt it."

"You doubt it? Who then?"

"Not you, is all I know. Jeptha, maybe."

"I'm a youngster," said Jeptha, wishing the two of them would stop bickering. It was keeping him alive and that was not his wish.

"He is not the oldest man in Salford!" said Margaret.

William Burling Jeter Jr. laughed with happiness. "Then bring him to me."

"The oldest man in Salford is dying," Margaret said. "He's in a hospital. Or he's in bed. The oldest man in Salford doesn't have time to waste in a bowling alley, begging for hot nuts."

"I'm not begging, honey," said William Burling Jeter Jr. "I'm just fine. Somebody else will get me my hot nuts."

"They're *mine*," she said, "so I don't know who."

"That nice Archie," suggested Jeptha.

He always did, that nice Archie, that profligate kid. Meanwhile Margaret wasn't going to smile for William Burling Jeter Jr. unless she knew who he really *was*. She turned to the old man, but his face was amused and aggravating, so she just said again, "They're *my* hot nuts."

"I know it, honey," Jeet said. "You hold 'em close. Hey Jep. I ever tell you I saw Sally Rand?" Only William Burling Jeter Jr. could make a story about a burlesque dancer dull—he began in the lobby, and lingered by the refreshment stand—Bud orange soda, made in Watertown, Massachusetts; Necco Wafers, made in Cambridge, Massachusetts, brought—if you didn't know!—by the explorer Mac-Millan to the Arctic so he could bribe the Esquimaux. It took a long time to get to Sally Rand herself. "I believe she was not nekkid behind her bubble but garbed in long underwear, still I'll be damned—Jep, hey Jep—hey, hey. Help!"

Midafternoon on a Saturday. The bowling stilled slowly. There is always shouting in a bowling alley: you want a beer, it's time to go, your mother's looking for you. Now the place fell quiet.

The silence scared William Burling Jeter Jr. even though he was the one who'd sounded the alarm. "Look," he said to Margaret Truitt.

Jeptha lay on the wooden bench. There was a tidiness to his body, ankles aligned, hands folded on his stomach, which didn't look like sleep.

What happened?

Nothing!

I'll call an ambulance.

Too late.

You sure?

I'm not.

Things went on in Jep's head all this while like that glass paperweight Dr. Sprague once gave him, *millefiori*, a thousand flowers, all shot through with color. *Mille-feuille*, a pastry, a thousand leaves. A thousand! Look at Jep, thought Jep of Jep. There's French in his head yet.

Young man, Jeet said to Jeptha, and that's when Jeptha Arrison knew he was really dying: he was a young man to somebody. Jeptha could hear the minuscule suction of Jeet's false teeth against his palate, could feel the cold velvet of his hand on Jeptha's throat. Young man. Jeptha Arrison. His own clothing being rearranged by a bunch of hands. His lungs seizing up.

Don't move him, said a boy's voice, and he hoped it would be the last thing he heard.

We have to! said a woman.

I loved you all, thought Jeptha, *with a few notable exceptions*. He wished he'd had the gumption to say it aloud. By gumption he meant life. He was dead.

But he could still hear. It was the last transmission of the earth into the head of Jeptha Arrison.

Why had Jeptha stayed at the alleys all those years he wasn't paid, was taken for granted? He was awaiting. What he reckoned, and what he always reckoned, was that Bertha Truitt was a chrononaut. A time traveler. He had read about it in a magazine. What else explains her apparition in the cemetery, discovered by a stranger, rich as Hector's pup? She fell through a rip in time. An empty cemetery. Then a woman in the frost. Three Berthas: Bertha; beneath her, a Bertha-shaped piece of dead grass; above her, a Bertha-shaped rift in the clouds. Where did she come from? The past. Then once she'd founded Truitt's, sometimes she would just disappear. He had written them down, those times. All of April 1911. Part of both June and July 1912. Seven hours of November 13, 1915. Off and on through the war. The only explanation, Jeptha believed, was time travel.

I don't remember her being gone.

You were not always there, Lu. She would bring things from the future: coins stamped with the wrong date. From the past, too, stale cakes, candles melted from the speed of decades. She came singing back on the wires—not like a ghost, nothing like a ghost. Like pneumatic tubes, whizzing faster than other people, and meanwhile Jeptha would be her flag, waving *here, here.*

Jeptha, LuEtta had said. You know she's dead.

We know she died but we don't know she's dead.

There's a stone in the cemetery.

But Bertha Truitt would have pointed out this truth: a stone in a cemetery is only ever evidence of a stone in a cemetery.

"Damnation," said Jeet.

"Who do we call?" said Margaret.

"His wife," said Jeet. "They live in Revere. They own an arcade on the boardwalk."

"Jeptha has a *wife*?" said Roy Truitt. "Wonder of wonders."

"Of course," said William Burling Jeter Jr. "Her name is Lu, LuEtta."

M argaret didn't call LuEtta Mood Arrison (really? *really* they'd married?); she let the hospital do it. She assumed that LuEtta would come by to collect Jeptha's effects, though she discovered he had not left anything behind, not a lunch pail, not a toothpick. She might come for his back pay, though Margaret could not remember the last time she'd paid him at all.

Still, she dug out a scrapbook that Bertha had kept. It was slap-dash, as nearly all of Bertha's handiwork was, but it included a clipping of the Salford *Bugle* the year LuEtta beat Minnie Barden in the trolley tournament. There she was on the front page, a rangy woman with thick hair and a heroic jaw.

"Good grief," said Roy. Then, "There's hope for all of us."

"Even you," said Margaret.

"Thank you, Mother." He flipped through the scrapbook and then said, idly, "I'm going to enlist."

"You're seventeen."

"When I'm eighteen."

"No," she said. "You'll take on the alley. Be the boss."

"You're the boss."

She said, "No I am not. It's not right. You'll take it, Roy. You're clever. You're a very clever boy."

"Is that a qualification for the job?"

She couldn't tell whether she was supposed to be insulted or not, which was probably a sign that she wasn't clever, but then again she'd never thought of herself as clever, and so why be insulted? Not clever but loving and tough and good with a dollar. She'd kept them afloat for a while now and her arms were aching with it.

"We need you here," she said. "To run the family business. Oldest son. How it's worked since the beginning of time."

"But *is* it," said Roy.

"Is it what?"

"The family business."

What had he heard? "Oh, for heaven's sake," she said, in too calm a voice. It was her habit when cornered to fuss with the candy in the glass counter, as though a nurse with incubating infants. "You're not allowed to join the army." Then she looked at him. "He was your father and he loved you," she said.

But Roy hadn't asked about love, and he knew his father was his father. It was the single fact he knew for sure about the man. "Anyhow," he said, "we need more pinsetters, now Jeptha's gone. You could ask Arch."

"Arch isn't suited." She shook a paper sack full of Mary Janes into one of the apothecary jars, was thinking of eating one, how sweet and chewy they were, thinking of how you could never get all the wax paper off and had to extract it later, masticated and damp, from your back molars. For Arch it was drink and for Nahum gambling and for Margaret it was candy, but she had strength of character, she stopped herself, though all she wanted was to eat all the candy in the world.

She handed Roy a Mary Jane. They were molasses flavored. She said, "I'll hire someone."

Under a pillow. Under a bed. Pieces at first, and then all of you, as you came into being, and then pieces of you again. At the kitchen table. In the old toilet. Beneath a bowling alley approach (lane one). That was good, close to family, you could hear them overhead though you are only a doll and you know it. Only a doll means you are ignored more and caressed more than any other member of the family. In the coat closet. In a bed, at last, under the eiderdown, pawed and beloved. In the bathtub, damp-bottomed. In a chair, in the basement, in a chair, in the basement, under the eiderdown, in the bathtub, in the basement. Wired to a cast-iron column. Then higher on the column. On a glass counter, nothing worse, nobody knows how to take care of you. In a suitcase. In a kitchen, in a suitcase on a trolley, under the ground. Love and lack of love and love again.

You can tell when you're underground even if you're also in a suitcase, even if you're made of wood and cloth. Sea air. In a penny arcade. In a glass coffin. (Not a coffin, a box. What's the difference? Dolls don't have coffins.) All along, one arm off, back on, one elbow broken, one foot on backward, eye gone from abuse, mouth half rubbed off, breast torn, brains leaking out. People think you're funny. People think you're unsettling. They are dismayed by your proportions. They want to lift your skirt. They don't want to think about what they'll find there. Do you have organs? A bowling ball, a small one, carved into the shape of a heart. Rubber, of course. Rubber and wood and cloth. How can they string you up so, when you're made of movement and clatter.

Sea air, sea air, years of it. You are the mascot of Arrison's Arcade, on Revere Beach. Suitcase, trolley, subway, trolley—all the same line, all the same car, just above and below and above again. Not carried kindly but with competence. Swung down the street and LuEtta Pickersgill Mood Arrison sets you down in the early morning in front of what was Truitt's.

LuEtta Pickersgill Mood Arrison's hair had gone roan with age. She was tall and lean, one of those women in her fifties whose figures had flattened, but glamorously. She gave the suitcase a pat and fought the urge to peer at the doll of Truitt one last time—she had taken its presence in her penny arcade for granted for so long she no longer knew how she felt about it, though when Jeptha had brought it home ten years before she'd wanted to give it a Viking funeral: obliterate it, but with respect.

Jeptha was dead, had gone to the hospital because he was dead, the Salford Hospital where he'd slept beneath Bertha Truitt's bed; then he had gone to the Salford Cemetery, where he owned a plot next to his first wife. He and LuEtta had lived these past years near the beach. They owned a little arcade that included eight Skee-Ball alleys, which LuEtta occasionally ran for the pleasure of her customers, *op op op*, center ring every ball. At Arrison's Arcade you could walk away with evidence of your good time: a gleamingly damp fragrant strip from the photo booth; a metal token stamped with a message you chose one letter at a time from the ID machine; a penny smashed into a lozenge, on one side raised letters that said SOUVENIR OF REVERE BEACH, on the other a faint elongated leftover Lincoln.

Carmine, her son, was stationed at Fort Benning in Georgia.

With Jeptha's death LuEtta was officially alone. She'd lost plenty of people—Truitt, Moses, Jeptha, and first and always Edith—but there had always been somebody else hanging around, heart-in-hand, asking for love. She'd thought then she was grateful. Now she was ashamed to discover how much she liked solitude, silence, the loneliness that Truitt had talked about as a pleasure.

It was two hours before opening. She planned to set the suitcase with the doll of Truitt down in the tiled trapezoid in front of the doors, to escape before seeing another living person. But as she came up Mims Avenue, she saw a slumping, smoking figure rattling his keys in front of the door. Not Joe Wear, though for a moment— Maybe time travel *was* possible, Jeptha. A teenaged kid. He had the look of somebody who'd been out all night and had come to sneak home before his mother found out. He looked up and saw her and gave a tired smile.

All right then: she'd deliver it, in Jeptha's name.

"Hey," she called. "You're one of the Truitt boys."

"Arch," he whispered, wincing up at the windows over the alley.

She nodded. They stood together on the worn-down black-and-white tile spelling out TRUITT. She would not look through the window; she handed the boy the case. She must have seemed to him an apparition. "From Jeptha," she whispered.

"What is it?"

"Look."

He balanced the case on one knee—it was difficult, he was still full of beer—and opened it, and saw the battered avid face, and though five minutes before he would not have remembered the doll on his own, he felt that swoony sensation of childhood unexpectedly returned: as though she'd fallen through time, back into his arms. Ever since Arch had been stood up by a ghost, he'd been unmoored, had twice been found by the police passed out in places he shouldn't have been—first in the passenger seat of a truck owned by his friend Phillip, who was busy stealing a rocking chair off some-body's back porch; then in the white leather examination chair of his girlfriend's dentist father at four in the morning. But this doll. He was drunk. He thought it might reform him. He looked up to thank the apparition—LuEtta was right, that was what she seemed like—but she had already gone.

LuEtta Mood Arrison was nearly to the trolley station when she thought she should have asked the kid to let her take a look inside Truitt's. Empty, she might have been able to bear it. Maybe Jeptha was right, and on the other side of some door at the alley, Bertha Truitt was straightening her clothing. Flying through time will knock the hat right off your head! It will twist your skirts! It will unbutton everything! Get yourself straight: then open the door and look for the people who love you.

Except of course everyone was gone. Leviticus dead, Jeptha dead, all of the cats of her personal acquaintance, her daughter gone. Why would Bertha time travel *here*? They had already missed her. Go back further. Use all your celestial stereoptical gizmos to find the right spot. Your darlings are alive, plenty of future ahead of them. It isn't too late to change things.

Don't go back for her, LuEtta. Remember what happened the last time you looked.

BETTY AMONG THE PINS

Minna had a trio. Margaret remembered her saying so but didn't know what that meant until one Saturday matinee at the Gearheart Theater, when she watched a wartime comedy featuring some dumb comedy team, a fat man and a thin man in suits. In a musical number set at a USO show, there was Minna in a cocktail dress, playing the drums behind a bass player and saxophone player, and singing: *Swing me, Daddy, to a reveille beat*. A trio. Three of them. A family. She watched Minna greedily, and though she knew it was impossible she believed in some way that Minna was able to see her in the Gearheart, would be able to sense her love. In the credits: Minna Sprague and her Canadian Cats. It was shocking to see a woman drum the way Minna did, with rapture and abandon. That was the province of men.

Her name out front! Margaret was proud: Minna, Minnabean, her dreamchild. She went to see the movie six times. Oh, mothering would be easy if it could be accomplished by cinematic means! Look at Minna twenty feet tall on the movie screen, safe and singing, beautiful. Meanwhile her boys, the Truitt boys, were slipping away from her. Roy was threatening the army. Soon it might be his choice.

Maybe he should do it. He was a boy both hard and soft—hard in his affection, for her, for his brother. Also untested. Sickly of spirit in some way. Anybody might take advantage of him. She supposed she had coddled him, by employing him as a pinsetter. He rarely spoke to anyone. Archie was soft where his brother was hard, and hard where he was soft. Arch would break a girl's heart and then cry to himself when he'd done it. He would kiss his old ma and then stay out all night. He drank. He drank so much that was the only way you could put it. Not, *he drank too much* or *he drank too often*. He drank.

They'd both been coddled, Margaret.

You spend a while thinking about ghosts and everything felt like a ghost, even your conscience whispering in your ear.

Now here was Minna, out in the world, and so happy. Her hair hot-combed glossy and straight, the front in bangs, the back caught in a snood. Her mouth wide and toothy. Of course it was a movie, but Margaret didn't believe anyone could playact at happiness. Not like that. Not happiness that made other people happy.

Margaret placed a newspaper ad in the *Bugle*. *Work for girls pinsetting. Please apply to Truitt's Alleys.* That was how they got seventeen-year-old Betty Graham, known as Cracker for her last name and because it suited her. She was sweet, but just, with a mouth kept bright with lipstick and a laugh like a rusty gate. People loved to make her laugh: nothing that unbecoming could be fake. Before the war, she'd worked at the Grover Cronin department store in Waltham, in Intimate Apparel. With gas rationing she needed a job closer to home.

"Do you bowl?" Margaret asked.

"*Yes*," she lied. She waited to be quizzed. She'd memorized scoring, jargon, dimensions of pins and balls.

"All right," said Margaret, "you'll do. Arch will show you around."

Cracker looked across the alley. There was a boy in striped coveralls sitting on a ledge at the end of the lanes. His hair was dark red. He had a dimpled chin and a cowlick she wanted to brush down.

"Ah, there he is," said Margaret, pointing in the other direction.

The boy she meant had been sitting at a table by himself, reading a magazine. He looked up and smiled. It was a smile of such charm and breadth that Cracker felt instantly insulted. She hated charm, *male* charm, unoriginal and automatic as it was. Margaret beckoned him over.

"This is Betty," said Margaret.

"Hi, Betty. I'm Arch."

Up close he had a newsprint smudge on one cheek, clean hands with bitten nails. You could see adolescence wasn't quite done with him, not at the jaw and shoulder line, though his blue eyes were grown-up, and tired, and fond of both her and himself. As though he was glad for her, that she got to talk to him. Lucky girl!

She did not like him.

"Betty's going to pinset. Show her around."

That made him frown. "Surely Roy—"

"Roy's working," said Margaret. "I'm asking you."

One woman made a difference: one woman brought more women. Cracker's friends came to watch her skip from pit to pit in her ballet slippers and then—because Margaret Truitt insisted—in a pair of old black boots with steel toes and ankle supports. It wasn't that Nahum Truitt had ever put a sign in the window that said NO WOMEN, not that he had changed anything about the place, not that once Nahum had disappeared Margaret had done a thing to discourage any particular woman from coming across the threshold. It was only the usual story: a low place that has contained only men for a good long time is deadly dull to most women. You could take one look through the plate glass window and see for yourself that Truitt's offered nothing that couldn't be had elsewhere, in better and tidier company.

Once there were a handful of girls coming to bowl regularly, their mothers came, too. They needed some cheap entertainment and conversation, to visit some minor violence upon inanimate objects. They watched Cracker Graham set their pins and laugh while she did it.

She was laughing at the beauty of bowling.

The beauty surprised her: she hadn't known. Maybe it wasn't beautiful from the front of the house, where you'd face people's posteriors, the soles of their lagging feet. Maybe it wasn't beautiful at the foul line, where you could see only the bowlers on either side of you, left, right, yourself. On the pinbody's ledge, you saw the whole chorus line of bowlers, intent, sizing up the pins, the lane, though it's the seventh frame of their third string and the pins are the same, the lane is the same. They touch the ball to the underside of their chins, or they hold it on one hip, like a Greek statue. They bite their lips. They approach, and deliver, and the ball comes down the lane, and the bowlers hope or despair. And they do this not in unison but not out of it either. Candlepin is hard; perfection is impossible; and yet some people are devoted to it. Cracker might have once found it ridiculous.

It was terrible to be only attendant to the beauty. She had to learn how to bowl herself. She needed a tutor.

Years later, Roy Truitt would wonder how his mother had managed to keep him from enlisting. He was eighteen years old! His decisions were his own! No, they weren't, not then: his decisions were his mother's. He wasn't sure how she accomplished this. Radio waves. Hypnosis. The old-fashioned maternal apparatus, guilt, helplessness, guile. Candy. Arch made his own decisions, entirely bad, and Margaret didn't care. Arch went out; Roy stayed home, listening to the Minna Sprague records he kept a secret from his mother, as she had kept Minna a secret from him. He'd bought himself a little player that could be stowed under the bed. *One more month*, thought Roy, *one more year*. He had registered for the draft and hoped it would take him. Meanwhile he'd turned himself into machinery: he could drop pins right-handed onto the deck perfectly while not losing his place in the book he was reading.

"Hey," said the girl his mother had hired. "Roy. I have a favor to ask."

He looked up from his book, volume five of a seven-volume history of the last war. Her voice was grave but her face was merry.

"Will you teach me how to bowl?"

"Sure," he said. "What's your average?"

"Zero," she said.

"You're either bad at math or bowling."

"I'm excellent at math. Zero pins divided by zero games equals an average of zero."

"You've *never* bowled?" asked Roy. The girl had rakishly rolled the cuffs of her coveralls, both wrist and ankle, and he found himself interested in her. Without looking he sensed that the bowler on his lane was winding up to roll the last ball of the frame.

She said, in a confidential voice, "I'm a quick study. Try me."

Roy Truitt was underground, had been underground for years, so subterraneanly turned around that he could not figure out which way to look for light. Here was Cracker Graham. She was not a beam slanting down from heaven, not the gilded edge of the rising sun, but she'd do: she was the glow in a darkened theater above a door:

EXIT. "Excuse me," he said—something he'd never before said in his pinsetting life—and he hopped down to his lane.

Pinsetting was dull. He had fallen years ago into the habit of pretending people were watching him, stopwatches in hands, timing him and marveling, though who in real life would actually pay attention? Now someone was. He plucked the pins up and set them on their marks on the plate. He assessed in his head: the center of each pin had to be exactly one foot away from the center of its fellows. Then he rolled the balls back along the return to the waiting bowler, one-two-three, waltz time. By then Cracker Graham was in her own lane, setting the pins, too slowly but with care.

"OK," he said when she'd finished. "Let us commence your bowling education."

They met Saturday mornings, before the alleys opened and the leagues came in; they started on lane one and worked their way to lane eight before they reset any pins. Cracker would have rather bowled in the crowded afternoon, surrounded by strangers: bowling, like dancing, was one of those things more intimate in a crowd.

"Your form is better than fair," said Roy.

"Are you flirting with me?" she asked.

"I don't know how to flirt," he answered.

Still, he was a good teacher, patient, scientific. "Here's the handshake grip," he told her. "Here's the semihandshake. Here's the overshoot." She'd imagined he would get behind her in the way of a lecherous golf instructor, his body shadowing hers, arm to arm, leg to leg, his breath tucked behind her right ear. Instead, he stood next to her, appraised her stance, and lectured.

"It's the dance of the pins and the ball," he said. "That's candlepin. Roll the ball and wait and see—the pins jump one way, you got a seven-ten split, you think the ball's gone, but then it hits the wall and comes back and maybe you have a strike. Nothing is for sure. Look down the lane. Read it. Some other houses oil the approaches to soup up the scores. We don't soup up the scores. OK, so roll. Good. Good. All right, you see how that broke at the end? That's fine, to have a breaking ball, but it means you need to adjust. You can pin bowl, or spot bowl, or a combination. Now it's time to play the wood. It's trickier than you think. Trickier than most people think. What's so funny?"

"You really don't know how to flirt."

At that he gave a dimpled smile of such promise any flirt would have paid money to learn it. "I told you," he said.

"You teach me to bowl," she said, setting the ball on her shoulder, her opposite hip cocked, "I'll teach you how to flirt."

"As though *you* know how."

She laughed. "Very good. See, you're improving already."

He looked at the pins uncomfortably. The four horsemen, right, three pin knocked over in front: if she hit the pin on the left, it would go spinning without touching the standing pins; straight on it might do nothing; on the left, it should convert the spare. That he understood. Flirtation flummoxed him, but so did ordinary conversation, which only sometimes obeyed the rules of physics. He looked at Cracker Graham, who seemed like a capable translator.

"Don't you have a boyfriend?" he asked.

"I did. He joined the navy. Just shipped out."

"And you're not waiting for him? Shame, shame."

"I don't wait," said Cracker.

"What if *I* joined the service?"

She looked at him. There'd been no question of waiting for Davey Cotter, who'd taken her virginity after-hours at Grover Cronin, in Intimate Apparel, and had apologized afterward, as though he'd accidentally eaten her lunch. She'd vowed to take it exactly that seriously. Roy was something else again. Roy was gravity. He was a big kid, with a kind of galumphing shape that Cracker found comforting and alluring, as though he might be her palisade. Davey Cotter had been a little guy with neat curls. Roy Truitt was large, both soft and muscular, with his uncombed red hair and battalion of cowlicks.

"I could try," she said.

She was what he needed, he understood: cemented to the bowling alley by duty, he needed an even greater duty to blast him free.

Early morning, Margaret in the alley alone, she thought. Unlock the door, lock herself in. Her shoulders went down. She was capable and by herself, nobody angling for a favor or money. Then, in the shadows over lane seven, legs dangling down. The deck was empty of pins. Four legs: two people sitting up on the ledge together. She had a sense that Arch had snuck girls in before, but late at night. After sunrise it seemed more debauched. As though they heard her think this, the boy dropped down, put his hand up to help the girl. They sat right down on the metal deck. It made Margaret's flanks cold to see. By then she'd walked to the foul line, picked up a ball. Not Arch: Roy.

They didn't hear her. Roy sat on a hip, one knee aimed at the girl, the other leg behind him, his foot in the gutter. They kissed. It wasn't their first kiss, Margaret could tell.

Margaret was a moviegoer. She went by herself to the Salford Theater every Saturday afternoon, hoping to see Minna again, contenting herself with love stories. The movies bruised her, then pressed on the bruise. That moment when the celluloid lovers, in profile, looked at each other, a minuscule tick of their heads, *oh!*, as though a kiss were something that needed to be tripped, like a bomb, another moment of suspense before the kiss. The mechanics of movie kisses were nothing that Margaret had ever experienced; movie kisses are all in profile but your own kisses are head-on. Movie kisses looked like they'd hurt. She couldn't get enough of them. They made her feel alive—not in any expansive resurrected way, but assessed, her pulse taken, a rubber mallet to the knee that made her kick.

Not this kiss.

Did it make Roy Truitt feel alive? Lifted from his misery, pulled into the air? He wasn't sure. It was his first day of kissing if not his first kiss. He had a sensation of watching his mouth from the back of his skull. Was that her tongue? No (he would realize in a week), her lower lip, which he seemed to have been thoughtfully sucking on for several minutes. For years he would suddenly remember that—he'd sucked on a human lip, believing it a tongue—and his brain would contract in unhappiness.

Why *is* he doing that? wondered Cracker, who had kissed plenty. She thought of Davey Cotter in Intimate Apparel, rubbing his steel-wool chin across hers, thrilling her, irking her, *ouch*, no, this (*too much thinking, Betty*) is better—

Roy wrenched his mouth away; Roy's mouth was *wrenched* away, bitingly—and he shrieked, and at the end of the lane Margaret Truitt shrieked: without thinking, she had bowled. A fast ball, sixty miles per hour. It struck Roy in the ankle, which was lucky. A bowling ball in the wrong place could rupture you. Could make you a genealogical dead end.

He was going, he was going, he was headed out the door. What his mother didn't know: this time he'd already packed his bag.

⁊

He never went to war, Roy. He never married. He wasn't the sort of guy for whom love trumped everything, who would have let his broken ankles mortar his affection for Cracker Graham. Indeed, whenever he saw her, his ankles ached. They'd been trained. Roy Truitt always learned his lesson. He would have made a good soldier, or bomb-sniffing dog.

Good thing he never married her. Shame Arch did.

4

ALL OVER YOU

On the boat to Italy, Arch dreamt. His mother was right, he was sleepy, congenitally, chronically. This was an advantage on the boat, the USS *Montrose*, which was so overcrowded the soldiers stood, lay, sat in shifts. Eight hours of each. A lot of the guys got anxious when it came for their turn in the belowdecks bunks. Their chance to sleep: What if they couldn't? Standing came next. Some of them, just out of bed, fainted from exhaustion. You could sleep when you sat down, but if you overindulged in sitting sleep, you might be too rested to sleep on your sleeping shift.

Not Arch. He dreamt in any position. He could fall asleep as a party trick. He made bets. "How can we tell you're not faking?" his shipmates asked, but once he'd fallen asleep—in seconds—there was no question. Look at him. He didn't snore. His mouth didn't hang open. He looked bigger asleep than awake, as though an equestrian statue, except a bunk instead of a horse. Standing he could doze and not tip over, and then he'd dream of otherworldly quotidian things, a grocery store that sold pulled teeth, a trolley line that took a sudden left turn into the ocean. Sitting dreams were about the unmet war: having to shoot only to discover that your rifle operated like a concertina, with buttons and bellows. Prone, he dreamt of his family—Roy, his mother, his long-gone father. He dreamt of Cracker Graham riding a penny farthing through the bowling alley, and wrote to her to say so.

All his life, insomniac friends would regard him with jealousy, his wakeful wife with loneliness, his children, alone and conscious, pining. He was the object of more hard feelings over his sleepfulness than any other of his bad habits.

Sometimes he thought Italy didn't wake him up. He dreamt through it. What else could explain setting up a hospital in a deserted fairgrounds, an enormous allegorical statue of a seated woman watching over him as he humped sacks of sugar into the kitchen? The Prima Mostra Triennale delle Terre Italiane d'Oltremare di Napoli—the first triennial exhibition of overseas Italian territories. First and last and never recurring no matter the interval. The allegorical woman in the central hall was Ethiopia, conquered by the Italians in 1935, already returned to Haile Selassie by the time Arch passed by her with his sacks of sugar—Arch, who had never met a statue he didn't suspect of being animate, biding its time, no matter how big, how misshapen, how dead-eyed or spraddle-limbed. Wax figures were alive to Arch, department store mannequins, the tractor-pelvised women of Henry Moore. Ethiopia would at any moment stand up and snuff Arch out with her helmet as though he were a candle.

The Mostra delle Terre Italiane d'Oltremare had been designed to strike awe, like the harpoon in Ethiopia's hand. Arch had been staring up at her when he met Joan, who had sidled up beside him and whispered, "Look on my works, you mighty, and despair."

"Ye," said Arch. "Ye mighty."

"Yeah, thanks," said Joan. She wore the brown seersucker uniform of the hospital staff. She looked like she should be doling out chocolates at a Fannie Farmer's. She said, "I stole something."

The uniform came with a wraparound skirt, in case the dress got dirty, reversible, in case the skirt did. She pulled aside one flap to display a white tablecloth.

"There are hundreds of them," she said. "I can show you where."

"I don't need a tablecloth. Where?"

They'd come ashore at the same time but hadn't seen each other—later Arch would speak of *storming a beach*, but Naples didn't need storming. There was nobody there. Even an abandoned cottage is eerie; even an abandoned bicycle. They waded, waddled, onto the sand, then began to set up the hospitals in the fairgrounds—three hospitals, plus another down the road at the thermal spa.

Joan was from Wyoming, a place that Arch had no notions about at all. She had brown hair with severe bangs, and a mole at the corner of her mouth that Arch found tragic: beautiful in its way but also unsettling. He never stopped noticing it. There was something mean about her that drew him, a wisp of cruelty that suggested she might push him down a flight of stairs just to see the look on his face. He went with her to the vast kitchens of the Imperial Hall, to the gleaming metal cupboards in the back. Hundreds of tablecloths in stacks.

"Take one," she said.

"I don't have a table."

"So what? You got a mother? Your mother got a table?" She kicked him in the calf; she was a kicker. "Don't be a chump."

"I'm not a chump."

"Don't be one is what I'm telling you."

In one of the outbuildings they came upon the dioramas celebrating the Italian military: boats, and mountains, and fields of battle, populated by miniature Italians in uniform. They each kidnapped half a dozen tiny servicemen.

What Arch really wanted: one of the many of commercial-grade espresso machines still wrapped in plastic, the Italian cousins of Bertha Truitt's Stanley Steamer, though how would he smuggle it out? Could he ever get it to work? He stole other things: covered silver dishes, pepper grinders, tablecloths to wrap them in.

Why did he steal? Because Joan made him. Because he wanted things. He *wanted* things. For revenge, said Joan, against Mussolini. Because he was frightened of war and needed talismans. Because the war would end and he needed evidence that he had been there. Because he needed evidence that he wasn't entirely good: the one sure way of dying in war was being a saint. The shifty would survive.

Because nobody was looking at him. Because Joan was looking at him.

They drove from Napoli to Sienna in a jeep, and the ash off Mount Vesuvius silvered their hair and eyebrows.

"This is how we'll look when we're old," said Joan. "Oh dear."

Arch pulled to the side of the road, beneath a tree with dripping lopsided pink blossoms that looked like lungs. They appraised each other.

"Yes," said Joan, deciding. She was the one who unfolded the blanket on the side of the road. They could feel the dropped pink blossoms beneath them, hear the ticking of the jeep. She was little. That was clearer as they lay down.

"What if the volcano erupts?" asked Arch, "I mean, fully," and Joan answered with a dirty laugh.

"Tell it not to," she said. "Take off your pants."

Later, he'd discover that he'd taken only silver lids and no bottoms to those covered dishes, and he told himself that this was because he'd felt guilty: he'd punished himself ahead of time. As he stole them, though, he did not feel guilty. He felt righteous. To feel guilty would have meant he was himself, watching himself do wrong. Deep down, said Joan, you're a good guy.

What about you, deep down?

Ah! I'm bottomless.

He was not himself. He stole because he was a thief.

A̲ll this time Cracker Graham wrote to him with news from home. Roy had left the alley, the apartment, Salford entirely.

> *I thought your mother would fire me, but she says with Roy gone she needs more hands anyhow, so here I am. I don't hear from Roy. I can't write to him because he'll have nothing to do with me, so here I am writing to you. I am a stinker.*

Cracker Graham was at the heart of it all, why his mother had broken Roy's ankle. When Arch had first seen Cracker in her coveralls and ballet slippers, he thought he might ask her out. Then he found out she was a year older than he was. He'd never considered going out with anyone older, and for a while he lost interest, and once he'd come around Roy was interested and that was that.

The letters back and forth were the longest conversation they'd ever had. Arch's stories were full of Italy, and no Italians; full of the war but no people; full of the bowling alley and full of Cracker Graham herself. He wrote everything he remembered about her: her father was dead. She hated the taste of peanuts. She loved egg salad. When she braided her curly hair, the plaits hung to her shoulders; loose, it came only to her chin. One day he'd been bowling with his girlfriend, Angela Cedrone, a little drunk, and when he saw Cracker he wanted her, Cracker, to throw him, Arch, over her shoulder and carry him off. (Angela was a tough girl. How else would he get away?) In a few months of writing he was signing his letters *love*.

That was all it took for Cracker to fall in love with Arch, for Arch to fall in love with Cracker.

How much of it was imaginary? They felt, reading each other's letters, known; they believed that being known made them over into their best selves. They confessed.

> *I am a childish person. I was always jealous of Roy. I used to give away my heart too easily.*
>
> *I cannot wait to see you. Everyone else bores me. I want to wrap you in cotton to keep you safe.*

It was for love of Cracker that he slept with Joan (he told himself): he wanted to make sure he wasn't making the love up. You had to test things: love, bravery, loyalty, you had to make sure your versions of these things were up to the task. Every time he slept around—and he did, all through their marriage—he thought of it as a test: *if after this I see that I am not in love with my wife, I'll leave her and end her misery.* But he was always in love with his wife. She didn't seem to think this news was as good as he did, but she was entangled, too.

HOW I CARRY ON

Broken-ankled Roy Truitt had gone, at last, to New York to look for Minna Sprague. He felt like a delinquent, but people saw his crutches and smiled at him, offered him bottles of Coke and spare sandwiches: they'd been told not to waste food for the sake of soldiers, and here one was, or so they believed. In the listings of *The New Yorker* he saw Minna Sprague's name and went to see her sing at a basement club in the West Village. He had never been to a jazz club, he had only ever heard music by himself, in listening booths or his bedroom at home when nobody else was there, had no idea that it was strange, this entirely mixed crowd, or that because Minna Sprague refused to perform in front of segregated audiences, this was the only place in Manhattan she played. She wore a white dress with cutouts under the arms that showed her lovely triceps, the better to swing her drumsticks, though mostly she sang. By then Roy had read the archive of the Salford *Bugler*, had combed the census, and had come to the conclusion that they were in no way related.

Still, he stood in the smoke and listened, and her voice—her ticking, overenunciated consonants, her round vowels full of longing, that hint of fury and foreignness—that belonged to him still. He was startled to discover that she smiled as she sang.

He sat through both sets, getting up the nerve. Then he approached her as she sat at a table with her bass player, a tall dark-skinned man whose glowering face looked as though it had been folded lengthwise and left with a crease. "Here, sit," he said to Roy, gesturing at his crutches. Roy shook his head. "I'm Roy Truitt," he said to Minna, and he handed her the packet of letters she'd written to her father, tied with its filthy blue ribbon. He'd brought them because they were hers, and because they were evidence. He'd brought them to make his mother furious. Minna held them by the edges. Then she said, seriously, "Come back to my place." It was one in the morning. The bass player gave them a ride there in his dark Hudson. Roy sat in the back with his crutches across his lap, and looked through the window at the dark city, dark because of the war.

She lived then in a vast apartment in a vast building in Hamilton Heights. She offered him a hand up the marble steps to the foyer. He turned it down, then regretted it. The walls of her sitting room were a dark green, a shocking color, thought Roy. A dress, an enormous signet ring, a feathered hat: such things were green. Not *apartments*. One day he'd have a living room this color. She was rich. He saw that now, then reminded himself that she wasn't actually a relative. Some bit of politeness and impertinence kicked in, and he hobbled over to help her with her coat.

"Thank you," she said, with a note of pity. He leaned in to catch her perfume but she only smelled like other people's cigarettes. Her voice was different than when she sang, dispassionate, European. "I have something for you."

The apartment was jammed with objects, paintings on the walls, books piled on the floor. Perhaps they *were* related. It was a familial accumulation. What she had for him were his mother's letters to her, kept in a cigar box, King Edward, five cents. "If you want."

A box of disappointment. He was done with his mother. Then he said it aloud. "I'm done with my mother."

"And your father?"

"Gone." Then, "He said he was your brother. Well, half."

She looked amused. Her expression was direct, both fond and damning. "You don't think so? The lawyers did. Shall I call you a cab? Where are you staying, honey?"

To his right there was a glass case, as though in a museum, with five bird nests inside. He said, "I've run away from home."

"No kidding? How old are you?"

"Eighteen."

"That's not running away from home," she said. "That is reaching your majority. What next? You were in the service, or no?"

He raised his crutches. "I've been turned down."

"College, then."

"Not sure how," he said.

"What in?"

"What in what?"

"What would you study?"

He wanted to impress her; he thought of the Latin and Greek in her letters to her father. "Classics," he said.

"Well, Roy Truitt!" she said to him. Minna Sprague, too, felt the odd hum of relation, despite his porridgey freckledness. She could sense in him a little interesting temper. "Perhaps I can help you."

"You'd pay for it?" He thought of how many hours he'd devoted to her, in listening booths, alone in the apartment. Surely she owed him *something*—

But Minna Sprague was acquainted with men, and boys, and even some women who thought she owed them something. "Ah, no," she said, laughing. "But I can help you get in, and I can help you get a job, and then your education will pay for itself. Have you heard of Englert College?"

"Wow," he said. "Yes." It was in western Massachusetts, the farthest western edge, a little liberal arts college that was coeducational and integrated, neither of which Roy had ever given much thought to but both of which seemed, in Minna Sprague's apartment, essential. "I do. You know the president?"

"I know the locksmith," she said.

He'd thought this was a joke—she knew the locksmith, who would pick the enormous academic lock on the front of Englert College—but she meant the actual locksmith, a man named George originally from Cypress who'd gotten his own degree at Englert.

"For Minna, anything," George said, and hired him immediately.

George imparted to Roy the romance of the lock. Locks were puzzles to which the solution was a key. Sometimes the key was the puzzle and the lock it fit into was the solution. The university had hundreds of locks, thousands: on dorm rooms and classrooms, faculty offices and buildings and laboratories, filing cabinets and gun storage. Locks were the school's lingua franca. Roy made keys till his ankle healed, and then the college was open to him. Once, working on an anonymous call, Roy had found a thin pale man handcuffed to a showerhead in a woman's locker room, wearing nothing but a black rubber swim cap and an overburdened ladies' girdle. Why did they even make girdles so small? What could you be girding? "You couldn't get rubber during the war," the man said apologetically to Roy, and then, with a dazzling smile, "I am Professor Hackert, of Calculus."

"You could have remained nameless," Roy had said, but Professor Hackert, like most people, could not quite sort out humiliation from pride.

Roy got his bachelor's, and then his master's, and then his first visiting job, at Englert. All those years ago, he'd been right. To change his life, all he needed was to talk to Minna Sprague.

R oy Truitt, visiting lecturer, took great bodily pleasure in his campus office, the enormous desk, the little typewriter stand, the floor-to-ceiling bookshelves, the window that looked onto someone else's window. He enjoyed dominating his leather ottoman with his leather brogues, flinging books to the ground, letting the ashtray fill. His students saw his disorder as a sign of genius. *Professor Truitt has read more books than anyone*, they said, though this wasn't true, and he wasn't a professor, not yet. He was twenty-three. He had inherited his predecessor's office as it was, with the books and the ottoman, the manual typewriter that reminded him of a skeleton in a natural history museum—a small dinosaur, one so unfortunately shaped it existed mostly as food for larger dinosaurs. An aquatic animal, probably, with an alphabetic spine.

The bowling alley in the basement of the student building was candlepin. Only the students bowled there. Roy Truitt didn't bowl. Once his ankle had healed, he was left with a ginger step. He had a sofa in his office upon which he napped; he took his meals at a diner a block away. The campus at night was his favorite place. His office was in a small brick building called Archibald Hall, named for the founder of the college, or for his wife, or for their children who had raised the money for Archibald Hall. The Archibalds. There was a painting of Mr. and Mrs. in the entryway, with green-tinged skin and tiny eyes, signed *Mary Archibald*. Somebody fancied herself an artist.

He had a key to Archibald Hall, issued by the key department. He had a master key left over from his time in the key department, and a series of lock picks if the master key failed him.

Just because you escaped your old life didn't mean you were all the way into the next: you still had to burgle, slink, steal. What was the first thing civilized man did? Figure out a way to keep others from what he loves. And what did uncivilized man do? Figure out a way to pick the lock.

His brother was not Archibald but Archer, he reminded himself every morning.

The first time Roy let himself into a colleague's office it was (he told himself) because he knew that the man had a copy of the Loeb Library translation of *City of God*—there was a sentence he wanted to verify. He'd taken Reggie Clayton's "Basics of Attic Greek" his freshman year; Clayton was a thin nervous man in his forties whose entire soul lit up when he read Greek. Standing on Reggie Clayton's Oriental rug, Roy felt he understood Reggie Clayton better. He convinced himself that this was why he'd done it, why he continued to do it, let himself into a different office every night, first in Archibald Hall and then across the quad into Butler. He'd collected his master's in classics, he'd get a Ph.D. next, but his education was incomplete. For instance, how did people who were brought up in houses live? They hung up their coats and displayed pictures of their families, they knew how to arrange furniture in a room, floor lamp, footstool. How else would he learn? He had invented himself but he couldn't civilize himself.

In the offices of his colleagues—his former teachers—he indulged in minor mischief of the shipshape sort, straightening framed diplomas, alphabetizing books, tamping down piles of papers. He felt first like a thief and then superior. No, he hadn't impersonated a ghost at Truitt's, but here he was, a poltergeist, a revenant. Perhaps he'd leave a message flapping in their typewriters. *Boo. I love you. You're out of athlete's foot ointment.*

Am I even human? Roy Truitt wondered as he chewed a sticky licorice cough drop he'd found in a colleague's middle desk drawer.

On the white cough drop box, the two bearded Smith Brothers, Trade and Mark. He sat at the desk and stuck his knees in the kneehole. These days he let himself into offices without looking at the name on the door, to make himself a detective. He examined the impressions left behind in a leather desk chair, breadth and depth of a colleague's bottom. He preferred breaking into the offices of male colleagues, who outnumbered the women anyhow. It felt less personal.

During the day he sat in his armchair and listened through the doors to his colleagues letting themselves into their offices. He waited to be caught. Every time somebody knocked on his door, he thought, *Here it is.* But it was only ever his students. Maybe he would find a wife among them. They were not so much younger than he was, after all. Melora Chalfen. Rose Pearlman. Any one of them might do.

Then one day the knock on the door was not a student, not a colleague who'd tracked him down, but Arch.

Arch sat down, like the students, on the uncomfortable chair on the other side of the desk. He wiggled his hips and nodded, as though he had never sat in a chair but found the experience satisfactory and Roy remembered this particular quality of Arch's: he always seemed to have just landed, amused and stymied by the customs of this new world. Was it a habit? A running joke? Arch pointed at the shelves. "Books," he observed.

"Yes. Well, Arch."

Arch smiled, and it unlocked both of them. "Well, Roy." He put his hand on the desk. "So, I've come to invite you to the wedding."

"Oh? Whose."

"You know whose," said Arch.

"Do I. I didn't know things had progressed."

"They've progressed," said Arch, sadly.

He didn't look like a man who should get married. He wore a

dingy short-sleeved shirt with a pattern that looked like canceled stamps and a dirty necktie with a pattern that looked like tarnished coins. Maybe his fiancée was waiting for them to get married before she started to look after him. Interfere. Whatever it was that made husbands comb their hair. Now, as though they were getting ready for the ceremony, Roy tsked and reached across the desk to fix Arch's tie.

"I thought it might be a tie place," said Arch. Roy could feel his voice buzz through the botched Windsor knot. "Your job."

"It is. What's *wrong* with you, Arch?"

"Why do people always ask?" said Arch in a mild voice. "Like I know."

"If you don't know, who does?"

"Seems like whoever asks the question has a pretty good idea what's wrong with me. At least they'd like to take a guess. Go on."

Roy sat back in his chair and looked out the window. Across the courtyard, the neighboring professor sat at her desk and unwrapped what looked like a present but turned out to be a sandwich. He had been in that office. She kept clean underwear in her center drawer. Without looking at his brother, he said, "You had a different girl-friend every week of your life, but you're marrying Betty."

"Nobody calls her Betty."

"I do," said Roy. "You can't take *that*."

"Roy, for God's sake. She wasn't ever really your girl. You dropped her the minute you broke your foot."

"I know that," he said irritatedly. "Very clear on that. But didn't you think—"

"—what?"

"That I might not like it? I might not like making conversation at family events. And I didn't *break* my *foot*."

Arch scratched his head with all of his fingers. It made him look like the dog he was at heart. "We don't have family events. This is the first one."

"Somebody's bound to die eventually," said Roy.

"I'm sorry!" Arch cried. "I just—oh God, Roy, really, I knew it was a bad idea. I did. *I* knew better, but my *heart*—"

"—who do you think your heart *is*?"

"Well—"

"You think your heart is separate from you?"

"Yes!" said Arch, as though asked at knifepoint his belief in God.

"You think there's some *intelligence* making demands? Demands that must be obeyed? Arch, that's just you. Not *your heart wants*. It's *you. You* want."

Arch put his hands on himself, at his clavicle, his lungs, his waist. Even from the outside, he could feel the way longing and love radiated from his torso. His heart pumped. It desired things. It moved those desires to his brain, where they displaced thought, duty, plans. "I can feel it," he said. He stood up, to display his whole body, its regions and faults.

"It's a fiction," said Roy. "Something the medievals made up to get out of things, and it caught on. Your heart is a brute organ. It traffics in blood. That's all."

"Not only," Arch insisted.

"Only. You're your head. Or your whole body. You come in one piece, anyhow. Do me a favor. Every time you want to say *my heart*, just tell the truth. *My heart wanted?* No. *I wanted. I longed. I broke*, to be honest, you can say that, too. That is what I say to you now. I am in front of you, and I am breaking. I can feel myself break."

At the end of the semester, the Friday of his brother's wedding at Salford City Hall, Roy Truitt, visiting lecturer, was found on the other side of the state, stuck in the trench coat of the tiny French professor, she of the at-the-ready clean underpants, the beautifully wrapped sandwiches. When she found him thrashing on the floor of her office, Roy looked like he was wearing some sort of psychiatric restraint. Caught in the act. He would be fired. He wanted to say "I'm not here." He wanted to say "I'm elsewhere." He wished he were at the wedding after all.

"*Mais qu'est-ce se passe?*" said the French professor.

"Lady," he said staring up at her, he an out-of-shape incompetent Houdini, no escape, no next semester. Had she really spoken French at him? She was from Secaucus, New Jersey. He should call her *mademoiselle*. Still, he liked the toughness of the word in his mouth, so he said it again. "Lady, lady. All sorts of things happen in this world. This is only one of them."

HE WENT UP

A rch Truitt came home from the war; got married; was given, for his troubles, Truitt's. "It's yours now," said Margaret, though she wouldn't give up her stool behind the wooden counter, nor neaten her stacks of dime magazines, nor sign over the deed. "Make any changes you like."

"All right," said Arch. The first thing he did was to order a new sign, light up letters that said BOWLAWAY.

"You can't just rename the place," said Margaret. "Surely. It's a sad name, don't you think? Bowlaway. Bowl away what?"

"Troubles," said Arch. "Sorrow. Hours. Whatever you don't want, bowl it away."

He hauled the mannequin up from the basement where he'd stored her, and wired her again to one of the iron columns. He put her high enough that people couldn't rub her cloth face. One of her eyes had nearly been worn away already; she seemed to wink. But visitors could reach her feet. The right one grew burnished, the left one stayed fine and dark: people always reach for the brighter spot, where other hands have been.

"Jesus Mary and Joseph," said Margaret. "Where did you find her?"

"Around," said Arch. "I love her."

She would be the one piece of history: Arch would modernize the Bowlaway. The first thing to go was the oak counter in the front, which had given the place the feel of a train station, or post office, or public library, where you might present yourself for official stamping. You could not enter without passing by whoever stood or sat there; whoever stood or sat there felt, variously, like a prisoner, a priest, a jailer, a mannequin in a shop window, a bird in a birdhouse. Arch had it ripped out.

"Why?" said Margaret.

"We need the room for the house shoes."

He'd already placed the order: eight dozen pairs of rubber-soled oxfords, each rentable for a nickel. Maybe *that* would convince Margaret to retire. She'd always been a persnickety woman, but her persnicketiness acquired teeth as she aged. She had a particular horror concerning the ground and the human foot. Feet were the lowest part of the human anatomy. She didn't even like seeing a stranger's anklebone.

"How wonderful!" Margaret said when the house shoes came in.

"You don't mind?" said Arch.

"Keep the lanes much cleaner! We won't have the general public dragging in who-knows-what on their shoes!"

The shoes meant that Margaret spoke to everyone, asked them a piece of personal information. Sometimes the men didn't know their shoe size and had to defer to their wives, or asked Margaret to look and guess. (These numbers Margaret committed to memory, to show off the next time.) Afterward, she wielded a giant can of Shu-kė-Ko disinfectant, which she sprayed into the open mouths of the shoes. A smart shot left, a smart shot right, miraculous sanitation! What she loved most was the warm leather of the returned shoes, the dark mushroomy smell of their recent occupation. The big shoes of the big men were her favorite. When those came back, Margaret pinched them together at the instep and felt the snug heat off the insole before she chilled them with her can of disinfectant. If she could have got away with it, she would have slipped her feet into them, for foot-to-foot communion. She had always hated feet because she had always loved them.

The long bar along the left wall went next, and the gum-stained pool tables, and Arch put in machines in their place: cigarette; baseball; a red Coke machine with glass bottles that you pulled out longwise by the neck. A jukebox (a terrible choice, in such clatter); pinball machines, a whole line of them, with the newest invention, flippers, and a big sign that said FOR ENTERTAINMENT PURPOSES ONLY: NO WAGERING. A new strength tester. A love rater. HOT STUFF, the love rater told Arch Truitt.

"Oh dear," said Cracker, who turned out to be A COLD FISH.

"See, darling?" said Arch. "It's broken, it doesn't know what it's talking about."

What Arch wanted removed was not just the old oak, nor the unused and outdated amusements, but also the past entirely: the alley his father had presided over, all the possible ghosts. The Ghoster, K. D., had ended up publishing a small article in *True Ghost Stories*, illustrated with his inconclusive photos, undoctored, and including the story of Leviticus Sprague, M.D., an apparent victim of spontaneous combustion who one night had gone up. So the Bowlaway got some ghost tourists, witch-ridden and twitchy people who'd gone to Salem and figured they might as well make the trip south to Salford: the quiet sort who dressed like puritans themselves, as well as the loudmouths who liked horror movies. Ghost tourists rented lanes and then didn't bowl, trying to keep the racket down. One day the Bowlaway was visited by a pair of women who called themselves combusters, a pair of sisters with tallow complexions and kerosene breath. You could tell they longed to burn, to be burnt, to burn somebody else. The brunette sister had sweet cutthroat dark eyes, the other was a champagne-cork blonde; the one as excitable as a book of matches, the other as still as unpoured accelerant. They'd brought a plaque they wanted to put up that said,

ON THIS SPOT
LEVITICUS SPRAGUE, M.D.
A VICTIM OF SPONTANEOUS COMBUSTION
"he is missed"

"No," said Arch Truitt. No more of the past. No more of the *forgotten* past.

"Why not?" said the brunette. He felt a flutter of admiration for her. She seemed the sort of woman who might murder in the name of love.

"All right," he said at last. But nobody knew where the spot was, and the plaque was installed behind the counter, where it could be hidden by the house shoes.

Cracker Graham wouldn't live in an apartment over a bowling alley, though she understood that wherever they moved, her mother-in-law would follow. Her cousins owned a red empire sofa that could never be abandoned; she herself had inherited a clawfoot buffet with a cracked tilted mirror. Previously she'd thought of the buffet as an elderly relative who needed to be taken care of—it wasn't its fault that it couldn't converse with the rest of the furniture—but now that she had a mother-in-law, the mother-in-law seemed like a piece of furniture. She would have to be installed somewhere.

Cracker's mother gave them the down payment to buy the house on Somefire Hill, a durable Victorian built around the time of Supersum but habitable. Margaret complained, and moaned, and declared she would miss her kitchen—really, just a hissing stove, an old refrigerator with a round rattling monitor top—and said she wouldn't go, and when she finally walked into her room at the house, burst into tears.

"I'm sorry," said Cracker.

Margaret shook her head. What she couldn't say: all she had ever wanted was a room like this for her own, she had gone to work as a baby nurse for it, had married for it, had children for it—she'd wanted it so long she'd become afraid of her longing, as many a religious heart decides to spurn what it desires. Now here it was: a double bed with a new mattress and two feather pillows, a pale purple chenille bedspread, a nightstand with a glass lamp flush and lumpy as the bedspread, a rag rug, a window with a balustrade, which looked out over the garden filled with flowers—Margaret didn't know what sort of flowers, she had always hated people who knew the names of things: birds, flowers, the constellations. Show-offs. Flowers themselves she loved, that flat-faced purple sort and the ones that looked like fireworks and the ones that smelled of lilac—why, they *were* lilacs, weren't they, even she knew that.

"I'm sorry," said Cracker again, and Margaret took her hand and squeezed it and in a voice of love and gratitude said, "You should be."

A pair of inventors had installed some automatic pinsetter prototypes at Whalom Park in Lunenburg, and the Arch Truitts went to see them. The machine swept the pins into the pit, brought them up on a conveyor belt, flung the balls back to the bowlers the way the pinbodies always had, with one good toss and gravity. Breathtaking, in a way, and also frightening: they did not work with humans, as the pinball machines did, but replaced them. Afterward, Cracker wanted to ride the Whalom Park roller coaster, and Arch pointed out that she was pregnant.

True enough, but she said, "So?"

"No wife of mine—"

"How many wives you got? That makes it sound like more than one."

"Sometimes it *feels* like it," he said. He set his hand on the underside of her stomach, which was bossy with child. He knew how to run his hands over a woman's anatomy—through clothing or not—as though his palm were magnetic, as though her soul were ductile, pulled around the surface of her skin. He did this now. Cracker shuddered. It astounded her that she'd fallen in love with him through the mail. He had a particular mesmerizing smell. She couldn't tell where it emanated from. Breath? Lungs? The interior of his nose? It seemed to come in puffs, though she could also detect it in the shallow wells of his collar bones, behind his ear: clean heat, starch ironed into a shirt, the sun on bedsheets. She thought, *I could find you in the dark.* Maybe it was her, too. This was the scent of the spell they cast together, what people meant when they spoke of chemistry.

"No," he said with certainty. "It's not safe."

She looked at the Flyer Comet in all its paleontological beauty. "I bet you can't fall asleep on it. Not even you."

He got a thinking look at that, then shook his head. "I have to put my foot down."

Later, this would be one of her biggest grievances against him, though she couldn't say why. Motherhood ruined her for roller coasters—it rearranged her inner ear, the nausea center of her brain: now when she looked at one she felt sick, though it wasn't like some lost pleasures, *what did I ever see in that?* She knew exactly what she'd lost, the plunging exhilaration of being dropped, rescued, dropped again, delivered to your beginning. She had wanted to ride the roller coaster. Arch wouldn't let her. It's amazing it wasn't listed in her writ of divorce.

"So we'll get them," said Arch.

She nodded. He'd been right about everything so far, every machine and modernization. Still, she'd worked as a pinsetter as Arch had not, and she knew that while it was better to have a machine sweep up the pins, pour them into the apparatus, set them down, it was sadder, too. Hand-setting was backbreaking, dangerous work, appreciated by nobody, the quietest thing that happened in a candlepin alley, a collaboration between two people.

They had to smash apart the pinsetters' shelf to make room for the machinery. The sound of the cracking wood was the most violent thing she'd ever heard, like bones, and she burst into tears. She'd loved that shelf and she had caused it to be broken.

"Why are you crying, honey?" Arch asked her.

She didn't know. She wanted to write to Roy to tell him, to ask. He might understand but he might not care.

The sound of the Bowlaway, in the 1950s! It was like a piano tumbling down a flight of stairs, then panting in pain. Arch had a knack for fixing the various machines, so he loved them the way anyone loves something or someone who is easily humbled and easily cheered. Children screamed in the alleys because they could. Bowlers shouted conversation. Babies cried, and their parents laughed at them, said, *do your worst, kid*. One of these babies was Amy Truitt, Amy of the fear of falling and the depthless sorrow, hiccupping Amy, shrieking Amy, Amy who smelled like Arch did, sweet and clean. It was something that ran in the family, like eye color and the width of feet.

When had Cracker stopped bowling? She had started during the war—she was no LuEtta Mood; that is, she was mortal—but she understood physics. She could convert spares with the exactitude of a surgeon. The problem was that the game, the long game, didn't interest her. Not the story of it. She didn't care if she won, she didn't care if she improved. (Later Arch would say, "That was the problem with you. You never wanted to win.") She wished she could pinset for Arch, but a robot had taken her job.

Instead she watched, along with everyone else. When Arch rolled, it was as though he knew, strike or split, half Worcester or full. He didn't make it happen, he foresaw it, turning away as the ball made its way down the alley. He smiled no matter what. LAUGHING ARCH TRUITT, the trade papers called him. He liked twenty-four-hour tournaments, tournaments to a thousand. The man could bowl forever. The automatic pinsetters kept up; as many people came to see them as the human bowlers. You could scarcely see the nineteenth century at the Bowlaway. Only the iron columns, the one doll high above. Elsewhere it was plastic, and ringing bells. Was Arch prescient, or simply a modern man who liked modern things? The game had changed, pins thicker, balls standard. A good bowler—Arch, for instance—could top 200 in a game, though it wasn't easy.

The overnights he dazzled, like a character from a tall tale—some of the old-timers who came around remembered LuEtta Mood, and told stories grown Bunyanesque: she bowled six days straight and only quit to go to church. She beat every woman in the house then every man then all comers and they told her to stop. She would not stop.

'Course, they said, that was then, and she was a girl. Reckon Arch could beat her. My money'd be on Arch, for sure.

No surprise when the local television station came, wanting him to bowl in front of the cameras. Not at Truitt's—the lanes were a funny length, dreamt up by a Victorian woman, they'd never do for a tournament—but at the new house in Boston, the Bowladrome. He bought handsome shirts it turned out he couldn't wear on TV—he had a weakness for loud patterns, a way to look a little ridiculous on purpose instead of by accident—and got his hair cut once a week. Bowling was made for television: unlike football, baseball, basketball, you didn't have to shrink it down to watch. It was already box shaped. It already had suspense; its quiet moments (the ball headed toward the pins) were as thrilling as its loud ones (their eventual meeting). On national television, it was all tenpin bowling, brutish and rewarding and sponsored by beer companies. New Englanders required candlepins. *Candlepins for Dollars*: a modest game for modest prizes, Saturday at noon. "I'm one step up from a test pattern," Arch liked to say, but he loved it.

He loved bowling. He wished he didn't: it felt like a family curse, one that Roy—who sent postcards from Lisbon and Belize and Tenerife, who had no dependents and no obligations—had escaped.

It is a curse to be good at something, Arch thought. He would take comfort where he could.

THE UNRELENTING BABY

All babies are beautiful," said Margaret dubiously, examining hiccupping Amy Truitt, then five months old. "When's the christening?"

"No christening," said Cracker. The very verb! To turn a baby more Christlike.

"You were christened your own self."

"No I wasn't," said Cracker. "I'm Jewish. That's why we got married at City Hall."

They were standing in the new kitchen then. Margaret closed the refrigerator as though it were a dirty book that had caught her unawares. "How are you *Jewish?*"

"Well, my mother is."

Margaret closed her eyes and tried to remember Cracker's mother, who lived now, already, in Florida. She reviewed the evidence—shortness, bad eyesight, a discombobulating glamour—and found it convincing.

"Well, that's *her*," she said. "My granddaughter will be christened. That's how *that* works."

The trick was, Cracker thought, keeping secrets from everybody. Margaret need never find out that because Cracker was Jewish (because her mother was), this meant Amy was, too. Her own mother need never hear of the christening itself.

Her own mother had been maternally standoffish, and Cracker had worried she would be likewise. Then she worried that she would be the opposite, she would crawl into their beds, watching them sleep, furious that she didn't know the content of their dreams. She would demand to know every first-star, birthday-candle, wishbone-splitting, wishing-well wish. She would say, over and over, the thing she would never say to a man: *Do you love me?* It was all she ever wanted to know.

Cracker held still and waited. She always had. Once somebody came close, *then* she could love, she was a pond of love, a lake. Depthless, she believed. Maybe she was right. In high school when her friends talked of crushes and marriage, Cracker kept mum. It didn't feel like fear, it was deeper, evolutionary, syncopal: talk of love lowered her blood pressure into the fainting zone. When Davey Cotter kissed her in the Intimate Apparel department of Grover Cronin, she had been surprised: she didn't particularly like him, but how to send him away? She had an idea she wasn't supposed to. She let him kiss her that day, and for months afterward.

Then Arch. Nothing cautious about Arch! Why everybody loved him: he was a spendthrift. Munificent. In his first letter: *Had a dream with you. Want to hear it? You were making me toast, and laughing. You rode away on an old-fashioned bicycle, the kind with a big front wheel. You looked beautiful. I take this as a sign I should write.*

If you came to her with love, she loved you. Even as a mother it was her way. That's why you hold still. It's a kind of camouflage, a blending into the native tree bark: *I don't care, I don't care, love me or don't.*

You better love me.

It worked. The children, those preposterous foreigners, declared their love even before they spoke the language, came and lay upon her and kissed her, doe-eyed, serious, or laughing uproariously. "You'll spoil them!" her mother-in-law would say. "They need a schedule." A schedule meant not just bedtime and mealtime but love. Amazing Margaret didn't want to check off affection next to diapers and baths.

Let them stay up all night. Let them eat when they want and what they want, wake up and pour a bowl of cereal, a glass of milk, mop up the mess.

It worked. First hiccupping Amy, who acquired a sense of humor, which she would later lose; then Brenda, the late arrival, always in that way an immigrant: determined to be accepted, do well, even when she didn't understand the jokes. She suffered from spasms of love. She'd kiss her mother's hand like a pantomime duke, sighing, murmuring *mama* [kiss], *mama* [kiss], *mama*, as though it were the only word of English she'd mastered. Cracker lay her hand on Brenda's back and felt the buzz of her blood. She braided Amy's maple hair and took such pleasure in the feel of it between her fingers, her daughter's back against her shins, she wanted to weep. "Ouch!" said Amy. "Hold still, pet," said Cracker in her gentling way.

(It worked for a while, anyhow. Once Amy and Brenda were out of the house they discovered the joys of a regular bedtime, hot breakfasts, bedroom slippers. All that stillness. They grew resentful. When they were children she had struck them as beyond reproach, entirely a mother, entirely theirs. Once they grew up and could see around the back of her the other parts, there all along, they felt duped. Her own desires! Her own ambitions! Hidden! She had been, they decided, a soundstage of a mother. They watched her friends, who adored her, who called her up and took her out to meals and fussed over her, who said *Your mother is such a wonderful woman.* You don't know, Amy wanted to say. But she didn't have any proof to the contrary, other than it had always been clear that it had been their job to love her, and they did. They still did.)

When the children were young, she was their mother. Not a full-time mother—she also worked as a wife and a daughter-in-law, did some mail-order work as a daughter to her own mother, off in Boynton Beach. She'd become a collection of other people's secrets. "Mama, can I tell you something?" Amy would say, and Cracker, full of hope, said yes. "I don't like Claire anymore." Well, that wasn't news. Who would like that pie-faced girl? She kept falling for it. Her children offered the most mundane facts prefaced by, *Mama, can I tell you something?* Yes, Cracker, said, every time, you can tell me anything. The children never confided anything she didn't already know.

The grown-ups did.

For instance, her friend had an elderly aunt who died. This aunt had been renting a house on the Cape, in Dennis, and it had fallen to Cracker's friend, Audra, to empty it, so Audra had cooked a week's worth of food for her husband and children and had gone to clear away the years of the aunt's retirement. Audra's husband was a dentist. He, too, was named Dennis. Her two girls were sweet and contained, polite in a way that Cracker had found both enviable and unreal. "I was worried they would miss me too much," said Audra. They were at the ice cream parlor. Audra angled her spoon under the dripping marshmallow. "And then I worried they wouldn't miss me at all."

"Did they?"

"Yes?" said Audra. Even her sundae was perfectly matched, stark marshmallow, off-white whipped cream, ivory ice cream, butterscotch. Audra's hair was butterscotch, too, her lips maraschino cherry. "But do you know? Betty, I would only say this to you: I didn't miss them. Not for a minute. I went for walks when I wanted. I swam in the sea. I ate whatever was left in the cupboards."

"You weren't lonely."

Audra put one hand in the air, as though swearing an oath in court, but on an ice cream sundae. "Not once," she said. "Betty, I knew I could tell you. You understand."

Cracker was glad that she was the sort of person her friends could tell terrible secrets to—she imagined she presented herself as a kind of card catalogue, where all the entries sat next to each other, each precisely the same size as the next, arranged for ease of location and not importance. She also wished she were not that person. Her friends thought she forgot their confidences. She didn't judge—mostly she didn't judge—but she remembered. *You understand*, Audra had said, but Cracker didn't. She didn't understand Janis drunkenly sleeping with the young mortician the day of her mother's funeral; she didn't understand Gladys's confession that she loved her littlest child, a son, better than all his lovely older sisters, and that the girls sensed this, and had become desperate to win her love, which turned her stomach. She didn't understand not missing Audra's nice Dennis, who fixed cars on the weekend and didn't drink and had once played bass in a jazz quartet. Of course not all families were happy! But Cracker didn't want to know the specifics. The visible world, that was fine, snappishness, ennui, misdirected flirtation. She would not turn away, but she wished to remain innocent of the causes.

She was known for her dislike of gossip and so everyone brought their gossip to her: they figured her for a lagoon. The affairs and the revenge affairs, the drunken incontinence, the lack of sex and the excess of it, the husband who cried for a month when his formerly secret mistress died, the woman who could not stand the smell of her child dying of cancer. "Like rotten cabbage," the mother said, then, seeing the look on Cracker's face, "I love her so."

By then her own marriage was falling apart. The wonder was that it had lasted so long. She thought she'd be embarrassed but she wasn't. All those things that she knew about other marriages, through confession and gossip, people likewise knew about hers, or made good guesses. Then one Saturday noontime she was watching Arch on *Candlepins for Dollars*, live television, and he absent-mindedly reached out and palmed the round underside of the rump of the ladies' champion, Anna Rzepka. Rzepka didn't even flinch. The camera cut away, cut back. In the intervening moment Arch had understood what he had done. It showed on his face. You'd have thought he'd lost the tournament, and just afterward he did that, too. No instant replay, thank God. Still, in living rooms all over greater Boston, Arch Truitt had idly fondled Anna Rzepka. By dinnertime people remembered it happening in close-up and slow motion.

Cracker, in her own living room, had seen it clearly, the stroking upturned hand, one finger above the rest intimately tickling. She looked at her mother-in-law, who was crocheting some ghastly circular object: a turtleneck for disadvantaged serpents. Then Cracker turned to the telephone and waited for it to ring. Isn't that what happened? No: in other houses, the phones were ringing, the chatter had begun. *Did you see that? Poor Cracker, poor thing. Well, it's no surprise.*

Nobody would be calling her. She turned her head back to the television. She'd forgiven him before, invisibly, at all the other signs: the hotel bills for tournaments an hour's drive away, the ringing phone with nobody on the other end, a sudden drop-off in their sex life, a new and startling expertise in bed. She'd known plenty and ignored plenty but they had never said anything. This was different.

"He's like his father." Margaret was still crocheting, jerking her fingers, circling the air with yarn in a genuflective way. "He wears his arm on his sleeve."

"Arm?" said Cracker.

"Heart," Margaret corrected. "He wears his *heart* on his sleeve."

"Yeah, well, look closer. That isn't his heart."

"Forgiveness is a blessing," said Margaret, to her moving fingers. "Don't forget that, darling."

He came home that night with one of his twilight hangovers, his hair combed back, his clothes hanging from his shoulders, a paper doll of a man. He had his bag over one shoulder, the balls stamped with his initials, *ACT*. He saw the look on her face. Probably he didn't want to be forgiven: you fuck up, you should feel like a fuckup.

"Sweetheart," he said. Alone of the Truitts he had that flat Salford accent. Sweet-hot. He winced at something, toothache, headache, conscience. Already he was guilty, repentant, on his way, he believed, to absolution. "I'll sleep at the alley."

"You will not," said Cracker. "That's my place now. You have a mother, remember?" The mother was dozing on the davenport; the mother (thought Cracker later) was why they did not fight, or fuck, or do anything that might jolt their marriage's fundaments, and save it.

She had children but she was not running off to Dennis, only down the street. She would come every morning and cook them breakfast, she would pack lunches and send them off to school. Like Audra she would not miss her family. She would not think anything until she thought the grand thoughts of her youth: she would imagine how she might be loved, how she might (through charity and hard work) be redeemed. That had been her plan, when she was a girl of fourteen. She was not the smartest girl in her class; she was only ordinarily pretty; she did not play an instrument; she could not sing. But she liked the idea of being good. Arch was guilty, there was no doubt about it, but maybe she was guilty, too. She planned to examine herself.

When she opened the door to the apartment she saw it hadn't stood empty in all that time. Arch had brought people here. Women?

Yes: there was a drift in the corner of womanly things, underpants and single stockings, cotton balls peachy with pancake, emery boards. But other people, too—beer cans and scotch bottles, the fat ashes of cigars, racing forms. It wasn't utter ruin, just bad behavior, medium fresh. He was a careless man but not a disaster. Once a month he cleaned the place. He hadn't slept with every woman who'd left a crescent lip print on a scotch glass. Really, only three or four over time. How many secret lives does one man need?

All of them, Cracker, all of them.

It felt like the sort of camp teenagers with a little money might pitch in the woods. She tried to clear things up. She got the old push broom from the alley and plowed the floor. *This is my penance*, she thought, still hoping she might attain goodness, *but for what?* Amid the garbage, the inevitable husks of insects and one twitching live one. The last drunk at the party. What kind of bug? She stepped on it. The crunchy kind. The worst of it: she'd been gone an hour and a half, and already she was lonely, she missed everyone. Amy, who was twelve, tall and pimpled and music-obsessed: her friends loved rock and roll but she was a folkie, perverse in the family way. Brenda, littler, little enough that she still let her mother pinch her bottom and sniff her neck. Who could Cracker confess to? *One day I ran away from home and you know what? I had to run back immediately.*

She missed Arch, too, but he had to go.

EVERY MAN
A PORTMANTEAU

The four months Arch lived above the bowling alley, his women treated him like a visiting dignitary from an impoverished country. They wanted him to be comfortable and also grateful, dazzled by the richness of ordinary things. They got rid of all the old beds in the apartment and moved in the wooden mission bed from Arch and Cracker's bedroom: she wanted a new one. She sewed him a quilt made of all the sheets and blankets of their married life. Cracker did not wish to sleep upon them or beneath them ever again.

"You could have just given them to me," said Arch. "They would have done fine. Now they're like—" He waved at the quilt, spread out on the bed. "It's like a mausoleum of blankets."

"Yes."

"Oh. Ah. OK."

He hoped he'd be let back in. That had been his life so far, old Arch, old dog—Cracker didn't know how many candlepin houses had barred him for drinking or gambling, and they always let him back in. How could his own family be different?

She was done cooking for him. His mother brought him meals in covered pots.

"Soup of the day," she said.

He peered into it, horrified. "It's casserole."

"Casserole's what travels."

He'd hidden some bottles in the alley mop closet, amid the sad faded feminine mops, because like his grandmother Arch liked to throw parties in the after-hours alley from time to time. The bottles were gone, dumped out by his mother, as all the liquor was everywhere else by his wife. *Good*, thought Arch. Otherwise he might unhinge his jaw and consume it all: vodka, bourbon, ginger ale, the pickled onions nobody ever requested. Mix the cocktails in his gullet. Anna drank beer, he drank beer with Anna, of the elastic muscles and sharp nose, the blood that pumped all through her body: Arch had never met a woman whose hands and feet were never cold. The climate of Anna was constant, warm in every region. It had all started with holding hands. He wanted to tell Cracker that.

He didn't want to be forgiven. That was work you had to take on for yourself. You had to find the work and do the work. (In the family he was famous for his laziness. They didn't know how he labored inside.) How would he manage it?

He decided to quit drinking. The decision came before the quitting, but he'd never considered it before. All his life he'd loved stories of solitary men against nature, Arctic explorers, round-the-world sailors, and this was how he convinced himself. It would be an act of bravery, one that might kill him. To set off on a life in which he would traverse Temperance. Perhaps he would sail off the very edge of it. One did not set off to cross the ocean thinking you might turn back. You had to make up your mind and *go*. He thought of the USS *Montrose*, how he sat and slept and stood in shifts, each day divided in thirds. Such order might help him now: eight hours of sleep, eight hours at the table, eight hours at the window staring out. In every attitude he shivered beneath the quilt Cracker had sewn him, as though condemned to it. A week passed.

Later a doctor would tell him he could have killed himself from such a sudden abstinence—this was in context of discussing all of Arch's favorite and possibly fatal habits—but now it was his wall of ice and he was determined to get over it. The rumbling in his head was not distant avalanches, not a scuppering wave, but always, ever, bowling.

His mother came to see him twice a day. As usual her fury manifested in frightening good cheer. He made himself sit at the kitchen table just before the alley opened, when she would appear with coffee and a cruller. She believed in the medicinal properties of the doughnut shop. "Honey! You look good, you look good!"

"Thanks, Ma." He turned up his collar. Awful, to be assessed by your mother. She reached over and turned his collar down. He wondered about asking after his wife and kids, but neither of them said a thing. She felt he was ruining his life. She didn't think he could stop, and she felt sorry for him, so she might as well straighten his collar as he tumbled away.

Because he'd given up drinking he had to give up drinking's Siamese twin, smoking. Instead, he ate. He consumed pounds of pistachios, which in those days came dyed red and dyed his fingers red, bought from Sutherland's Market down the block. Cherries, too, which were in season, and which turned his fingertips a muddier red, black around the nails. Any kind of fiddly food eaten one at a time, to occupy his hands and mouth. Olives didn't work for some reason. Grapes could but they weren't time-consuming enough. The floor of the apartment was scattered with nut paper, cherry stems, the arboreal remains of grapes. Oysters were tempting but impractical. The expedition began its second month. It was too late to turn back, and more dangerous. In his cabin above the bowling alley, he kept on.

He visited the girls, took them on Sundays into Boston, when everything was closed because of the blue laws. He imagined that they'd demand he explain himself—how come he lived at the alley? When was he coming back?—but their questions concerned candy, and could they stop walking, and why couldn't they see a movie. Those he could answer.

How to explain to Cracker that he'd changed his life? Why, through television, of course. He went back on *Candlepins for Dollars*. He would not stray, never stray, to the women's lanes. Drinking, he was baby faced; now he had a jawline, cheekbones, a pointed upper lip. "Laughing Arch Truitt," the announcer still called him, but he did not laugh so much. He concentrated on the lanes. He spoke to the pins. One week he kicked the ball return and the station told him he was on probation. Drinking, he assumed that drink was what made him a bowler. It unknotted his shoulders. It made him forget grudges. But surely it kept him back, too. Sober, he thought, prayingly, *Well now I'll be champion*. But it didn't work that way. Lots of the game was luck, which was why he liked it. Every ball was a test of luck, every box, every string. He still thought that, but it was a long story. Your luck could worsen. You could keep failing, get worse, reveal yourself as a failure, a jinx. Your own jinx.

Cracker didn't watch him. How could she? Instead she tried to think of him as merely a man who—like most of the men of the world—made their money mysteriously and elsewhere.

His fingers were dyed red from pistachios. His stomach hurt. He'd given up everything to get his family back and had forgotten that the first thing he'd given up was his family. What did she *do* with her days? She sat and waited for him to come home. He sat and waited to be invited.

He went back to work in the alley. Every morning he went downstairs and his mother said, "Good morning, dear!"

"Good morning!"

"How did you sleep?"

"Like a bear."

"Brought you breakfast."

"Coffee first."

"Brought you coffee. Looks like a nice day. Oh, those shoes, somebody put 'em back any which way."

People came to the alley to shake Arch's hand. He wasn't the best bowler on *Candlepins for Dollars* but he was memorable: his smile, those billboard cowboy teeth, straight and white; the way he'd been caught goosing that big Polish girl on local television. So he devoted himself to the Bowlaway. He gave lessons. He cleaned the balls and tended to the balky pinsetters. One day to his mother's amazement he saddle-soaped every shoe in the place, including the numbers stitched on the heels: he used one of the stubby scoring pencils to work the soap through the seams.

Then he went upstairs and watched television and disassembled pistachios with his fingertips. Look at the shells! It seemed like there should be something to do with them. The thing to do, of course, was throw them away, but he couldn't: they were evidence of the only progress he was making. He began to stack them. He would make an obelisk of pistachio shells. He said aloud, "I've gone mad."

If you've gone mad you don't know it. But what if you say it aloud?

He went to bed, got up, drank his mother's coffee from the plaid thermos, ate his mother's cruller. At noon she presented his lunch, saying, as she always did, "Soup of the day!"

This lasted until the Tuesday morning his mother said, "Good morning, dear!" and in return he burst into tears.

"You're drunk," she said, and—certain he had been seen for the first time in ages—he tearfully agreed. He remembered Roy saying the same thing to him, decades before. Maybe he was only truly visible when drunk.

He'd been good for so long! Four months! Not so long for most things but a world record for him and good behavior. The only way to make four months seem less like forever was to continue to be good for even longer and that was impossible, he couldn't do it, not all by himself like this. There was booze somewhere in the apartment, he had realized, even though Cracker had hauled away most of the debauchery in her seven-hour tenancy: when he'd moved in it had smelled of piney soap; she even seemed to have had sunlight installed, which had never been a feature of his childhood. He'd let the apartment get so foul so quickly the place might have generated booze—or, more likely, she only cleared out the bottles where a nondrinker might look. At the very back of the under-the-sink cupboards in the kitchen, he found a half-filled bottle of gin. He sniffed to make sure it wasn't cleaning fluid. Then he tasted it.

Once he'd loved gin, but then at fourteen a bottle had bit him pretty hard, and thereafter the smell reminded him of his torment, a vomitous night, how he and his friend Trevor Peters had to try to hose the puke out of each other's hair at two in the morning, and how they woke up in the bathroom, Trevor in the tub, Arch flat out on the towel next to it. That's what gin tasted like to him, complicated bare-bottomed humiliation. This gin was particularly foul, body-temperature, old-lady scented. It took the paint right off his soul. He kept drinking it. He ran his tongue around the lip of the bottle.

Gin was the soup of the day. He drank it. He had been so *good*. Now he said it to his mother, weeping. "I've been so *good*."

She answered bitterly, "Well, it surely doesn't seem like you enjoy it."

What good was goodness if you did it miserably, they both thought, but in different ways.

Margaret called Cracker. "You better come get your husband," she said.

Cracker had scarcely spoken to Arch since he'd left. His mother had brought back reports, said he was not drinking, he was making amends, once she got him to go to church she was sure he could return to the marriage.

"I don't care if he goes to church," said Cracker, not sure she wanted him to return to her, either, but maybe, maybe. As for church—he hadn't gone to church since he was ten.

"Darling, he *has* to go to church. Any day now."

When Margaret called and said, Come down to the alley, she figured that was it. Arch had gone to church. Just like Arch to go to church on a Tuesday morning, with all the little old ladies at morning mass. But here he was, and she could tell: that man had not gone to church, not unless he'd already drunk the bars and package stores of Salford dry and had broken in to steal the sacramental wine.

He watched her come in, her dear peculiar gait. He tried to pat himself together, as though he were clay: pat pat on his shirt, his pants pockets, his hair, pat pat the tears away. Oh, she would never forgive him, he could see that. Or she would but he'd need to die.

"What's *wrong* with you?" Cracker Truitt asked her husband.

"Nothing death won't fix."

"Don't talk that way."

"I'll die of *this* place," he said. "I gotta go."

"Where will you go?"

He shrugged. Then he said, "Roy. Roy'll take me in for a while. Roy'll make me walk the straight and narrow."

Roy would make him give up drinking; Roy would get him walking around Lake Quinsigamond in Worcester, would pound his chest and suggest deep breathing. Roy owned a female dog named Leslie who barked in the background of their occasional phone calls, and when Roy said *Sit. Stay. No . . . no . . . Good girl*, the dog fell silent. Arch was rooting for the dog. He had no intention of going there.

"Who gets custody of *me*?" asked Margaret.

"You have custody of yourself, Mother," said Cracker. "You're seventy-two years old."

She was weeping. Her handkerchief was small and lavender and paper thin, like her eyelids. "But where will I go? To the home!"

"Of course not. Of course not. Here—"

They put their arms around her in an intricate knot, so they didn't touch each other. How like her, to make the end of everything seem like the end of her.

"No, you'll stay at the house, of course," said Arch. "You *live* there. For heaven's sake!"

Margaret had imagined leaving with her son, and she had thought that wouldn't be so bad, in a way. They'd stay in motels in twin beds. Or if the room had one bed she'd sleep at the foot of his. She'd liked it, these weeks of taking care of him—he was the younger kid, the hobnobber, always talking to somebody else. For a few months she'd been the first person he spoke to in the morning and the last person at night. Why not hit the road together? She'd keep him from straying the way he had. Buy a hot plate to hot up soup. Breakfast in doughnut shops. See New England and its candlepin houses. It was what she should have done years before with Nahum—in her old age, she'd forgotten that he'd invited her and she'd said no, now she could see him walk away from her, she should have hailed him, *Me, too, I'll go!*

"We'd miss you, Mother," said Cracker. "The girls would."

"Oh, thank the Lord," said Margaret. "What about you, Arch darling? Will I see you?"

"I'll try."

"Trying's enough," declared Margaret.

Arch laughed, smeary tears still on his cheeks. "Then I'm a saint. I'm a champion. I'm the best who ever was."

Later, as she left, he said to Cracker, "Will we get divorced."

"What for?"

"In case you want to get married to somebody else."

"Baby," she said, "rest assured. You ruined me for that." Her way of being nice, not saying, *that for me.*

They made Roy come pick him up. Once Arch had been loaded into the car, an absurd Renault 15 he'd brought back from Paris, Roy stood with Cracker on the front porch. "I'm sorry," he said to her. He wore a green jacket the same color as the car, one shade grassier than pool-table green. "I really am."

"You don't seem sorry."

"Of course I am," he said. Then, "I mean, I should have apologized years ago. For my lack of gumption. I sometimes wonder—"

"Oh no," said Cracker. "No, for Pete's sake. You would have hated me soon enough."

"I doubt that," said Roy. When he had seen Cracker Graham's mouth was as wide as ever, her lipstick as red, her long limbs as tan, he did not feel a flutter in his heart, but a snapped cable. If Arch had destroyed her looks he would have been happier. He'd only smudged the outlines.

"I would have been terrible to you," she said again. "I just don't have a sympathetic heart."

He laughed. "Are you kidding? What have you done with your life! You're a professional sympathizer! You think I would have been more work to sympathize with than Arch?"

They looked to the Renault. Arch had passed out in the passenger's seat, his cheek smashed up against the window. He looked peaceful and plastic.

"A *lot* more," she said. "I mean, you deserve it, but *tons.*"

What a thing, to marry into a family! What could be more perilous? And yet people did it all the time. They married and had children, every child a portmanteau, a mythical beast, a montage.

Arch did not abandon his family. He visited the girls, and sent postcards whenever he traveled, all the places candlepin bowling took him: Springfield, Massachusetts; Providence; Sacco, Maine.

> *Dearest girlies, I have been to the beach. A seagull took my roast beef sandwich! I think I may join the draft dodgers and go to Canada, not that I have a draft to dodge but because I would, if I had to, I wish I had when it had come to me. I didn't even know it was possible. Love, Daddy.*

"He didn't even see combat," said Cracker, reading it. "His big excitement is he stole a bunch of silver lids."

"Lids?" said Amy.

Cracker mimed covering some casserole. "The Italians left a bunch of covered silver dishes. But he ended up with lids and no bottoms. Oh God, he took it badly. He *cried*. I don't know what happened to them."

"Well then that's why," said Brenda. "The war made him compromise his morals."

Cracker laughed, a creaking gate always. "Sure. I guess. He was pure before?"

"He was *always* pure," said Amy, age fifteen, passionately. "That's why when he did something bad it was poison to him."

Too often Cracker could not sleep for wondering where Arch was in the world. Years later, even. He never disappeared, as his own father had, he was just a radio station who some days was clear and others nearly overwhelmed by static—though enough of his voice beneath the crackle you still could hope that with gentling he might come through. Had he remarried? Cracker might wonder suddenly in the night. Was he drinking? He called his mother and his daughters on no regular schedule. He and Roy came to see their mother—at the alley, mostly, and then Arch might roll a few frames. Once a year, every other year. His life was a mystery. *I'll tell you everything*, he'd once told her, and she'd said, *God, no*. She was never the type of woman who'd fall for the promise, the threat, of everything. She tried to convince herself she could live on nothing instead.

MEN FROM MARS

Jeptha Arrison hadn't been born in a bowling alley, not ever, but Arch Truitt was. It was an event that had embarrassed everyone involved so much they never spoke of it: Margaret's modesty protected by the oak counter, though Nahum had urged her to stretch out on the pool table. Was he crazy? Don't ruin the felt. Give birth someplace that can be mopped up. The doctor who arrived five minutes too late pronounced the sudden labor and delivery typical. Not for me it isn't, said Margaret, and the doctor laughed with such condescension it was like a sword run through her body that missed all her organs. She would feel the injury the rest of her life.

Arch Truitt was born in the Bowlaway; that is, Truitt's Alleys; that is, in the middle of a swamp. Bowling was what he knew in the front part of his brain, before the expulsion. The back of his brain was fenland. Why he had to drink so much. He had to keep up the damp. He was mostly marsh.

They weren't a walking family, they'd driven everywhere, walking was for layabouts and geniuses. "Dr. Sprague walked," Margaret once said, "in order to think." She said it as though a walk was like college. Yes, you could go, but you better be sure you could stick it out, and she surely wouldn't sponsor you. "Who was Dr. Sprague?" asked Arch, but Margaret only shook her head. Sometimes she thought Roy had inherited some of Dr. Sprague's seriousness and melancholy, thinking things he shouldn't; Arch might have inherited his thirst. Never mind inheritance was impossible. They'd never met. He was only maritally part of the family. But couldn't certain qualities be heavier than others, and drip down through the generations anyhow?

Roy, who'd gone to college, went for walks. He encouraged Arch to come with him. So Arch set off, and, being a swamp, sought out the swamp.

This was in the summer. They lived together in Roy's enormous Worcester apartment, actually three apartments knocked together, the sort of place that, growing up, Arch had literally dreamt of: a floor plan that made no sense, bedrooms beyond closet doors, a kitchen the size of another person's apartment in the middle, another smaller pointless kitchen in a far corner. It was big enough they could live in companionable silence when Arch wasn't on the road or with a girlfriend. The living room was green, like Minna's living room, which Roy had seen during the war, a vow he'd kept, perhaps the only one. Now they were on vacation, down the Cape, surrounded by marsh. They were out too late on the beach and walking back to their car. Roy had gone ahead—when they were children he was always slower, because of his weight, because of his clockwork. They were men now, and he took pleasure in outpacing his brother when he could.

Arch lagged behind. He was a city kid and the lack of streetlights in nature always struck him as eldritch.

A flash above his head, so bright it had to be fatal or divine. Some bird was saying calmly, as though half-dead, *help-help, help-help, help-help*. It knew nobody would.

He stopped and listened. Ahead, a salty glow. He walked toward it, and stepped into a clearing, and into a bog.

Which way was home, by which he meant the parking lot?

The bog got its fingers into his shoe.

What happened then: peace fell over Arch Truitt and he sat down. Sat down in a bog. Yes, he was drunk. He could hear strange tinkling music, and across the bog he could see some sort of creature burrowing along the edge.

Who are you?

I mean you no harm.

That's not what I asked.

Do you mean me harm?

I will help you however I can, Arch thought, and believed it. He'd known that flash of light was not of this earth. It was a spaceship crashing down. Arch tried to stand up but no man is light on his feet in a bog. Once he'd finally managed it the creature was gone. He thought it was. The bog had taken his shoe. Then he saw more lights, orange through the scrubby pines one direction, and a more alien light throbbing the other, and he went toward the throbbing, and found Roy there in the parking lot, next to a police car all alight. Roy's shoes were in his hands, pants rolled up, feet black with mud.

"Oh my God," said Roy. He dropped his shoes to the ground and stepped into them in disbelief. "I thought you were dead."

"Why would I be dead?" asked Arch.

A policeman got out of the car. He was very tall and thin, but with a sweet round boyish face. He would be boyish all his life, you could tell. "You need to go to the hospital?" he asked Arch. He had the worried voice of feigned bravery, alto, marbled with baritone.

"Why on earth?"

The policeman pointed at his bare foot.

"I don't think that's a medical condition," said Roy. "Come on," he said to Arch. His hands were shaking. This had been an emergency and he wanted to drive away from it.

"What were you to up to?" said the policeman, suddenly suspicious.

"Walking," said Roy.

"*Well*," said Arch.

"Well," said the policeman with a mean encouragement—everything that had been boyish about him stayed boyish, but spiteful and stunted. "What were you up to?"

"We're *brothers*," said Roy, as though that explained everything.

"I'm talking to *him*. Your *brother*." He examined Arch's face, eyes, jawline, Roy thought for a family resemblance—was it there? was it convincing?—then said, in a petty, vulcanized voice, "You look familiar."

At that Arch gave his best smile, the magnanimous one that made you glad to know him. "Maybe from television."

The cop straightened up. "Oh! Yes! You!" He put his hand out for a shake. Arch took it. "You're an actor," the cop said.

"Then you know me," said Arch.

"Sure," the policeman said less certainly. "All right, then. You're OK?"

"We're OK," said Arch. "Thank you. Appreciate it."

The Truitt boys waited for the cruiser to pull away. Then Roy backed into something—a tree?—and there was a sound that went all through the car and dented their hearts, then he pulled forward, backed up again, a vibrating crash—a pole?—and then eased away.

"We should look at that," said Arch.

"It's *fine*," said Roy.

They swung out of the parking lot. Arch said, "You called the police?"

"You were gone *five hours*," said Roy. "I thought you'd drowned."

Five hours? No, not possible, but on the other hand the orange glow had been dawn—here was the sun, glazing the bay—and they'd left the beach at night.

Roy said, "So now you're an actor?"

"He recognized me, didn't he?"

"You look like some Cape Cod cat burglar," said Roy.

"I *am* on TV," said Arch.

"Sometimes. You're an occasional Saturday afternoon candlepin bowler."

"I'm an actor," Arch said peaceably. It *was* only occasional these days. "Maybe I never was that good a bowler, I just acted as though I was one and the pins believed me."

"What on earth are you talking about?"

Arch felt as though he understood his own life for the first time, not spelled out in words, not something he could translate to another human being, but shining all around him as the car moved through it. He should have taken that talent elsewhere. He *could* have been an actor. He could have been nearly anything. He still could change his life.

"I saw a UFO," said Arch. "That's what took me so long."

"You saw a cop's flashlight."

"I heard music."

"Must have been a boardwalk on the other side of the bay. Sound carries across water."

"I know sound carries across water."

They drove a long time in silence, and Roy said, "I believe you."

"Believe me what?" asked Arch.

"What you said. About the spaceship."

"The UFO," said Arch, thinking it sounded more scientific. But the ship, the object, wasn't the point: it was the creature who'd spoken to him thought to thought. He couldn't work out how to put it.

"Yes," said Roy. "I believe you."

Arch studied Roy, resolutely piloting the old Renault. A perversity to drive that car in the States. Nobody knew how to fix it, and they weren't inclined to try. Roy's face, as always, was that of a captain who'd vowed to go down with his ship, but not quietly. "You don't believe in UFOs," said Arch.

"I believe you," said Roy.

"You don't believe in ghosts."

"Whatever you tell me, Arch," said Roy, and he looked away from the road for a moment, and his eyes were filled with tears, "I believe. I owe you that."

Arch sat back. For a moment he was irritated at Roy—these tears! this pity! when Arch himself felt entirely happy and at peace—and then he accepted the belief (but not the pity), the brotherly affection, as he had accepted plenty of things from Roy over the years. Roy was a monk; Roy renounced things not for God but for his brother.

As for Roy himself—it had come upon him then that if any living human could talk to the dead, to the galactically misplaced, to babies dreaming in their prams, it was his brother, as innocent a sinner as ever lived.

Home. Before Roy got out he said, "I think we should open a bowling alley."

Arch nodded. He said, "You hate bowling."

"I don't," said Roy. "In another life I might have loved it. We'll do everything differently."

"Tenpin."

"Sure, why not," said Roy. "Half and half. Stay at home. Run the pro shop."

"All right," said Arch. "I will."

Roy got out and looked at the back of the Renault. The bumper was half off, and there was a crack in the rear window.

"Vandals," he said.

Arch laughed.

"*Vandals*," said Roy threateningly.

"OK," said Arch. After all, he was changed; he believed, too. He knew things now that Roy didn't and he looked toward the blue morning sky to confirm them. There was a finial atop the nearby church steeple that Arch had never noticed before. A message from another world. It fattened and diminished, fattened and diminished. It flew away. It was a pigeon.

He always looked for it afterward, and he always missed it.

GOD AND BOWLING
AND CHILDREN

Cracker did enter into marriage again, she already had. She was married to that parody bride, her mother-in-law. They went about planning a life together. Leagues, birthday parties, more pinball machines, move out the pool tables. Cracker hired more help, an evening manager named Walter, a weekend manager named Ida Jane. She bought a hot dog roller, a little oven, expanded the candy selection, got a new vending machine that dispensed not Eskimo Pies but Fudgsicles and Dreamsicles and Popsicles. She sold factory-made cookies that came stacked three to a round pack, wrapped in crackling cellophane, salty, awful, addictive. A bowling alley was a place for children now; children had trash taste. The balls were always sticky. The little hand dryers at the end of every lane blew up billows of powdered sugar and cheese popcorn dust.

"You'll look after me?" Margaret asked Cracker, like the abandoned child she was.

"Of course."

"Even if your own mother gets sick? Even if your own mother needs you?"

Cracker laughed. "My own mother will *never* need me."

Her own mother—Arlene Levine Graham Buchsbaum—was still hale and cheerful in Boynton Beach. Mostly she required that her granddaughters be shipped down for summer visits; they came back brown limbed and green haired, with souvenirs from obscure and troubling tourist traps: Zarkland, Murray's House of Snakes, Little Batavia. Occasionally Arlene came north for a visit. She was always amused by Cracker's love for Margaret.

"When you were little," she would say, smoking in the garden, "you had dolls of all nations. Now you have a little Catholic whose hair you comb."

"I don't comb her hair," Cracker lied.

"You always were the motherly sort." Then Arlene gave Cracker a folder with instructions: when her two-story house was too much, she planned to move to a nearby retirement village, and here was the pamphlet; when she needed more help, to the Jewish Home the next town over, pamphlet; when she died, to this cemetery here, where Mr. Buchsbaum, her second husband, was already interred. Pamphlet. Her first husband, Cracker's father, was buried—like Bertha Truitt—in the pamphletless Salford Cemetery, but who would visit Arlene there? Shady Palms was the popular spot, among her set.

How could Cracker explain it to her mother? Margaret *loved* her. Margaret, who had been (according to her sons) an exhausting, shrieking mother; who'd been a grandmother concerned mostly with what might kill her grandchildren (chills, their own misbehavior, maternal neglect). Her relatives were doomed stocks in which she had better not invest, but she had come into love like a late inheritance. "You're so wonderful to me," she would tell Cracker, and she would stroke Cracker's shoulder, or seize her hand and kiss it—shades of toddler Brenda! "I really love you, honey. You know that?" She had given up knitting for crossword puzzles and consulted Cracker. "You're so smart, you'll know this." Her eyes were clear and blue. She called Cracker *Honey honey* and *darling girl*. A junk shop had opened up in the block over from Truitt's, and Margaret liked to pick up presents for Cracker there—little bisque figurines of Snow White and the Seven Dwarfs, old windup monkeys who played the drums. "I thought this would appeal to your sense of humor," she'd say, with something like admiration, as though the monkey, goggle-eyed and toothy, were a book in German she herself could never hope to understand. She started to clean more, she flew at the windows like a songbird, with Windex and a rag. She made lemonade with saccharine and biscuits that never rose. She set the table, all spoons.

Only later would Cracker recognize the love at the first glimmering evidence. She should have noticed when she shampooed Margaret in the kitchen sink with the slow-moving emerald Prell. Her mother-in-law had stopped dyeing her hair the childish brown she favored (the kind of brown nobody else would choose, that generally darkened after childhood into something more interesting). Here were her gray roots, like a kind of sadness radiating from her skull. Beneath the wet hair, Cracker could feel the seams of Margaret's skull as it had come together in utero, infancy, and childhood, in the nineteenth century. She felt dents, too, and one ovoid lump. They would tell a story, if only you knew how to read them.

Margaret was wild in her mind. Bowling took over everything. Hadn't it already? Worse. She dreamt of bowling, she told long stories about bowling to strangers, to her fellow parishioners at St. Elias's, the moral of which was always: gravity brings down all things eventually. In her own head she heard the sounds of the pins. She knew it was boring but she couldn't help it. The Bowl-Mor pinsetter, it's still the best, it breaks down but I know how to fix nearly anything by now, you wouldn't think an old woman like me would be so clever at mechanics but it's like those machines are my children, I know they're about to get a fever or a jam or a crazy notion and just like that I'm there to fix and soothe, I put those babies to bed. A candlepin ball weighs 2.5 pounds. The pharaohs bowled. Bertha Truitt introduced the sport of candlepin bowling to the people of Salford, Massachusetts. A curious woman. She could bowl for hours and never improve.

Margaret you are crazy if you think people want to hear about bowling. But bowling and God, that's all it was with her. The people at church were driven round the bend. Bowling or God or both. Or dark predictions about children, or murders from her pulp magazines. She believed in the everlasting light of God and in the darkness and depravity of mankind. She had read the Bible three times in her life cover to cover, and hundreds of murder mysteries and true-crime books. That's a lot of murder, Margaret. Sure and murder has been with us since the beginning or directly after: Cain and Abel, funny how she couldn't remember who was the murdered one. There is more to life, Margaret, than murder and bowling and God and children. O yes then what.

Just cuddle the baby, don't tell the new mother—Amy this time, she married young and had a son, she lives in Salford—don't tell her all the ways her neglect can lead to his death. Just lock the door, don't explain how a man intent on slitting your throat can climb a trellis and open a window and get to you as silent as slicing a cake. Just watch the leagues bowl. People bowl for the bowling of it, not because they wish to hear about the history of bowling, who invented it, who refined it, what it means.

At the bowling alley Margaret narrated her own movements with the calm detail of a wildlife documentary: "I'm standing by the corn popper. Why am I standing by the corn popper? I was looking at the league schedules, and now I'm here." More than once when she retraced her own steps she ended up in the men's room, making nobody happy.

"The Little Sisters is a nice place," Cracker reminded Margaret. "You used to say so yourself when you volunteered there." If only she could speed up the process of Margaret losing her mind, so that Cracker could get her into the nursing home without her noticing it. Slide her in sideways.

"They tell you when you can get out of bed," said Margaret in a passion. "They tell you when you walk and eat and—*everything*. They own your body."

"They don't own your body, Mother."

"Possession is nine-tenths of the law," said Margaret darkly. "You're their slave. It's slavery. Except nothing gets done."

"It's not—"

"Is money exchanged?"

"Yes."

"When I was little it was called baby-farming. I don't know what you call it now. I will be sold for parts."

Cracker only wanted Margaret out of the house, to pace at the Bowlaway away from the stove, the bathtub, the iron, the steep back-stairs. All the deaths that Margaret had predicted for the children seemed to be gunning for her: drowning, burning, the horrifying attentions of unscrupulous strangers.

"Everyone asks for you," Cracker would say.

"Who's everyone?" asked Margaret, already anxious.

Margaret, neglected, was found in her nightgown on the porches of neighbors. "Ah, Margaret," said the neighbors, next door, across the street, "it's nice to see you." No it wasn't. They wanted to call the authorities, but they weren't sure what authorities to call.

The neighbors believed themselves to be good people, sympathetic, of course they would save the life of a poor soul adrift. The first time somebody took Margaret into their living room, offered her a cookie and a cup of tea, listened to her tell a story about bowling, oh, it was *wonderful*. Poor old woman, and such a teller of tales! They'd certainly remember this day! She got home safe eventually, it was a pleasure to have her. No trouble at all. Goodbye, Margaret! Come back anytime.

But she would. For the same visit, with variations: a different nightgown. Different next of kin: "I am looking for my husband. I am looking for my Minna. I am looking for my mother, I misplaced her, have you seen my mother?"

"Who's your mother, darling," said the around-the-corner neighbor, a weight lifter named Henrik who looked like a Saint Bernard to Margaret; she cowered, held her hand up so he could sniff her acquaintance. Instead he kissed it. "What's your name, my love."

"Margaret Vanetten," she said, and then, dubiously, "Truitt."

"Oh, Truitt," said Henrik. "I know Truitts. Let's take you home."

They kept taking her to this house that was not hers!

The old woman wasn't Cracker's responsibility *really*, was she? Was possession nine-tenths of the law? That's what children said on the playground, when *finders keepers* was no longer binding. Margaret had two sons. Surely it was their turn to pick up the weight. Where, for instance, was Arch? He was no longer on channel 5, not banned but beat for good. The last time she'd seen him was at Amy's high school graduation, where he had worn a trench coat against the rain and also (thought Cracker) to disguise himself. He'd kept his hands in his pockets. Then Brenda had graduated and moved away, and there was no reason for Cracker and Arch to meet. Years ago now.

That left Roy.

She called Roy on a Saturday afternoon, and Arch answered. She recognized his voice instantly and hung up, her fingers on the kitchen phone's hook. She counted to five and lifted her hand and listened to the inhuman dial tone, the voice of God telling you that you need not be alone.

She dialed again and this time when Arch answered—irritated, she had given him enough time to sit back down only to have to stand up again, it was a husbandly irritation—she said, "It's Cracker. We need to talk about your mother. Is that Arch?"

"It's Arch," said Arch. "OK. Let's talk."

RETURN TO ME

C racker Graham sat in South Station, waiting for Arch Truitt. Would he be wearing a trench coat? Would he have his old familiar head? He might have aged hundreds of years, or not at all. Every time somebody about the size of Arch, as she remembered him, walked into the vast waiting hall, she stood up, though the person was not always even a man.

Then there he was, not in a trench coat but a denim jacket, blue jeans a shade darker. She'd wondered whether they would hug, which showed how she'd forgotten her once and future husband, who never hesitated in the face of an embrace. He hugged her. She felt the old brass button on the cuff of his jacket behind her left ear: what she needed. That sweet smell of him.

"Car's this way," she said. "You look good." He did, ramshackle around the edges, but pink and not yellow, his long hair combed back.

"Roy takes better care of me."

"Better than I did."

"Better than me of myself. No one bosses like a brother."

"Color in your cheeks. What are you doing these days?"

"We own a candlepin house. Me and Roy."

"This candlepin house?" she said, pointing to the sidewalk by her old Impala. She unlocked the door for him, then opened it with a chivalrous flourish before going to the driver's side.

"Thanks. No, not this one. We bought a house in Worcester. Got a little pro shop in it. I run that. People come to see me."

"Laughing Arch Truitt," she said across the roof of the car.

Laughter transformed his face in just the way it always had. "Yeah, well," he said sheepishly. "You might not believe it but some people want to shake my hand."

"*I* want to shake your hand."

But they couldn't reach across the car roof. Instead, she rattled the keys in an affectionate way. They both got in. Cracker started the engine, pulled into traffic.

"You don't mind driving in town?" he asked.

"Not anymore. Not for ages."

In the years of their marriage she'd been a nervous driver. Indeed, she had never driven a sober Arch anywhere; she only took the wheel when he was sodden with drink and cheerful enough to let her do it.

"You own an alley with *Roy*," she said.

"Why not?"

"I would have thought he'd give it up. He hated it, didn't he?"

"Our place is different."

"You wouldn't recognize *our* place," she said.

"Oh, now it's yours? Huh."

They were at a red light. She ran her hands around the steering wheel in a caressing way. "You don't have a car?"

"Don't drive. Seizures."

—

Maybe this was a lie to cover up drinking, or maybe it was the truth and the seizures were caused by drinking. Surely there was nothing about Arch that didn't touch drink.

"You still drinking?" she asked.

"Nah," he said, as though answering a different question.

"You ready to see your mother?"

He reached over and touched the dashboard, like a painting on a wall he meant to straighten. "Remind me. She's a little woman, right? Sweet in her way?"

"Sweeter, you want to know the truth."

"Holy cow."

"She's forgotten all her grudges."

"Nice for her," he said. "I'm nervous. Can we stop for a drink?"

"I thought you weren't drinking."

"I'm not *drinking* drinking."

"Not *drinking* drinking," she said. "What is that in fluid ounces?"

"Forget it," he said.

They crossed the bridge over the mouth of the Charles that would take them to Salford.

"Roy never married," she said at last.

"No."

"Lady friends?"

"*May*be. Look, I can't talk to you about my brother."

"Your brother. Why not?"

"Because you don't know why not."

"I didn't break his heart," she said.

"Sure," said Arch, who wanted to protect Roy. Chiefly, how *boring* Roy was. Roy's entire existence was devoted to boring things: locks, history. Not until those things became interesting, but until the dullness was so utterly mapped anyone could understand the topography: the heights of boredom, the depths of boredom, the bedrock, the gravitational pull. He was terrifically interested in grammar. He thought he might write a book on the representation of stained linen in Homer. Then he would start his magnum opus: a history of bowling. Even Arch didn't want to read that. They would sell it at their bowling alley, which was called, simply, Bowl.

"Ah, Roy," said Arch. "Listen, I gotta honor his wishes. You know?"

"All right. I invited Amy and Ben over for dinner, and the baby, Bobby. He's wonderful."

"I met the wonderful Bobby," Arch said in a cheerful voice. "I met Brenda's guy, too. Lars."

"Oh."

"Oh God my mother makes me crazy," he said. "Will she know who I am?"

"Of course! Don't worry."

"Almost prefer it if she didn't, you wanna know the truth."

She looked at Arch then, his flinty blue eyes, his hair that needed cutting. They were in Salford. "Let's get that drink," she said.

Oh, the darling!" said Margaret when she saw Arch. "Oh my sweetheart! Lift me up! Lift me up so I can kiss you!"

He did. He scooped her up in the way of Rhett Butler, or the Creature from the Black Lagoon. She kissed his cheek and beamed.

"Now I'm done for," she said happily.

"Done for, Mother?" Cracker asked.

"Taken *care* of," said Margaret. "Now we'll be all right, won't we."

Years ago Amy had so relentlessly admired a neighbor girl's canopy bed that it had been given to her, and it was here, after dinner with his mother, his wife, his daughter and grandson, that Arch Truitt was put to sleep his first night back in Salford. It struck him as unhealthy, or spiritually unsound, to sleep under a canopy. Your hopes would fester and choke you. Your nightmares would never dissipate. Eventually he got up, found Amy's plaid-and-duck-patterned sleeping bag in her closet, and went to sleep in the little room between bedrooms that had once been the nursery.

Even he was not sure why he'd gone there. To be close to his mother, or to Cracker? Like a spy or a household pet? The sleeping bag was soft and musty, like a chrysalis. Perhaps he would bust out a new man. He could hear the noises of the women on either side of him, lights snapping off and on, creaking beds, sighs unintended for the ears of men, which he was stunned to realize sounded exactly the same as the other sort. All those years it wasn't him that caused that exasperated noise he could never decode, the satisfied noise! It was life itself!

He hadn't brought a pillow; he could feel the seams between the floorboards with the back of his head as he tilted back to look out the one window in the room. What he could see: tree branches and stars, the mobile light of satellites, or UFOs, or meteors. When he was a young man the mysteries of the world seemed like generosity—you can think anything you want! Now the universe withheld things. It was like luck. Luck once meant anything could happen. Now it meant he was doomed. But maybe it didn't need to.

Maybe he could have this one thing he had loved and never stopped wanting. To be part of a family. To be loved by his wife.

Cracker snored. His mother cried in her dreams. He fell asleep, of course. He was Arch Truitt. Longest love story in his life.

He was woken in the dark by Cracker tripping over his toes.

"What are you doing here?" Then, "She's crying."

"I know she's crying."

"Then why are you asleep."

He stood up in the sleeping bag then let it fall around his ankles, stepped out of it. Sleepy whimpering in the other room, and Cracker's familiar shushing, *ssh, you're all right, I'm right here.* He went in. His mother was in the covers up to her neck. She had the puppety look of the dentureless, and he thought if there *was* life on other planets, and they *did* come to take us over, they would look for the sad creatures who kept their teeth outside their bodies at night.

"She didn't even wake up," said Cracker. She slept in the same sort of long loose nightgown she always had, which concealed the shape of her body with its shape and revealed it with its sheerness. White, with one pale pink rose at her breastbone. "Why were you sleeping on the floor, funny man?"

The funny man said, "I missed you."

n north Salford, by the fens, lived a woman who could not stop adopting wild animals. This was in the olden days. As a child she took in frogs and snakes and pantry mice. Then rats. A raccoon, a possum. She eyed a skunk but drew the line. The animals chewed the walls of her little house. It was their house, too. The neighbors called the police.

"Humans were not designed to live with animals," the visiting policeman said to the woman.

"That's exactly what they *were* designed for!" the woman said.

That policeman didn't understand. He had never fallen asleep with the bulk of a raccoon in his bed. That humped heat off the humped back. The chatter. The *weight* of animals. Their tails. She wanted her own tail, she dreamt of it, and when she woke in her bed tailless she felt amputated, as though something that was by rights hers had been taken away. At least she could live with the tails of others. Sometimes there were two raccoons in the bed, and one spring a set of kits. If animals weren't meant to live in houses, how come they learned to open the refrigerator, work the kitchen faucets? She wasn't a bad-looking woman, said the neighbors. She could marry, have children. As though the dreams of other people were hers! As though what people found attractive was likewise attractive to a raccoon. She preferred animals. She dreamt, like animals did, of chasing things, and undeserved beatings.

At the end of her life—she was not old, she was never meant to be—she found an animal on the edge of the fens, a sweet-faced wild cat, big as a German shepherd—or was it a wild dog? No, not wild, the animal had an air of domesticity. It must have been forsaken by another human. It came snuffling up, it reminded her of the possum she'd taken in ten years before, whom she in her head called Sugar, though she never said names aloud. Perhaps she was discovering a new species. It had human eyes, hunched therianthropic posture like a little accountant, a black damp nose. She had dreamt of owning a nose like that, too, a cold wet animal schnoz that telegraphed love and health. An understanding passed between the woman and the creature. She turned. It followed.

Two weeks later she was found on her kitchen floor. Kicked to death. Throat torn out. Whatever had done the job broke down the kitchen door from the inside and was never caught.

"We warned her," the police told the newspaper.

Cracker Graham had read this story as a young woman and took it to heart. When the authorities come to your house and say, *No more,* take it seriously. Listen to your neighbors, your relatives. Even so she respected the torn-apart woman. To have something you were willing not only to *die for* but also to be *killed by.* She imagined the woman on her kitchen floor, already knocked down and bleeding, offering her throat, thinking, *Ah, you see, my townspeople? I am not dying alone.*

Cracker decided to take Arch in.

THE OLD WOMAN
OF THE ROOFTOP

The marriage was not dead; the marriage had been buried alive. Look at it in its coffin. Stare and you can see it breathing. What's worse than giving up on something or somebody you only *think* is dead?

The bed was new. The drinking glasses were new, bought at the grocery story. The cats had died and not been replaced: Cracker was done (she thought, she thought) taking care of living things. The marriage was neither old nor new. They were not teenagers, they were middle-aged, and therefore grateful. Arch had forgotten the particular swing of Cracker's limbs, the laugh that could sound dirty or childish. Cracker had forgotten the pleasure of telling somebody else to do things she did not want to do herself. There were no children in the house, only a hard-of-hearing old woman. They did not have to whisper.

Mostly Cracker had left things alone in the house, but she had let things build up. In the kitchen there were too many little tables and carts—a cart for spices, a cart for measuring cups and spoons—because every drawer was filled with a different category of detritus: menus and rubber bands in one, broken spatulas in another, baby clutter in a third. Arch imagined turning the whole house over and giving it a shake to see what fell from its pockets.

Whenever he suggested getting rid of anything, Cracker said, "No, I like that. Leave it be."

Leave it be meant Margaret, too. They forgot they'd thought they might put her in a nursing home.

"I'll clear out some of the stuff in my mother's room," Arch said.

"That you're welcome to. I'll take her to the alley, get her out of your way. Who knows what you'll find?"

"The Truitt Gold," said Arch.

"Yeah, right," said Cracker. "Please, try and find the Truitt Gold."

In the closet, in the nightstands, beneath the bed: years of presents. Margaret had put them there, all those tokens of good intentions. Enormous loafs of soap wrapped in patterned paper, little shell-shaped guest soaps, bath oil in bottles, bath oils in little plastic capsules that were meant to melt away in water, everything lavender, hyacinth, violet. They must have thought she was very filthy indeed. Evidence of both love and disappointment. What would you like for your birthday, Grandma? Oh, nothing, she would say. Or, I'll love anything you give me. A lie. Since childhood she'd only ever wanted one thing: a box filled with a substance she couldn't imagine that would change her life.

Now Arch found it all, boxes and tubs of soap and bath oil, drifts of embroidered handkerchiefs. She never used anything and she never threw anything away. He could not tell what it all meant. Why had she kept it? Sentiment or reproach? He filled a plastic garbage bag, then another.

Beneath the foot of the bed was a suitcase filled with old family papers. A sheaf of old tax returns over some rubber-banded letters

from his father, still in their envelopes. His handwriting was terrible.
Arch drew one out. *My dearest pink and cream girleen*, it began, and
wincing, he put it back in the envelope to read later, or to hand down
to the girls. Brenda loved that sort of thing. He imagined calling
her at college on Sunday and telling her. Beneath the letters was an
ancient document that said on the outside of the fold, LAST WILL AND
TESTAMENT.

Old, New, Last Will and. It looked that ancient and consequen-
tial. Like anyone pinched for money, Arch Truitt had dreamt of
inheritance from somebody he'd never heard of, wouldn't mourn.
And why not? There were sawed-off limbs in every direction on the
family tree. A rich relative wasn't out of the question: a Truitt they'd
never heard of, Margaret's birth family, even a Sprague who'd run
out of descendants.

He unfolded the paper and read it.

*I leave my worldly possessions to my husband, Dr. Leviticus
Sprague, with one exception. Truitt's Alleys and all contents I leave
to Joe Wear, as promised so long ago. I am Bertha Truitt, age fifty-
seven, April 7, 1918.*

He ran to the Bowlaway.

H ere you go, Mother," said Cracker. They set her by one of the
unused lanes—Tuesday mornings they gave senior citizens a
discount, it was a quiet time—and handed her hot coffee from the
vending machine that also dispensed chicken soup and cocoa. The
light from the fluorescent bulbs showed all the fingerprints on her
eyeglasses. She looked daft. She *was* daft. The line of gray in her hair
was nearly around her temples now.

"Ma," said Arch. "How did you end up owning the alley."

"The family business," said Margaret, fiddling with her paper cup. "I should say it ought to come to me. And to you."

"But—how did *Papa* come to own it?"

"He inherited it from his mother."

It was hard to know how to accuse your mother of grand theft. (Was it *grand* theft? He wasn't sure what made a theft grand in the eyes of the law.) Arch took a sip of his own coffee. It tasted—like all the drinks in the machine—faintly of chicken soup. Why would a human being want such a thing? He was filled with anger toward the disgusting coffee and the ridiculous machine that had made it. He tried, "Was there a will?"

"I'm sure."

"But did you see it?"

She shook her head and laughed. "I'm under interrogation!" she said, then, "what kind of place is this anyhow?"

Cracker put her hand on Margaret's shoulder. "We're not interrogating."

"See there," said Margaret. "It's yours now. I give it to you!"

"*We* don't want it," said Arch. "What happened to Joe Wear?"

"Joe Wear." Margaret put her hand over her mouth. From the outside you could not tell whether she was remembering or failing to remember. Even inside she was not sure. She saw the very letters of his name but could not find his face. "Joe Wear," she said again. "He got run off is my guess."

"By who?"

"Anybody might have done it."

But Arch remembered the name. *Joe Wear* was the boogeyman who'd lived in the rooms above the alley before they did. When something inexplicable or inconvenient occurred, his father blamed Joe Wear. *This damn bad knife Joe Wear left behind. This faucet never did work after Joe Wear balled it up.*

"Where'd he go?" said Arch.

Margaret looked placidly at the candy in the counter. "Who? Oh darling," she said. "I am tired."

He couldn't stand it, her calm, the impossibility of knowing what had actually happened. "Maybe you should go back to Little Sisters of the Poor," he said.

Margaret turned to him. Behind the fingerprints and thumbprints, her eyes were panicked. "The orphanage?"

"The old-age home," said Arch. "Let them take care of you."

"I'd rather die," she said.

Arch shrugged. So she was forgetful: she'd forget this. He could say anything to her, at long last. "OK," he said. "You'd rather die. That's fine"

"Betty!" said Margaret.

"Leave her alone," said Cracker to Arch. "It's been fifty years, nearly. Jesus, Arch. You want more coffee, Mother?"

"I always want more coffee," said Margaret cautiously, though she hadn't drunk a drop.

Arch kept thinking that if he asked in the right way his mother would confess. Her memory wasn't gone entirely, just illegible in spots, like a letter long-ago wept over. It was hard for Arch not to take it personally. It felt like forgetting things was something Margaret was doing *to* him.

"You can't take umbrage," said Cracker.

"Umbrage is all I *can* take," said Arch.

Just like his mother to hold on to her secrets till her memory failed. He kept looking at her. If his parents had stolen a bowling alley out from under somebody, what else might they have done?

"I think she should go to Little Sisters of the Poor," said Arch to Cracker. "I think it's time."

"I thought you didn't want to put her in a home."

He shook his head. "All I can think," he said.

"So we'll see if we can find Joe Wear or his descendants."

"It's not that," said Arch. "It's, who would I have been? I *hated* that place."

"*Roy* hated that place."

"I am not Roy!" Arch roared. "And I hated that place! He got out and I got swallowed up."

"You mean you married me."

"That's not what I mean."

"You married me and you had kids. I guess I know you didn't like that, you walked away from it."

"That's not what I meant," said Arch. "You're not listening to me, nobody ever listens to me."

She was quiet. "Go ahead," she said. "Here I am listening."

He said, "I don't know. I don't know. I feel like I got trapped and I only realized once I started to starve to death. And it's nobody's fault but that old woman's, and she doesn't even know what she did."

"She did her best," said Cracker, because that's what you said in these cases. "And we don't know what she did, either. Nothing would make me happier than getting rid of the bowling alley. I mean, sell it. We can't give it away, all the years we've put into it."

"I thought you were the moral one."

"I'm the practical one," said Cracker. "We'll sell it. We'll move your mother someplace she can be looked after. Mass every day if she wants, volunteers who'll play cards with her. Then we'll decide what to do with the rest of our lives."

The next morning Margaret took the bus in the dark to the bowling alley and unlocked the door. Everyone thought she was past such things, buses and bus fare, keys and locks. One day you'd handled all the keys of your life and it was somebody else's turn. She wore her nightgown and house slippers, but she carried her pocketbook. Nobody questioned an old woman, as long as she had the authority of her pocketbook.

She locked the alley door behind her. The place was hers. Not everyone has the privilege of locking people out. She'd missed it. She closed the toothy key in her fist. She was headed home.

The candy counter was full and lovely. She filled her pocketbook: lemon drops, her favorite, Mary Janes, though how would she chew them? Up the interior stairs to the old apartment. It had a forsaken smell, as though a pan had been forgotten on the burner over the tiniest flame, but for months. The quilt tossed over the sofa looked like the Sunday funnies—not jokes, but soap operas, Rex Morgan, M.D., Mary Worth, Smilin' Jack, people in airplanes and under duress.

She had a sense she was escaping but she was not sure from what. Cold storage. Betrayal. Arch was mad at her. He'd yelled, who never yelled. She found the hidden door in the front closet and opened it up. At first she despaired, the ladder was so far overhead, but then she saw an old suitcase and she used it as a step. She was a very old woman but she could climb a ladder, so little and light it took no more effort to move her body up the rungs than it had to cross the floor. At the top she found the slide bolt but could not budge it.

Then she did. Not adrenaline but memory. As a young mother she had done this, come up to the roof. Old Margaret Vanetten Truitt got to the top of the ladder and realized this was the tricky part. The tops of ladders took scramble. Bertha gave birth at the top of a ladder! Nearly. Why had she ended up there? In emergencies you got yourself to the highest point.

Margaret dragged herself out, unfolded herself. The lights of Salford! Not really. She was only two stories up, and it was five in the morning, the darkest time. Cold up here—Margaret was always cold—and she could only just see Phillipine Square, the dark of the movie marquee, Sutherland's Market store across the street. *Nobody knows where I am*, she thought, though that wasn't true: in the apartment building behind her, an old man in his living room looked out and saw her in her nightgown, then turned back to his television. She walked to the edge. There was a wine bottle here. Maybe one of the boys had found the roof.

Windy higher up. What did that? The hatch slammed shut over the ladder. She would never be able to bend over and yank it back up. Anyhow, she'd lost the key somewhere and she was furious for reasons she could not remember except they were genuine.

If I fall off the roof, she thought, and the idea filled her with pleasure. She put a lemon drop on her tongue and was surprised to find not a tooth in her mouth. She'd left them at home. She was so light she'd fall silent as any New England precipitation, and in the daylight whoever found her would wonder what height she'd fallen from, an airship or heaven, an addlepated stork. Dropped from the claws of the Salford Devil, flying down Mims Avenue. The Salford Devil herself, a flying woman, but old, weary. *They'll think I killed myself.* That'd be a funeral! That'd show them! But she didn't like to cause trouble and so she went backward onto the roof. Not so light after all. As soon as she fell the bruise began to form, dusk of skin pressed up against the dusky tar paper of the roof in the dawny light. Above her, some wooly clouds unraveled like a chewed sock. *Not a cloud in the sky,* she thought bitterly: how it ought to be. Joe used to sleep up here—he had told her so—and then she could see his face, squinty and sad. Alone, he made it sound, but she wondered. Not too many places a man like Joe Wear could go with a sweetheart, in those days or these, and her heart was filled with benevolence for him and then the benevolence drained away. Good. Drive 'em out. Let 'em find other neighborhoods to ruin.

Oh, the wind would teach her a lesson for that, it grabbed the hem of her nightgown and pulled it up past her haunches to the underside of her tiny breasts. *I'm not wearing underwear!* she thought, as though somebody had stolen it, but she never did when she slept: even a pious woman needed airing out. There was the wind, puzzling over her lower anatomy. She began to weep with the shame and pleasure of it. Nobody had touched her below the waist since that old fraud her husband and nobody would, not even for purely sanitary reasons. She would not go to the home, to have immigrants wipe her bottom, no matter what her children said. She would not have her bottom parted and cleaned by strangers, or even by family, though here she was parted, the wind was parting her, her bottom in the back and in front what Nahum called, intolerably, her nelly. Old Mr. TV saw everything. *I will die of exposure!* Less embarrassing to be seen by someone her own age but also worse, worse, and with enormous effort she rolled underneath the lip of the roof as though under the sooty wing of one of God's own angels.

When they found her bed empty and unmade they could not imagine what had happened. She couldn't have left it on purpose, she who believed an unmade bed was as sordid an object as found in a modern home. Where's Margaret? They searched every corner of the house, and the yard, and the Bowlaway, and the public library half a mile away. The police went door-to-door.

Where *was* she? Had she taken the train? Had she started to walk? Had she been pulled from her window by a kidnapper (*you're coming with me, don't forget your purse*) and been driven far away in a dark car? She had wandered off again, she was old, the family was prone to wandering. But to disappear so *thoroughly*. And also: When? There was a whole stretch of hours they had not seen her.

They should have put her in the home, where she would have disappeared the usual way, via slow evaporation.

FATHERS FORE

Arch went to college bars to drink away his guilt. He, who had never been to college, believed college students were honest. They wouldn't rob you, anyhow. They wouldn't *kill* you. They were dumb, in their way—this idea he got from Roy, that any grown man could outdrink them and outthink them. Then he was sitting in Father's—which number? Too? Fore? Won? he couldn't remember—in odd company when the lights came on. The bars closed at 2:00 A.M. and the package stores hours before that but Arch was a drinker who'd fallen in with drinkers: they were still thirsty. Two boys and one quiet girl. It was *essential* they have another. Where could they go? "I got a bottle at home," said Arch. "I got a car," said one of the boys. Arch rode up front. He knew how drunk they all must have been; he was full of admiration at the driver's skill, this long-haired beetle-browed boy. The other boy (shorter, in a flat scally cap) sat in the back with the girl (Italian, Arch thought, brown hair parted in the middle, blue jeans and a plaid shirt shot through with gold thread). He felt the rattling of the car but he thought they were holding still, it was the road that was moving beneath them, under their wheels and far away behind them in the dark.

If the night had gone differently, Arch might have woken up the next morning, astounded to have survived the mere drive home. *What a stupid thing to do!* he might have said to Cracker, who would have answered, *It's time to forgive yourself. Drink at home, if you have to drink.* Instead, he unlocked the door to the Bowlaway and said to the kids—Jordan, Terrence, and somebody else, Arch couldn't remember whether the girl was Jordan or the beetle-browed boy was. Terrence was the cap. "Come in," said Arch. They all did.

They drank in the dark of the alley, whiskey that Arch kept under the counter, mixed with Coke from glass bottles pulled lengthwise from the upright vending machine. "Don't you have a key?" asked Terrence the Cap, as Arch counted out quarters. "Somewhere," said Arch. "All the keys of the world are somewhere." The key was on his key chain. He unlocked the machine and swung the door open so they could help themselves.

"Wicked," said Jordan, or not-Jordan, the boy.

"What kind of bowling is this?" the girl asked.

"Candlepin."

"What the fuck is that," said the girl.

"Language," said Arch. "You're not from New England."

"Sorry. Pennsylvania," said the girl. "You own this place?"

"No," he said. "Mr. Joe Wear owns it. I just work here." He said, "Oh well."

The bowling-alley gloom had taken the gloss out of the girl's hair. Arch wanted to know what her name was. He was old enough to be her father. Arch had no designs on her, not so much as a doodle, except that he wanted her to like him. Terrence the Cap and Beetle-brow were trying to figure out how to turn on Pong till Terrence gave up and went to rifle through the candy behind the front counter.

Arch was a grown man looking after children. "Maybe it's time to call it a night."

Terrence the Cap unwrapped his candy. A Sky Bar, the worst kind of candy there was, five compartments of not quite chocolate filled with not quite caramel, not quite coconut, not quite fudge. "You got a key to this safe?" He kicked at the small lockbox under the counter.

"Nah," Arch said. "They don't trust me with it."

"It's dark in here," called the beetle-browed boy.

"Bowling alleys aren't famous for their light," said Arch.

"You got electric," said the Cap.

"Don't want to attract the cops," said Arch. Which was true enough. He'd had too much of the police, with his mother missing; he didn't want them to find him drunk and out of place. He should be holding a vigil. Candlelight: she'd like that. If only she knew he was burning himself down from the inside. She'd been missing six weeks, was surely dead, but who knows where. He looked at his company. Where had they come from? No, not just how they had all ended up here, middle of the night, the Bowlaway, but who *were* they, who did they used to be? These children, they were so young, they used to be babies. They might have been nice babies. He tried to see it, their round baby heads, the pudge of their arms.

"What's in the safe?" Terrence asked.

Arch got up to lean on the counter. He looked at the safe. It would be empty—Ida Jane, the night manager, would have taken the day's receipts to the night depository—but that wasn't a good story. Nobody ever wanted a safe to be empty. "The Doomsday Code," he said.

"Nah, mush," said Terrence. "Really."

What Arch hadn't realized: they were all strangers. The girl and the beetle-browed boy, one of them named Jordan; the guy in the flat cap, who was younger than the other two; Arch. They had met that night. The girl (her name was Julie, she'd only said her name was Jordan) was on the edge of dropping out of Radcliffe, she wasn't failing but she knew she would; the beetle-browed boy, Marcus, was from Florida, and had enrolled at BC only to discover how much he liked to drink; Terrence the Cap was only ten miles away from home, seventeen years old, underage, in debt, in trouble, and already (he'd decided) doomed. Terrence had seen in Arch a countryman, drunk and frayed. Pliable. Starved for admiration. Terrence tried to pick up the safe, but it was bolted beneath the counter.

"Leave it alone," said Arch.

"Whose place is this?" said Terrence.

"The boss's."

"Who's that?"

"Mr. Joe Wear," said the girl.

"Why not call it a night," said Arch. He tried to make his voice paternal. In the fridge upstairs Arch kept a six-pack of beer he didn't intend to share.

"Is there another safe? A bigger one?"

"No," said Arch. "Yes." There *was* a safe in the basement, enormous and flowered, though they had never in his memory used it: just another one of those ancient objects that had come to rest and never moved. Why hadn't they? A safe might have changed everything. "All right," he said, "it's time to go."

"Show me the safe."

"I can't," said Arch.

"I think you can."

"Knock it off, man," called the other guy to the Cap. You could hear the bravery in the middle of the words, but he couldn't quite force it all the way to the edges. "Got it," he said, as he found the outlet and plugged in the Ping-Pong game.

Terrence turned and regarded him with disgust. "What's your *name*?" he asked, as though he suspected the guy was just the kind of jerk who didn't have one.

"Marcus," said Marcus. "Let's go."

"Shut up, Marcus," said Terrence.

Marcus tried the door, but Arch, like his mother, had locked it behind him. He wanted to go home. Cracker would be furious, and would forgive him. That's what he needed.

"I'll let you out," said Arch, finding the key.

"Not going," said Terrence. "Show the safe."

"Don't be a child," said Arch. Then he looked at Terrence and saw that he *was* a child, a kid. Not a twitchy small guy, just not full grown, and the boy's childishness suffused Arch's heart and ossified it. Arch thought he'd never hated somebody so much in his entire life. Terrence Fanning, his little steel eyes and overripe lips. "You fucking boy: when there's a grown man telling you what to do, you *do* it."

The kid turned. Unhappiness gave him a hunchback. *I've done it*, thought Arch, *he's going*. Then the guy came charging at him, shoulder first. He knocked Arch off his feet, into lane three.

On the ground the two of them stared at each other. Terrence Fanning weighed nothing at all; Arch would knock him off once he caught his own breath. They were both doomed, which is to say they'd both always courted that feeling of doom. They loved it, the shadow over the sun that meant your own fuckups were not personal: they were ordained and condemned by God. Neither could help himself. "Fuck you," said Arch from the floor.

Moments before, Arch had seen him with flashbulb clarity, every pimple, the fine wales of his corduroy cap. Now Terrence Fanning disappeared into a column of rage. He was gone. He couldn't see Arch Truitt, either. The flame of fury had shot up all around him. How had they gotten here? They didn't know.

A bowling alley is a warehouse for blunt objects. Terrence Fanning belonged there; he was a blunt object; so was the ball he picked up in his hand; so were the wailing witnesses behind him. Neither doomed man was looking at the other. They jolted, jolted, hollered.

When it was over Terrence Fanning stood up. There was a candy smell that he knew came from his brain and meant his life was over. Candy required candy: he walked behind the counter and helped himself to several rattling boxes of Lemonheads and Boston Baked Beans. His shoes were bloody; he picked out a pair of piebald bowling oxfords with the size stitched on the heel, larger than he usually wore because he was self-conscious about his little feet. Somebody was weeping. It was him.

"Give me a ride home," he said to Marcus, who was also weeping. Only the girl was dry-eyed. That was just like a girl, and he wanted to hit her so they'd match.

"We have to call an ambulance," she said in a steady voice.

"He's dead," said Terrence Fanning, age seventeen, of Adams Road in the Nonantum neighborhood of Newton, Massachusetts. Now he was calm, too. He stubbed out the tears on his cheeks with the heels of his hands. "Give me a ride, *Marcus.*"

"What about the safe?" asked tearful Marcus.

"There is no safe," said Terrence Fanning.

Behind them, Laughing Arch Truitt whispered into the floor, "Don't leave me." Who was he talking to? "Don't *let* me," he said. He didn't finish the sentence. He could hear the ball that had done him in wobble stickily down the gutter toward the pins. He didn't want to be saved. He only wanted somebody—the calm girl, the terrified boy, his gray-eyed murderer—to sit beside him as he died. Nobody did. His mother was close by, of course, but already dead, and no company at all. They would find her on the roof the next day, as they swept through the crime scene, the Bowlaway, old Bertha Truitt's, her body an answer to one mystery, but not to most.

5

AMONG THE ARTISTS

fter giving up Superba Minna Sprague saved everything that
had touched her, imagining a museum about her extraordinary
family—her father's family; she had inherited everything —
but it was a hodgepodge, a hash, a gallimaufry. Her children didn't
want it: they lived spare and settled lives in the Midwest, of all places.
Easier if there had been a single story. Her father, the distinguished
black doctor and writer. Or Almira the cellist, who composed music in her farmhouse bedroom till the day she died, age eighty-six,
the last of her siblings. Benjamin the businessman and gentleman
farmer. Even Joseph, the quietest Sprague, who made strange vision-
ary drawings on grocery store bags with pencil and saved them in
wooden egg crates. Almira had thrown out all the drawings but one
after Joseph's death, though she had saved dozens of his fine white
shirts, which Minna now owned. If you knew Joseph—in another
life he would have been the hero! the genius! instead of the most
minor Sprague—if you'd known him the drawing, now framed in

Minna's parlor, would have meant something. Here was Almira, her body like a cello; here was Benjamin built of barrels and wheat. The sun on the horizon was a dozy eye about to close. Where was Joseph himself? The graphite hand in the corner reaching down, pinching a penciled pencil, as though the drawing were drawing itself. But nobody knew Joseph anymore but Minna, and the drawing was only picturesque, one more detail among too many details. You couldn't make sense of it. She wished she owned all the drawings and damn the shirts. No, keep the shirts. She was, like some of the men who collected her recordings (always men), a completist. It was like a vitamin deficiency.

So when Roy Truitt called her she said, "I want everything."

"Oh," he said. "I mean, I was calling about the bowling alley—"

She *did* want everything. But you couldn't ask. Or you could ask, but then you'd have to laugh it off as a joke, which she did now. She'd helped him out and then she'd never heard from him. "Of course not. I don't need anything. My children don't want it. That godforsaken place."

"You have children," he said, in a voice of irritating wonder.

"Yes, I have children," she said. "Grandchildren, too. What do you think?"

There was a long pause. She couldn't tell what he thought, though she was generally good at discerning the various discomforts that incited silence.

"It's nice to hear your voice," he said at last.

"I never heard from you."

"I'm sorry," he said. "I—I've had a hard time."

"Did you end up teaching?"

"A little," he said. She had saved his life, in order that he might bungle it in ways he'd never foreseen. He'd blamed her, he saw now, though really he should have thanked her. "Now I own a bowling alley, somehow. Not my mother's. I don't know how it happened.

Thank you," he said. "I should have—anyhow, the alley, Truitt's, was left to somebody. We're trying to track him down. Joseph Wear. We're not sure—"

"I know Joe," said Minna. "Let me get you his phone number."

All those years before, thirty-nine years old and suddenly liberated, there were a lot of things that Joe Wear had never done. He had never been out of New England—the farthest he'd gone was to New Hampshire, to see his aunt Rose and her new family one summer day, where he verified his dislike of lakes, and cabins, and Protestant ministers. He had never danced. Had his picture taken. Had a dream of flying and woke to earthbound disappointment. Married, of course. Had a pet. Bought a piece of furniture himself: not so much as a pillow. Been at ease.

(Never danced? Not once.)

Until one day coming out of the Bowladrome on lower Broadway in New York, Joe in his coveralls and boots, shaking out his limbs for the walk to his boarding room, when he came upon a man and a woman.

The man spoke first. "Hey," he said. "I know you."

Joe tilted his head.

"We've met before."

The man was all forehead, with black curly hair around the edges. He held his head as though he wished you to admire the magnificence and plenitude of his forehead. His chin was tucked into his muffler, he had a beard and mustache that likewise suggested that his face was beneath notice, his bespectacled eyes were weak, his nose (he unfurled a handkerchief and blew it) faulty, but his forehead! It gleamed beneath the streetlight; his wife bent away from its dazzle. She wore a brown cloth coat fixed with a pewter pin shaped like a lobster. (She was the important one, though Joe didn't know that yet.) It was entirely possible, thought Joe, that he'd met the man in a bathhouse but they had not paid attention to each other's face, and that the moment the man remembered in the presence of his wife he would shriek and scuttle away.

"I'm pretty sure not," said Joe.

"Yes!" said the man. "At the Jackdaws."

"Oh," said Joe, relieved. "No, that wasn't me."

"It was," said the man. "No, I'm sure of it. The *Jackdaws*," he said. "Thanksgivingtime, or thereabouts. You were sitting on Abigail's lap."

"I don't know Abigail."

"Very likely!" the man said. "Not a requirement, for entrance to her lap. Constance, tell him: we've met."

The woman was very small, with a round face and round red glasses. She seemed to be wearing a round sailor's hat. "Leave him alone, Manny."

"I will not! Not only," said Manny, appraising his wife, "will I *not* leave him alone, I will very threateningly take him to dinner, and I will pay the bill, and we will discuss the Jackdaws, and we will introduce him to Arthur, and we will crack open our fortune cookies and follow the directions therein. What do you think of *that*."

"Well!" said the woman. "Can't argue. You like Chinese food?" she said to Joe.

"I guess I might," said Joe, though he was thirty-nine years old and had never tasted it.

They went to Chen Wei's on Thirteenth. Arthur turned out to be their favorite waiter, a Chinese-looking man in his seventies who wore a red bow tie and spoke English with a disorienting County Cork accent very much like Joe's aunt Rose. Joe couldn't figure out why they wanted to introduce him, though they shook hands. Arthur was so old that every time he showed up with a plate Joe half stood to help him with it. This incensed Arthur. "Lookit," he said to Joe, "lookit," but he was so mad he couldn't finish the thought. To make peace, Manny made them both sit down and went to the kitchen to get the plates himself.

"Oddest thing," said Manny. "Chinese makes my forehead sweat. You don't believe me, I can tell. He doesn't believe me, Arthur. Feel my forehead!"

Arthur said, "The man does not want to feel your terrible forehead."

"Sure he does."

"He does not," said Arthur. "No man alive wants such a t'ing."

"Listen," said the woman to Joe. "What do you do?"

"Manage a bowling alley."

"Really?" she said. She sounded genuinely touched. Her voice was buttery and odd. He found he trusted her. Now Manny was trying to convince Arthur to touch his forehead. "I'm wondering if I could paint you. Mostly I don't paint people. I paint shipyards. Or train yards. But—no, please, I'd love to paint you."

"Well," said Joe, "I don't have too much time—"

"I'll pay you, of course," she said.

A month later he was sitting naked on a stool in New York City, surrounded by strangers and entirely relaxed. Men and women: they drew him with bits of charcoal. There were twenty-five faces in the room and thirteen of them were Joe Wear's.

It was as though he had to be turned into a stage prop before he could turn back into a human being. What had he been? He wasn't sure. Not human the way the rest of the world had been, because being human meant getting along with other human beings, same as being a fox meant running with foxes. Who thought of him in the world, when he was not in front of them? Not a single person. Though it had been a case of mistaken identity, Manny and Constance had seen him that night. Three months in New York City and he'd concluded that he was as invisible there as he'd been in Massachusetts, and then somebody had said, *I know you*. Constance particularly. Of course she painted him naked, that didn't surprise him—what surprised him was that he felt not a single scrap of modesty. He didn't care. To be looked at was no threat.

Soon enough Joe was posing for artists everywhere in the city, in studios and classes. They liked him for his angularity, the honest muscles of his trade, his ability to hold the most punishing poses for ages, even if it might put him into bed spasming the next day. Then Constance introduced him to yoga. Like laundry for muscles: it was as though he had himself steam cleaned and steam pressed and folded perfectly back into his body's compartments. He still ached, limped, stiffened up, spasmed, but it allowed him to model day after day.

It was an age of murals: Joe Wear appeared as sailors and Gods, as Columbus arriving in America, as John Smith, as Powhatan greeting him. He had never known what it was like to be beloved. He took advantage of it. An authentic tough among all the artists: he actually knew how to fix things. The artists splinted and patched but no repair they made ever lasted.

At one show, at the Louska Gallery, you could see a two-foot-high plaster maquette of Joe Wear looking at a pink and green water-color of Joe Wear who was turning his head in the direction of a disembodied leg of Joe Wear, knee like a boulder, foot kicking aside a flying ladder. Joe Wear, the real one, bone and muscle, came to the opening in his coveralls. (The artists loved his coveralls. They asked where he got them but he wouldn't say. "I came by 'em honest," he'd say, and they knew it, it's why, in their dungarees and fishing sweaters and leather sandals, they loved him.) Like Cracker Graham he'd figured out that a casual roll of his cuffs, ankle and wrist, gave him a louche, alluring look. Then he realized short-sleeved coveralls were even more effective. The opening was in March. Another man would have shivered in the thin coveralls and canvas tennis shoes, but Joe Wear loved the cold, the way it made lesser mortals say, "You must be freezing! How do you stand it?" He felt the cold and shook it off, in order to be admired.

When Ethan Olcoff showed up at the Louska Gallery, he was wearing shorts and sandals, a long-sleeved striped sailor's shirt tucked into a belt. He had dark curls and blue eyes and a long nose that sliced at Joe Wear's heart. Constance whispered in his ear, "His father invented the shopping cart. You'd think he could afford socks. Well," she said, pulling back to regard Joe, "I suppose you'll keep each other warm."

Ethan's father had not invented the shopping cart, but he had made certain clever refinements, and moreover had owned a small chain of grocery stores in Tennessee called Purity Markets. "Haven't you met me?" Ethan liked to say. "I'm the Purity heir." Ethan was rich, and restless with it, and eleven years younger than Joe. He owned a house in the West Village. Joe gave up his job at the Bowl-adrome but not the paraphernalia: he, too, would be an artist. He carved figures out of bowling pins, men who seemed, from whatever angle, to be turning away from you. He carved patterns into bowling balls and inked them and made prints, rolling them down the paper. Sometimes he remembered carving legs out of bowling pins for Dr. Sprague, and he thought: *I should have done something better with my life, I should have gone into medicine.*

He moved into Ethan's house in the West Village, he who had lived only in rented rooms or dark apartments loaned by his employers. To live somewhere with a dining room, a library, a rooftop garden. It took him many years to sit in a chair after dinner, to just sit, so used was he to walking miles to get his head straight, to avoid the way a ceiling lowered itself like a twisting press upon your bed.

To think that home was a place you might want to stay: it was Ethan, of course, who convinced him.

The only unhappiness was that Joe Wear could never really love Ethan's cooking. "Tell me how you like it," Ethan would ask, spooning the bouillon over the darling quenelle, and Joe would panic. He had been educated and liberated a thousand times over by then, he was a dumb kid brought up in the Dolbeer Home who knew the difference between chiaroscuro, sfumato, and contrapposto, a Hepplewhite foot from a Queen Anne, he'd learned music, he'd learned poetry at least a little, but a dumpling was a dumpling was a dumpling to him and he refused to pretend otherwise. Their friends tasted Ethan's food and their eyes fluttered. "How do you do it?" asked Constance, tasting Ethan's Poulet au Pot, and Joe thought, but did not say, *It's boiled chicken*. Once a year they had a screaming fight about it. Constance said, when Joe told her, "You're not fighting about the food, the food stands for something else." No: they were fighting about the food. Who could take food that seriously, and that frivolously, at the same time?

He could still remember what it was like to be fifteen and hungry, actually hungry, and the beautiful drama of finally eating.

Joe had thought of Bertha Truitt over the years. She was the first unconventional person he'd ever met. Bertha Truitt was why he had not turned away from Manny and Constance outside of the Bowladrome in 1931: he recognized them, they were Bertha's countrypeople, he might emigrate and join them. Then the oddity of oddities: one day, at one of Ethan's parties, Bertha Truitt's daughter showed up with a crowd of musicians. She was a singer, a good one, and a drummer—Joe couldn't tell how good. He didn't know about drumming. Jazz was one of the dull spots in his understanding, alongside abstract art.

It was odd to figure out the connection, but no odder than anything else in his life. Minna got along with Ethan but was wary of Joe, though he had once carved her a little cow out of a bowling pin.

Maybe *because* he had. They didn't know what they wanted from each other.

Ethan had been dead two months when the call came. Joe Wear lived in the house in the Village alone, among the fish forks and the soup tureens. The moment Ethan had died, in Cedars Sinai, of pneumonia, Joe's inclination had been to join the army, though he was eighty years old and a pacifist. There must be some way to be shipped far away from home and killed, for a good reason, in another country.

Roy Truitt explained that they'd found a will, an old one. Not notarized, but it left the alley to Joe. They would talk to a lawyer—

Time was he might have said yes. It'll be mine then. I'll have it. Once he had people who loved him he'd seen how ill he'd been treated all the years before that. By Bertha, he'd thought, but if she'd left him the alley after all—then he realized he'd been at peace with Bertha some time.

Well, he'd come to see the place. Not to own it, of course. Just to see it before it was demolished.

Phillipine Square had been revised. The Gearheart Olympia was now the Salford Cinema, with four screens, advertising real butter on their popcorn, as though real butter on popcorn weren't an ordinary human right. A sports bar, a women's clothing shop that looked like it had seen better days, with outfits hanging in the window both revealing and frumpish: turtleneck halter tops, batwing minidresses. Sutherland's Grocery was still there, with its pygmy shopping carts. A car mechanic. Cessidia's Bakery, going strong, aniseed scented. A dry cleaner's. Summertime, and all the brick and asphalt heated up.

Joe Wear arrived by subway—the subway stop was new, too, a direct line from South Station in Boston. He stood across the street from Truitt's Alleys, though it wasn't Truitt's Alleys anymore, but the Bowlaway: the sign in fancy script was beat up, the *B* faded and cracked. *owlaway.* A cursed place. Roy Truitt had told him there'd been a murder, his brother, it had been in the papers. Nobody would bowl there ever again.

Joe had forgotten the angles of Salford, how none of the streets met one another straight on. They looped and slanted. They radiated. He crossed the street and knocked on the glass door—plate glass, put in since Joe had left—and a man came from the inside to unlock it.

Neither Joe Wear nor Roy Truitt was what the other had expected. Joe Wear wore a suit both expensive and casual—what the clothing in the window of Belinda's Boutique hoped to be—in a pale blue gabardine, with a pleated shirt beneath. He had a ruched face, beautiful broad shoulders—he was a mythical creature with the body of a youth and the head of a geezer, though his body hitched when he walked—and a haircut that, like his clothing, spoke of money. Steel gray hair, and a glorious white mustache, the sort that reminded you that only certain men should be allowed mustaches. Roy Truitt was fifty years old by then, his red hair ebbing away, which was a shame, thought Joe: it was a face that could have used a good head of hair. He did not look like his mismatched parents, nor like an averaging of their qualities. He looked like a bowler.

"Mr. Wear. I'm Roy Truitt."

"Roy." Joe patted his own pockets, as though for protection. "*This* place." Then he said, surprised, "I *hated* this place."

"It'll do that. Let me get the lights."

They shook hands absentmindedly in the way of New Englanders, a kind of tired duty that was more intimate than the glad-handing of any other region of the country.

Truitt's had been renovated piecemeal over the years, but the change, to Joe Wear, was total. Automatic pinsetters, of course, the pinboys shelf ripped out. Blue plastic benches to sit while you waited your turn, and overhead projectors for the score sheets. The long bar had been replaced by a series of machines: pinball, ice cream. Somebody had left the video Ping-Pong plugged in. Ghosts played it.

Joe Wear's wooden counter was gone. He'd imagined standing behind it. Trying it on for size: a bit of time travel. But it had been demolished, replaced with a long glass counter along the wall, behind it all the empty matching shoes arranged by size. What would happen to those shoes?

Above the pin decks, wooden cutouts: an angry anthropomorphic ball, legless but with cocked arms, charging at a cringing crying pin, beneath them the die-cut slogan BOWL! FOR THE FUN OF IT!

"This place," said Joe Wear again. "You got a buyer?"

"Not yet. This is my first time here since—" Roy shook his head. "Burn it to the ground, is my opinion. My sister-in-law's, too. Betty. Arch's wife."

"Make sure and look in the safe," said Joe Wear. "Before you light the match."

"What safe?"

"In the cellar."

"Yeah, I don't think that's been used in all the time I've been here. My old man is the last person who opened it."

"You should check."

"He would have cleaned it out."

"I'm telling you."

"What is it that you think is in there, Mr. Wear?"

"Gold bars. Ham sandwiches. Who knows. Gold bars," he said again.

"Well, I'll have to get the door blown off."

"Seventy-six; thirty-three; two."

"Is that—you remember it? Must be somebody's birthday."

"It's nobody's birthday. You should look. I'll write it down."

"You'll come with me," said Roy Truitt in a pleading voice. He caught Joe Wear by the elbow. The man was in his eighties, Roy should have left him alone, but he knew he needed him, and for the first time in his life, maybe, he thought he could ask another person for what he needed. "We'll look together."

Joe Wear patted Roy's hand. "All right. I can do that."

The cellar stairs were the same, board risers, a splintery banister.

"Can you make it?" said Roy.

"I can make it yet," said Joe Wear, clinging to the banister. Splinters dug into his hand.

The basement smelled mineral and ancient, like its dirt floor. There was a slope of empty liquor bottles in one corner, and the enormous safe, black, funereal, a hearse, a mausoleum, painted with flowers and the words EXCELSIOR SAFE & LOCK CO., SALFORD MASS.

Joe Wear said again, "Seventy-six; thirty-three; two."

It was empty. "I thought it would be," said Roy.

"There'll be a false bottom. Bertha loved a false bottom. You got something? Here—" Joe handed over his penknife. It was important that Roy Truitt do the work himself.

"Oh," Roy said. "I see."

It took some prying up, but there it was. No ham sandwiches, but nestled below a thin steel plate: twelve pounds of gold, not in bars—not in big bars, as Roy imagined, despite himself—but little ones. "Ingots," he said. "Bullion. These can't be real."

"Believe they are," said Joe Wear. He knew it for a fact. When he'd left decades ago, he'd taken two of them. "Bertha put her faith in gold all her life."

Roy Truitt was panting, sitting in the dirt by the safe. He said, in a heartbroken voice, "Well, they're yours, then."

"Nope. It ain't bowling related, even."

"'And all contents,'" said Roy.

"You couldn't pay me to take it," said Joe Wear. "I don't need it and even if I did—no."

"There a curse on it?"

Joe Wear laughed.

Roy said, "Might explain some things. Well, we'll give it to the widow Truitt." Roy was shocked at how mocking that sounded. "My sister-in-law. Betty. Cracker."

Now that he was on the ground, Roy wasn't sure how he was going to stand up. He was old now, stiff and stout, concerned all of a sudden with stepping off curbs, standing up, crossing one leg over the other. Worse to do it in front of an audience.

"Let's see if my legs'll hold me," he said.

"You got a limp there, I noticed."

"Once upon a time my mother broke my ankle," said Roy, which sounded so awful he laughed.

"Margaret did? She drop you as a baby?"

He shook his head. "With a bowling ball. Mother of the Year. I was eighteen."

"Margaret Vanetten!" said Joe Wear. "Though somehow—no, I believe she would. It fits." He offered a hand to Roy Truitt, who shook his head and pulled himself up on the safe. "Me, I have a birth injury. If you wondered."

Roy nodded. Then he said, with some pleasure in his voice, "The old man used to talk about you."

"Christ," said Joe Wear. "Really? I hate to think what he said."

"He cursed you," said Roy cheerfully.

"No surprise there."

"For your absence."

"He liked an absence himself."

"I guess he did."

"Do you—" said Joe Wear, and then he stopped, he wasn't sure what he was going to ask.

He had thought over the years of Dr. Sprague, Jeptha Arrison, even Margaret. Bertha Truitt, of course. But the person who troubled him decades later was Nahum. He could make no sense of the man, the strange compelling heat at the heart of him, the meanness that could kick in, the way he would abruptly turn and tease. *Hurry up, Joe Wear, stop dancing.* The way he might come back with a box of maple long johns from the bakery and offer one, fine, and then a second, all right, here comes the third, well it's yours now you've touched it—he would badger and insult until Joe had somehow eaten five just to shut him up.

How old would he have been? Ancient, but he was a con man, he might have conned death.

"Your father's not still alive?"

"No matter how you do the math," said Roy. "Let's go up."

Genealogy says that things happen in chronological order, but also all at once: we wouldn't be interested in this nineteenth-century cobbler from Salem, North Carolina, if he were somebody else's dead. While your quiet life is occurring over here, in Eastham, Massachusetts—a yearly vacation with another family in a rented house by Coast Guard Beach—you are surrounded by sixth cousins. One of them is vacationing in a time-share in Provincetown, minutes away, and another is in Foxbury, Ohio, tending to his dying wife, who as it happens is also your twelfth cousin—this will be discovered not by you, but by his great-granddaughter, in another twenty years—and your other sixth cousins are spending their money wisely, and are going bankrupt, and are converting to the Bahá'í Faith, and are having their pubic hair removed (for surgery in one case; for aesthetics in another), and are attempting to donate a box of old books to the public library book sale. The ordinary person understands a handful of relatives: parents, grand-parents, aunts, uncles, the more palatable first cousins. People look into genealogy to find ancestors, but ancestors beget descendants in all directions, until the little boat of your family is swamped with cousins of every degree and removal. It's possible that one or two will be interesting but mostly the study of genealogy will make you believe that being one of your people is common as dirt. Well, it is.

Upstairs, Roy Truitt turned on the rest of the lights, lit up the wooden Bertha who had been looking down at them all along, a crick in her fabric neck. She'd been wired up on the iron column since LuEtta Mood Arrison had brought her back. The two men didn't see her yet.

"I'm sorry about your brother," said Joe Wear. "I've heard that's bad, to lose a brother."

Roy Truitt rubbed his face. "There's no word for it."

"Heartbreaking," said Joe Wear.

"No *actual* word. Like *widow* or *orphan*, what I meant, for some-thing that happens all the time. You got a brother, one of you will outlive the other. Or a sister, I guess."

"There's not a word for a lot of things," said Joe Wear.

"Sure," said Roy Truitt.

Joe Wear put his arms out like divining rods and breathed in. He shut his eyes. "Here's where my counter was," he said.

"I remember that counter. How's it feel?"

"Can't tell. Like nothing. Like I was never here."

"Story of my life," said Roy Truitt.

"Yours? Take the alley but leave me that. It *was* my story. This place! Hey," said Joe Wear, looking up, and he saw her. "Well. Well, Bertha now."

"*That* unholy object."

"Careful. I made her. Can we—you got something to take her down."

"Probably. Let me look. *You* made her? Guess I heard you were an artist."

"Her arms and legs. Your grandfather—your step-grandfather— he made the rest."

"*He* wasn't an artist."

"No," said Joe Wear. "A doctor. Minna's father. Dr. Sprague. An educated man, like yourself. Surely your mother—"

"My family wasn't much for stories. I mean, Arch was. He was the one."

Years later Roy Truitt's niece would go looking: there was DNA to test, and databases full of genealogies. You could discover amazing things about who you were without leaving the house. Roy was an old man by then and had outgrown the genealogical urge. "I wish to remain a mystery." To yourself? "Particularly." What Arch had liked about the unseen world: you could think about it but you could never solve it. Mysteries were full of promise, were a pleasure to contemplate. Facts were disappointing, and Roy had put all his stock in facts and had been, all his life, disappointed. "Leave me out of it," he said to Brenda.

"You want her?" Roy Truitt asked Joe Wear now, gesturing at Wooden Bertha on her column, and that nearly made Joe Wear roar that he would see the Widow Truitt and any so-called Truitt descendants in court, he would take the whole place so as not to have to ask for this, which was his: he would not ask permission. "Of course," said Roy. "I can mail it for you."

"I'll take her with me," said Joe Wear.

Anybody who looked through the window—and people did

peer in, a month after the murder, they dared each other to—would have seen an angular older man climbing atop a stool steadied by a stout middle-aged man, handling what would have looked like to a suspicious eye the corpse of a child, rigor mortis set in, something ghoulish—no. A doll. Two men with a doll. Well, that was even more suspicious, wasn't it.

The two men laid her out on the glass of a pinball machine, a newish one, Disco Dan.

"I'm sorry," said Roy. "She's lovely in her way. I wonder how she got here. Thank you," he said. "Mr. Wear. We're very thankful."

Bertha. Joe's Bertha. She would surely need restoration; there were toothmarks in one ankle. The head that Dr. Sprague had made was so dear, and so bad—it couldn't be replaced but perhaps, perhaps. Or not. Leave her as she was. Her skirt was split down the middle, for cycling; her limbs were willy-nilly. Stretched out on the darkened pinball machine, she looked as though she had just dropped out of the sky. She should: she had. We all fall out of the sky. That's where we come from. Joe Wear gathered Bertha Truitt in his arms, and took her out of the bowling alley, out of Salford, out of Massachusetts, out of New England, so they could start again.

ACKNOWLEDGMENTS

This book is highly inaccurate, even for a novel, but two books helped make it a little less so: *The Game of Candlepin Bowling* by Florence E. Greenleaf (as told to Paul C. Tedford) and *Dark Tide* by Stephen Puleo. My remarkable late great-aunt Jessica Bernstein's unpublished memoir of her World War II service, "Sir, I'm from Indiana," was hugely helpful and inspiring. Thanks, too, to Colin Dickey, author of *Ghostland*, for some timely ghost advice.

And many thanks to: Paul Harding, Paul Lisicky, Ann Patchett, S. Kirk Walsh, and Michael Taeckens; Henry Dunow, Arielle Datz, and everyone at Dunow, Carlson & Lerner; everyone at Ecco, including Daniel Halpern, Miriam Parker, Sonya Cheuse, Emma Dries, Sara Birmingham, and particularly the wonderful Megan Lynch.

I have been very lucky to work with Robin Robertson for literal decades: I cannot thank him enough.

It goes without saying that the influence of Edward Carey is every page of this book, and that without him nothing for me—neither work nor life—would be possible, or good. It so goes without saying that I forgot to mention him in the first edition of the acknowledgments. In my defense: any attempt to summarize for the public what he means to me would be revolting, unbelievable, and insufficient.